CW00557509

£1.00
1102
0303 50p
20p

*Trading the
Future*

Trading the
Future

G.F. NEWMAN

Macdonald

A *Macdonald* Book

First published in Great Britain in 1991 by
Macdonald & Co (Publishers) Ltd
London & Sydney

Copyright © G.F. Newman 1991

The right of G.F. Newman to be identified as author of this work has been asserted
by him in accordance with the Copyright, Designs and Patents Act 1988.

*All characters in this publication are fictitious
and any resemblance to real persons, living or dead,
is purely coincidental.*

ALL RIGHTS RESERVED.
No part of this publication may be reproduced,
stored in a retrieval system, or transmitted, in any
form or by any means without the prior
permission in writing of the publisher, nor be
otherwise circulated in any form of binding or
cover other than that in which it is published and
without a similar condition including this
condition being imposed on the subsequent purchaser.

Photoset in North Wales by
Derek Doyle & Associates, Mold, Clwyd
Printed and bound in Great Britain by
BPCC Hazell Books
Aylesbury, Bucks, England
Member of BPCC Ltd.

A CIP catalogue record for this book is
available from the British Library

ISBN 0 356 20020 5

Macdonald & Co (Publishers) Ltd
Orbit House
1 New Fetter Lane
London EC4A 1AR
A member of Maxwell Macmillan Pergamon Publishing Corporation

For Rebecca,
who's waited too long

Prologue

MADONNA WAS BLASTING FROM THE Porsche at about
100 watts as it drew alongside his two-year-old
finance-company-owned Cutlass, drowning all other
traffic noise. Shapiro jerked around and looked at the
driver, who was wearing dark glasses and voguing in his
rearview mirror. Without pausing the attractive young
man glanced in his direction, a look that seemed to assess
and dismiss him: Jew. A familiar knot of tension
tightened in his chest. He couldn't breathe. Right then he
hoped a truck would roll over that goddamn sports car,
and the arrogant bastard driving it. Goddamn him and his
devastating good looks. Guys like that, without even
removing their shades, could deny with a passing glance a
people, a culture that had existed since the dawn of time,
while he had been struggling to deny it for thirty-five
years. He ran into them the whole while, they were born
seriously rich or lucky or good-looking. White Anglo-
Saxons who lived in expensive Co-ops out in Dumbarton
Oaks and partnered classy downtown law firms; WASP
charity-ballers who got any damn thing they wanted.
They didn't do daily battle with rush-hour traffic in from
New Carollton to try to conjure items in the administration that basically didn't submit to logic. No way was this
guy a goddamn cog in the government machine, one
whose contribution made no noticeable difference.

Pat Shapiro had been born neither rich, lucky nor
good-looking. He was a presidential advisor on agriculture with an office in the West Executive building
adjacent to the White House. Contemporaries believed

1

his proximity to the seat of power helped shape the decisions that made some difference. Every once in a while he demurred and confessed his cog-like status, but guys who had gone into commerce, some of whom were now millionaires, figured he was being modest. Making forty-three thousand dollars before stoppages, and with a federal ceiling of sixty-eight thousand, he knew he'd never be seriously rich. Maybe he could have lived without either a Porsche or making a million bucks a year had his relationship to power been truly influential. His analytical mind had a capacity for shrewd assessment and accurate second-guessing but neither would make him rich doing his job. Had he been a commodity broker he may have had his first, or second million in the bank, instead of pursuing this dumb public service ethic that helped keep the country running while other guys made millions. He regretted his career choice, but knew that venturing into the marketplace now would mean starting way back on a lowly rung.

These were familiar rush-hour thoughts, goddamn them. He saw the Porsche power away through a gap, and tried to follow, but left it too late. A blaring horn got him back on line. He would have made better time taking the subway to Farragut Square, but he held a coveted reserved parking space at West Exec, so struggled in by car. There had been pressure on him to relinquish this in favour of more senior advisors from the private sector – people rich enough to have their drivers circle the block. He would have quit for sure had he lost his parking privileges. A real stand on principle! He forced air out through his nose to keep from screaming as a horn blared behind him. He wasn't keeping closed up. A Mercedes broke the rules and changed lines to fill a space ahead of him. When he broke the rules he always got caught. The driver of the car behind sat on the horn again. Along this section of 17th people were ready to kill for advantage; their rage was ugly and out of control. His chest hurt worse and he couldn't breathe properly. Suddenly he was back in Philadelphia, suffering an asthma attack, with his father making him stand in front of an open window with a matchstick clamped between his teeth while he breathed in and out for the count of four. He had struggled to get enough air past the matchstick and into his lungs against the rising tide of panic.

He rolled down the window and sucked in air on quick shallow breaths. His panic subsided.

Further along 17th the traffic eased, and on State all but disappeared. The gate on West Executive Avenue was guarded by the uniformed secret service. The pretty face was unfamiliar, so he automatically reached for his identity tag, but couldn't locate it.

'It's here someplace, chief,' he said, looking through his driver's mirror at the auto that stopped behind him.

'Pull out of line, sir,' the guard ordered. 'You're holding up the Secretary of State.'

Clamping his teeth together, Shapiro breathed in – Screw yourself, and the Secretary of State – his status was diminished like this a dozen times a day.

'There you go.'

He showed the pass and clipped it to his coat. The barrier came open. Glancing back, he saw the wispy kid in uniform saluting the occupant of the blue Lincoln like he was genuflecting. That security pass should have been checked too.

The West Exec, like most government buildings in the capital, was built of limestone and laid out on a grand scale, reflecting the past wealth and power of the nation. Here, the large rooms, with high ceilings, noisy plumbing and bad light, were in short supply. The number of advisors needed close to the President had outgrown the building. His own second-floor office was eighteen feet square and twelve high with a pair of tall windows that didn't open. An ugly air plant sat at the bottom of one. It was noisy and he avoided using it until the temperature became unbearable.

He felt safe here, while the world got filtered through his computer terminal. He switched on the coffee machine, then the screen and logged on. Other computers talked to his while he had coffee and skimmed the papers for stories concerning agriculture; he closely read those

3

dealing with grain. All reflected American concerns. By his second cup of coffee he had noted increasing alarm among bankers over the troubled farmers in the Midwest. There was too much grain around, more than the First World wanted, or the Second and Third Worlds could afford. His immediate task was to devise a response for the President to farmers' complaints of crippling debt and low grain prices, and to Grain Association lobbyists' demands for bigger tariffs so that American wheat could compete more easily in the heavily subsidized world market. His advice rarely went directly onto the President's lips.

The problem with his best solutions was that they were long-term. Politicians rarely wanted two-, three- and four-year plans. Next year's scheme to pay farmers not to grow wheat was no answer, for next year could as easily bring a deficit in wheat following a winter without snow in the Midwest, or another summer without rain as climates became less and less reliable. Then there could be real shortages in wheat, with prices through the roof. Farmer and banker alike wanted salvation now. He knew what that was: the Russian wheat harvest failing badly. But this wasn't something they could leave to chance, for all the signs were that their grain harvests were improving.

The situation for the American farmer and American banks was going to get worse unless action was taken. He knew what action, but didn't know if it would be politically acceptable in the present climate. Russia was no longer perceived as the Evil Empire of yore.

He glanced at his watch and thought about Wilf Fear, a CIA advisor, who worked along the corridor. He wanted to run his idea for Russian wheat past him, but not in either of their offices. At this time of the morning he knew he'd catch him in the first floor cafeteria. That was neutral ground. If the CIA man turned him down or dismissed his idea as crazy then he'd let it drop. With any kind of encouragement he'd pursue it.

1

DESPAIR, LIKE A DARK CLOUD, seemed to follow her husband as he arrived back. His meeting at the bank clearly hadn't gone well. The only time such a meeting had gone well in her experience was when their first farm loan had been agreed, having inspired the bank manager with their hope and enthusiasm.

Grace was across the farmyard in the converted barn feeding their thirty-eight milk cows. These were kept inside all year round. This hadn't been their intention. They had started out with plans for a sustainable system of agriculture, but mounting debt and a sixteen-hour day had changed that. The cows went from feeding shed to milking parlour; then to the exercising ring and back to the shed.

She finished pouring pelleted feed into their troughs, then paused to stroke one of them between the eyes, not wanting to find out what Colin had to tell her. Cows were much maligned, misunderstood and misused. It upset her even to think about the treatment they received in the cattle markets when they didn't respond fast enough. Being around cows for the past two years had taught her to let them make up their own minds. Deep inside an unheeded voice told her that this wasn't any way to keep a cow. But she knew they had to earn a living, as difficult as that was becoming.

'Go on,' she said. 'Eat your feed.'

In the littered yard, where boots were always needed and broken plant rusted in heaps, Grace saw her hopes being trampled in the muddy ruts, while all her potential

5

seeped away like the polluting liquor from the silage clamp that had been the source of several complaints. Maybe the bad feeling she sensed from her husband was affecting her, but she knew the time had arrived to stop wondering what point it was they were struggling to prove, and change the course of her life instead. That would bring added difficulties. But unless she at least tried she would hate herself for a long time, and the situation between her and Colin would get worse.

Avoiding her husband's bad news, she said, 'The vet's been. The cows have mastitis.'

Colin nodded, like this was bad-news day. 'I thought we'd avoid that – keeping them in.'

'He said the problem's becoming worse with intensive milking. It's causing the cows' immune system to break down.'

'They don't tell you that when you start these wonderful schemes,' he said. Grace heard resentment in his voice, as if he was incapable of making informed choices. Often that was the way, the result of being on his knees.

'We've borrowed too much converting to intensive milking.'

She knew he wasn't going to quit or even think about it. 'We have to milk them out every hour, and not send the milk in.'

'Great! – no milk cheques.'

Watching him stride into the house, she wished she could make things better. Her own plans would inevitably make things worse initially. Her interests, at the age of thirty, lay elsewhere. Without her unpaid labour the farm was completely uneconomic. Colin could make a better living as a contractor. Spraying chemicals for the agribusinesses that surrounded them had become part of their economic reality.

In the house she found Colin slamming around like a frustrated child. He couldn't cope when anything went wrong. She said nothing but got a crock of soup from the stove and brought it to the table.

'I sometimes wonder what it's all for.'

'What did the bank manager say?'

'Those milk cheques barely cover the interest on our loan. He wants me to sell the thirty-acre field. The only piece of the farm I own.'

'It's not the end of the world.'

It was a blessing in disguise – she glanced quickly away in case he had recognized her thought.

'It puts us into a tighter corner. I won't sell that field. I won't. We need those milk cheques, whatever the vet says.'

She didn't argue. There was no point. She knew what he planned to do with the milk, and what the consequences would be if they were found out. The phone started ringing like an alarm. She left Colin to answer it, and went to the sitting-room to get their daughter, who was on the floor, sucking her thumb, clutching her dog-eared teddy while watching an Indian woman on the TV demonstrating how to make a sari.

'Rose. Rose!' – suddenly irritated that her daughter so often disappeared into her own world.

'Lunch is ready,' she said, grasping her shoulder. 'Television off. Wash your hands.'

'Just a sec, Mum.' Everything was just a second to the not yet five-year-old.

'Now.' Grace stabbed off the set. 'Go and wash your hands.'

In the kitchen Colin's mood had changed. He was smiling. 'It was Mace Hodges – Shearing wants some spraying done – their winter barley. They've had another breakdown. They work those machines far too hard.'

'Can you fit it in?'

'I certainly can. They won't keep me waiting for my money.'

'Remember I'm going to Norwich tomorrow – for my interview.'

'Oh – we'll talk about it later.' He glanced at Rose as she came in. 'Did you wash your hands, sweetheart?'

'Yes. And Teddy did.' She didn't say when.

'It'll help keep the bank quiet, Grace. It will,' he said, without looking at her.

She felt angry, but didn't respond. The atmosphere had

7

changed again. Her needs might not have existed. Getting back into university to complete her degree course would be difficult enough even with his support, but he would barely talk to her about it.

'It can't be helped,' Colin said, not hiding his irritation.

'Don't argue,' Rose said. 'Teddy doesn't like it.'

'We're not arguing. Just eat your soup.'

Rose started to cough, and ate hardly any lunch. Each winter brought recurring bronchitis that left her wracked and sleepless. Only lately Grace had noticed how her coughing seemed related to what was going on between herself and Colin. Whenever they rowed Rose's cough grew worse. She tried not to argue for Rose's sake, but it was difficult.

In bed that night, anxiety about her interview prevented her sleeping. She listened to Rose coughing, remembering earlier how she had found her with Teddy's paws clamped over her ears. She no longer tried to see Colin's point of view, or understand why he wanted to go on struggling with the farm. Norwich University held far more appeal. If she made it through her interview and got an offer she would accept the place, even if it meant moving into town. She suspected Colin knew this too.

'We chase from one end of the farming year to the other. Still we get nowhere.'

He always included her at times such as this. It felt like one more bolt to her escape hatch.

'You work too hard for too little in return,' she whispered, wanting him to agree that there was no point in going on.

She was terrified that this was all there was, with hope seeping away, while she waited for Colin to fall prey to accidents around the farm machinery as increasing tiredness became the dominant feature in his life.

Without warning Colin turned around and pulled her against himself. The tension between them seemed to have no effect on him. Their arguments were reduced to simple physical needs. She couldn't readily face being alone, and even thinking about it depressed her; however, if that was the eventual price of getting back into higher

8

education, she knew she would somehow find the will to meet the challenge. She could be very wilful.

Colin was gone when she got up to do the milking, and he hadn't returned by the time she had showered with Rose and given her breakfast. She started to get angry, believing her husband was doing this intentionally to prevent her going to the interview. That made her more determined. Who could she leave Rose with? There were no close neighbours, and none with whom she had that sort of relationship anyway. Maybe she could take Rose along, but then she'd worry in case that suggested she couldn't organize her life.

'Have you had enough to eat, Rose?'

'Teddy wants some porridge,' she said as she pushed a piece of toast against his stitched mouth.

'Don't be silly. I haven't got time this morning.' She caught her look and softened. 'Can you wait for Daddy? – God knows where he is.'

She wouldn't have time to get his breakfast now and wouldn't offer to. She hated going in a rush, with no time to collect her thoughts; their eight-year-old Ford Escort was no longer reliable.

The door opened, startling her. Colin appeared, bringing a branch of frothy cream-coloured meadow-sweet. It was not only late but rare in East Anglia, where plough and the 'cide sisters conspired against it.

'I walked across the fields. I picked this.'

'That's nice.' Uncertainty made her hesitate. What was he saying? She remembered his tenderness last night and felt herself being drawn back. He might talk about their hopes once more. 'I have to go.'

'Yes. Rose'll be fine with me. Won't you, sweetheart?'

Alarm replaced her uncertainty. 'You'll lose your spraying certificate if anyone sees you – then what'll happen?'

Letting a child under thirteen up in the cab of a working tractor was an offence; so was having one around a spraying operation. She didn't see any immediate alternative – Colin not taking the cash contract? It wasn't even a remote possibility.

9

'You can barely see across those fields. No one'll notice her in the cab. They've given me all the barley to do,' – the reason for his good mood, Grace realized. 'They're stuck for machines.'

'You will be careful, Colin.'

'Of course. Go on or you'll be late. I'll get my breakfast.'

He gave her a kiss.

The escape hatch was thrown wide open, and Grace flew.

The two-hundred-acre field of emerging winter barley was billiard-table flat. Walter Shearing, the farm owner, had had a computerized leveller working here for weeks scraping and spreading anything suggesting itself to be a bump, eradicating any low cold spots to ensure that crops crew as evenly as selective breeding would allow. With the forty-foot boom on the back of his 90hp Ford, Colin worked in arrow-straight lines with boring monotony. Counting the money earned by acres he sprayed relieved his boredom. Looking back at the edge of the field as he raised the boom bars for the tight turn, he saw Rose feeding her teddy bear a piece of biscuit. She was propped on two cushions behind him in the air-conditioned cab, keeping up a one-sided conversation with Teddy under the drone of the engine.

On completing the turn, he stopped his tractor by the chemical trailer as the mix gauge on his spray tank showed only a few gallons off empty.

'Stay there, Rose,' he said as he climbed down, pulling on his rubber gloves. He should have been wearing a zip-through disposable overall and mask for this operation, but such paraphernalia ate into profits. He was always careful with his mixes. From the chemical trailer he mixed two blue unmarked ten-litre drums of fungicide into the tank along with a twenty-five-litre drum of herbicide and seven hundred litres of water. Two and a bit of the mixes were needed to fill the tank on his rig. Automatically he looked at the sky before climbing back into the tractor. The bright, clear autumn day gave him the inclination to breathe deeply, but not around this spraying operation. He travelled up and down the field twice with this load when the first problem of the day occurred. He had almost willed it by telling himself how his run of luck was too good to last. A hose blew on the spraying bar. Not a major problem, but he wasn't pleased at having to shut down to cut in a new section and replace the taps. Time wasted meant money he could otherwise be giving to the bank, to avoid selling his thirty-acre field.

'Dad, I want a wee,' Rose said from the cab door.

'Can you hang on, love? If I don't get this tankful on before dinner, I won't finish today.'

'Teddy wants to go.'

There was no arguing with Teddy's needs. He lifted them down.

'Go by the trailer. Be a good girl and come straight back.'

He watched her go along the narrow unploughed margin land and disappear behind the trailer. He smiled to himself as he thought about her with Teddy, how she would hold him and pretend to let him pee like a boy, then she would even make him wash his hands. Maybe she needed a brother. That would sort out several problems, he decided.

Dropping first a spanner, then a nut off the clip holding a hose, he had to get on the ground and search. He hardly noticed how long Rose was gone.

He called her name when he didn't immediately see her. 'Rose!' She appeared at once from around the opposite end of the trailer and ran back to the tractor. 'You didn't touch anything, sweetheart?'

'No, I didn't. Dad, I'm hungry.'

'Can you have a biscuit for now? Then we'll go back to the house.'

With the repair finished and Rose and Teddy safely back in the cab, he steamed on until lunchtime. His anxiety about further breakdowns never quite leaving him. They returned to the house for the sandwiches Grace had left. With Rose and Teddy eating them in front of the TV, he went over to milk-out the cows. He didn't

11

pour the milk away, but into his refrigeration tank. Then he injected antibiotics directly into the teats of the five cows most affected with mastitis and hoped that not too much of it would show up in the milk. If the random tests revealed it there he'd lose his milk cheques anyway.

'Have you had enough to eat, Rose?'

'Yes. Can I have a drink?' She hadn't moved from in front of the TV.

'Can you get it, sweetheart? I've got to make some more tea.'

In the kitchen Rose said, 'Is Mum going back to school?'

He shook his head without thinking about the question. If he did he would get angry, and things would start to go wrong. 'Come on, let's get your drink, then get this spraying finished.'

Darkness had fallen by the time Grace got home. She couldn't quite believe that she was back at the house, that she had been away the whole day, freed from the increasing drudgery; that she had been accepted into university and treated like an intelligent human being with opinions that others were concerned to hear. It was the most wonderful feeling and she didn't want all that the farm now represented to diminish it. Finding Colin spraying by the arc lights on the cab of his machine brought her back to earth with a bump. It said there could be no let up. Rose was asleep on the pillows, her thumb in her mouth.

'How are you getting on?' she asked as Colin lifted Rose down. Grace wanted him to ask her how she had got on but knew he wouldn't think to.

'S'been endless breakdowns,' he said. 'God knows what he's putting on here. Whatever it is, is clogging the pipes.'

'Poor things. You're worn out. Come on, lovey.' She carried Rose to the car and settled her. Still Colin didn't ask about her day.

'They offered me a place.'

'Well, it's nice to have brains.' He turned away.

12

That reaction was the best she would get. She wanted to run after her husband and tell him she was going to accept the offer come what may. Instead she stood and watched him haul himself back into the machine. Nothing else seemed to matter to him more than holding onto this crummy way of life. She felt like crying but willed herself not to.

'I left Teddy in the tractor,' Rose said at the house.

'Daddy will bring him. Do you want a nice bath before supper?'

Rose shook her head. 'Don't want no supper.'

'Let's wash your face and hands, lovey.'

'Don't want to wash.'

'Come on. I got you a nice present in Norwich. A pretty dress like the girl had on in the *Secret House*. I got us all a present as a celebration. They told me I can go back to university. Isn't that good?'

Neither her excitement nor anything else could penetrate Rose's tiredness. She cried for Teddy.

'Daddy will soon be back with it, sweetheart.'

But he wasn't. Rose was over-tired and wouldn't sleep. She started coughing. Grace gave her hot blackcurrant drink and lay with her until she eventually slipped into a fitful sleep. The bouts of coughing that followed brought her upstairs several times. They seemed to last longer each time. She considered calling out the doctor, but knew getting him there would be difficult, so she put off the decision until Colin got back. Hearing the start of the *Nine O'Clock News* on the TV from the sitting-room, she began to worry. Still Colin hadn't returned. She knew just how the dangers of spraying increased when it was done in the dark. She wanted to go and tell him to stop, but couldn't leave Rose.

Eventually she heard Colin arrive back. In the kitchen she found him getting the supper, and at once could feel his heavy mood.

'Rose will have to see the doctor,' she said, trying to draw him into an area of mutual concern. 'She has a headache and a sore throat.'

Colin nodded. 'Why didn't you call him?'

13

'What's wrong?'

'I've been out for twelve hours. I have to get my own food.'

'It's not the end of the world, is it? I know it's a long hard day . . .'

'It won't get any shorter. Not for me. Not now.'

'Colin . . .?' She suddenly remembered the shirt she had bought for him in Norwich, but didn't feel like offering it to him in the teeth of his self-pity.

'How can you go back to university, with everything here?'

She closed her eyes, refusing to buckle.

'Walking into college today, getting accepted like that, it was like walking into spring after a long winter.'

'Oh very poetic. What am I supposed to do – go broke? What about the cows? Did you milk them out?'

She had completely forgotten either to feed or milk them. Her shame turned to anger: 'You go and see to them.'

She rushed back upstairs to Rose.

The cough seemed to deepen through the night and she complained repeatedly about her sore throat and aching head. When Colin finally called the doctor he refused to come out.

'He said give her Junior Disprin and plenty of water,' Colin told her in the bedroom where Grace was sponging Rose's face and neck.

The painkiller did the trick, and for a while Rose slipped into sleep.

In bed her husband reached out to her, bridging the gulf.

'I'm sorry, love – I just see myself swamped. God, I'd like to walk away. I'd like to go back to agricultural college. I'd even take a job with Mr Shearing, if he offered it – instead of just contracting.'

When Colin softened she couldn't fight him and suspected he knew it. She held him now. 'I won't take the university place. I can't.'

'We'll manage. Somehow. The more we try to improve things here the bigger the debt gets. Intensive milking was a mistake. It's a bad joke keeping cows like that really.'

14

That was an enormous climbdown for him. He didn't easily admit he was wrong, and she wasn't sure where it came from.

'I went into it with you, with my eyes open.'

She hoped he would insist that she went back to college. Knowing a place was there beckoning would prove too frustrating for her.

Rose cried out, and Grace got up. 'She really does need the doctor.'

Colin sprang from bed and went downstairs.

'If my wife says Rose needs a doctor, I expect you to come,' she heard him shout over the phone. 'If you don't I'm going to ring the police, and ask them to send an ambulance, and I'll tell them why.'

Grace remembered hearing someone threaten that in a radio play she and Colin had listened to through earphones in the tractor cab. In the play, after the doctor had agreed to call he wrote on the record: troublemaker. This forever prejudiced their medical treatment.

'It's a respiratory infection,' the doctor said, giving her an antibiotic in the thigh. 'Try phoning before surgery if she needs another visit, Mrs Chance.'

When cows got sick they hesitated about calling the vet because of the cost. Delaying those sorts of decisions never unduly worried them, even when inevitably some were left too late. During the first part of the morning she watched Rose carefully, but finally decided she didn't need a second visit from the doctor. She gave her another Junior Disprin for her headache. Rose asked for her teddy to make it go away.

Bringing it from his tractor, Colin said, 'Going to give Daddy a kiss goodbye?' He kissed her. 'Bye, sweetheart.' He gave her another one on her damp red lips. 'You'll feel better soon.'

Grace followed him to the yard. 'Colin, Rose didn't get near any of the spraying yesterday?' she said. 'That might have caused her headache.'

'Don't be daft. Of course she didn't.'

He was clearly affronted by her suggestion and she felt guilty for making it.

15

*

If he hadn't been delayed with milking and feeding the cows he'd have finished the two-hundred-acre field by mid-morning. Now he estimated he'd be done by midday. He swung the tractor around and lowered the boom and watched the spray cloud rise, then as he turned in the cab he saw Mace Hodges, the farm manager, driving along the tine lines. Colin stopped and climbed out.

'Half an hour, Mace, I'll be finished here.'

'Good work.' Mace automatically assessed what remained. 'Leave that, Colin. Your girl's been taken to hospital.'

'What happened? When?'

'They didn't say. Take the landrover – I'll finish off here.'

All kinds of thoughts assailed him as he drove into Bury St Edmunds. Grace's anxiety came at him and he wondered if somehow Rose could have got near the mix; perhaps they should have called the doctor sooner, and called him out again. Perhaps she'd had some other sort of accident. Traffic was congested and delayed him; then no one at the hospital could tell him which ward Rose was on. He learned that she was in the operating theatre, but no one said why. He assumed she had had an accident, but couldn't begin to think how.

The theatre corridor seemed a thousand miles long when he eventually found it. The person sitting at the far end bore a faint resemblance to Grace, like some ghost of her had brushed past long ago, leaving an imprint on this woman. She was unmoving, holding a plastic cup in her hands. Something was terribly wrong. Fear began to oppress him. Why didn't she get up to meet him? He tried to shut out his thoughts as he started to run, his movements seeming uncoordinated, carrying him forward not very fast. Not fast enough. He froze when he reached Grace and she looked up. She was ashen and her eyes were deep and dark-ringed and full of tears. He let out a wail of despair, tears springing to his own eyes. He wanted to protest, send back the message that was

16

hammering on some tight drumskin over his brain, but all he could do was sob as the coffee cup slipped from Grace's hand and crumpled on the floor, sending out an ominous dark brown stain over the green tiles.

2

A NUMBNESS SETTLED OVER GRACE in the days following Rose's death. Every thought and memory of her deepened the suffering and so she tried not to think about her. But the more she avoided thinking about her the more numb she became. She wanted to scream; she wanted to escape from her body; she wanted to die, believing it was her fault alone that Rose was dead. If she hadn't wanted to go back to college, if she hadn't gone off for her interview, if instead she had stayed and looked after Rose, she would still be alive. She couldn't deny the conclusion. The pain it caused, despite the numbness, was like a barb embedded in her flesh, and every movement or effort to escape caused it to tear at her.

Night-time merged unnoticed with the daytime; mealtimes passed without her eating food. Occasionally she was aware of Colin's presence as he attempted to comfort her, and only vaguely knew why she was taken back to the hospital to talk to a doctor.

'The cause of Rose's death was a viral infection,' he told them. 'This completely closed the bronchus.'

'But Rose was in hospital,' she protested. 'She was in intensive care, that sort of thing should have been prevented.'

The familiar paternalism from the doctor, who seemed to have no more idea than she had about what to do with his feelings, made her situation worse. Somehow the explanation wasn't enough.

A week or so after Rose's death Grace found herself at her lowest emotional point, wanting simply to take more and more valium in the hope of drifting away forever. When Colin came to talk to her about the funeral arrangements he was like a complete stranger who offered her neither comfort nor security, and she turned away from him. He returned later and raised the subject again. Why did Rose have to be buried now? With such indecent haste? The thought of her child going into the ground was unbearable. That was so final. She didn't want to have to get to that point.

'Grace, we've got to bury her sooner or later. The pathologist has finished his examination. We can't delay it any longer.'

It was then she saw clearly why he wanted to hasten the burial, recalling how he had agreed with all that the doctor had said. A part of her mind now emerging from the fog reasoned that these doubts weren't rational, that she should stop them. Instead they loomed larger.

'I'm not going to bury her until I get the truth about her death,' she said, not looking at her husband, fearing what she might see.

'It only prolongs the agony, Grace. I can't go on like this. I can't. We've got to make the funeral arrangements.'

His frustration and helplessness were transparent, and with a tiny, clear part of her mind she felt sorry for him. This was a difficult time for Colin. He was lost in emotional turmoil, his physical strength was of no use to him now. She began to weep. But pain immediately closed off that healed space.

In Rose's bedroom, where she finally went looking for comfort among the clothes and toys, she discovered what she understood was the reason for her continuing unease beyond grief. Tiny fragments of thought that somehow told her Rose had died as a result of pesticide poisoning were pulled together, when she found Teddy smelling of chemicals. Tears streamed from her eyes. She was unable to see the teddy without seeing Rose dragging it around, Teddy sharing everything she did.

She pursued Colin in the yard, where he was hooking up the plough behind his tractor. 'Rose was poisoned!' she said. 'You can smell the pesticide.'

19

'What? What are you saying? Don't I feel bad enough already?'

'I want to know why she died, Colin. We killed her.'

Anger flared from her husband. 'If you'd stayed home and looked after her, she'd still be alive,' he said. He clawed at the air as though his frustration was inexpressible. 'I'm sorry, I didn't mean that.'

Grace didn't know her next move. He blamed her too. 'I can smell the pesticides. I can.'

'This is madness. Let it go. Forget it.'

She wasn't about to. Understanding why Rose died was the only way she might come to terms with her death. Tackling Colin seemed the obvious starting point. But he was denying his part. Grabbing the teddy, he hurled it across the messy yard; never a man to argue logically where physical expression was possible. Now he hauled himself into the cab of his tractor.

A sick feeling came over her as she watched him drive out of the yard. It was like the last remnants of their marriage and the plans they had had for the future were leaving too.

The vet who came to check the cows with mastitis knew of their problem, but avoided speaking of it. He became embarrassed when questioned about the possibility of Rose being poisoned.

'I don't know what to suggest, Mrs Chance.' He avoided looking at her. 'Pesticides can cause problems to both humans and animals if not handled correctly. Why not talk to your family doctor?' He was shifting his weight from foot to foot and glancing towards his car.

'The doctor got the diagnosis wrong. Now he's siding with the hospital – to cover himself, I suppose. They all do it.'

'Doctors won't often speak against colleagues.' He gave her a fleeting look. 'I know a doctor who might give you a sympathetic hearing – she's a psychiatrist.'

'I'm not going mad,' she said.

The young vet laughed. He looked at his watch. Animals were obviously far easier to deal with than humans.

20

'You could at least talk to this psychiatrist,' Colin said.

'Oh yes,' she responded. 'That so easily shifts the burden from you, doesn't it.'

He didn't argue back. Not then.

They would lapse into a respite. Some lasted a few hours, or a whole day, with neither speaking and so avoiding mentioning the fearsome trigger words. When they did all her doubts re-emerged through the unease.

Following him into the bedroom as he was getting ready for bed, she said, 'I want to know what you were spraying. I think it may have been what killed Rose.' That had been her tack for two days. Eventually she would wear him down. She always did.

She watched him climb jerkily into his pyjamas, remembering how he had sometimes buttoned Rose into them. She closed her mind's eye against that image and quickly went out, knowing what she had to do then. Colin gave her no alternative. She had to take action to avoid going mad.

Collecting Colin's keys from the kitchen, she drove over to Shearing's farm; without thought of concealment she parked in the austerely tidy yard. She once had had a friend whose house, like this yard, had nothing out of place. She would tidy a cup as she used it, Grace remembered. She didn't see her any more. There was only one padlock key on Colin's ring. It fitted the chemical store lock. Clicking on the torch as she slid back the door, she let the beam run over drums of pesticides. They provided few clues. But at that moment she was ready to believe any one of the 'cide sisters might have caused Rose's death.

She leaned against a large drum of tractor oil, wondering about her next move, suspecting that answers to all her questions were here if only she had the means of digging them out.

Lights coming on in the store and yard startled her; she froze like a rabbit galvanized by car headlights.

'Stay where you are. I've called the police.'

She didn't recognize the farm manager's voice straight-away, but decided the police were just who she needed. After all her daughter had been killed.

21

The following day when Colin went over to Shearing's farm to collect their car, Walter Shearing, the owner, was waiting for him.

'It's outrageous that Mrs Chance makes such accusations. I don't know why she would say this. All I've done is express my concern. If she were my wife, Colin, I'd get professional help, and soon. Going round saying our chemicals killed Rose – of course, you shouldn't have had your daughter with you in the tractor cab,' he reminded him. 'But that doesn't change the facts of the situation. The pathologist didn't hint at pesticide poisoning being the cause of death.'

'I'm sorry, Mr Shearing. Rose didn't get near any of that.'

Shearing nodded. 'I would hope not, Colin, for your sake. Look, if there is anything I can do.'

'She won't go and see the psychiatrist. I can't make her.'

'Can't? You're her husband, man.' He smiled. 'You might have to make that decision for her if she's incapable. It's for her own good.'

At first Grace was alarmed when Colin told her he'd made her an appointment at the psychiatric day-centre. Only after constant badgering did she finally agree to go along there with him, not having the energy to go on fighting him. But thinking about what he might be up to frightened her. Not even at her worst moments of despair did she believe she needed psychiatric help. Her being mad would be too convenient for those conspiring to conceal the real cause of Rose's death. Despite what Colin believed, she intended undergoing psychiatric examination, but had other plans for this trip to town.

A sudden feeling of panic assailed her as she climbed from the toilet window at the day-centre; any doctor hearing about this action might believe she was mad! It was too late to turn back. Her bag, which she had pushed through first, was on the ground, Teddy's head poking through the zipper at one end. She dropped to the ground herself and glanced quickly round. Anyone seeing her climbing from a window of a psychiatric hospital might raise the alarm.

She didn't care where the bus that stopped in the street across from the hospital gates took her, as long as it was away and as quickly as possible. A partially disabled man approached slowly and the driver waited for him. Grace waited almost holding her breath, expecting Colin to come after her at any moment. He didn't. Two other buses were needed to get her out to the Agricultural Department Advisory Service offices on the opposite side of Bury St Edmunds. Before leaving home she had telephoned the scientific officer who had offered to try and identify the chemicals on Teddy.

Dr Carne was tall and stiffly upright with silver hair. He reminded her of her father. The association made her uncomfortable. She felt that coming here was perhaps a mistake and she wanted to flee immediately. She stopped herself by choosing to ignore the feeling.

'We know Mr Shearing's farm, Mrs Chance,' Dr Carne said. 'He's a careful farmer. With a good safety record.'

'His farm is terribly tidy,' she said, making it sound less than a compliment. 'I'm not saying he's a bad man, Dr Carne. I just want to know if the spraying could have caused Rose's death. I think it might have done. She was fine before.' Grace was having difficulty in keeping her responses rational as she fought back tears.

Dr Carne smiled, but still she wasn't reassured.

'I'll get some tests done, Mrs Chance. There will be a small charge . . .' He didn't pursue the matter. 'I'll ring you in a few days with the results.'

When that call came through Colin answered the phone, even though Grace had been waiting for it as if on tenter hooks. She tried to grab the phone, but he pushed her away.

'A number of chemicals impregnated the teddy bear's coat. None of them is likely to have caused your daughter's death. The predominant substance seems to be diesel oil.'

A nervous chuckle came out of Colin. Finally he said,

23

'Thank you very much, sir. Would you mind telling my wife?'

Listening to what the scientific officer had to say made Grace feel slightly sick. Something was wrong with the situation that Dr Carne described. She wanted to believe him, and didn't know what was stopping her.

'Is that an end to this nonsense, Grace?' Colin asked.

She shook her head slowly, barely suspecting the trouble her refusal to accept his findings might cause.

'God, do you know what you're doing? You've cost me Mr Shearing's work; the bank's about to foreclose. So far everyone's being so kind to you. Unless you get help with your problem, I'll do something you won't like. Believe me, Grace, I will. Be warned.'

That jolted her like an electric current. Now she saw in Colin a ruthlessness she had hitherto only suspected. Perhaps it was only noticeable because she was no longer prepared to subjugate her feelings. At that moment she was prepared to walk out of his life, even to risk being on her own, for regardless of whether what she believed about Rose's death was real or imagined, he wasn't prepared to give her any space.

Walking out wasn't practical if she hoped to make any real discovery. Instead she agreed to seek help, reasoning that if she truly did need psychiatric help then she should submit to it; if she didn't she'd have nothing to reproach herself for later.

'Is it a silly notion?' the psychiatrist asked as she made them instant coffee. The milk was sour, so they had their coffee black. 'People often get poisoned by pesticides.'

The doctor was about twenty-five, and although Grace was glad to have someone of her own generation to talk to, she believed that all wisdom was received and therefore accumulated with age.

In the deserted sitting-room where two dozen assorted chairs formed a circle, the doctor said, 'Why do you believe pesticides stopped Rose's breathing? The hospital pathologist seems to think they didn't.'

'I don't know. I'm just convinced they did. Maybe I should be a patient here – like Colin seems to want.'

'What about Colin? Doesn't he share some responsibility?'

This was the most sympathetic response she had met. None of the previous noises of sympathy had meant anything. But it changed nothing. She shrugged. 'I should have stayed at home that day. Then Rose would still be alive.' She buried her face in her coffee mug, fighting back tears.

The young doctor gave her some space, before saying, 'Does feeling guilty change anything, Grace? I think what you really need is to understand from someone you can trust, how your daughter may have died.'

'Everyone says her breathing just stopped – it sometimes happens. That it wasn't anything to do with the pesticides Colin was using. I wish I could somehow be convinced that it wasn't the spraying.'

'Do you want that to be the reason?'

The question puzzled her and she looked at the younger woman for the first time without averting her eyes.

'I just want to know the truth, instead of being fobbed off. It's almost like there is some sort of cover-up going on. I can't say why. I don't know why there would be. It's just something I feel. I have to find out the truth or I will go mad.'

'There's someone at Cambridge who might be able to help. His field's biotech – plant genetics. But the impact of pesticides on the environment is something he's always concerned himself about. I could ring and ask him to talk to you. See if what you think happened is possible.'

'Would he be able to tell me how Rose died?'

'He might not have time to help, even if he can. But at least you're trying something. Action of any kind is really the best remedy to depression. You can trust him. I do.'

Grace looked at her, wondering what she was saying about this man, if she wasn't a bit in love with him.

While she had no misgivings about trusting the man she sat listening to, as he paced up and down at the front of the small lecture room in the Cambridge library, she did wonder if he was the right person to help her. Dr Redford plainly didn't like farmers and the harm he perceived they were doing to the environment.

He was an American, and his anecdotes were about the American farmer; however what he was saying didn't only relate to American farmers for she recognized her neighbour, Walter Shearing, in this man's putative farmer. Dr Redford moved on to attack multinationals who were, he said, increasingly dominating the marketing of seed and chemicals, and using unfair leverage on farmers to make them buy their toxic wares. His talk was stimulating, she found, and her mind, instead of staying filled with her problem, was teeming with questions. She wished she had taken notes.

'. . . Paradoxically,' Dr Redford was saying as he returned to the small dais, and glanced at his notes, 'aid isn't helping the Third World solve any of its agricultural problems. Instead it's helping create total dependence, which the multinationals are wickedly exploiting. The more seed companies that get bought up by the oil and chemical giants, the less chance the Third World has of ever finding the means of feeding itself. These companies are now starting to control seed supply through patenting: they are coming to dictate the environment in which the seeds grow also. Their seeds respond only to their chemicals. Soon we could have a situation where seeds will be worthless to the farmer – unless he buys the company's chemicals also.'

He stopped abruptly and straightened his papers. He didn't ask if there were any questions, but glanced around the fifteen or so silent faces, lunchtime refugees from the cold and damp Cambridgeshire afternoon. They seemed vacant or were searching the floor, unsure if the talk was over, not wanting to be the first to leave.

Tension spread through Grace's chest, making her breathless, as a question she was afraid to ask began to fragment in her mind. She looked around hoping someone else would be the first. Her hand suddenly shot up and her mouth went dry and she couldn't get the words out.

26

'Your wheat, the wheat you're working on to fix nitrogen from the atmosphere,' she finally managed around her thick, seemingly uncontrollable tongue. 'Wouldn't that bring a lot of problems too?'

Seeing him smile, she assumed she had said something foolish. She flushed with embarrassment and wished she hadn't come or asked such a stupid question.

'Producing two tons of grain from a medium poor acre, and without chemicals, is that a problem?'

Anxiety subsided. An argument marshalled itself. She said, 'But there's huge over-production of cereals. More than farmers can sell most years. They're being paid not to grow cereals.'

'All the result of high inputs here in the West – and at considerable cost to water aquifers and to soil structure. Millions and millions of acres erode beyond productive use every year as a result of current intensive farming methods. Russia alone lost 1.5 million acres last year. A nitrogen-fixing wheat not only halts those problems, but gets places like Ethiopia feeding itself within a single growing season.'

'But they would then sell the produce to the West as a cash crop.'

'To feed cattle here to feed humans. Sure,' Dr Redford conceded. 'Pretty damn stupid. Nitrogen fixation won't solve politico-economic problems.'

He looked around for other questions. There were none. She saw him glance her way again and she blushed without knowing why. Perhaps because she thought he knew who she was.

'Are you near to fixing nitrogen in wheat?' There was a tremor in her voice as she approached him outside the library.

'We don't yet know how to transfer a single one of the Nif genes into wheat, much less all seventeen *en bloc*. Getting the genes to express themselves will likely prove an even bigger problem.' His statement assumed she was familiar with what he was talking about. 'Are you a plant breeder?'

'A farmer. I'm Grace Chance.'

27

'You know most of the problems, Grace. I hope you enjoyed the lecture.'

As he turned and started down the steps, Grace felt foolish and confused and wasn't sure if Dr Clarke, the psychiatrist, had in fact spoken to him. She had given her the lecture details.

'Dr Clarke . . .' she began as she went after him, seeing this as her only opportunity. 'She phoned you . . .'

'Oh sure . . .' He continued along the street. 'I told Ali I'm not the person to help. You need a chemical pathologist. It's a long time since I did any of that stuff.'

'Dr . . . but you are concerned about the use of pesticides, Alison said.'

'The problem is, Mrs Chance, my own project is all backed up.'

It sounded like a flat refusal. Grace stopped in the street, ready to flee and was surprised when Redford turned back. She blushed again as he looked her up and down, and hated herself for being so inadequate.

There was a long silence through which he continued to stare at her. She looked away, and looked back. Why didn't he speak? He had a slightly haunted look, like something long since gone still held him in its spell. That made her curious about him.

'I guess I can listen to your story.' He looked at his watch.

'I'm sorry. You're very busy –'

'Yes. I'm giving a radio talk at four-thirty.'

'Dr Clarke thought . . .' she looked for the opportunity to flee, hating this man for his abrupt manner.

'Let me get you some tea,' he said. He seemed determined not to do more than listen.

In the familiar surroundings of his rooms in the sixteenth-century building at King's he visibly relaxed as he made tea. 'Have you eaten anything?' he asked. Grace realized she hadn't since breakfast and now felt hungry. She watched him trying to toast a crumpet by the gasfire. It fell off the toasting fork into the grate as he overheated and backed away from the flames.

'Two years, and still I haven't got the hang of this,' he

said. 'King's reached pre-eminence for left-wing radi-
calism in the sixties and early seventies. Can you believe
such traditions survive to this day?'

She was about to ask why he bothered with them. 'Have
you tried an electric toaster?' she asked instead. Even
though she preferred practical people, she didn't like the
way her husband dismissed every academic as being incapable of tying shoelaces.

'Kids get taught how to toast these at school here.'

Finally she took the crumpet, resited it on the fork and
toasted it in a couple of minutes. There was no butter and
the organic jam he offered her was covered with a film of
mould, which she scraped off without comment. She was
aware of him watching her the whole time and felt very
self-conscious. Pushing some books off a wing-chair, he
settled in it with his crumpet and tea to listen to her story.

She went over the details, not all of them in the right
order. It sounded a bit confusing to her and she wasn't
reassured when Dr Redford looked at his watch.

'It would be a hell of a lot easier if you'd accept the
autopsy finding. Maybe the spray didn't cause your daughter's death.'

That she couldn't accept, even if she couldn't say why.
'I'll read chemical pathology when I go to Norwich if I have
to.'

'That's real persistence.' He sat forward and poured
warm water from the kettle over his used tea bag.

'I can't let this drop. I won't. I know I'm right.'

He nodded. 'Sometimes that gut feeling you get is
enough. Getting pushed in the opposite direction only
seems to increase the feeling.'

Grace almost smiled. Here was a highly qualified scientist giving her some encouragement. She didn't know what
to say.

'You're burning the crumpet,' he told her, interrupting
her thoughts. 'The best I can do, Mrs Chance, is have a
colleague here run some checks on the pesticide, assess if it
was the likely cause of your daughter's death. What was it
being used?'

She stopped scraping the burnt crumpet. 'I don't know.'

29

'Didn't that scientific officer identify it?'

'If he did, he didn't tell me.'

'I guess I'd better call the guy and ask him.'

When Dr Redford made the call the response he got visibly caused his attitude to change, along with some of her uncertainty about him.

Dr Carne said over the phone, 'I'm intrigued, sir, but I don't know Mrs Chance. I didn't run any tests for her.'

'Rose's teddy reeked of pesticide,' Grace protested as she paced agitatedly, picking her way through the papers and books that littered the floor. 'I did go there. He did examine it. He did.'

'Did you get the teddy bear back? We'll run our own tests.'

'No – I was in such a state. I didn't think.'

'Why would the guy lie?'

'I don't know – he's covering something up.' Panic assailed her as she saw what she imagined was disbelief enter his face. She wished she hadn't said that. 'You think I'm mad. That I made this up.' She wanted to persuade him by argument, not tears.

'Ali Clarke wouldn't have sent a flake down here.' He smiled. 'Here's what you do, Mrs Chance. Either you get Teddy back, or get me some clothing your daughter was wearing during the spraying operation. Or alternatively let me know exactly what your husband was putting on that barley.'

'You mean you believe me?'

'Why would anyone invent such a story? Get that clothing, or the bear – maybe we'll find out why this guy is lying.'

She felt confused as relief and uncertainty rushed at her; then anxious, for she wasn't sure if she could provide what he needed. She didn't want to appear a fool or an hysteric. This man's opinion of her mattered to her right then. It was all she had to hang onto.

Darkness had fallen by the time she got back to the farm. The dark, combined with Colin's hostility over her neglect of the cows, was oppressive. But at that moment she felt less burdened than she had in a long while, someone who mattered was prepared to give time and energy to her doubts about the cause of Rose's death.

Seeing a cattle truck pulling out of the yard, she felt a little sick and tried to ignore the reason why.

'Where've you been?' Colin said. 'He wasn't going to take the calves it got so late.'

She closed her eyes, remembering how the cows moaned when separated from their offspring; how the calves cried as they were penned at the market.

'I didn't want them to go.'

'That's stupid. They'll eat us further into debt.'

'I have to get Rose's clothes,' she said, avoiding thinking about the calves and their future. The image of them wouldn't leave her mind's eye.

Colin pursued her into the house.

Rose's bedroom had been stripped. All that remained was the bed, dressing table and wardrobe. Grace wrenched open drawers and cupboards, a sense of alarm and loss leap-frogging one another. There was nothing of Rose left, not even a button that had come astray.

'Where are Rose's things? Where are they?'

'I couldn't bear looking at them,' Colin said.

'They're all I've got.'

'I gave them to the Oxfam shop.'

'You can't –' Alarm appeared in her voice. The last traces of Rose were gone. It was as if Colin were trying to deny she had existed. 'If I don't get them back I'll never forgive you. Never.' Her words laid a wall of ice between them. 'I've got to get them back.'

Colin grabbed her as she tried to push out of the bedroom.

'Grace, the shop will be closed. You can't get them.'

Wrenching away, she fled, not knowing which Oxfam shop Colin had taken the clothes and toys to, but she assumed the one in Bury St Edmunds.

It was closed, as a moment's pause would have told her. Distraught and without thinking at all, she hammered on the door, somehow imagining that if she continued to ring the bell and bang on the door, eventually someone would open it. She simply became more upset.

31

This was all part of a plan to stop her getting to the truth of Rose's death. She saw it clearly and said as much to the police officers who eventually approached her. They looked at her like she was drunk or disturbed.

'I want her clothes. I want them. I have to get them.'

'The shop's shut, love,' the policewoman said. 'It won't be open until ten tomorrow. It says so on the window.'

As if to deny this, Grace hammered harder on the door.

'You'd better come with us.' They put her in the back of their car.

At the police station she alternated between tears and physical protests. In lucid moments she thought how she might defeat this conspiracy. The police talked about Sectioning her to spend seventy-two hours in a psychiatric hospital until she calmly gave her name and where her husband could be contacted. But then she felt threatened. Colin would side with the police; later when he came to the police station she was certain he had.

'Grace, I'm taking you home.'

'I don't want to go home. I want Rose's clothes back. You had no right to give them away.' She had difficulty holding down her rising agitation.

Colin crouched and took her hands. She saw him giving the police an apologetic glance. 'Grace, stop this, or you'll be back at the psychiatric hospital. They want to take you there now.'

'I haven't been . . .' she began. Then she saw how manipulative he was being but still couldn't control herself despite the danger. 'Why are you trying to cover it up? Why?' She sprang up and flew at the door.

'Hospital might be best,' the sergeant said.

'I want Rose's clothes back. That's all. Why can't I get them?'

'I could contact the manageress of the Oxfam shop, sarge,' the policewoman suggested. Grace held her breath at this. 'We could get her to open up. It would save a lot of bother.'

The sergeant considered this and finally agreed.

The elderly manageress of the Oxfam shop grumbled as

she unlocked the door, complaining that nothing was so urgent that it couldn't wait till morning.

Grace pushed in past her as she put on the lights. The racks of clothes smelt sick and tired.

'Today's lot are in the stockroom,' the elderly woman said.

Recognizing the apple box of toys from Rose's bedroom, Grace plunged her hands into it, lifting things out in a carrier bag. She found the dress and cardigan Rose had been wearing that day on the tractor. The smell of chemicals was still on them.

Tears slid from her eyes and down her cheeks as she remembered Rose. The yearning she felt was sharp and painful. More than anything she wanted her back. Next to that she wanted to know why she had died. Wiping her eyes, she looked up and saw Colin watching her, seeing in his look the fear of someone suddenly caught out. The chasm that lay between them seemed to open wider then. They were miles apart and growing more distant.

3

THERE WERE MORE SCIENTIFIC WAYS to test if the
condition of a field was right for ploughing than by
putting the toe of a boot into the soil or taking a handful
to see how it felt, but that was the way most farmers went
about it. Standing with his farm manager on this
five-hundred-acre field, Walter Shearing wondered if he
shouldn't employ a little more science. Back in early
summer he had had his entire crop of spring wheat fail
spectacularly here. There was no logical explanation for
it. The government Advisory Service had told him it was a
bad case of Take-all, a dormant soil-borne virus which
good husbandry kept in check. His farming methods were
second to none and he didn't accept the explanation.
Take-all when it appeared, mostly reduced yields. The
field with its grey underformed wheat was a pitiful sight,
and especially galling as it meant the loss of two hundred
thousand pounds plus. But for the dry autumn the stunted
wheat would have turned black and rotted away
altogether.

'It would take the plough, Mr Shearing,' Mace Hodges
said, letting the friable earth fall through his hand. 'We
could get in the whole crop of canola.'

Shearing had wanted the physical evidence of the
wheat's failure intact until he had received full
compensation from the seed company, but if he didn't
take action soon, he would miss the winter planting and
lose more profit.

'Who would you put down here, Mace?'

'It'd make sense to get going with five tractors. I'd bring

34

in Colin Chance as well – if that's okay.'

'When is our big Fiat going to be repaired?'

'They promised us the computer engineer yesterday – this weather might not hold.'

If the weather changed and the soil became cold and wet, damage from their heavy machines would undo the gains of higher yields from winter planting. The structure of the soil was becoming ever more fragile and likely to collapse and erode.

He thought about the call he'd received late last night from Donald Carne, the ADAS scientific advisor, concerning Mrs Chance. He didn't really want further involvement with that family, but did want to put the failure of this five hundred acres far behind him now and get the field back into profit.

'There's no one else you can get instead of Chance?'

'There's no one else available – not with the weather like this.'

'Take him on if you must. I daresay the poor bastard can use the work. I'll chase our seed suppliers about compensation. Get it organized right away, Mace.'

It hadn't been his intention to run this farm in East Anglia. When he inherited six hundred acres from his uncle, he had been a lawyer, and although not happy in that expensive service industry, he was a partner in a large City firm and making a good living. The farm had been undercapitalized and the wrong size. He knew where to borrow money, and soon bought a neighbouring farm. His first two managers both proved unsatisfactory, having strong opinions and a reluctance to consult him. On buying out another neighbour, and with loans of over a million pounds, he took control directly, and found Mace Hodges who fitted his style of working. Within four years he had reduced his debt to under half a million long-term, with a two hundred thousand operating overdraft, bought a fourth farm and rented two others. He wanted the land belonging to his only remaining immediate neighbour, Colin Chance, and given the current bank rate, knew it was only a matter of time before he got it. There was no economic need of that land, it was a tidying operation. He liked order. For that reason he liked monoculture; hundreds of acres of wheat or field beans or rape with not a single weed intruding. His farmyard displayed the same order. Machinery not housed in the machinery shed was lined up like cars on a sales front. Everybody visiting there commented on how neat things were. None of which proved any guarantee against the unforeseen chaos of breakdown or crop failure.

Dr Carne arrived shortly after the farm manager's departure and parked his car on the edge of the field next to Shearing's Mercedes. His distinct unease amused Shearing. This was a man who enjoyed what he obviously liked to think was their friendship. He more than earned the drinks he sometimes got invited to at Shearing's Queen Anne manor house, and the even less frequent games of golf.

'It doesn't get any better,' Carne said, looking over the rotten wheat.

Here in the pale wintry sunshine he wondered if this man wasn't over-reacting to the phone call he'd received from the Cambridge scientist about Mrs Chance.

'Did you find anything to help me get my compensation?' he said.

'We still think it was duff seed.'

'Spinetti don't accept that. Not all five hundred acres failing.'

'Possibly their polymer coating set up some chain reaction with the Take-all virus.'

He nodded. 'That sounds promising, Donald. It was certainly Take-all that wiped out this wheat, but no one's worked out why so devastatingly, or how the chemicals and fertilizers the seed company wraps around each seed in its polymer coat triggered the problem.'

'We're looking for similar cases of chemical damage to seeds. There might be something for you there.'

'What happened to the Chances that's so urgent?' He looked at his watch. He had an appointment with the bank manager.

'When someone gets a bee in the bonnet, I'm never sure what to make of it. Mrs Chance seems to have one in

36

her bonnet. She's got Dr Joshua Redford from King's College to help her identify the cause of her daughter's death.'

'Is he a pathologist?'

'A plant geneticist. He might be listened to.'

'Is there something to listen to, Donald?'

'Well, no, I suppose not.' He blushed. 'I thought you'd like to know.'

The hospital pathologist's report on the child's death settled all his doubts. Nevertheless he decided then to help the family beyond the work he would give Colin. He didn't want Mrs Chance making rash accusations that might eventually get her into trouble. That would create more bad feeling.

'Is Mrs Chance any better, Colin?' he asked his neighbour when he came over to talk to the farm manager. He assumed her illness to be mental.

'She can't get over Rose's death. It's early days.'

'These things take time. You're not getting much done,' he speculated.

'If it wasn't for your work . . . I'm mostly working for the bank anyway. When you have a good year, everyone else in farming does too. You never seem to get ahead.'

'Don't I know it, Colin. Everyone assumes because you're large there aren't problems. They're simply larger – like the overdraft.' He pushed into the office, motioning Colin to follow.

Here the same order prevailed. Everything went onto the computer, which showed exactly what the stock position was on seed, fertilizer, pesticides, crop rotations; inputs down to the finite penny, and projected returns per acre. Enough information to keep any bank manager happy, except when chaos descended. Profit on the five hundred acres of wheat had been the means of bringing his working overdraft under its ceiling. He carried no insurance against the loss. When a farm got over a certain size, premiums outweighed the risk covered.

'Spinetti Seeds confirmed tomorrow's meeting,' his secretary told him. 'They'd prefer it was informal – without lawyers.'

He nodded. 'Get me some tea, Molly.' He went into his office with Colin. 'No one has any notion still why that five hundred acres failed – apart from Take-all.'

'That makes no sense, Mr Shearing. You set wheat there the year before.'

He didn't want to discuss his troubles. He opened a drawer in his desk and took out a cheque-book and wrote a cheque. 'This doesn't mean I'm responsible for what happened to your daughter, Colin – it's to help you through this bad patch.'

Colin Chance stared at the cheque for a long while, and for a moment Shearing thought he wasn't going to accept it.

'I don't know what to say. The spraying wasn't the cause, Mr Shearing. It wasn't.'

Shearing felt irritated. 'If I thought so, Colin, I wouldn't offer that. Mace will send some work your way.'

'I appreciate it. I've been thinking about getting out – we put a lot into the farm with nothing much to show. Grace wouldn't care.'

'Land's not making its price. It'll get better, hopefully.' He didn't sound hopeful.

'We'll take this as a sort of loan, Mr Shearing,' Colin said.

'Anyway you like, Colin,' – letting him salvage his pride as he steered him to the door.

'Mr Richards phoned, Mr Shearing,' his secretary said, when she brought him his tea along with the computer printouts. 'He wants you to call at the bank before your lunch appointment.'

'Oh does he?' He was unsure whether she knew who would run that meeting. So many people had an inordinate terror of bank managers. He had no such fear. 'Is this what's happening over the next six months?'

'I've included the expected trade-in price of the old combine, but not the anticipated cost of a new one.'

Imminent income in relation to future borrowing was what Dick Richards, the manager of the area bank, wanted to talk about. Shearing met him for lunch three times a year to discuss his requirements. As far as the bank was concerned it was good business, which he was never slow to point out.

The parking space that came free immediately outside the area bank building in Bury St Edmunds caused him to smile with pleasure. He ignored the stony look from a woman driver who was waiting to reverse her car into the space, deciding she was stupid for hesitating. Parking was at a premium in the old market town.

'Walter.' The bank manager stepped from his office beyond the first-floor open-plan customer service area. His smile was unctuous, his handshake damp. 'You're looking well. Still playing squash?'

Shearing disliked small talk. The day was always too short. He preferred bald statements, fast exits.

'It's hard work. I'm developing my golf instead.'

They went round like this while Richards poured him a glass of sherry and brought it in to him in the deep armchair in his office. The bank manager was in his late forties, putting him four or five years older than himself. His hair had receded further, he had dry skin on his forehead along with red patches. The stress of the job was possibly proving too much for him. An altogether unattractive man, he thought. Early in their relationship he had decided Richards had a weak character, but he had yet to find a way to use this to his advantage.

'I thought it would be useful to review your current position before lunch, Walter.'

'Fine.' He wanted to suggest skipping lunch.

'See what your borrowing requirements are.'

'Is Region getting jittery, Dick?'

'Area has no difficulty making a case for the farmers to Region. It's Head Office, they feel over-exposed after writing off so much bad debt here. We don't look like getting back much on what's left.' He opened a buff folder. 'You're on three-two-seven, at two and a half above base.' He never put in the three noughts.

'I need a new combine – assuming I have wheat next year.'

'Is compensation for that lost wheat any closer?'

'I will at least get my inputs. That still leaves me short

two hundred and forty thousand.'

'That would put you back within two hundred.'

'I do have three thousand acres to secure it.'

'Region's concerned that land prices are unrealistically high. They are in a sense. If they started to slip . . .'

'They would need to slip a long way,' he said. 'I could take my business across the road.'

'I hope not,' Richards said, rubbing his hands and conjuring a smile to his face. He glanced at the file and said without looking at him, 'Your house is unencumbered, Walter. Would you leave the deeds on an informal basis?'

'I think not. There's more than enough on the table.'

He certainly would take his business elsewhere if the bank reached for his manor house.

'Let's have lunch – I'm not about to let you go, Walter.'

The set lunch in the Tower Restaurant wasn't any inducement to stay. He watched the bank manager score the tablecloth with his fork as if nervous about something. Extra security for his farm borrowing hadn't been mentioned.

Finally Richards got to it.

'Could I ask a favour, Walter? This is terribly embarrassing, but I don't know what else to do. If I increased your borrowing to four hundred, could you loan me five?'

'Been playing the equity market?' he asked.

'It's nothing like that.' The bank manager gave him a fleeting glance. 'Oh well, I lost a bit. I sold too soon. My wife has to go into hospital for a mastectomy.'

He didn't believe him, for he doubted if a mastectomy could be got for five grand.

'Doesn't the bank have a medical insurance scheme?'

'Not for spouses, I'm afraid.'

Taking out his calculator, he computed the figures as he thought about the proposition. There was a way.

'If I got £400,000 at 1.25 above base instead of 2.5 that would free £5,000 in a full year. You'd be welcome to that. We could review the situation later.'

The bank manager closed his eyes. He didn't see the

triumph in Shearing's smile. The day was decidedly improving, and leading him to some unexpectedly optimistic outcome to his meeting with Spinetti Seeds.

The air conditioning unit in his Mercedes filtered out the poisonous diesel fumes from a heavily laden truck as he followed it along the untidy drive of Spinetti Seeds out at King's Lynn. Watching it turn towards the processing plant as he headed for the double-storeyed office block, he decided the vehicle was overloaded. He had sent off many overloaded twenty-ton grain trucks from his farm. The risk the driver took was less of going out of control, than being stopped by the police and made to unload the excess weight. The advantage to drivers on piece-work outweighed the risks.

'I have an appointment with the products manager.'

The receptionist located him in the quality control room, and directed Shearing to join him there.

The move might have been calculated to show that their process couldn't possibly have caused his seed to fail.

'We make certain our seeds germinate through the coatings we put on, Walter,' said the red-faced products manager.

'Germination wasn't the problem. You saw that field. If it wasn't duff seed, that leaves bad husbandry. The Advisory Service believes your chemicals caused a chain reaction with the Take-all virus in the soil.'

'Impossible.'

That degree of certainty irritated him, believing no one could be that certain about anything. Especially not a wholly unattractive man with an irritatingly prominent Adam's apple that slapped up and down as he spoke.

'I need to get onto that field. The longer this drags on the more compensation I'll look for.' He didn't tell him he had already made his decision, regardless.

'Our managing director is prepared to make you an offer,' the seedman said, surprising him.

'Are Spinetti accepting responsibility?'

That wasn't the position the moon-faced MD took

where he sat across the table from him in the boardroom. He slowly shook his head. Here they were served tea with biscuits baked from Spinetti's wheats. He removed his round glasses and carefully wiped his moist eyes.

'Any offer of compensation is a gesture of goodwill to a favoured customer, Walter.'

'How much goodwill am I worth?' he wanted to know.

Not much, was how he interpreted their offer to refund just the cost of the seed. He took out his pocket calculator and came up with £316,000, which was the price per ton × tonnage per acre × acres planted.

'You'd have needed everything right, including your market,' the products manager protested.

'Of course. That's how I farm – to make money, Winston. I'd accept my inputs to settle this. That's £134.20 an acre.'

The products manager thought £67,000 a lot of money, while the MD was prepared to recommend it to his board.

They were like a hard and soft man double-act and suddenly he felt cheated, knowing he had settled too cheaply. Something was very wrong about this whole episode, he decided, but right then couldn't even begin to guess what it was.

4

J AK REDFORD MOVED WITH A graceless shuffle that ran
his shoes down at the heels, and his gait gave no clue
that he was a marathon runner. He had taken up running
nine years ago. He knew the precise day, the moment, the
reason. He had sprinted then, like he was trying to get
away. But no matter how hard or fast he'd run his
thoughts were always with him. Until he discovered
marathon running. Then he knew he wasn't a sprinter at
all. That was reflected in his work also. Having taken a
major change of course late in his career, there had been a
hard, sustained haul needed to get where he wanted to get
in his new field. It required the single pointed dedication
that he applied to running. When he ran long distances he
found he got high. The longer and harder he ran, the
higher he got. Thoughts got lost like in a meditation,
losing first the past; then the conscious stream; then the
self, and finally the ego. Thinking of himself as little more
than a field of energy disturbing the air he moved
through. Mile after mile became effortless. He didn't
want to stop. When he stopped the thoughts returned. It
was a long time before he had been able to draw a veil
over them and let them rest.

Crossing the lawns between the science labs at
Cambridge, he heard his name called, and turned. Roy
Worlaby was hanging out of a window. The chemical
pathologist was a sprinter.

'I've got some results on that child's clothing.' Worlaby
signalled him over in his peremptory fashion and shut the
window when he changed direction.

Beneath his white lab coat Dr Worlaby dressed like an ICI executive in striped shirts and polka dot neckties. Those were the only visible parts for he always wore a lab coat. Redford had never run with him and didn't know if he ran in a lab coat, but figured he might. He was the kind of guy whose major concern was about his status. His lab coat confirmed what he was.

'There were quite a few chemical compounds on the child's clothing,' Worlaby said. 'We failed to identify some of them.'

'Mrs Chance was hoping for a fatal cocktail,' he told him. He thought about the parcel of clothes she had brought him. Her anxiety about leaving them. There was a real reluctance on his part to get any further involved in this, but something was taking him forward. Maybe the woman herself. It seemed hard to imagine her as a farmer, or even a farmer's wife. The fact that the scientist at the Advisory Service had almost certainly lied intrigued him most. Why? He couldn't leave such a question unanswered.

'Any of these compounds in large enough quantities might kill a child,' Worlaby was saying.

'They'd have shown up in PM.'

'Perhaps – if the pathologist knew what he was looking for. What is interesting, Jak, are the protocol sheets on what I suspect is the most likely product's active ingredients. It looks decidedly fishy.'

'Falsified?' He felt a sudden chill that he knew was entirely to do with his past.

'Well, maybe. I'd certainly doubt that the animal testing which the authors describe would have produced the published results.'

'You mean they *are* likely to cause respiratory problems?' he said. The more excited he got, the more chilled he felt paradoxically.

'I've got a couple of my little gardeners digging out more information,' Dr Worlaby said. 'I don't wish to venture too far along this speculative limb. If you can let me know the exact pesticide cocktail being sprayed, I daresay I can provide a totally clear picture.'

44

In theory that should have been pretty easy to discover, he figured, as he sensed himself being drawn back. Not just to Grace Chance at her farm for more information, but toward his own past and a place which he had made great efforts to avoid.

Mrs Chance was feeding concentrates to the cows in the intensive milking parlour. She looked a real mess, but he noticed little of that, only her eyes. They were dark-ringed with grief and fatigue, but the clear brown irises showed anger and defiance and intelligence and sadness all at the same time. Picking his way through the piles of dung that littered the ground, he wished now he had on boots rather than trainers. The information he had he could easily have given her over the phone. But he found himself seeking excuses to meet her again.

'Couldn't your friend identify the product by a process of elimination?' Grace asked, tidying the loose strands of her dark red hair back behind her ear.

'With time and an unlimited budget, I guess. There are over eight hundred synthetic pesticides on the UK market, with a thousand-plus active ingredients,' he explained. 'Maybe it came in from the US. Stateside there are no less than thirty-two thousand.'

The figures visibly shocked her.

'How can anyone doubt what killed Rose.' She pulled at her anorak like she was suddenly conscious of how she looked. 'My husband won't tell me what he was spraying. If he even knows.'

'Is that legal?'

There was a clear reluctance on Colin Chance's part to talk to anyone. He was subsoiling on contract for Shearing, and didn't disguise the pressure he was under as he leaned out of the tractor cab. Jak had to ask his questions above the engine noise.

'I'm sorry, Dr Redford. The matter's closed.'

'No it's not. It's not,' Grace responded. 'Not until I know.'

'Let it go, Grace – please.'

Tension between this man and woman was so badly fraying their relationship that Jak wondered how they

45

shared the same house, much less the same bed – if they still did. He did think about that.

'If we identified the chemicals, Colin, we could resolve this.'

'I can't tell you. I don't know.'

'You don't know what the hell you were spraying? Don't you guys have to carry a licence to operate a spraying rig? What were you spraying to kill?'

'Not my daughter! Not her.'

He jumped clear of the subsoiler bar as Colin socked the tractor into gear. The machine stopped immediately and he tensed as Colin jumped down.

'I shouldn't have done those tank mixes without knowing the product, of course not. But Rose didn't get anywhere near it. She didn't.'

Nothing Jak heard convinced him of that.

Unable to get any further information here he went with Grace to talk with the farmer.

'I run a safe, efficient farm,' Shearing protested without being accused of a thing. This intrigued Jak more.

'No one's accusing you, sir. Mrs Chance wants an end to her uncertainty over Rose's death.'

'The post-mortem did that, at least for reasonable people. I'm sorry, Mrs Chance. I know this has affected your health – that you're under a psychiatrist.' He glanced at Jak. 'The money I offered was simply to help them over this patch.'

'Please. What was Colin spraying?' Grace said. It was an emotional appeal that got Shearing mad.

'I won't be hounded like this. You'll simply have to accept the pathologist's report. Those sprays weren't responsible for your daughter's death.'

Shearing's face and neck muscles locked rigid and his face reddened before he turned away and disappeared into the farm office.

'Is something eating that guy? We're not getting any-place, Mrs Chance.'

'Yes I'm sorry,' she said like she thought he was quitting. He wanted to tell her he wasn't.

'Let's talk to the scientific officer at the Advisory

Service. Who knows, maybe he's changed his mind.'

The increasing concern he was feeling about what might have happened to this woman's child was a bad sign, he knew. It would start taking precious time that should have been devoted to his own project.

Anxiety chased surprise across Dr Carne's face as he came into the ADAS reception area and saw Mrs Chance. Jak tried to keep surprise off his own face. But his smile wasn't simply a greeting.

'Dr Redford, Mrs Chance,' Carne said. He looked askance at Grace as he ushered them through to his office.

'I guess you're pretty busy, sir.'

'Department cutbacks are causing some staffing difficulties. At least one still has a job, Dr Redford, and some funding.'

In his office he retreated behind his desk.

'I can only repeat, I didn't talk to Mrs Chance or examine the doll.'

'It was a teddy bear,' Grace said.

'Whatever it was, I didn't examine it.'

'You saw the pathologist's report?' Jak asked.

Dr Carne hesitated. 'Yes. Mr Shearing showed it to me.'

Jak glanced at Grace, to see if the same questions occurred to her that came to him: Why did Shearing have the report? Who gave it to him? Why show it to this man?

'You're lying,' Grace said. 'I did come here with Rose's teddy.'

'I will try to help, of course, Mrs Chance. But I do object to being called a liar. And in my own office.'

'You are. You are lying.'

Carne was getting steamed.

'Mrs Chance, let me handle this. Look, why don't you wait outside?' Jak could see she wasn't happy about that as he rose and put his hand on her arm to guide her. He saw her confusion, and tears clouded her eyes. She fled the office.

'Jesus, my patience is about to run out,' he said.

'This must be quite upsetting for her,' Dr Carne said.

'Quite . . .? Emotions just get in the way.'

This was one scientist addressing another and he sensed

Dr Carne begin to relax. Scientists were objective, they didn't get emotional or threatening.

'I don't really understand your interest in pesticides. Now, if you were looking at Shearing's other problem – all the wheat he had fail – I could see why you'd be sparing the time.'

'A friend asked me to help the lady. God knows why I agreed,' he said. 'I'm beginning to wish I hadn't.'

'She is very pretty,' the scientific officer pointed out.

'She sure is.' He wished he could convince himself that that fact had no influence on him.

'Shearing was using a trinurion herbicide – we recommend a cypermethrin fungicide.'

'Is that still used here? The EPA banned it in the USA.'

'I can't think why – the Advisory Committee on Pesticides here decided it was safe.'

He gave him a look, wondering what kind of people they were on such committees that they dared to pronounce any pesticide safe.

'A colleague at Cambridge – Roy Worlaby – found dichlorpronine on the child's clothing. That was banned years ago Stateside.' He had every reason to know it was.

'Dr Worlaby.' Carne wrote the name on his pad. 'Nothing showed in the blood or urine, not according to the pathologist's report. Look, are you going on with this?'

'I don't have the time – not even for a pretty woman.'

'Ah. Would you care to take a look at the spring wheat Shearing had fail?' the ADAS scientist asked. 'You'll find that far more interesting, I'm sure.'

'Was the failure to do with spraying methods?'

Dr Carne smiled. He asked his secretary to get the file from the laboratory. When she found Grace there searching cupboards, Jak was forced to dismiss her as being mentally and emotionally unbalanced. It placated the scientist's fury.

'What a charming guy – real helpful,' he said when he finally emerged from the building carrying a cardboard box of soil and root samples Carne had given him.

'He's a liar!' Grace said.

'I guess he didn't like you snooping around his laboratory. That isn't the way to get him on our side. Get in the car.' He put the box on the rear seat. 'Your neighbour had a big problem with Take-all.'

'He can rot in hell with his wheat.' Grace looked at him. 'Couldn't you see he was lying? Couldn't you? He was.'

'Sure,' he said and started the car. He glanced at Grace, enjoying her bewilderment. About the only thing Carne was right about was her being very pretty. Her freckled nose made her look girlish; she had a full mouth, the kind that made him want to lean right over and kiss. That red hair suggested enough volatility to make life interesting, perhaps too interesting for a scientist! It was a long while since he'd had such thoughts, and they were like awkward strangers stumbling around in his mind. He would never be able to do anything with them.

'He greeted you in the reception,' he explained. 'I only gave the receptionist my name.'

'I thought . . .' She blushed. Then snapped open her bag. 'Look, I found Rose's teddy in the lab.'

'Hey, great! I figured I was a detective.' He enjoyed detective work. To him that was the best kind of science. Doggedness usually determined success. He was dogged. Marathon runners had to be.

The possibility that through helping Grace he was stirring up feelings best left undisturbed had occurred to him from the start. Randomly he was finding his thoughts were seeking her out, comparing her to his wife, considering what a relationship with her would mean, if it could be sustained intellectually. Thoughts of her caused him to pause from dressing. He judged her intelligent, and sensed a doggedness equal to his own. They were pluses in any possible relationship. Clearly she wasn't achieving a fraction of her potential on that messy little farm. He had avoided any emotional involvements since his wife had been killed. There had been opportunities. Now he didn't know how much control he had over this awakening side of his nature. Or what it would mean as the lady concerned was already married.

49

What he had refused to consider in pursuing this was that problems which he had even less control over might arise and rebound on his own project to fix nitrogen in wheat. There was no way they could. He was a research fellow at one of the most prestigious universities in the world. He had a three-year contract funded by an oil company to do pure research. None of his funding was, as far as he knew, directly linked to commercial potential – researchers often suffered interference and oversight from the companies that made huge investments in university departments. But he believed that vested interest couldn't touch him. His line of reasoning on the pesticide poisoning was that it was a local incident and not proven anyway, even though dichlorpronine gave him serious pause. If the lady got the answers she wanted, then the entire episode would fade into history, and she would presumably disappear from his life. So maybe he was stupid to get himself stirred up like he was.

Hearing the vacuum cleaner as the bedder circled the piles of books on the floor in his two rooms at King's, he turned and smiled. After she had been in cleaning, cups foamed with washing-up liquid bubbles when he subsequently used them; and papers stuck to his desk which she swamped with sudsy water. When he complained she would smile and say he had too many papers anyway!

'Is this too loud for tea with the dean, Cherry?' He held a necktie against his chest. Mostly he went tieless and sometimes didn't shave either.

She switched off the vacuum cleaner. 'You on the carpet, Dr Redford?'

'Am I going to get my ass chewed off? I guess not.' In truth he didn't know why the dean had invited him. But it wasn't so unheard of that it was worrying.

In contrast to his own rooms, those the dean occupied were neat and orderly. Books seemingly undisturbed for a hundred years were arranged by author or subject on his dusted shelves. The dean had the same air of permanence where he stooped at the grate for the copper kettle that was boiling on an electric ring. Jak tried to imagine him functioning in an American university, where deans hustled finance, parleying political aspirations the whole while. He watched the white-haired man with the pink fleshy face make tea in a china pot and bring it to the table. His movements suggested years of habit.

'So few people make tea properly these days. There are even tea machines.'

'I guess you don't rate tea-bags?' He had expected other academics to be here and was puzzled by this one to one meeting.

'In a cup presumably? They contain the worst dyed teas. The wood pulp the bag is made from interacts badly with the bleach used for whitening it when immersed. Dioxins are released.'

He guessed it was going to be one of those meetings.

'Is your programme progressing, Jak?' the dean asked when they settled, with what he called a real treat – refined strawberry jam on refined white bread.

Resisting telling him what resulted from eating refined white bread, Jak said, 'Sometimes I figure we're this close to getting the Nif genes to express themselves in wheat. Other times . . . who knows?'

'I can't think that you won't.'

This kind of flattery made him wary. The dean had a reputation for acerbity, which probably explained his fondness for strawberry jam.

'There are many distractions: political, social, economic. Pure research must hold itself remote, especially in these economically restrained times.'

'It's a real world out there, Dean. Things happen that we don't necessarily like.' He sensed himself being forced into some kind of corner.

'A large part of that world awaits the means of feeding itself. What a prize. Stick to the single-minded ruthlessness that science demands. Political questions, even those with a small "p" are not the remit of the pure researcher.'

'Do you have any small "p" in mind?'

The dean poured himself more tea. 'It's from the Uji region of Japan,' he said. 'The only tea that's fit to drink.'

51

The conversation moved on and didn't return to the possible small 'p' political activities he might have been involved in. And Jak was left wondering if the dean had got the right guy.

The real purpose of tea with the dean wasn't something he suspected until a couple of days later when he pursued Dr Roy Worlaby, whose manner became preoccupied to the point of being evasive. He followed him around his laboratory, peering through his microscopes, waiting for him to give him the information he was after.

'Did the tests on the teddy bear finally tell us anything, Roy?'

'Not really. I'm not sure I can be much help. I have a lot of my own work, Jak,' – never once looking at him.

'Am I missing something?' He made the possible connection with those small 'p' political activities now. 'This wouldn't have a bearing on the dean's friendly tea, where nothing gets said, but concern is conveyed at my political involvement outside my academic remit.'

'That's nonsense, Jak.'

'Then what the hell is going down, Roy?'

Turning to look at him for the first time, Worlaby said, 'When you finish here, Jak, you'll go home, where you'll go into industry, or get a chair at one of the Land Grant universities. Nothing is certain when my contract runs out.' His eyes searched the floor.

'How did the British ever lose their goddamn empire?' he said. 'Stateside heads of department tell you to butt out. Here you get tea, and the old knife slips between the shoulder-blades.'

'You're being somewhat melodramatic.'

'You bet! I'm getting the boom lowered.'

'My research is funded by the British Agrochemicals Association. I'm risking their support.'

'Because of an accident to a child on a local farm, Roy? Can you be serious? Or is there something else?'

Dr Worlaby strode along the laboratory away from other researchers and began sorting through slides. Jak went after him.

'From the chemicals we found on the teddy bear the

computer identified the formula of a fungicide as the most likely candidate. It's called Resolution, it's made by Aggrow Chemicals,' Worlaby said, like he was in a confessional. 'An unfortunate name – Aggrow, I mean. They are an influential member of the British Agrochemical Association.'

'That's fairly on the nose, Roy.'

'I can't see that it helps. The product is only in development as yet. I don't believe its active ingredients would have caused the child's death,' Worlaby said.

'Before you figured their protocols could have been faked.'

'That opinion was hasty – certainly mistaken.'

He felt himself getting pushed further back to a place where fear and loathing held sway, and logic and intellect had no power at all.

'Is this one any more sound, Roy?'

He walked out of the lab without hearing Worlaby's reply, figuring it wasn't important. When you depended on chemical companies for research funding, you tended to bend a little in their direction. It was easy for him to take the moral high ground, not having that kind of funding. But when the chips were down he liked to think he would maybe do the right thing now.

His work on trying to get a beneficial gene in one plant to express itself in another was being less rigorously pursued. The reason was that the questions troubling Grace were increasingly troubling him, and he too began to subscribe to the notion of some kind of cover-up. Previous dealings with chemical outfits led him to that conclusion. Pursuing Aggrow Chemicals would, he believed, be a serious error. Then when he learned of the American company which owned Aggrow Chemicals, he doubted if he could go on. But some inexplicable force seemed to be dictating his actions, taking him straight back to his past. All he knew at that point was that he didn't want to go back and unearth whatever was there.

A billboard ten feet high and twenty feet long proudly proclaiming, 'Growing for a better future', spanned the front of Aggrow Chemicals' building in Essex.

53

'I dreamed up the slogan,' said the pleased-looking Peter Beale, the marketing director. 'I believe the statement, too, Dr Redford. I must say I somewhat resent your questions. They sound somewhat like accusations.' None of his resentment surfaced. He kept smiling throughout their meeting.

'We certainly have nothing to hide here.' Beale paused as if expecting an argument, his thick lips parting like slabs of raw meat. 'It's wholly unjust, Dr Redford, that in the late twentieth century there are places in the world where children are still starving. I tell that to my kids when they won't eat their food. They're never impressed. Basically our work is to help farmers grow more and better grain, for all those hungry kids. Unfortunately that advertising slogan is carried by a rival's product – I wish I'd dreamed up that one.'

'Nothing wrong with the objective.' He had heard it many times before from chemical companies.

'There are of course toxicity levels in all agro-chemicals,' Beale conceded. 'But the combination you describe wouldn't have had such an effect, unless the child were chronically ill. Was she?'

Uncertainty caused him to shake his head.

'I would suggest Dr Worlaby identified the wrong product.' His smile broadened. 'Resolution isn't yet available in this country.'

Jak felt disturbed by that statement, and wondered why Beale hadn't told him this over the phone, then guessed he wanted to assess him and what information he had.

'Could I look at the work-up sheets on the product – now I'm here?'

The challenge surprised Beale. His smile momentarily slipped, revealing something else.

'That is too commercially sensitive,' he said.

Maybe he only imagined the fear he saw behind the smiling mask, he thought as he left Aggrow. But there was something more that worried him, something he couldn't identify right then, and that worried him too.

'The more questions I ask,' he told Grace, 'the more brick walls I run up against.'

'Will you go on asking, Dr Redford? Will you, please?'

He looked at her. With that tone in her voice he guessed he'd have walked through fire had she asked him to.

'Would Dr Worlaby help any more?'

He shook his head firmly and started to smile as he remembered what was troubling him from his meeting at Aggrow. Beale had referred to Dr Worlaby's findings. He hadn't mentioned him by name. He saw Grace's puzzled expression, but said nothing to her.

'Can you do some research on this?' He didn't want to admit not even to himself why he asked her. His own researchers would get it done faster.

'Is there no way of getting the protocol sheets?' she said as he took her through the Cambridge science library.

'Not if somebody is lowering the boom.' He opened an index file in the ante-room. 'Here you have references to field trials on the active ingredients in pesticides. Some papers are published in the periodicals on the shelves in the library. Others the librarian will summon up for you as you identify them. Photocopy the results where either dichlor-pronine or trinurion is involved. Cross-reference any variations on that combination. Here – trinurion combined with oxadixyl, so check that too. Can you handle that?'

'Oh, I should think so,' Grace said.

'You know where my rooms are if you need anything. Stop by. Maybe we'll have some tea or burnt muffin.'

It was with an increasing feeling of disappointment that he found she never visited his rooms to ask questions. The bundles of xeroxed references she produced each day were left at the porter's lodge. Slowly he was facing up to the possibility that he was in no way physically attractive to her. But he had a strong sense of denial that left his ego intact.

Jessie Mann, his senior research assistant, found him in his office, where he was contemplating whether to go and offer to buy Grace lunch and what the consequences could be. She had been digging up references for two weeks, and he felt the need to make contact even if she didn't.

'That seed you brought from the Advisory Service offices,' Jessie Mann said. 'There seems to be some new genetic material that's fully expressed itself in it.'

They had sprouted the seed in agar on Petri dishes in controlled environment cabinets that duplicated ideal climatic conditions. Other batches they had grown from single cells chopped out of the sprouted wheat.

He knew Jessie Mann had out of curiosity been looking at why all five hundred acres of the farmer's wheat had failed. This work had little bearing on the thesis she was writing for her PhD.

'What do you figure you've found, Jessie?'

'Maybe I'm getting spots before my eyes. I thought it was a novel or mutant gene. It seems to be a bacterium gene similar to the Nif genes.' She saw his look. 'It's not. I sampled wheat at random from the batches we have been growing, each plant carries the same gene. None of the wheats we have been growing from other sources do.'

The excitement he felt at this was immediately marred by anxiety: he was a competitive animal suddenly faced with the prospect of someone being ahead of him. The seventeen nitrogen fixing genes – the so-called Nif genes – although clearly identified, had yet to be transferred into wheat. The biggest, and so far insuperable, obstacle to the Nif genes being expressed in wheat was that wheat was a plant while these particular genes were bacteria. For that reason the thrust of his work was instead to try to identify the gene that enabled the legumes to form the nodules that harboured the rhizobia bacteria that fixed nitrogen. If Jessie Mann's observations were correct something had occurred in gene transfer along the conceptually far more difficult route. When he examined her findings his anxiety only increased. They needed to repeat the experiment by growing another batch of the seed, and plants from single cells; then another, and yet another, each time establishing if the new gene from a bacterium was there. Then would come the mammoth task of discovering what its primary function was.

Meanwhile he wanted to know more about the seed. Dr Carne wasn't forthcoming. All the scientist could tell him was the name of the supplier. So it was to them he turned.

The day he picked for visiting Spinetti Seeds found the

reception area bedecked with flowers like they were expecting royalty.

'Are they all for me?' He couldn't not say something about such a conspicuous display.

The receptionist smiled. 'It's the Russians. We have the Russians over buying wheat seed.'

The products manager was tied up. Their twelve o'clock appointment slid away. As he waited he occasionally caught glimpses of the entourage gliding out of one of the dusty pre-fabricated buildings into another. The tour looked presidential, and he wondered if he might tag onto it unnoticed. But he guessed it wouldn't tell him much, and the guys in the lumpy suits were more than likely KGB – one of their main functions. Suddenly he found that world fascinating.

The party finally arrived at the reception area, and he saw hope of getting to the products manager. The receptionist glanced in his direction as the Russians swept through. At its head was an animated man, in round spectacles, who was obviously the boss of Spinetti, with a short balding Russian who, from the cut of his suit and detached manner, was obviously the leading buyer. The receptionist didn't forget him, but buttonholed the tall, stooped products manager, who finally came across to him.

'Dr Redford – sorry to have kept you so long. We have Aleksei Krevenko the head of Exportkhleb over looking for a lot of seed.' He glanced round and lowered his voice, making his prominent Adam's apple jump. The Russian's name meant nothing to Jak, but he was rather surprised that they were coming to Britain to buy seed.

'You had a hybrid vigour wheat seed fail on a farm in Bury St Edmunds – I'm looking at the reasons.'

The products manager glanced round again, showing alarm now as the party of Russians went through the double doors to fall upon the buffet lunch spread out there.

'What's your interest?'

'It's pretty unusual. The whole five hundred acres going down. ADAS had no information on the seed.'

57

'It was Prairie Red, a hard spring wheat we imported from Kansas. I can't think that we'll repeat the exercise. It could prove costly – we reimbursed the farmer.'

'I'm interested in the seed's history. It seems there's some new genetic material in there.'

'Breeders are doing all sorts nowadays with the help of plant geneticists.' His Adam's apple jumped up and down.

Figuring this man probably wasn't very well informed about the seed, he said, 'This is a bacterium gene.' That meant nothing to the products manager.

'Crocker-Giant of Kansas developed the seed as a universal high yielding wheat for all climates and latitudes. You'd need to talk to them.'

'Do you have any information at all on it?'

'Only the yields. The hagberg and protein content.'

'What are the Russians buying?' he asked.

'That's what we want to know, Dr Redford. Yes indeed!'

The meeting was over, and he left, but with a lot of unanswered questions.

5

TIME SPENT IN THE CAMBRIDGE science library passed quickly for Grace. She found herself so absorbed that she almost put aside the tragedy that took her there; she was doing something about Rose's death and that helped close the floodgates on her pain. Slowly through the plethora of detail, that she struggled to make sense of, came a growing awareness of at what cost in human tragedy, advances in scientific farming were made. The science she wasn't able to understand, she asked the librarians to explain rather than bother Dr Redford. Her only other contact in the library was with a student who tried to pick her up. She was shocked at first, thinking of this place as she did a cathedral. The second time the student approached she was flattered, and saw herself as less of an outsider. She told herself she was too busy to accept either of his invitations to go for coffee. She was too busy, but she was scared also. The student was good-looking and flamboyantly dressed, and his interest helped give her confidence.

The story she stumbled on in *The Times* was easy to interpret. Several children had died in Mexico from what was believed to be a pesticide accident. The report was circumspect, but left the reader in little doubt that the reporter didn't believe the official version. It quoted a local doctor who stated that the children weren't accidentally sprayed but had been used as guinea pigs to test the effect of the pesticide. Remembering the friendly little guinea pig Rose had had, she found herself wondering why such animals were used for testing, especially as they didn't seem to make the chemicals safe for humans anyway. The fungicide wasn't familiar to her, nor the manufacturing company, but the symptoms described were similar to those Rose had suffered. A breathless nausea came over her. She sat at the library table for a long while, thinking about the dozens of pesticides she had read about there and cross-referenced, just a few dozen out of the hundreds being poured onto the land and into the atmosphere; that she and Colin had used, along with millions of other farmers and gardeners. A seemingly endless stream of poison. Until now she had been concerned only about Rose's death. But there were hundreds, possibly thousands, of similar deaths throughout the world. All as pointless. All leaving someone angry and helpless. Her eyes filled with tears as she thought about the children in Mexico suffering and dying like Rose. Nothing of what she read mitigated her own guilt. She should have been able to prevent Rose's death.

It was some time before she recovered herself, but she didn't feel like going on with her work today.

Finding herself at a watershed and feeling confused about her own part in the stream of poison – yet not being convinced that farming could survive economically without chemicals – she decided to talk to Dr Redford. But she wasn't sure if she wanted him to absolve her or condemn her.

He wasn't in his rooms. The lodge porter thought he was out running but didn't know how long he would be. She decided to wait, not wanting to return to the farm. Colin wouldn't understand but would blow up and tell her they were living in the real world, that he had to make a living. She feared he was right.

She waited for what seemed like a long while on that stone bench in the weather-eroded college entrance. She was getting cold and considered going into the town for tea, but was afraid of missing Dr Redford. She wanted to go to the college refectory, but lacked confidence; there someone might have challenged her, recognizing that she truly wasn't one of them.

Jak Redford came hammering into the entrance and stopped when he saw her. Grace got flustered, uncertain if this was a serious enough reason for bothering him.

'Are you waiting for me, Mrs Chance?'

'I didn't know you were jogging – I may have found something.'

'Why didn't you wait in my rooms – you must be cold.' She let him steer her across the quad.

'I thought it might be intruding.'

'So you freeze to death out of politeness. I guess I'll never understand the English, Mrs Chance.'

With a tremor of anxiety, she said, 'You could call me Grace.'

'Sure. You could call me Jak instead of Dr Redford.'

'Oh. I thought your name was Joshua.'

'So it is – Joshua Alwyn Kennedy Redford.'

In his rooms an awkwardness settled between them. There was no reason to prolong this meeting that Grace could think of and she sensed impatience in him. It made her more nervous and caused her to wonder about the value of what she had found.

'Look, I need to take a shower before I go to give a lecture. Why don't you put the kettle on? We'll have some tea.'

He disappeared into the other room.

The kettle was empty and there was no water in this room, and she didn't quite know what to do. Standing by the fireplace, she noticed the trophies on the mantel, and flushed with embarrassment.

'I'm sorry,' she said when he emerged half-dressed. 'You're not a jogger.'

'These days I get through the marathon at about a jog.'

'You were sixth in last year's London marathon,' she pointed out, reading an inscription.

'One time I'd have been in the first three.'

'Do you run a marathon daily?' she said, afraid to stop talking.

'That would be like a mountaineer climbing Everest every day. I manage about ten miles.'

'Gosh. How do you find the stamina?'

61

'Potatoes basically – and a desire to win, Mrs Chance,' he said.

The way he continued to use her title, despite her invitation to use her given name, stopped her being more familiar.

'Look, I may have found something.'

She spread her latest batch of research papers on the floor as there was no other space anywhere, and knelt to sort them while he made some tea.

'A company called American Chemicals did some trials in Mexico on a dichlorpronine-based pesticide about nine years ago.' She glanced up at him. He was standing as if frozen with the box of teabags in his hand. 'They accidentally sprayed pesticide on some children in a field.'

He shook his head. 'Smartkill – it was called. They stood the kids in the field and sent over the spray plane.'

'Oh, you know about it?' She was surprised.

'The product was banned soon after by the Environmental Protection Agency. It still gets made in the US for export to countries that don't have our kind of controls.'

'Some of the children in Mexico suffered symptoms similar to Rose's,' she said, stretching the facts in the newspaper story as she tried to take the initiative. 'It was reported that some of the children died. The company denied this.'

She stopped suddenly and looked at him. Seeing his face turning ashen, she wondered fleetingly if he was ill from his run. 'Are you all right?'

He nodded. 'American Chemicals own the British company Aggrow Chemicals – you figure they are using the same product here, Mrs Chance?'

'How could they?' she said. 'Don't pesticides have to pass stringent Ministry tests? I don't know how stringent those tests are, but the sales reps always maintained they were impossibly restrictive. I can't see why they would let it in here if it is causing such problems elsewhere.'

'We need your husband to confirm if that's what he was using – so we can compare the active ingredients with what we know about the sprays used in Mexico.'

That immediately plunged Grace back to the dull,

onerous life she had on the farm. She would have happily never returned to it if there had been a viable alternative.

Her questions to Colin later that evening opened up hostilities that had been gathering momentum ever since the accident.

'What are you trying to do?' he demanded. 'Send *me* mad? Is that what you want?'

She was stung by that. He was implying she was mad.

Refusing to react to him, she said, 'I just want to know for Rose's sake.'

'Let it go, Grace, please. Give me some peace.'

There were tears in his eyes when he turned to her. She wanted to remain detached but was unable to ignore anyone crying. She hated herself for weakening like this. She hated him for being weak also. She wanted to turn away and leave, but found herself reaching out and holding him instead, having as much need then to hold onto someone herself. She too began to cry. This was a familiar pattern; they would make love; she would answer her own physical need with a man she cared less and less about; then he would carry on like nothing had happened, and she would find herself thrown back, liking herself less and less.

The cow staggering into the milking parlour, where he was chaining them into the stalls, meant only one thing. The cow slipped and went down onto the deck like a drunken sailor and looked around in distress. That confirmed his worst fears. The problem was notifiable by law, and Colin knew what this would mean to him economically, to the worsening prospect he had of hanging onto the farm.

Nothing was going right. If there was something that could go wrong it did. He couldn't work out why he had such bad luck, or how to break it. He seriously began to wonder why he kept on struggling with the farm when it brought nothing but misery and hard work. The litany of disasters dug him in deeper. This cow going down with bovine spongiform encephalopathy meant the Ministry of Agriculture insisting it be culled, also possibly his entire

63

herd. While compensation meant he would get market value for the beast, his income would vanish with her milk. He decided not to inform the vet, but instead hoist the cow on the bucket of his front loader and drop her into the slurry tank. Then run her into market and sell her as a damaged carcass, saying she had slipped into the slurry pit and drowned. She would go into burgers and pies. He hoped none of his other animals had the same problem. If they did he would be finished. There would be no income, and he certainly wouldn't be able to borrow any more money to rebuild his dairy herd. Not that he'd choose to. What he would really like was a job where he could put on a suit and drive around talking to other farmers, maybe a rep for a fertilizer company. Farming on this level was a nightmare. He couldn't bear to think of the plans he and Grace once had had.

As he got the cows chained onto their stalls, he put the suction cups over their teats to milk them, first drenching the mastitis-affected animals with antibiotic. As he put the hypodermic into an affected teat, he noticed it had collapsed. He checked the others. Two out of the four had collapsed. That was half his income from this cow gone. He cursed and slammed his forearm into her flank. She was another destined for the burger trade.

After he had all the cows hooked up, he stepped out of the parlour and glanced across the yard to a blue Metro, which belonged to the local environmental health officer. His more immediate concern was whether this man had seen the cow with the staggers. If he had there was no way he could do what he planned.

'Mr Chance,' the environmental health officer said, appearing from around the side of the slurry tank. 'Your silage clamp is *still* leaking and *still* polluting the stream. It's killing all the aquatic life.'

'I can see it myself,' he protested. 'The silage is stable now.'

'But the rain on top of it causes liquor to leach out. And your slurry tank is leaking. That's another source of pollution. You've done nothing about either since my last visit.'

'You can't keep up on your own. I've got the bank on my back – the cows are badly infected with mastitis.'

'I know the problems. But you've got to deal with this pollution.'

It was his third warning.

'Why don't you go after my neighbour? He's a worse polluter! The sprays and fertilizer he puts on all gets into the river. He can bloody well get away with it.'

'You have thirty days to remedy the problem or we'll take action through the court.'

'What about Shearing?'

This man clearly didn't want to hear about that. He turned away.

'Shearing's probably bribing someone in your department. Those who can afford it get away with murder.' He hated Shearing at that moment. 'The likes of him always cause a bigger burden of bureaucracy to fall on the small farmer. You people have to pick on someone.'

Later in the pub, where he went to escape the increasingly hostile atmosphere at home, he was bought a drink by one of Shearing's farm workers. The farm-hand told him they were taking out hedges and draining some wetlands. The anger Colin felt about that was to do with the fact that it was work he could have done with. Since the winter spraying finished he hadn't had any work from Shearing. Removing hedges was something else the big farmer got away with.

'That piece of wetland is a Site of Special Scientific Interest,' he pointed out.

'I expect the boss will pay a small fine for destroying it if he's caught. No one's going to make him restore it.'

'How come I didn't get some of that work, Dave? I thought you blokes were pretty busy.'

'The boss got a bunch of cowboys in to help us.'

Colin realized at once that he had been bought off over the death of his daughter. The two thousand pounds from Shearing was to keep him quiet. Grace was probably right about the unlabelled pesticide he'd used on that barley somehow killing Rose. He felt sick with rage and left the pub not knowing what to do. He thought about going to talk to Grace, but knew she'd demand the evidence. He decided to get it.

He no longer had a key to the padlock on Shearing's chemical store, but a crowbar snapped the hasp effortlessly. He didn't think about the retort carrying through the clear frosty air, or associate the distant dog barking with what he was doing.

The blue unlabelled drums he had mixed the spray from were nowhere to be found, but as he searched he tipped over other drums as he thought about what Shearing had done to his family. He wanted to pay him back, so poured diesel oil onto some rags, then put a match to it. This was madness, he told himself as he watched the flames spread. He knew he could go to prison. Good sense made him try to put out the fire, but as it spread, panic caused him to run.

'Colin!' Mace Hodges said, as he hurried across the yard from his bungalow.

The rottweiler was barking wildly and throwing itself against the wire fence of its pen.

Colin froze briefly then ran out of the yard without considering retrieving the situation by helping Hodges to extinguish the fire.

The police arrested Colin on the road before he had reached his own farm. He refused to go quietly.

'It was bloody stupid,' Walter Shearing said, pacing up and down in front of him at the police station. 'Bloody stupid, Colin. You could have burned down the whole chemical store and half my machinery if Mace hadn't heard you. But I don't want to be vindictive, I don't want to press charges.'

That surprised him.

The police inspector seemed surprised also.

'It's not that simple, sir. He assaulted one of my officers.'

Shearing stopped pacing and looked in his direction, then motioned the inspector outside. Colin was amazed that this man could treat the police the same way he treated his hired help.

What Shearing said he didn't know, but when the

inspector returned to the charge room on his own he punched him in the side of the head without warning. Colin went sprawling out of his chair and tried to scrabble away when he was helped up, fearing another blow.

'You strike a policeman again,' the inspector said, 'you'll get a lot worse. Now get on home – your wife's outside. You can thank Mr Shearing you're not being charged.'

Colin said nothing, but didn't feel a bit thankful.

He and Grace walked in silence to their car. He was unable to talk. Grace seemed to have nothing to say to him. When finally she looked at him he started to cry. Huge sobs stuttered out of him without any control.

'Pull yourself together, Colin. For godsake. You could be in prison.'

'I can't go on, Grace. I can't. I've decided I want to sell up. Everything reminds me of Rose. What those sprays did to her.'

'It's a bit late now,' Grace said, and walked on ahead to their car.

Colin blew his nose and watched her go. He suddenly turned and ran back the way they had come, ducking around the first corner. He didn't care if he never saw her again.

After analysing the whole of Grace's research material from the library, Jak Redford saw clear culpability on the part of Shearing in the death of the child. It wouldn't be easy to prove that the dichlorpronine-containing product Resolution had been used, not without a reliable witness. But with a couple of imaginative leaps they could talk to a lawyer about maybe suing Aggrow Chemicals, along with Walter Shearing, and so put pressure on them. It was a legitimate excuse to meet with Grace again.

'Let us assume that Resolution is somehow available here, and was the unlabelled product being used by your husband,' he said, pacing up and down in his laboratory. Today he noticed the faint cologne Grace had on. More and more he had started noticing what she was wearing, and thought perhaps she was taking obvious care when she

67

came to Cambridge. 'Its active ingredient is dichlorpro-nine, which mixed with herbicide trinurion resulted in respiratory problems in rats in two of the studies you turned up.'

'I hadn't noticed,' Grace said. 'Would the effect be the same in humans? Do laboratory rats and humans really have anything in common?'

'Unfortunately for the rat there seem to be some similarities in the two nervous systems. We know for sure one of the products used by your husband contained trinurion. Combined with information about those kids killed in Mexico with a similar product to Resolution, I figure we could start a lawsuit.'

Grace remained silent for a long while.

Uncertainty came at him. Maybe he was trying to push her too hard into a course of action that would possibly affect her for the rest of her life. Maybe he wasn't thinking through the consequences. It would doubtless put a lot of pressure on her marriage. Maybe that was what he wanted.

'I'm giving a talk in London this evening – Look, I set up a meeting with a lawyer I know. I thought it would be useful.'

'Today?' Grace said.

'Can't you make it? This firm is pretty high-powered, but Mark Bailey, the partner I talked to, he has a kind of social conscience. More important he doesn't have farming connections, so that won't affect his advice.'

'I'm not sure. I wouldn't be able to afford such an expensive action.'

'Well, talk is cheap. Mark won't charge for this meeting. I got that much out of him.'

The firm's spacious offices in an imposing post-war block in High Holborn suggested that even to think about hiring them would be costly.

Mark Bailey, one of the twenty-seven partners, raised the question of cost at the outset.

'High court actions are pretty expensive, Grace.' He scrunched one of the ginger biscuits he had had sent in with the tea. 'There's no point pretending otherwise.

68

Aggrow Chemicals will fight it expensively in order to run you out of money, especially if they are culpable. They would also pay money into court towards any damages and so make you liable for your own costs from the moment that payment went into court if any award to you didn't exceed their payment.'

'What about some kind of legal aid funding, Mark?'

'Grace might qualify if her prospects of winning were good enough. We couldn't rely on that. We could start, then ask the government to take this over in the public interest. But it's doubtful if they would. Not with the Ministry of Agriculture representing the sort of vested interest it seems to.'

'I wouldn't be able to afford this, not even if we sold the farm.'

Mark Bailey scrunched another biscuit and furrowed his forehead. 'I don't want to foster false hope, Grace. But who knows, Aggrow Chemicals might fall at our first puff.' He smiled.

'But the chances are they won't.'

'How about your company taking a percentage, Mark?' Jak asked. 'Like lawyers in the US.'

The solicitor laughed. 'This is not America. We're not allowed to undertake contingency actions.'

'Class Actions?' Jak said, confused by English legal jargon.

'No – taking cases for a percentage – there are no Class Actions here either. Look, I'll write to Aggrow, Grace. I'll be fairly bullish. See what happens. That won't cost you a thing.'

'Is money getting to be a problem?' Jak asked, surprising himself as he and Grace walked along High Holborn.

'Nothing much around the farm generates income at this time of year,' she replied. 'Our overdraft is creeping up, and the bank is getting more difficult about cashing cheques. They're the usual problems small farmers have.'

He didn't invite her to his lecture at the Royal Society, but hoped she wouldn't make an excuse not to go as he drove her towards Carlton House Terrace. Despite the time he had spent with her, he felt no closer to her, and no nearer to understanding what made her settle for the kind of life she had.

As he was parking the car she said, 'Why are you going on with this? What will you get out of it? That sounds ungracious, I'm sorry. I don't want you to stop looking. But I'm worried about taking so much of your time.'

'You haven't met too many marathon runners, Mrs Chance,' he said, feeling elated at her concern. 'Your feet get sore, your muscles burn, your head is light and still you refuse to quit.'

Grace glanced sideways at him.

'I found something interesting on your neighbour's farm. It ties in with my own research.'

'To do with the wheat that failed?'

'You're pretty smart, Mrs Chance. That problem with Take-all looks like it was somehow genetically engineered.'

'Take-all comes from a soil-borne virus.'

'Sounds crazy. There's no pesticide for it. Good husbandry pretty well keeps it in check.'

'Shearing's farm is well managed.'

'Sure. Everything looks wrong for the problem on that scale. There is a new bacterium gene in those plants. We haven't identified its source.'

'You can identify a gene from bacteria within a plant, and the effect it has?'

'We're not quite that smart yet. But the multinationals figure we'll get there – that's why they're grabbing seed companies.'

'But why engineer a wheat to fail?'

'If that's what has happened, it means somebody's way ahead of me. No one's published any of the work that I've seen. I need some more information – I'm hoping maybe that guy Carne has it. Or Shearing.'

He got nowhere with the farmer, and wasn't optimistic about the agriculture advisor having that kind of information, but pursued him anyway. The man's manner was evasive and he wondered if Dr Carne had talked with Shearing.

'I can't challenge your authority, Dr Redford, but some-one developing a wheat to attract Take-all? It seems unlikely.'

'It makes no kind of sense,' he conceded. 'Maybe you and I should talk with the guy who sowed it.'

'Mr Shearing? He was compensated for his crop.'

'I'd like to know why the seed company paid up. I tried calling him. He wouldn't talk to me. He'd take a visit from you, I guess.'

'The notion is so far-fetched,' Dr Carne said.

'It sure is. But that's how it looks.'

'I suppose I did get you into this.'

When they called out to the farm Shearing was busy, clad in a white fumigation suit, helping dust potatoes in the huge store to stop them sprouting and reducing their market value.

He waited in the yard with Dr Carne, who tried to make conversation about biotech developments that would eventually dispense with the need of the chemical farm.

'I figure Environmentalists will get us there quicker,' Jak said. 'Most of the progress will come from demands for a safer environment.'

'The warm weather's causing my spuds to sprout,' Shearing said as he removed his helmet. 'They'll start to look like bewhiskered prunes.' He smiled. 'You're getting your lines crossed, Dr Redford. I didn't have any sort of problem with Take-all.'

'I guess somebody's information is getting screwed up someplace,' Redford replied. 'You didn't lose five hun-dred acres, or get compensation?'

Shearing laughed. 'I'd soon go broke.'

'I got soil and root samples from your five-hundred-acre field.' He looked at Dr Carne.

'Ah, no,' Carne said, avoiding his eyes. 'Those came from a test patch we planted ourselves, Dr Redford.'

'We've been here before with some questions about pesticide,' Jak said, not disguising his surprise. 'Where is this patch? I'd like to take a look.'

'I'm afraid I can't say, our computer is down at the moment.'

He nodded slowly. He couldn't wait to stop by and tell Grace of this development. 'You're full of shit. Jesus Christ, you guys are so full of it.' He headed away to his car, feeling steamed and amused at the same time.

Something *was* being covered up here, he had no doubt about that, nor that he would go on pursuing it. He'd enjoy pulling those two assholes to pieces.

He found Grace in the yard outside the milking parlour. She was talking to someone but he couldn't see who. Not wanting to interrupt, he still felt guilty at maybe listening to a private conversation. She was standing watching the cows. When she approached one and stroked it, leaning her head on its broad flat back, he realized she was talking to them.

'I can't blame you,' she was saying, and then, 'I can't go on. I can't . . . Nor can you really.'

He tried to creep away, when she turned and was startled at seeing him.

'I called to the house . . .' he said. 'Are you okay?'

'It's a long while since I've talked to the cows. Colin used to all the while in the early days – before they became machines.'

Grace wiped away her tears. 'They won't go in. Who can blame them really? When life becomes unspeakably miserable and uncomfortable, there has to come a point when even creatures as supposedly stupid as cows refuse to go on. I think perhaps they've reached that point. Their only thanks for their suffering is to end up in some crummy beefburger. I can't bear to think about that. I'm not even sure if I can bear to see them being milked any longer.'

'Don't they have to get milked somehow?'

'They'll be uncomfortable until they drop their milk. Not as uncomfortable as they are now. They'll dry up.'

'Along with your farm income?' It needed no seer to divine the economic future here.

'I'm going to turn them out into the field, let them behave like real cows.'

She threw herself into that like she was afraid the notion would vanish.

72

The cows pranced and bucked when they reached the field. Grace smiled as she watched them.

He considered her tear-stained cheeks and her old farm clothes, sensing she was terribly vulnerable, and finding that even more attractive.

She turned and noticed him looking at her. He didn't know if she saw anything in his look, but her hand suddenly tidied a loose strand of her hair, then reached to cover a missing button.

'Am I interrupting your chores?' He followed her to the house.

'I don't want to carry on with this – Colin left.'

'He just let out? What are your plans?'

'Prove how Rose died – then take up my degree course at Norwich. Would you like tea?'

'Sure.' He felt pleased she was still planning on going to college. He was scared of her investing too in him, even though a part of him might have welcomed that kind of commitment. It had been a long time. He refused to explore the thoughts further.

Over tea he said, 'Where are the five hundred acres of wheat your neighbour lost?'

'He's ploughed and planted the field.'

'I guess it's still there.'

They went, as night fell, armed with a trowel and Safeway plastic bags to pick up some soil samples.

'Why would he deny losing his wheat?' Grace said. 'Everyone around here heard about it.'

'Something's going down. The guy from the Advisory Service is in on it. Maybe they're looking to destroy a lot of wheat, then somehow corner the market.'

'Is that possible?'

'I guess not. Not with an outfit the size of Shearing's.'

'But the Advisory Service is government backed. Maybe it's a way to control overproduction?' Grace speculated.

'The British government sure could afford the kind of research involved. That doesn't tell us who did it.'

A tractor appearing along the edge of the field startled them. An arc light on its cab swept an area away from them.

73

He pushed Grace to the ground. Then carefully reached out and pulled the white and red Safeway bags close to his prone body, brushing her shoulder as he did so, feeling its warmth, enjoying its softness. The arc of light passed nearby. The tractor swung round and went back along the track to the road.

Neither he nor Grace moved.

'Do you think he saw us?'

'Somebody sure did for them to come looking. Let's get out of here. These soil samples will do.'

They climbed off the ground. 'Mrs Chance,' he said, feeling suddenly closer to her for having shared this danger, and daring to make real contact. She turned. With a slightly trembling hand he reached out and brushed some mud off her face. She held his look. That tremble of expectation affected his whole body. He wasn't sure what was happening and was still less certain what to do about it. He waited too long. The moment passed and he regretted letting it go.

6

NEWS THAT THE DEAN HAD been looking for him at his laboratory, if unusual, caused Jak Redford no sense of alarm. Nor when the dean showed up again later that morning.

He was running tests on the soil he had got from Shearing's field. The level of the soil-borne virus Gaenmannomyces graninis was about the highest recorded, and he couldn't believe that was accidental or coincidental.

The white-haired dean stopped alongside him and peered through the adjacent microscope. He wasn't about to offer him tea-bag tea.

'Interesting?'

'Gaeumannomyces graminis,' he replied, showing no curiosity at the dean's unexpected visit. 'Fifty thousand parts per million – give or take a dozen or so.'

'The significance?' – like he was addressing a student rather than someone *Nature* referred to as a leader in his field. Jak felt mildly irritated.

'There's going to be a real problem for farmers growing wheat on this soil for years.'

'Conclusion?'

Getting more irritated now, he said, 'What can I do for you, dean?'

'The petroleum company funding your work has axed you.'

'The hell they did. I have a year to run on my contract.'

'They are the sole source of finance – I did point out that your contract hadn't expired. I'm afraid they suggested you might sue them.'

'I sure will.' The suddenness of this, the equilibrium with which the dean delivered the news made him suspicious. 'How can they come on like this? There's been no warning, no faculty discussion that I've been part of.'

'The axe swings perilously close to so many. I argued your case with the utmost vigour.'

'What's the story, Horace? Am I touching a raw nerve or two someplace?'

'This isn't personal, Jak,' the dean said. 'I wouldn't like it to be thought otherwise.'

'It feels pretty goddamn personal to me, Horace. Goddamn it, I've got a hell of a lot invested in this work.' Grace came into his thoughts. He might not see her again. 'Am I being denied access to my laboratory?'

Clearly the dean hadn't expected this tack. When funding vanished, work almost always stopped automatically.

'Oh, of course not, my dear fellow. But your project being non-specific as it were, the science department won't be able to provide funds for you to continue – as much as we would like to. These really are economically constrained times as far as pure research goes.'

'I figure I'll go on with this using my own money a while.'

The dean seemed surprised. He simply retreated.

Jak knew he was being more angry than realistic. He had no idea how long he could continue for. If somebody was putting pressure on him the next move would be to take away his facilities, or bill him for them. Then there would be no way he could go on either with his own work or with helping Grace in her search for truth.

Existing as he did in the somewhat drawn-off world of academia, where most intrigue related to faculty pecking order, which he chose not to involve himself in, he was able to believe that any conspiracy theories around the campus were mostly fantasy. The axing of his research funding wasn't because of what he was getting into, he told himself. Only the reassurance carried little conviction.

Mark Bailey wasn't a fantasist. At least not in his assessment of him. Nor an alarmist. He was a large, round, moderately ambitious English lawyer with two large feet planted firmly in the ground. The phone call he received from Bailey was at first surprising, then not a little worrying.

'I've had my office burgled, Jak.'

'Gee, that's too bad.' He wondered what it had to do with him that it was worth a phone call. 'Don't you guys have security?'

'No more than is reasonable. These things just don't happen to solicitors like us. It's the sort of thing that happens to solicitors in places like Euston and Waterloo.'

Solicitors in the vicinity of London train stations didn't mean a thing to him.

'That's where the radical leftish firms are.'

'They are? Is there any way I can help, Mark? I'm having one or two problems myself right now.'

'Oh, what kind of problems?'

He told him briefly about losing his funding, still puzzling at a busy lawyer taking time out in his morning for this call.

'That means you can't continue with your work?'

'That's how it will stack up. Did you lose anything in the break-in?'

'One file is missing. It makes no sense at all.'

Then he knew the purpose of the call. 'This is connected with Mrs Chance.'

'Yes. It's one very slim file containing details of her claim against Aggrow Chemicals.'

He said nothing but felt breathless.

'Burglary is supposed to leave the victim feeling violated,' the solicitor continued. 'All this has left me feeling bemused, and it's disturbed the routine of our morning. My partners seem to think I might be mixed up in something sinister . . . Am I, Jak?'

'I guess,' he said. 'Just what the hell it is I can't tell you right now. I don't know.'

'I might have forgotten the whole incident only my girlfriend has just phoned to say that both my car and our flat have been broken into.'

'That is pretty heavy, Mark.' He closed his eyes, as if

77

trying not to get sucked back into that stuff.

'It is very sinister, I'd say. It can't be just a coincidence. What am I to tell the police?'

'There's nothing to tell right now.'

'Jak?' Mark Bailey said with uncertainty in his voice. 'I'm not an exponent of conspiracy theories, but this certainly feels like one of some sort.'

He hesitated, trying to deny what all this was telling him.

'I'd make a pretty sure bet that Aggrow Chemicals, or maybe their parent company, American Chemicals, are somehow involved, Mark.'

'Do you have something to substantiate that?'

'Nothing that would impress the police. But, Mark, they kind of like to play to win.'

The phone call left him feeling slightly sick and trembling. As a result of his own experience with American Chemicals he had changed the entire course of his life. He had done so on little more than suspicion. Now, because of some fairly minor run-in with a subsidiary of that company things seemed to have come full circle in his life. He was back at a point where he was ready to run again. There was no real point in staying on, he told himself, not without funding available to him. That wasn't running, he argued, but merely bowing to the inevitable.

Even accepting that American/Aggrow Chemicals were capable of all kinds of dirty tricks, burglary not least among their repertoire, he still made no immediate connection between helping Grace with her investigation and the two men who wandered into his laboratory a couple of days later. He was under the emergency shower he sometimes used after his morning run. When he shut off the water he heard cupboards being opened and closed and assumed it was his research assistant. She was the only help he had left.

'Hi, Jessie,' he called. 'You want to take a look at those DNA enzymes I tagged earlier. Real interesting.'

The silence that followed puzzled him. Stepping into his tracksuit pants, he moved along past some large

78

controlled environment cabinets to find two guys going through filing cabinet drawers like they owned the place.

'If you're looking for drugs, you're in the wrong department,' – guessing drug abuse wasn't their problem, despite the menace coming from them.

'Laurence James,' the larger of the two said, producing his identity.

It said he was a Home Office immigration official. The photo needed updating, he noticed, glancing at the short balding man, who possibly believed time had stood still for him.

'That's Detective Sergeant Lynch.' He indicated the edgy, bearded man who continued to check through the drawers.

'Do you need any help?'

'Your assistant won't be coming in today,' Lynch informed him. 'She's been arrested.'

'Did you get the right guy? Jessie arrested? What the hell for?'

'What's your resident's status, sir?' James asked.

'I'm a research fellow. My work permit is in order. What is this?' he demanded.

'Does your work have military or strategic application?'

'Are you serious?' He didn't like minor officials coming down on him, but he could handle that kind of trouble. 'This is crazy.'

'Just answer the question, sir.' Lynch made the 'sir' sound like an insult.

'I'm an American citizen. I don't have to take this shit. If you want answers from me, you'd better give me some. Why was Jessie arrested?'

That caused confusion between these two men which suggested something wasn't quite right here. At once doubt assailed him over his assessment, never having been a person to allow intuition to guide him through any situation where reason or intellect could be used.

'She was picked up on a drugs charge,' the Special Branch detective said. 'With an official from the Israeli Embassy.'

'This has something to do with my resident's status?'

'Your relationship with this particular Israeli official raises questions of your own desirability, Dr Redford.'

'I figured Israel for a friendly nation.'

The immigration official was now perspiring heavily.

'Hey!' Jak grabbed a folder and slammed a drawer. 'If you want to do that, get a warrant – or do you have one?'

'It's an informal visit, sir.'

'Then be sure and warn me not to be around if it ever gets to be official.'

He showed them the door, wondering how he'd handle this if they refused to leave. He was just about mad enough to hit one of them.

Afterwards he found himself shaking so much he had difficulty getting the coffee pot set over a bunsen burner on one of the sterile benches. These men were part of the same problem. But for their English accents they might have stepped right out of his past. He remembered the indifference in the official's voice as she explained how his wife and child had died; the mouth he had focused on had seemed somehow detached from the woman, it had been slightly hare-lipped and shaped like a cracked button, and had hissed the words, an accident, an accident . . .

As he calmed down he glanced about the room, wondering how long it would take him to put his papers together and get out. What excuse would he give to Mrs Chance? He decided to write her a note, then resisted the idea. If he returned to the US in these circumstances he would be right where he had been nine years ago.

The options open to him were to go back and find out what happened or go forward. He wasn't sure if he was brave enough for either and wanted to stay put where he was. Right then he decided to set about finding out if Jessie Mann needed any help and picked up the phone.

The phone ringing as she was about to leave to see the bank manager was bound to be more bad news. Grace almost didn't answer it. A minute later and she would have been gone anyway. It was the lawyer, Mark Bailey. He told her that Aggrow Chemicals were prepared to make an offer without prejudice of £4,000 compensation over Rose's death. The offer confused Grace. At once she felt vindicated in her actions, but then hurt that anyone could think so little of the death of her daughter.

'Four thousand doesn't seem a great deal,' Bailey said, 'but it is in line with the type of settlement courts award. Perhaps you'd like to think about it. I did discuss it with one of my senior partners. It's unlikely that you would get more.'

From his tone she knew he was telling her to settle. 'I don't want more,' she said. 'I just want someone to say that they were responsible for Rose's death. That the chemicals they're polluting everything with are to blame. Is that what they are saying?'

'No. I'm afraid it isn't.'

'Then why are they making this offer?'

'To avoid adverse publicity in today's environmentally sensitive climate. Aggrow Chemicals would require that you forgo any future action.'

'Only if they admit full responsibility.'

'Frankly, I think we'll wait till hell freezes over for that.' He hesitated. 'I'm not quite sure what's happening here. Has Jak Redford spoken to you recently?'

He seemed surprised when she told him no. She wondered if he thought there was something more between them than in fact there was.

'I had my office and flat burgled. And my car broken into. The only thing taken was your file.'

A feeling of relief flooded over her as she stood in the kitchen. This was almost as good as the pesticide manufacturer admitting full responsibility.

'What did the police say?' she asked.

'That I should be glad my office and flat weren't wrecked. Charming, isn't it?'

'I still haven't got any money to pay you, Mr Bailey – but will you continue with this – there might be something left over from selling the farm.'

'I can hardly drop out now, Grace. I'll pursue Aggrow to the next stage and reassess the situation then.'

With that, she flew to her meeting with the bank manager.

81

She knew what he wanted, even though he had difficulty in getting to it as she sat in his office. He wanted the bank's money back. She decided she wasn't going to make life easy for him and stared across the desk. He refused to look at her. His eyes glanced everywhere else, when not on the fat folder in front of him.

'It's not a pretty situation, Mrs Chance,' Dick Richards said. 'Your indebtedness now stands at £68,000. With your husband gone, the farm income is precarious, to say the least.'

'No. It's non-existent. That's why I've decided to sell,' she added, seizing the initiative.

'I see.' He glanced over the computerized bank statements. 'We haven't seen any milk cheques recently.'

'You wouldn't have. The cows have mastitis – I've stopped milking them.'

'Putting them into calf again will be expensive. You'd need . . .'

'No – I've just told you, I'm selling up. Everything.'

Richards scanned the file again. 'Even with selling your milk quota, the total price is unlikely to cover your borrowing. The bank expected you to make a going concern of intensive milk production, that's why we loaned you the capital to build and equip. You've only been going for just over two years.'

'I'm sorry.' What Grace really wanted to say was that she thought the bank equally to blame for encouraging them to borrow as it had.

'You realize we will look to you for any deficit.'

'I was hoping there might be something to spare – I'm starting back at university.'

'I wish I shared your optimism, Mrs Chance – about there being any surplus from a sale.' He rose. The meeting was at an end. 'I'll write to you formally calling in your loan. I have to protect the bank's position. I suggest you try to come to some sort of settlement with any other creditors, as you don't want them bankrupting you.'

'How can I with no income?' Grace asked, her spirit vanishing.

'Delay them. Explain that you're selling up and will

make some settlement then.'

'But you just said there won't be anything left.' She saw his suggestion as dishonest, the means of protecting his interests.

'I do have to think about the bank. Thank you for coming in.'

'You know it's just as much your fault – the way banks keep on encouraging farmers to borrow more and more. It is.' She was determined not to cry.

'I can't get into a philosophical discussion about this.'

He opened the door as if with great difficulty.

Clearly he didn't choose to understand what she was saying or acknowledge his own responsibility in any way. But she felt better for saying what she had. The knowledge that the farm would be going and that she would no longer have to struggle to keep it running lifted a great weight from her shoulders. Now she could concentrate on what was important.

7

EIGHT CALLS HE MADE TO the products manager at Spinetti Seeds and eight times he got a promise from his secretary that she would have him return his call. With each subsequent call he convinced himself that the man was avoiding him because of his part in what had happened to Shearing's wheat. What had happened to it was still far from clear. Or why.

Finally he knew if he was to go any farther with this investigation he had to drive out to King's Lynn and lay siege to the products manager's office. Even that offered no guarantees. The man still might not talk to him, and he could avoid him physically at his place of work almost as easily as he could on the phone.

He chose his time carefully, and following a twenty-five minute wait, caught the products manager as he came through the reception area returning from lunch. Straightaway he denied he had been avoiding him, but stammered when he said it and grew red in the cheeks.

'I don't know what the hell is going on, but I aim to find out,' Jak told him. 'Either you can give me some answers or I'll find them someplace else. But I am going to get that information.'

'Wheat being genetically engineered to attract Take-all as you suggest is pretty far-fetched, Dr Redford.'

He measured the man with a long look. 'Are you a plant geneticist, sir?'

'Well, no, but even so.'

'Then what's the basis for your statement?'

The products manager looked more embarrassed. 'I can't see why anyone would do such a thing.'

'Nor can I yet. A couple of years ago the whole notion of transferring genes from one plant into another was pretty far-fetched. Right?'

'I'm sorry, I didn't mean to insult you.'

'A new bacterium gene is repeating itself identically in the wheat Shearing lost. I haven't traced its source, but I figure that's what made it susceptible to Take-all. If I can't get to take a look at those breeding records, get me some of the seed you supplied to Shearing.'

The products manager looked like he was about to run. He glanced at the receptionist, then back in his direction, and smiled.

'That's not possible. We haven't supplied seed to Shearing's farm in years.'

Jak nodded slowly, not a bit surprised by the response. It confirmed all he suspected. 'You dumb asshole,' he said. 'That is *so* dumb.'

With that he walked out, knowing there was nothing more he was going to get here, that he would have to finally go after Crocker-Giant. Calls to their offices in Kansas got him no place, but some kind of sixth sense told him his calls worried them.

Although growing more paranoid by the day, as he dug deeper into what for him was a real mystery, he wasn't prepared for the second visit he got from the immigration official and his unsmiling cop. They were physically searching his laboratory when he arrived, going through drawers and opening files without even pretending to neatness.

He remembered who they were immediately and flew at them, slamming the drawer Sergeant Lynch was searching, almost trapping his fingers.

'I guess you guys dug up that warrant.'

'The vice-chancellor gave permission for your lab to be searched, sir.'

'It's real good to know your friends.' He was too mad to pick up the phone and check that. 'What did you find?'

They fielded that one.

'Under the 1971 Immigration Act,' Laurence James said, rising to his full height, which he guessed was a couple of inches short of his own five eight, 'I'm serving you with notice of intention to deport you.' He handed him the notice.

'What shit is this?' he protested, trying to understand what was going down.

'The Secretary of State no longer deems your presence conducive to the public good. Under Section 15 of the Act you have fourteen days in which to give notice of intention to appeal, sir, or risk being deported.'

Just like that! A bolt from the blue cloaked in official language that shifted the blame onto some distant minister. After they had departed he called the American Embassy. The official he talked to wasn't helpful, pointing out that he was a guest here and that if he misbehaved he should expect to be asked to leave.

'Hey, what is this shit? I haven't misbehaved.'

'Then I advise you to talk with your lawyer, sir. If this proves to be a case of unfair deportation we would gladly take it up with the Home Office for you.'

He felt less than reassured.

The dean wasn't helpful. If Jak hadn't been so mad at what was happening he might have seen his evasiveness as something more than embarrassment.

'I'm powerless to help, Jak, I'm sorry.'

'This is crazy, Horace. Those moves with Jessie Mann are a smoke screen. She said she met the guy from the Israeli Embassy at an exhibition of Brazilian native art in London.'

The dean smiled a mock apology.

'I was contacted by a man from the American Embassy,' he told him. 'He explained how Special Branch had been obliged to release Miss Mann. However, he did say that she was the prime suspect for information that was still arriving at the Israeli mail drop. I've always believed you sound, Jak.'

'Then why the hell are they deporting me? If those cops have got something, why don't they haul me into court?'

'If a mistake has been made, the Home Office will

quickly remedy it. They're scrupulously fair.'

With that he dived through a door and was gone.

Jak saw no point in pursuing him. Instead he went back to his laboratory. But with the problems now pressing in on him he couldn't put his mind to the details of gene manipulation.

Had he known what was in store for him at his laboratory the following morning, he would have stayed the night, dug in, held his ground. The lock on the door had been changed when he arrived.

'I don't believe this shit!' He threw his shoulder against the door and didn't even rock it.

The lodge porter confirmed with some embarrassment that he wasn't to be given access to the lab without a senior member of the administration being present.

All the dean would say was, 'I'm sorry, Jak, it should have happened when your funding ceased. It was remiss of me.'

'You've gotta know a hell of a lot more than you're telling, Horace. What is going on? Something connected to what I found at Shearing's farm? Is the government directly involved in this shit?'

'We had rather hoped your work would produce a wheat that might prove the salvation of the Third World. You seem to have got yourself mixed up in a mess instead.'

'I figure someone has cracked the genetic code, but in such a way that it could wreck the entire wheat growing capacity of the First World, Horace.'

The dean merely blinked in surprise.

'I need to get into my lab, Horace. That's the only way I can investigate what is happening.'

'I'm afraid that is no longer possible.'

There was a finality about the statement that left him reeling.

Word flew round the faculty. Lecturers and researchers avoided him as though he was suddenly contagious; they would doubtless talk to him again but now they needed time to adjust. Perhaps no one was treating him any differently, that this was only how he was perceiving it.

He headed over to the library, where he vaguely hoped to find Grace. At least that would assure him of a concerned response. She wasn't there, so he decided to drive out to her farm to talk with her, but then hesitated, wondering what real help she could give. She had a good, logical mind and could possibly make sense of all this, as he sure couldn't.

Perhaps instead he should go and talk to a lawyer and have him kick up a ruckus about his possible deportation. There were a couple of law dons who he was sure would advise him. He stopped – maybe they too had word on him like the people in the science faculty.

Emerging from the library, he saw Grace coming up the steps and suddenly ran forward to greet her like he had no control over his feelings. He wanted to embrace her just because she was a friendly face, but thinking about it stopped him.

Taking her arm, he led her quickly away, talking rapidly and excitely. They walked along by the River Cam, where he calmed down completely as he explained what had happened. The calmer he became, the more demonstratively outraged Grace got. She paced agitatedly.

'How can they stop you having your own research papers?'

'By locking me out – they figure the oil company paid for the work.'

'How can you stay so calm? Don't you feel like hitting someone?'

'I was pretty mad. I thought about punching the dean out.' He didn't know if she knew how old the guy was.

Grace stopped pacing and looked at him.

'He's like seventy.'

Her look said she still didn't get it.

'I plan to break into my lab tonight. Are you any good at burglary? There's nobody else I'd trust.'

She didn't hesitate.

A wave of emotion shot through him. He felt very flattered that she would get into that with him, but didn't quite understand what it meant. Right then anything seemed possible, even burglary.

Emotions of a different kind almost took him out of control when they slipped past the porter's lodge late that night. There was something about deceiving authority that was both exciting and scary. He had felt that way ever since he was a kid. There were students around still, so their presence went uncommented on. Right then he was more terrified of making a fool of himself in front of this woman than of getting caught.

The laboratory door was locked as tightly as it was this morning. Somehow he expected something different, and illogically felt hurt by the apparent lack of trust. He rarely locked the door.

'How are you going to break in?'

'I don't know. I've never done this kind of thing before. Have you got any ideas?'

Grace started to giggle. Tension caused him to, but anything could have been the trigger right then. Here they were planning to break into his lab to steal his papers and neither had any idea how to go about it.

'I guess it is pretty funny. Maybe we could break a window in the door.'

That made Grace laugh harder. 'Did you bring a brick?'

'Have you done this before, Mrs Chance?'

'My name is Grace,' she said and laughed again.

The act of burglary was almost as intimate as sex, and still they hadn't managed to get to first names. Maybe she figured he was socially inept, or worse . . .

She pulled an edging stone from around the root of a climbing rose and handed it to him. It had a sobering effect when he hit the small pane of glass nearest the latch lock. The sound echoed across the quad, causing them both to tense, ready to run. Nothing happened. The only sound they heard was their heavy breathing. He opened the door and was about to put on the light, until she stopped him and offered a small torch from her zip-through jacket pocket.

'Gee, a flashlight! You have done this before.'

They worked uninterrupted sorting out the essential papers he needed, and finally staggered from the lab thirty-five minutes later with four full Safeway bags. Tomorrow the science faculty would know at once who had taken them. The question was what would they do about it? He figured nothing, believing that most of them saw the injustice of what had happened to him and were accepting it without protest only because of fear for their own funding. Counting on that, he planned on taking a crack at Roy Worlaby's lab for the protocol sheets on the pesticide that had killed Rose.

'I don't want to see you get into trouble,' Grace said. 'That's real burglary, not like your own lab.'

'We won't get a second shot,' he told her.

They didn't even get the first. The brick crashing through the lab door window set off an alarm bell. That was Roy Worlaby for you! They ran with what they had.

The door to his flat was ajar when they climbed the narrow creaking stairs to the second floor of the sixteenth-century building. He hadn't left it open that morning, he was sure of that. Right away he figured this was the work of that detective and guy from Immigration.

'Why would they behave like this?' Grace challenged.

'This sure as hell isn't how I live, Mrs Chance. Why wouldn't they? They're kicking me out of your goddamn country.'

The flat was a total mess. He picked through the litter, collecting books and papers, trying to assess what if anything was missing. Nothing was. Certainly nothing that was stark by its absence.

'Will you call the police?'

'You figure they'll be interested? They didn't get too excited about Mark Bailey's burglaries!'

'Perhaps they'll think you're an absent-minded professor who left the door open.'

'Is that what you figure?'

'Me?' Grace said. 'No, of course not. Would my opinion matter anyway?'

'Sure it matters. Why wouldn't it?'

He thought she blushed as she looked away and he felt embarrassed too.

'Whoever's doing this might search you at the airport,'

she pointed out. 'Especially if there is some official involvement. They'll know your papers are missing from college.'

'How am I going to keep them safe?'

'The only place I can think of that might be reasonably safe is the roof space at home. At least it's dry.'

Driving out to her house, he tried to figure what this invitation meant. If it meant anything at all. If he should proposition her. If she was expecting that. Nothing else she said led him to believe it was so. He grew anxious as they got nearer the house in case this was a missed opportunity.

He passed the Safeway bags to Grace on the step-ladder, and she put them into the loft space. He was aware the whole time how close he was to her slender, well-shaped legs. Should he say something? Should he do something? How could he be forty-one and so sexually indecisive? As she reached down to haul up the last bag, the unstable ladder wobbled, causing him to automatically grab her ankles to steady her. They both laughed self-consciously and he removed his hands.

'I'm sorry, I thought . . .'

'Yes, the ladder's a bit wobbly.'

That's all it was. He felt angry with himself for letting this chance contact go for nothing.

So preoccupied was he with the uncertainties of a possible relationship ever getting started that he was scarcely aware of what he was doing or saying. In the kitchen all hope of something happening grew dimmer with each subsequent statement and action of his. Picking up a framed photograph of Rose, he realized that it was likely to remind her of the reason that they were together rather than lead to any romantic overture. But it was then he got a surprise: less from the flood of memories it brought about his own child, than from the fact that they had remained so sharp and painful after all this time. The reason was, he suspected, that rather than confront and deal with the pain, he had run from it. This wasn't the moment to open up that whole episode, as he was feeling all too vulnerable. Until now he had been fully occupied pursuing his new branch of

91

science, telling himself that plant biotechnology consuming his every thought was a positive response, that he wasn't running from anything.

He set the photo down quickly when Grace spoke to him, as if caught doing something he shouldn't have been doing.

'Excuse me?'

'Are you going to appeal against deportation?'

'I've got no place to work here now,' he said. 'There's no real point in staying on. Can you dig out some information on who could be in back of this? Figure maybe it's whoever genetically engineered that wheat to fail. You could also look into the possible moves that chemical company could be making since we started looking for the cause of your daughter's death. I can't think of any other reason for Mark getting burgled.'

'But why didn't they search here?'

He glanced around the place. It wasn't exactly the neatest house he'd been in.

'Who the hell knows. Maybe they did. If you could somehow get a look at Shearing, and that seed supplier. They could be connected with the oil company that funded my research. When you look at Aggrow Chemicals, see if they have some connection with my work. Be careful around those people.' He stopped and looked at her, unsure how she was going to handle this. He saw tears in her eyes before she looked away. He didn't know why she was crying and was scared to speculate. He was going back to America and she'd have to do all he asked on her own.

'Can you handle that?' he said after a while.

'I'll try. What exactly am I looking for?'

'You won't know that until you find it, Grace,' he said, using her name quite naturally then. There was a moment of surprise between them. He felt elated like he had passed some test. 'Any kind of connection. Shearing may have a brother on the board of the seed company, or in Aggrow Chemicals. Don't worry about how tenuous the connection might be.'

He wasn't sure how she might fund herself doing this

scuffling around. He was uncertain about offering her money, so didn't.

'I think perhaps I should forget suing Aggrow Chemicals,' she said, 'and take their offer instead. I would go on looking for the answers I want anyway. It just means not pursuing the company through the courts.'

'Their product killed your daughter. If you could show that in court it would be a strike for a safer environment.'

'I'd settle for the satisfaction of knowing why Rose had to die.'

'The smart thing, Grace, would be for you to come over to the States and start a Class Action against American Chemicals – the parent company. Resolution looks a whole lot like their product Smartkill – it's got to be the same product under a different label.' She didn't respond. 'Grace? It won't bring Rose back, but it'll be something for those kids in Mexico and every place else they've gotten poisoned. You've got to know American Chemicals won't sit still for that happening. But lawyers Stateside run for a piece of the action.' He paced around, wondering if he was saying too much. He stopped and took hold of her suddenly, causing her to start. 'I've just had a great idea, there's a friend of mine working for the Christic Institute. They're a religious legal outfit who take on public interest cases involving major social injustice. Rory's a real interesting guy. He was a priest, then quit and became a lawyer and worked with the Securities Exchange Commission for a while before joining Christic. He's a great marathon runner.' That might have been the only recommendation anyone needed. 'Why don't I talk to him about your case when I get back to Washington? What do you say?'

He was running out of steam and badly needed a response – before he leaned in and kissed her. The idea just popped into his head, but thinking about it made him back off and let go of her.

Another brain-storming idea flashed at him and he seized her again. 'Look, why don't you get on a plane with me, Grace? Come out to Washington and talk to Christic yourself.'

93

She looked at him. Then as he leaned forward to kiss her, the door flew open and her husband walked in, startling them.

'Don't let me interrupt,' he said. 'I'm only collecting some things.'

He went through the kitchen and out into the hall.

An awkward silence fell between them. He felt Grace withdraw, shutting down her emotional antennae, leaving him stranded. She started after her husband, then turned back, but didn't say a thing.

Jak felt more awkward, thinking about how he would've handled this had he kissed her, guessing the guy was outside the whole while waiting for it to happen. The asshole.

'You going to be okay?'

Grace closed her eyes and nodded and went out.

He sat in his car a while and watched the two of them pacing around the bedroom, arguing. Her demanding an explanation, him saying how they ended up with nothing.

Most of what was being said was indistinguishable and he was glad. He felt like a sneak. There was no way he could intervene between this husband and wife and not because the guy was a lot heavier than him. He was glad now that he hadn't kissed Grace as he drove out of the yard; it would have meant starting something he couldn't follow through.

On principle he paid a visit to the American Embassy in Grosvenor Square to protest about his deportation. He got angry at the indifference of the official who took his details at the front desk, before telling him to wait while he had someone talk to him. He returned shortly afterwards and showed him into a small office decorated with the American flag, a portrait of the president, and a couple of pictures of familiar American landscapes, which made him wonder where the US government managed to find such dumb interior decorators.

Soon they were joined by a man who he perceived to be in a lot of pain from the way he lurched in on his two sticks. He'd have figured as much from looking at the man's deeply creased face, and decided that what he was suffering wasn't simply physical pain. His gait seemed to defy gravity as he stabbed at the floor ahead of him with his sticks, then swung his legs through and levered himself forward. Believing that this war vet had been wheeled in to disarm him, like you were out of line if you got mad at a cripple, he got more angry at what he saw as a cheap tactic.

'Kicking me out of the country without any charges getting laid against me is a gross violation of my civil liberties,' – using the words like a baseball bat on them.

The deep lines in Wilf Fear's face dropped like canyons when he smiled, but the smile indicated no pleasure. 'The smart thing to do, sir, is to get while you can.'

That totally disarmed him. He was confused, unsure whether this man just didn't give a shit about his rights or knew something he didn't.

'Hey come on, I'm a fully paid up American citizen. You guys should fight this one for me. That's why you're here, goddamn it. That's why I pay taxes.'

'The US Government doesn't want this becoming a major incident,' Wilf Fear said.

'What?' Jak demanded, getting out of his seat. 'I didn't do jackshit. Do you know what's happened to me here? My whole research project is wrecked. That's two years' work. That's work that could give us a wheat that doesn't need any chemical fertilizer. Do you know what that would mean, damn it?'

The man with the sticks clearly wasn't impressed.

'Did you talk to your lawyer?'

'Screw you,' Jak said.

As he walked out of the embassy, he was feeling bruised and disgruntled, and more than a little scared, but not sure of what. He was less sure what he was going to do right then, other than to return to the US.

95

8

THE FOURTEEN-HOUR FLIGHT FROM West Africa via Paris, France was tiring. Ordinarily Pat Shapiro had no problem sleeping on planes, especially not in the first-class cabin. Anxiety prevented him doing so now. His waking nightmare was of falling asleep and losing the attaché case he kept close to him.

He looked at his watch, then at the cabin attendant, and at his case on the seat next to him. The stewardess smiled and asked if she could get him anything. He said no. He had been telling ladies 'no' for the past nine days, and most had been offering more than hot towels and drinks. He hadn't needed the advice of the American Embassy agricultural attaché to avoid casual sex. He had no difficulty in saying 'no' to women in general, nor to the particular offers from the country's Agricultural Minister, a brother-in-law of the president. The young boys were something else, but still he said 'no'. However, he had had to be careful about how he said it. The plan was for Hirshorn to go on supplying the West Africans with as much grain as they could use. The problem was they could use more than they could afford. Not only had they not paid for their last two shipments, but they had also defaulted on the payments for their flour mill. That had really got his boss mad. Caddy Hirshorn saw feeding the developing nations as a personal crusade: the stalled payments for wheat he could live with, but the flour mill was something he had raised hard currency to get built, and in the face of a lot of opposition in Washington. Regular payments were needed to meet the interest.

The agricultural attaché had explained how President Moselle was using all the country's hard currency for weapons.

'Have they tried eating weapons?' had been Shapiro's response.

He had taken five days to get a meeting with the Agriculture Minister, and only then after he had called Caddy Hirshorn in Oklahoma to stop the ship with thirty thousand tons of No 2 grade US wheat that was due in.

The minister had been furious at this imperialist behaviour.

'It's not imperialism, minister,' Shapiro had said. 'It's business.'

'A business that leaves people without bread.'

'As soon as we receive the next instalment on that flour mill, we'll start delivery again.'

'In the meanwhile our people go hungry.'

There had been no logic to the minister's argument, only emotion.

Shapiro had indelicately brought up the question of West African arms purchases, causing the embassy attaché to blanch. He didn't care. He had been sent here to sort out a problem that neither their local manager, nor the American Embassy could solve, and he hadn't been about to fail his boss. There had been bread queues in the streets, and food riots shown on TV, along with anti-American demonstrations. The assessment of the CIA was that these had been stage-managed.

Two days later the minister had summoned him from his hotel, where the distracting offers of casual sex partners had continued.

'President Moselle Leon has ordered you paid.' The open attaché case on the table had been stacked with $100 bills. 'Two-point-five-million. That covers what is due under the leasing agreement on the flour mill. It is also part-payment on the wheat. You will instruct your ship to dock and unload its cargo immediately.'

The money had given him an anxiety attack. He had feared getting mugged as he left the ministry and having to explain to Caddy Hirshorn how he had been suckered.

In fact the Minister had provided an armed escort right to the door of his plane.

American airports after first-class travel were an anti-climax. There was never first-class processing at immigration and customs. He shuffled on line with everyone else.

The overweight customs officer at Will Rogers Airport glanced at his declaration, almost not seeing what was written there. His eyes shifted to the bags, then to Shapiro's face.

'You bringing in two-point-five-million dollars, sir? D'you want to open this up,' – pointing to the attaché case.

He slowly unlocked the case, enjoying the moment.

'That is two-point-five-million? Where d'you get this money, sir?' – like the only source was dope.

'The West African Minister of Agriculture.'

The customs official called a colleague over. Then took him to the office where he consulted with a more senior officer.

His story was too straightforward to appeal to bureaucratic minds used to a legion of deceivers. As more customs officers were consulted the customs hall ground to a halt. Steam began to rise off the tired travellers.

'Come on, guys, I'm bushed. Here it is again. Hirshorn' – whom they all knew, because the company was synonymous with Oklahoma, families having worked for them for generations – 'built a flour mill in West Africa; we shipped wheat to them; when they missed some payments, the boss cut off shipments to their – our mill.' That they visibly enjoyed. Someone had once likened Caddy Hirshorn to Teddy Roosevelt, both in looks and for speaking softly but carrying a big stick – 'Soon they had food riots. Then they came up with this,' – pointing to the money. 'The missed instalments. So how about it?'

One of the more senior officials came back from talking with Mr Hirshorn on the phone. 'Your boss said you be sure and look in at his garden party.' He closed the attaché case and signed the declaration ticket. 'Do you need an escort?'

Shapiro didn't want another thing to delay him.

98

The new 911 Carrera on the airport parking lot gave him a buzz as he caught sight of it. This was his third Porsche. He had purchased his first used 911 three years ago, a month after going to work for Hirshorn. He could almost meet the instalments on this 911 out of the car allowance he opted for instead of a company car. Initially he had gone to work learning the diverse structure of the company, which was owned primarily by Caddy Hirshorn and his family: grain trading, financing, the poultry and feed lots; paint, printing, shipping and agricultural chemicals. Their prime business was grain, which was where he spent most time before going to work as Caddy Hirshorn's executive assistant.

The automatic lock on the car door snapped open and he tossed in the attaché case and put his suitcase and valise behind the seat. The engine roared, then purred. He listened to it as if it were a concerto. Life without such a car now would have been miserable. He couldn't stop such thoughts recurring; the two-point-five-million dollars sitting on the seat next to him, the open road before him and a fast car beneath him, had provoked them. If he got no more raises, and no bonuses it would take him twenty years to accumulate this kind of money, assuming he never spent a dime. Here he could just take it and drive, or take it and not drive, but instead invent a mugging. Trusting him like he obviously did, his boss would believe any story he came up with, and not miss the money badly. Could he get away with such a scam? Sure he could. It would hurt Hirshorn no more than losing loose change from his pocket. He stopped right there. Caddy Hirshorn was the kind of man who had never once in his life lost loose change. What he gave away was noted to the last cent, along with what he got back in return. If he took this money Shapiro knew that somehow, no matter what remained on the surface between them, their relationship would change. Maybe the change would be as subtle as crossing the state line from Oklahoma to Kansas. The sign announces you have left Oklahoma and entered Kansas, where everything looks the same – the cloudless sky, the ploughed fields, crows rising off the telegraph wires. The only difference was that you were no longer in Oklahoma. Mistrust would have entered between them. He admired his boss too much to want that. And as badly as he wanted to get seriously rich he knew he'd have to find another way. His salary of a hundred and twenty-five thousand dollars a year plus bonuses wasn't it.

The post-colonial house on the grassy knoll seven miles west of the city was built six years ago. The man-made knoll was landscaped, the avenues of trees hauled in by truck and planted with a crane; as with the house itself they looked like they had been there a long while.

That feeling of permanence was something Arkadi 'Caddy' Hirshorn worked at harder than most. Seeing himself as the guardian of all he owned, he wanted only to pass stewardship to his children, who in turn he expected would pass it to theirs. That was what life meant to him, an emotional, spiritual, economic continuum comprising family, church, business. The baton had been handed on since his great-grandfather had got the company started in the mid-nineteenth century. There had been hiatuses – a notable one was caused by great-uncle Gunston, a gambler, who had almost ruined the family before dying in a riding accident. Caddy's father had brought them back from ruin, while he had made them market leaders.

Six days a week he worked, and on the seventh he worshipped in the church he had helped construct with his own hands. After the family got back from church he made them all brunch. About every two months or so he'd pick a Sunday to fix lunch for people he considered special. Today that was upward of fifty gathered on the wide terrace, half of them children, seven of those his own.

Abraham, his eldest son at fifteen and with his mother's striking dark hair and eyes, approached. He picked at food from the table near the spit where twenty chickens were roasting.

'Dad, Aunt May said when do we get to eat?' He glanced over the browning carcasses.

Caddy wiped his fingers on his apron. 'What do you

think, Abe?' he said, challenging him. He knew what Abe's answer would be and anticipated his own annoyance.

'Looks fine to me,' Abraham said.

Caddy nodded. The fact that his son didn't eat meat would have been a no-win situation had his mother not decided to support his right to choose. Owning poultry plants and feed lots like he did, he could see there might be a problem with Abe taking over from him. That he could live with, but not with having his son tell him it was unchristian to eat the animals that shared this planet. He knew clearly enough what was Christian and what wasn't. He went to church regularly therefore he was Christian; he gave a part of his income to the church, therefore his business was based on Christian principles.

'Anyone can make fine, son,' he said. 'What I'm making here is perfect. Tell Aunt May to hang in there.'

Seeing Shapiro step onto the terrace, he signalled to him.

'Pat! Glad you made it.' He grasped his arm.

'It's a real honour, sir,' Shapiro said.

These lunch parties were legendary.

'Did you get a drink?'

Caddy didn't drink alcohol, but had no objection to other people doing so. A maid appeared with a tray of drinks.

'That was a lot of money you brought across.'

'It's safely in the bank.'

He nodded like there could have been no doubt. The bank manager, who had given up his Sunday to take the deposit, had called him.

'Some men might have been tempted to head south.'

A laugh crept out of Shapiro. 'Where could I hide? Hirshorn has offices in every corner of the world.'

'Not even tempted, Pat?'

'I'm doing pretty good. Yes, sir.'

'You're going to do a lot better. How long will it be before West Africa defaults again? Before we're seen to be starving emerging nations into submission? I don't want that kind of image – I feed the world.' He spread his

101

hands over his food. 'Tomatoes and cantaloupes picked yesterday in Mexico. Chickens from our plant here in Oklahoma. Strawberries from California. All of it perfect. All of it meeting a great human need.'

'Default needn't come into things with the provisional deal we worked out with their Agriculture Minister – a way to get them PL480 food aid.'

'If we can get it on. Go up to the house and change. This is ready.' He slapped his shoulder. 'You did real fine, Pat.'

Then turning to the children closest to him, 'Let's get you folk started on this good healthy food.'

The clear perception he had of himself was a smiling provider who fed the world, and with wholesome food. Nothing he liked better than to see eager children crowding in at feed-time.

After food came entertainment. The only child among them who was reluctant to perform was his youngest son Mark. He played the recorder, but as he introduced him, Mark who was eight, blushed and hung back near his mother. The guests gave him a round of applause, but still he hung back.

'Come on, son,' he said. 'Play that piece you learnt in school.' He waited impatiently.

Finally his wife eased Mark forward onto the stage, which was a raised level of the terrace. Caddy smiled.

'Just do your best, son,' he said, then went back to where his brother-in-law Gordon Dulles was sitting with the only non-family vice-president of Hirshorn, Herb Fixx, and Shapiro. They were discussing West Africa's chances of getting food aid. Dulles was pointing out problems.

'To every problem there's an equal or greater solution, Gordon.' That was the philosophy he lived by.

'This one means turning President Moselle right around. The State Department won't aid pro-Iraqi regimes.'

'What's your assessment, Pat?'

'Their agriculture minister indicated they would sway in the wind to meet the State Department's demand. They need grain.'

'How much weight does he carry?' Dulles asked.

'He's the brother of the president's favourite wife.'

102

That was a point of mirth.

'I can tolerate those people dealing secretly with the Iraqis,' Caddy said, 'but they are not Christian.'

'At least they're eating wheat, Caddy, not each other.'

'We'll start lobbying. Get those folk enough to eat in case they start into cannibalism again.' He raised his hand. The discussion ended as Mark began to play.

In Washington the lobbyist was seen as a helpful soul who brought oil for the machinery of government, along with jobs and prosperity to the states of the congressmen, whom he hustled on behalf of vested interest.

Hirshorn employed three firms of lobbyists to ease the way or plead particular causes. But when wheat was involved, Caddy liked to talk with people on Capitol Hill directly. If only to know that he still could. He would fly in by the company's executive jet, pack a close schedule, then fly back to his family.

They got in to Washington National at around seven and took breakfast with two senators on the Foreign Relations Subcommittee. Neither favoured West Africa getting food aid, but as both represented states with grain interests they wouldn't oppose the plan.

A lady senator from Vermont offered her support because she didn't want women and children starving, whatever their colour or beliefs. He knew she saw him as a powerful ally.

The Subcommittee wasn't tied up by the time they got to lunch with Senator Charles Harvey. He wasn't a man who liked to feel outmanoeuvred, so Caddy allowed him to hold sway.

'I'll be sorry to have to disappoint you, Caddy,' Harvey said through his cigar smoke. 'Not even I could swing US aid for West Africa, not after they were caught supplying Iraq.' He didn't chair the committee, but was its most influential voice.

'That's too bad. They have women and children starving, Charlie,' he said, like there was no commercial interest involved. 'We have grain poking out of our socks!'

103

'Sure. And those people have been using hard currency to buy grain. PL480 would free that for arms – not American arms.'

Therein lay the problem, he guessed.

'Tell me what you need, Charlie. Pat's got the ear of the president's favourite wife's brother,' he said, making the senator laugh.

'Any influence Hirshorn could exert that would be good for America would be good for Hirshorn.'

There was no such thing as a free lunch for anybody!

'Pat can stay on in Washington and talk to the West African ambassador. We know just what they want besides US wheat – armaments – ostensibly to stop terrorist incursions.'

'The US Administration would have no objections to maintaining the body of such a state,' the Senator said, 'just as long as it got its head right and stopped its rhetoric in the UN.'

Before flying back to Oklahoma, there was business Caddy had in New York with a commodity broker in Wall Street. He didn't need Shapiro or anyone else at that meeting.

The broker was Armand Bequai, who had offices way up in the Manufacturers Hanover Trust Building, a 900-foot-high skyscraper with a pyramid-shaped roof. The views from the windows were marginally better than the modern art on the walls. But neither interested Caddy, whose attention remained fixed on the screens that were a lexicon of prices.

Bequai hovered around him like an overstuffed bird of prey, a huge bill dipping toward the tally, small round eyes deepset in his pockmarked face. He didn't look at him as he spoke. Few people could, Caddy found, when they had things to say they figured wouldn't please him.

'All the computer predictions say wheat's going to be spilling everywhere next July. The market's moving against you, Caddy.'

Those words from this man would have sent any other client into an orgy of selling.

'You want something on the margin?' he joked.

Commodities were traded on margin accounts. For every 5000-bushel wheat contract, 5 per cent of its value was put down as a deposit on the margin. This had to be maintained throughout the entire period of trading. If the marker moved against a customer he settled his losses to the broker at the end of each day, or had him collect his profit from the Clearing Corporation. That was the way profit and loss was accounted in all futures trading.

Bequai smiled now like a man unused to smiling.

He had traded for Caddy privately, often secretly, for the past twenty years and had never once called for margin deposits. But never before had Caddy traded against his own company, and for such amounts. He could understand why Bequai was worried. Or maybe he, like so many others, believed the rumours about his health.

'May wheat is down two-point-nine cents. The hundred contracts we bought yesterday lost fourteen K when trading resumed today. What I'm buying, some of Hirshorn's own brokers are selling.'

'I'll see wheat on the floor, making less than farmers grow it for,' he declared. That situation was getting pretty close without help from either of them.

'Today's prices will look high when the Commodity Credit Corp gets done auctioning government stocks. They sure have to do something or they won't have anyplace to store what they buy in to guarantee next year's price to farmers.'

The whole notion of government intervening in the market drove Caddy crazy. He wanted all tariffs and supports removed entirely, knowing his company could trade better than any of the competition. A free market would regulate the amount of produce grown and the price it made. All things being equal, he had faith in American farmers producing food as efficiently as any in the world, but none in the Administration's ability to solve the continuing farm crisis. His plan would go a long way to doing that, besides making him a lot of money. His public profile was inevitably high, but behind that façade he was a private person who preferred to operate behind closed doors, without undue attention. That was getting

105

harder and harder these days with everyone in business constantly watching everyone else in business to try and make sure they didn't get too far ahead.

'Where are the opposition, Armand?' he asked, taking information from the broker and the screens.

'Trying to second-guess you.' He paused.

He saw Bequai's round eyes flash in his direction.

'I had to fire one of my people, Caddy.' He paused again and sighed. 'He was signalling International Grain about your moves.'

Caddy nodded, accepting this as if it was of no importance. Having instigated similar moves, he saw it as an almost legitimate business practice. But where Oscar Hartmine at International Grain was involved it became a personal affront that couldn't go unpunished. There were old scores to settle with him dating back to the seventies when the Russians had bought almost the entire US wheat surplus. The world believed the Russians had slipped in and stolen the American wheat. In effect they did, but only because Hartmine had reneged on the cartel Caddy had organized to control the price. That was a long time ago, but he had a long memory. Now the time to settle with Hartmine was approaching.

'We limited the damage some. But they know you're buying wheat.'

'I appreciate you telling me, Armand. I guess Oscar is still smarting from the beating he took over our raid on Crocker-Giant.'

'That kind of beating a body can live with. He sold his stock at a large profit. I figure the Stock Exchange Commission are smarting more.'

'I don't see any kind of problem there. Not now that lawyer they had on the case has quit. What was his name?' He had purposely forgotten.

'Spelman. Rory Spelman,' Bequai said.

'Spelman,' Caddy nodded. 'Guys like that can't live with anybody making money.'

He thought about how close the young lawyer had come to exposing a major nerve, but obviously hadn't realized how close or he'd never have quit like he had.

Maybe he wouldn't have, had Hartmine not backed off, when his levered buyout failed. Hartmine had done no more than second-guess their illegal moves. He was a grain trader who survived by his gut feeling. There had been no logic in his pursuing the seed company – other than to block Hirshorn. Through the intervention of friends on Capitol Hill he had got the SEC off his back; however, if International Grain had the scent of the main deal, which buying the seed company Crocker-Giant was but a part of, then the danger of exposure might return. He thought about accelerating his plans for Hartmine, but decided the time wasn't right to do him maximum damage.

'Will he talk, this guy you fired?'

'I guess if the circumstances are right, he will. We could maybe buy him off.'

He looked at the broker and shook his head. 'He'd just up the ante as the prize got bigger. The prize is going to get big. What have you bought for me, Armand?'

Leaning round at his desk, Bequai tapped onto the computer keyboard and 2.72 million bushels went up on the monitor. He wiped it immediately like he didn't want this information to escape into the ether.

'Small contracts spread through nominee accounts. No volume bulge that's alerting the CFTC. The real problem with this equation, Caddy, is getting the floor back under wheat before you liquidate.'

'I'm not going to. I want every bushel delivered.'

That surprised Bequai. He said, 'That is going to be a real problem. The regulatory body will look at those purchases real close.'

'Make good and sure they're well spread out, Armand, every bushel.' He looked at the broker. 'I don't want my board knowing any of this. Not yet.'

'That could cause me more problems. Yes sir.'

He nodded. Bequai was also buying wheat futures for the company, dealing on a daily basis with Gordon Dulles. This would be a real test for him. He enjoyed testing the loyalty of those who worked for him.

'To every problem there is an equal or greater solution, Armand. I figure you can handle it.'

107

The broker was at risk of not only losing his licence, but of going to jail if any of this went wrong. But then Bequai would make a lot more than his fees on this deal. In return Caddy expected him to be more discreet than the dead.

9

MORNINGS IN THE HIRSHORN HOUSE were noisy with seven kids, four dogs and three cats running around, being pursued by his wife or the maids with football helmets, homework, musical instruments or scoldings for trailing water from the pool across the marble hall. The kids only swam before breakfast if their Mom did. The noise and confusion disappeared as Caddy returned as he did at eight-fifteen every weekday morning. He started work at six when his floor at the headquarters building was quiet apart from the soft hum of computers. He made a point whenever possible of taking breakfast with his family, and dinner, no matter how much work he had.

'Morning, Martha,' he said to the maid as he entered the wide hallway. 'Are we all here?'

''Cept young Mark. He ain't feeling good, Mr Hirshorn.'

'What's wrong with him?'

'He got an awful upset tummy, sir,' the maid said.

'Have him come down, Martha.' He recognized his wife's diagnosis here. Being the youngest, Mark was inevitably treated as the weakest, which he knew wasn't good for him.

Conversation dropped as he entered the dining-room, and lifted up again after he had greeted everyone. Despite his intense feeling for his family, it was never to him they turned to settle squabbles, always Mom. He thought that was as it should be. Caroline gave them what they wanted; sometimes he overruled her decision. She encouraged Abe to challenge his values, while he forced

109

him into a corner making the boy defend his position as his own Daddy had done with him.

'We'll wait for Mark to get here,' he said, as if only then noticing his absence.

'He wasn't well, Caddy,' his wife said. 'I'll have the doctor stop by.'

He smiled. She was a good woman, a good Christian mother, still beautiful and always loyal, but in this matter she was wrong.

'It's better that he joins us.'

All eyes fell on Mark as he entered.

Caddy reached out his hand to have him come to him.

'Are you feeling better, son?'

Mark glanced at his mother before nodding. His father respected him for this gesture of loyalty.

'Good. Never give in to illness. Give it up to God.' He gave the boy a kiss and a hug. 'Sit. I'll say a prayer.'

With heads bowed – 'Bless this food, dear Lord, and all who grew and prepared it. Make all who eat it humble and grateful for your bounty. Amen.'

The maids served breakfast.

This was what he loved about family life, the excited chatter as the day was arranged; his childrens' aspirations and tribulations, knowing that he could simply reach in and help them to achieve any of their goals and resolve any problems they might have. He never did so unless they put in equal effort. His own father had refused to help when he stumbled, being concerned solely to prepare him for the world. He was more than prepared. That was what he wanted for his children.

As he discussed the ball game that was being organized with the older children, he noticed Caroline reach out and squeeze Mark's hand. He opened the conversation to include his youngest son. Sarah, his eldest daughter, wanted to know if girls could bat too. Abe thought not. He was resolute about that.

'What do you say, Mark?'

Mark looked at his Mom, then said, 'I think they could.'

'Yes, they could, Mark,' Abe argued. 'The question is, should they? The game's far too aggressive for girls.'

'Then why do they want to play it?' Sarah cut in.

'That's stupid,' Matthew said, 'it's a boy's game.'

Caddy had no abiding belief in sexual equality, but Abe was having to defend his position against Sarah's assault. His whole family had something to say. This was family life at its best. As he glanced along the table he saw Caroline's raw-boned face find a well-practised smile that said everything was fine in the world. Where she could make it so, it was, and where she couldn't effect the outcome, she provided all the necessary support. An area of concern where he was grateful for that support, even though he wouldn't readily talk about it, was over his health.

After breakfast the children got a kiss and words of encouragement from him. He took Mark on his knee and put his arms around him, smelling the delicately perfumed skin that boys of his age had, enjoying it.

'Just because you're the youngest, Mark, never allow yourself to become the weakest. God pities the weak. He aids the strong. Which do you want to be?'

Mark glanced at his mother, and said, 'Strong.'

'Good. You have a nice day, son.' He kissed him on the lips.

Afterwards Caroline joined him and put her arm around him. He stiffened instinctively as she touched his back.

'I'm too soft with him.'

'That's what mothers are for.'

'You're seeing Kurt Blumenthal today. Would you like me to go with you, Caddy? I'd like to.'

He smiled at her anxiety.

'I'm only stopping by his office,' he said. 'If I have time.'

'I'm sure it's not the same problem.'

He wasn't sure at all.

'With God's help I'll run Hirshorn a while longer.'

When kissing Caroline goodbye, he lingered, and wondered if she saw that uncertainty in him. He did want her to go with him to see his physician, but couldn't take up her offer in case she saw it as a sign of weakness in him. If she hadn't, he would. He despised weakness.

At fifty-one he was strong of wind and limb; he could work hard and could swim tireless lengths of his pool.

111

Refusing to accord his health importance was to deny the problem. He saw Kurt Blumenthal at the hospital on his lunch break. The problem that brought him here was a whorl-like lesion beneath his left shoulder. Two similar lesions had been removed during the past eighteen months. Both had been pre-cancerous. He feared this one was as the doctor carefully excised a tiny sliver of the lesion and placed it in a Petri dish for a biopsy.

'Fine, Caddy. That's all I need.' He dressed the small wound with a band-aid and went off into his adjoining office.

'You want to sit,' Dr Blumenthal suggested when he joined him.

He glanced at his watch.

'We completely eradicated the previous lesions with the laser therapy – patients here have something to be grateful to the Hirshorn Trust for.'

'Kurt,' he said. 'I don't need the testimonials.'

'Your body scan showed no metastasis, but I'm afraid this new lesion looks worryingly similar to the previous. The histology report would need to confirm that before we decide on a course of treatment.'

'Maybe God is calling me to account,' – believing as a good Christian he gave his best.

'You could try easing up, Caddy.'

'That isn't the kind of advice I pay you for, doctor.'

Blumenthal stepped back instinctively.

'Let's get this examined, then we can think about booking you in for some more laser treatment. We will get this licked, Caddy. I promise you.'

He had no doubt about that. He would bring to bear his will, his prayers, and his money.

His wealth and that of his company was reflected in their headquarters building, an enormous neo-Georgian house in landscaped gardens on the edge of Oklahoma City. It was a nice place to work, and few of his employees quit ahead of retirement. Job satisfaction and company loyalty were high in Hirshorn, where he made sure everyone on the payroll had a face and name – too many for him to know personally, but he knew all the

112

vice-presidents and managers of the various divisions who in turn knew the first names and spouses' names of all their people – often their concerns too. That was the Christian way, the way he got the best from people.

The executive offices grouped in a horse-shoe around the central boardroom on the top floor were decorated with bleached walnut panelling, and gave no preference or higher status to any member of the board. Each had similar responsibility over the various divisions. Their assistants and secretarial staff numbered the same. Caddy had two extra secretaries to deal with work generated by Pat Shapiro.

Shapiro was there to meet him at the elevator. His expression said he was the bearer of bad news from the assistant secretary he'd been in contact with in the Department of Agriculture.

'The trouble we've been hearing about in the chicken processing division is here at last,' Shapiro said.

'How bad, Pat?'

'Agriculture plans on publishing a report stating that seventy per cent of intensively reared chickens contain dangerous levels of salmonella.'

'Seventy per cent could close us down. Only in the US?'

'The problem's world-wide,' Shapiro said. 'We won't be able to import from our plants abroad if the report bears out.'

'We'd better make sure it doesn't.'

That was the first item on the agenda of this afternoon's board meeting.

'Why the hell isn't the Department liaising with the industry?' Herb Fixx wanted to know from across the long polished table in the boardroom.

'They have been, Herb,' Shapiro informed him. 'All the way down the line. Either the requirements set by the Federal Inspectors are not being met, or they're insufficient.'

'Are we accepting the Department's findings?' asked Jack Devine, a Harvard law graduate married to Caroline's younger sister.

'Salmonella's a persistent problem. We're increasing

113

levels of antibiotics in feed to reduce the risk of other infections. But chickens go on shedding the bacteria.'

'Kids thrive on our chicken,' Caddy said. He was angry at the bureaucracy coming down on him and wasn't about to accept it. 'Let's not scuttle around here like criminals. Criminals we're not.'

'A counter-offensive is needed, Caddy. I eat chicken every day. Have done for as long as I can remember.'

'I guess it gets cooked properly, Herb,' Shapiro said. 'That's where the problem comes from.'

'What could this cost us?'

'Pre-tax earnings in the poultry division last year were ninety-seven million,' Devine said. 'With our expansion programme we're looking for one hundred and thirty million. How aggressively will the Department pursue this, Pat? Do we know yet?'

'No. I'm finding out. I guess they'll wait for our response to the report being published.'

'Sales'll take a dive around publication, Caddy. But the public have pretty short memories. Shit, most people can't remember what they ate for breakfast.'

'What about the purity of our product?' he said, looking over at the young lawyer. 'Of course you're right. But we can't wait around for the random response of the marketplace. Take over publicity, Herb. Use everything to limit the damage. Either we stop this report going out, or we get chicken so much editorial coverage that's all folk will want to eat anyhow. Whatever it may or may not have wrong with it.'

The next item on the agenda was wheat futures. Attention moved to the bank of monitors, seconds later the prices were clattering out of the printer for those present to have in front of them.

'July No 2's at an eleven-year low.' Caddy showed none of his pleasure in his voice, even though he was having to meet margin calls on some of his recent purchases of wheat futures.

'People are dumping ahead of the government auctions,' Michael Whiteman said.

'Good.' He acknowledged his cousin, then clearly

surprised him by saying, 'Let's buy ahead of the demand.'

'What demand? The computer says sell through September.'

'The market's coming back.'

When he made such statements nobody argued because few people knew wheat like he did. But when he said, 'I'd like a corner,' there were more than surprised reactions. He knew some of the men at the table were now wondering if his illness was affecting his judgement. His eyes moved slowly across them. Only Gordon Dulles didn't respond. He looked like a pirate behind his black eye-patch, and at most times would behave like a pirate when the opportunity presented itself.

'The CFTC still has its three-million-bushel speculative ceiling,' Whiteman pointed out, without overstating the obstacle.

'Times are hard, Michael. Who is going to call foul when wheat's not moving anyplace but into store?' Shapiro argued.

Computing the figures, Dulles said, 'A hundred names could hold eight million tons of wheat.'

'Is that what we'd be looking for?' Whiteman asked.

'Eight million tons is a lot of wheat, but not a corner,' Caddy said. 'Let's think about putting together four hundred million bushels by having family and loyal employees buy for us. We can do that, I guess.'

'Twenty-five million tons! That represents more than half the entire US domestic consumption of hard red. The price will skyrocket.'

'If we can hang onto its tail I'd guess we'd turn a profit.'

'The regulatory board will come at us every which way.'

'We won't be speculating, Michael. We'll be buying for delivery.'

'Then why risk trouble with the CFTC by going into the futures market in the first place?' the cautious lawyer asked. 'Clearly there will be serious problems, Caddy.'

'If we start in with options we can control the price more easily. If we buy physicals the price will jump as traders anticipate shortages,' he said, telling them nothing they didn't already know. But it did not hurt to remind them. 'In no time we would be looking at wheat around six dollars a bushel, instead of under three. This way the price will still rise, but not so high and in a more orderly fashion. The Board will expect us to liquidate before the Spot. Trading on margin accounts won't hurt our cashflow; it costs us nothing to store the grain.'

'You figure there's going to be a market for this wheat, Caddy?'

'I could be wrong about that.'

'I sure hope you've got the inside track, Caddy. You're talking three-point-five billion dollars' worth of wheat – at today's prices.'

'I can't fault your arithmetic, Jack,' he said.

Finding the market for the amount of wheat he wanted was something he had devoted considerable time and energy to over the past three years. It wasn't something that was worrying him right then, like the five hundred tons of their finished hybrid vigour seed missing from their elevator facility out on the gulf port at Galveston. That seed had taken a lot of money to develop to its current stage; it was the means to create the market for every bushel of wheat he purchased.

'How did you find out about that missing seed?' he asked Shapiro, as they returned to his office.

'Mark Kuhfuss came clean. He figured it's an error.'

'That's an expensive error, Pat.'

'Is Kuhfuss reliable?' Shapiro asked.

That wasn't something he had considered. He trusted the plant manager and wondered why Shapiro was raising this doubt.

'Mark goes back a long way with me.'

'But do you trust him?'

'All he knows is he's storing a very special wheat seed. You'd better go out there when Gordon goes tomorrow.'

'To Galveston?' Shapiro seemed surprised.

'I rely on you to find out exactly what happened, Pat. Look into it.'

Having his assistant go along with his brother-in-law was another means of testing Shapiro. He was yet to be convinced of his unswerving loyalty, despite the good service he gave the company.

*

The concrete grain silos, rising 150 feet off the dock along the ship canal dominated the Galveston skyline. Each was capable of a 1500 ton throughput every eight minutes. In a twenty-four hour period they could clean, grade, blend and ship 200,000 tons of wheat; mostly hard red from Texas, Oklahoma and Kansas, brought in by railroad.

Mark Kuhfuss, the elevator complex manager, had seen leaner times than these, but not much. They were shipping a lot of grain, but on margins so thin.

Stopping on the iron staircase from his second-storey office, he looked across at the ship tied up alongside their dock. The loading gantries were funnelling grain into the holds with hardly a trace of dust where the operators kept the mouth of the funnels close to the rising surface of the grain. Before the process of coating grain with mineral oil had been invented, loading grain was a risky business, the dust being highly combustible. He enjoyed seeing how smoothly all this operated, and wondered why he was being summoned to meet with Gordon Dulles away from here. The thought jarred as he crossed the lot to his auto. He guessed whatever it was Dulles wanted to talk about wasn't something for the Federal Grain Inspection Service to know about. Being around the facility the whole time it was operating they didn't get to miss much.

Gordon Dulles was waiting on the parking lot at the Galveston Mall on Broadway. Shapiro was with him, which he guessed didn't bode well. For no reason he could figure he didn't like the boss's assistant. The neat little guy was real smart, quick to learn and extremely polite – he guessed it was this last point that set off some warning light about him. Shapiro had a sneaky politeness that didn't reassure.

After the exchanges about health and family, Dulles got right to it. 'What we want here, Mark, is grain ships going out from this terminal underloaded.'

The baldness of the statement, the audacity of the demand shocked him.

'I've been shipping grain a long while, Gordon,' he said, with anger in his voice. 'Suddenly you come down here and tell me how I should ship it.'

'Margins are real tight, Mark. They're getting tighter. Soon you'll carry our profit in your pants pocket. Ships headed for modern ports like Antwerp or Rotterdam, load those an eighth of one per cent below manifest. Those headed for the old ports of India, Africa, the Far East, they can go out underloaded a full three per cent. But not those to Japan.'

'That's great business, you get away with it, Gordon.' He glanced at Shapiro, figuring he would support either one of them. But he was keeping his powder dry. 'Grain doesn't grow in the goddamn silos. How do I explain this extra grain – assuming the Federal Inspectors don't spot the underloading and kick my ass all the way into Federal court?'

'Our accountants will enter deliveries down here by truck.'

'That's a real bitch, Gordon. Two tons go down the chute, two tons get logged by the computer. No other way for it.'

'Those inspectors are just plain human. Like you and me. Right, Mark?' He paused and gave his old pirate smile.

Kuhfuss didn't respond. He knew inspectors who took bribes over the grading of grain, letting wheat that was no better than US No 3 through as No 2, but he couldn't see any of them going for this, and he wasn't sure if he wanted to try any of them.

'You got the *Blue Ribbon* going out with forty thousand tons for West Africa. Take off three per cent, that's $129,000 before we add in the subsidy.'

'Government aid wheat. That gets me five in the Federal pen.'

'Only if you're caught, Mark,' Dulles said. 'This is a company affair.'

Kuhfuss looked between these two men, hoping one of

118

them would say who had ordered this done. If it had been ordered done. Neither did.

'Tampering with computer records – Jesus Christ.' He blew down his nostrils. Maybe he'd have to call Caddy Hirshorn about this. Hear what he had to say.

'Is that how you're short five hundred tons of Prairie Red?' Shapiro asked. 'Someone tampering with the computer records to cover a thief?'

'You want those answers,' he replied, 'come to the office. That's where I do my business!'

He climbed back into his auto and drove away. Glancing through his rearview mirror as he pulled off the lot he saw the two of them talking as they walked across to their limousine. Trying to figure what they might be saying only made him more mad.

The entire Hirshorn terminal grain facility was computer controlled, from weighing grain in the silos, to coating it with mineral oil, and loading it. Every operation was displayed on the monitors around the forty-foot operations room, and all movements were recorded on the IBM mini they had *in situ*.

How did Dulles and Shapiro figure anyone was going to steal anything out of this system? He knew there wasn't a system devised by man that couldn't be beaten, but was willing to bet neither of those two assholes had any notion how it might be done. It hadn't been done anyway, not the five hundred tons they were looking to find. Mark Kuhfuss was getting mad again. He was a grizzly old grain man, who looked like he would be more at home in the yard driving a Cat, than tapping out terminal keys with his thick hairy fingers. But he knew his computer like no other employee in the Galveston operation, and it showed as he searched down the movements of Prairie Red. The wheat seed was a special hybrid being stored here for Crocker-Giant, prior to shipment for purchasers, and he wasn't dumb enough to divert any of that. But accidents happened as it got moved around the terminal from silo to silo to prevent spoilage. Some of it had gotten bagged and shipped out.

'There's some of it,' he announced as a set of figures

appeared on the monitor. 'Fifty tons that got shipped to Spinetti Seeds in King's Lynn, England.'

'How the hell is that?' Shapiro demanded. 'That grain wasn't supposed to go anyplace without Mr Hirshorn's personal okay.'

'An operator screwed up,' he told him. This was just the kind of problem that could expose everything else that then was getting past the company. It was a dumb mistake, no one made a cent from it.

He looked toward the Federal Grain Inspection Service office. Behind the half-glazed partition all five inspectors were following this discussion. He glanced at Shapiro and thought about conducting this investigation in his office. But then thought to hell with it.

'The operator concerned gave the right instructions for the wrong wheat. It happens. It was shipped way back in February for Crocker-Giant – they own Spinetti. I'd guess it got planted back in the spring.'

Dulles said, 'It caused a hell of a lot of problems for us, Mark. You'd better take care of the rest of that wheat seed like it's a baby.'

For some inexplicable reason Mark Kuhfuss found that statement added to the unease he felt about this seed. Right then he didn't know what he could do with that feeling.

10

'IS THE TREATMENT CONCLUDED?' SHAPIRO asked his boss. 'Is that it, sir?'

Caddy Hirshorn was dressing in his hospital room. Initially he hadn't believed it possible to have skin cancer removed, even by laser, and leave the same day.

'Until they find another lesion,' he said.

'You walk into hospital. You have major surgery. You walk out. You've got to have one pretty sound constitution. Yes, sir.'

He paused and looked at his aide. 'What did you hear about this, Pat? What are the rumours going around?'

'Some of them are pretty wild. You're as good as dead. Your judgement is off on account of the drugs you're taking.'

'Good.' He nodded. 'Let's feed the rumours some. This is helping the price of wheat. If chemotherapy is throwing out my judgement, where's that going to leave the opposition?'

'In no particular hurry to follow you, I guess.'

He nodded. 'I don't want to hear that I'm dead yet. That was our wheat that got planted on the east coast of England? No mistake about it?'

He stepped through the door as his assistant opened it.

'Absolutely no doubt. Crocker-Giant are worried in case Galveston shipped more than they're telling anyone.'

The hospital staff stopped and smiled like he was the President as he went through the lobby. Caddy had to admit that he enjoyed being rich enough to receive this kind of attention.

121

'Mark Kuhfuss insists they didn't. But they sure shipped this batch. I still can't figure him shipping this in error. It was so dumb!' He glanced at his boss.

'Maybe. When my Daddy set me to learn the grain trade it was with Mark Kuhfuss. Twenty-nine years ago.' He remembered that period with affection. Unlike his Daddy, Mark never once rode him for making mistakes, and he had made plenty.

'I kind of feel more than a personal interest in this whole project, kind of being responsible for getting it started with you. I want to help get it into profit finally.'

'I appreciate your concern,' he said. Then waited. 'Is that all you got to say to me, Pat?'

Shapiro closed his eyes, a second or two too long for Caddy not to notice. 'I just got a feeling that Kuhfuss could somehow threaten this. But I should keep my thoughts to myself as I can't pin anything down.'

Earlier doubts about the loyalty of his assistant surfaced again. A slight feeling of unease that made Caddy want to go on testing him. There were things he knew Shapiro knew about and wasn't telling him and he wanted to know why. He knew he should let this man go right now. That once doubt had been allowed to enter into a relationship there was no redeeming it. Ruthlessness was called for. But he was inextricably tied up with Shapiro in a deal that he brought to them three years ago, one which he had quit his safe government job for. The whole ambitious plan had been a long-term gamble that Gordon Dulles had persuaded him to take. He hadn't needed much persuading. If they succeeded in it they would change the face of grain trading. If he moved too early against Shapiro or misjudged it, the man could do him a lot of hurt. He would wait, learn to live with his doubt. But finally, if it was deemed necessary, he would dispose of the problem ruthlessly, effectively, and without damage to Hirshorn.

'Let's make sure the rest of that seed goes into the ground in the right place, Pat. Call Mark Kuhfuss. Tell him I'm coming out tomorrow to look things over.'

He had planned to spend the day with his family, using some of the time to give thanks to God that he had come

122

through surgery. Now he would do that in the morning and fly out to Texas in the afternoon.

As the Lear jet approached Galveston with clearance to land at the small municipal airport, Caddy had the flight attendant tell the pilot to overfly the elevator complex. The sight of the 152 silos with the superstructure flying conveyors off the railyard to the docks was a pleasure he took too infrequently. Freight cars bearing blue and orange Hirshorn colours were lined up like cigarette cartons as they dumped grain into the chutes.

'I get a lot of satisfaction knowing those silos are filling and emptying as naturally as breathing.'

'Without the kind of throughput you're getting here, they'd scarcely make a buck,' Shapiro pointed out.

'I've known thinner margins, Pat. All the while you can trade you can make money. You shave your unit costs; push down your demurrage; find a return cargo. Our boats are bringing back copper from West Africa at prices so low Hirshorn can afford to store it. Any depreciation of the asset we'll take as a tax write off.'

He had seen enough. He told the pilot to land.

Mark Kuhfuss was waiting for them and he greeted him warmly. Theirs was a special relationship, one of many he had with certain employees who had shown particular loyalty.

'What's the story, Mark?' he asked, walking up to his office, holding Kuhfuss's arm.

All the information was laid out in anticipation of this visit.

'The computer went down. A manifest clerk shipped fifty tons of that prized hybrid vigour wheat seed for regular Prairie Red seed. The simplest mistakes are usually the worst, Caddy.'

'Is fifty tons it? Not five hundred?'

'That's it. We reweighed the rest. We're holding 128.9 thousand tons.'

'That problem in England was expensive,' Shapiro pointed out. 'We had to wait almost a year to learn about it from you, Mark. Did you can the manifest clerk?'

Kuhfuss shook his head. 'He could have covered it by blending in the fifty tons he should have shipped.'

'You'd have seen the movement in the computer.'

'Maybe.' Kuhfuss stared at the lean, sharp-faced assistant. 'You can hide an awful lot in the computer.'

Shapiro glanced at the Federal Inspectors' office.

Caddy followed his glance and thought about what was riding on this wheat seed.

'Mark, handle this personally. The Russians are going to make a grab for this seed,' he said. 'Real soon. The whole shoot. If they need more we'll blend it with our regular hybrid vigour. Will you take care of that, Mark?'

'There won't be any slip-ups, Caddy.'

Employees like Kuhfuss responded to his personal touch. He believed there wasn't anything they wouldn't do for him if the asking was done in the right way. He had no problems about Kuhfuss getting it right. On this visit he took the opportunity to look at the seed stock they held; the throughput they were making on wheat, the demurrage they were giving. His plant manager was maximizing the potential of this operation. Other elements that went to making the grain division profitable were in somebody's control elsewhere: the policy that told brokers in Kansas, Chicago and Minneapolis what to buy; shippers in New York when to ship, feed lots in Ohio and San Francisco how much to store. He kept abreast of it all. His only concern about the future was in not knowing which of his children would take over from him. His own Daddy had often told the story of how at the age of twelve, he was ready to wrest control of the company from him. None of his children who were already aged twelve and over showed any interest in business.

'I figure he suspects something,' Shapiro said as they headed out to the airport. 'I know you go back a long way with Mark, but we're talking three or four billion dollars here.'

'I hope that your CIA friends keep their act together. Now we have a very different kind of Russia to deal with. Mark won't hurt us with his suspicions.' He smiled, belying his unease.

The tiny, claustrophobic elevator that ran up the side of the nine interconnected silos was rickety and caused some people problems. It held four at a squeeze, and wasn't exactly fast. There wasn't a day which passed without Kuhfuss making a trip to the top of the silos. From the top a body could see clear across to Oklahoma one way and Cuba the other! Up here he could collect his thoughts and clear his lungs.

Stepping off the gantry, he approached a large inspection hatch on the silo and cranked the ratchet open. He switched on the arc lamp and looked at the wheat seed, almost wishing it wasn't there, along with the seed that was in ninety of the other silos. Small pieces of information he was picking up on the deal involving this wheat that he now learned would be going to the Russians disturbed him. Somehow he knew it had to be connected with the three million bushels of wheat futures he had been asked personally by Caddy to hold in his name. That move meant he could avoid the three million bushel speculative limit set by the Commission. It was wrong but he had no problem getting involved with this kind of deal. What truly bothered him was not having an overall picture of what was going down. Caddy Hirshorn wasn't a guy to give anyone information they didn't need, nor was he the kind of guy you went right up to and asked what the story was. The situation left him feeling pretty frustrated and guessing, sometimes wildly. The only thing he could figure was some kind of corner was being sought. But that didn't make sense. If the Russians bought this whole pile of hybrid vigour seed they were likely to become net exporters of wheat rather than importers and the price would go down as a result. So taking a corner, if that was the plan, would be dumb. The more he thought about the situation the more frustrated he got.

A Ford LTD bumped across the railroad tracks and swooped into the yard. Watching it, he decided the two men in suits who climbed out looked like cops, even from this distance. Their flashing some ID seemed to confirm it.

He headed for the elevator.

'Mr Kuhfuss,' his secretary said as he stepped into the office. 'These two gentlemen are from the FBI.'

They rose from their chairs. Kuhfuss's eyes settled uneasily on the black agent. Being from Georgia, he hadn't questioned the way of life that segregation had brought until the civil rights movement had swept through his neighbourhood. But blacks in positions of authority still made him uneasy.

'My name is Quick. This is Special Agent Johnson. Could we talk in private, Mr Kuhfuss?'

In the office, Special Agent Quick said, 'We're investigating short-loading of grain out of this facility. We need to ask you some questions, sir.'

'That's great business, if you get away with it.' He didn't miss a beat. He had been expecting this visit if not so soon. 'We have one of the most modern storage and loading facilities in the US.'

It meant nothing to the FBI agents.

'The loading manifests are controlled by computer,' he explained, 'and printed automatically.'

'You saying there are no short loads to unmodern ports?'

'What the hell would the Federal Grain Inspectors be doing? They're here twenty-four hours a day. It happened all the time before they got started. Not any more.'

'You figure someone is trying to cause trouble?' He didn't respond. 'You mind if we ask some questions around here?'

'Be my guest,' he said. He was real glad about this investigation. Now he would get an opportunity to tell Caddy how he was unhappy about the whole deal.

'We'd like to take a look in your computer.'

He glanced uneasily at Johnson. 'That holds details our rivals would pay a lot for.'

'We could get a warrant, Mr Kuhfuss.'

With a slow nod, he said, 'You'd need to, boy.'

Whenever potential problems got to a pitch that they required executive action, Caddy Hirshorn always found the smartest thing to do was pitch right in and make the decisions directly. Certainly the moves being made by the Department of Agriculture could potentially affect a large piece of Hirshorn's earnings.

'Does the Department realize what it would mean, shutting down our chicken plants, Pat?' he asked when his assistant brought him the latest USDA intelligence to his office.

'Jim Kempinski's saying they just want the chickens and the plants cleaned up some.'

'That's not possible unless guys someplace invented a new kind of chicken. I didn't hear about it.'

'They're working on it, sir. One hundred per cent plastic!'

The assistant secretary who Shapiro had been in contact with over the Hirshorn salmonella problem had alerted him to possible injunctive action by the Department.

'We have twenty thousand workers in our chicken plants,' he reminded him. 'Most of those jobs could disappear.'

'Any threat to jobs will swing some powerful congressmen behind us. Especially in the Southern states.'

'Did your friend get us up and running, Pat?'

Shapiro smiled.

'Our scientists can make statistics prove any damn thing we want basically. Certainly the USDA is worried that a judge will be as persuaded by our argument as theirs. It's a lottery, sir.'

'If this goes to court, a lot of damage gets done meanwhile. We need to come up with something better than that.'

'It seems the Public Health Committee wants its day. The chairwoman's family got real sick from eating contaminated chicken – she took it up to the Director of Information.' He paused. 'The rumour is Joe Newberg's getting in a lot of sack-time there.'

'Did that come from your assistant-secretary friend?'

Shapiro looked at him and nodded. 'The only way Newberg will back off is if we deal with the salmonella problem.'

'Betty Shorr's the chairwoman?'

'He gave me this in confidence, sir.'

127

He waited, wondering what his assistant was saying, and guessed the statement was to impress him with his loyalty.

'Bottom line,' Shapiro said as they headed along the central corridor to the Hirshorn boardroom, 'we can expose the relationship between the information director and Betty Shorr. We totally discredit their judgement. Force them to resign.'

'People who are prepared to cheat on their partners can't be trusted at all.' He believed that God eventually punished such sinners, but in the meanwhile help was needed. 'Presumably they have families?'

'He has a wife and three kids. She has two children.'

'That's pretty despicable. Get some private investigators working on it. Have them look at any of the other Committee members who support this woman.'

'I already did, sir.'

'Well done, Pat.'

In the boardroom Gordon Dulles and Herb Fixx were checking over an advertising layout that extolled the virtues of chicken.

'Is this how we're going to beat the USDA threat?'

'We're lining up congressmen with plants in their states, Caddy,' Dulles said. 'Every state in the Union apart from Maine – they have local opposition over environmental damage from plants.'

'Our advertising people came up with this little fella. Willy Chick.' Fixx held up some chicken cartoons. 'The happiest thing on the farm.'

'Who's it appealing to, Herb?' He felt little attraction to the project.

'Kids. Parents of ethnic minorities. Blue collar workers. My grandkids love him. Try him out on your kids, Caddy,' Fixx urged. 'We have a schools information pack about the chickens' welfare; hygiene, nutrition. Quotes from athletes, movie actors. All raising the profile of chicken.'

'Other producers benefit too, Herb,' Shapiro pointed out.

'I'm not interested in joint campaigns. Earnings in the

128

poultry division last year were $97 million. Make healthy chicken and Hirshorn synonymous. Meanwhile what are the plans to ensure kids don't get sick?'

'If the meat gets cooked right, the organisms get killed,' Fixx told him. 'The USDA want a warning label.'

'That identifies a dirty product, not a healthy one.'

'Advertising won't clean it up.'

'We've got scientists working on a feed with micro-organisms that excludes salmonella from the gut,' Fixx said. 'The problem is chickens need high doses of antibiotics to reduce co-factoring. That's going to bring us into confrontation with the FDA. They want new tests running on these drugs. That could take three years. The other possibility is irradiating carcasses. But there's still powerful consumer resistance to that.'

'I don't want food irradiated,' he said. 'It encourages carelessness. Producers will figure they can let go hygiene and zap the bugs.'

'The real problem is with the Food and Drug Administration wanting long term testing to continue to see what the health risks are on these antibiotics. A lot of lobbying needs to get done, Caddy.'

'I'm confident we'll find an equal or better solution, Herb. Let's make Willy Chick squeaky clean.'

There was no question but they had to come out looking clean and pure if they were to maintain profits in the poultry division. Thinking about the problem in relation to his own kids as they headed off for school, he knew how he would feel if any of them got sick from contaminated chicken meat. Any of them might, except Abe. He considered telling them not to eat chicken anyplace but at home, or to follow Abe's vegetarian example. He thought about the Chicago meat packer from whom he had bought some feed lots. Over their lunch to close the deal the man wouldn't touch his own product. When asked why he stayed in the meat packing business, he had said, 'All the while suckers want to eat it, why not?'

Such thoughts vanished when he saw Mark Kuhfuss in the doorway of the dining-room, speaking with Caroline. He had taken an early morning flight in from Houston.

129

He waved him in and rose from the breakfast table.

'Get us some fresh coffee, Martha,' he said to the maid. 'We'll have it on the terrace. Do you want some breakfast, Mark?'

Kuhfuss smiled. 'I'm fine. I ate on the plane.'

The terrace was enclosed in glass and heated for both the comfort of swimmers during winter, and the collection of orchids and sub-tropical plants. Kuhfuss talked knowledgeably about the plants until the maid departed. Then he raised the problem he had called him about last night.

Accessibility and the fact that Caddy gave anyone a hearing without recriminations made it possible for an employee to talk to him about problems at work.

'How serious is this difficulty with the FBI, Mark?'

Kuhfuss hesitated. 'Real serious – if they get a warrant and find the wheat we're hiding in our computer.'

Caddy nodded, his gaze not leaving the elevator manager's eyes. 'Why are we hiding wheat?'

The laugh that came out of Kuhfuss said it all. 'I guess because I bought a bunch of shit from a huckster. I should have known you weren't in back of this, Caddy. I should've known. I was gonna call sooner. We're short-loading by up to three per cent.'

'My Daddy made a lot of money that way. But he didn't have Federal Inspection on his back the whole while.'

'You build a better mousetrap – mice get smarter.'

'Three per cent sounds more like a rat. Who order it done, Mark?'

'I take the rap. I should've checked with you.'

'Fine, Mark. I'll stop it out of your bonuses! Meanwhile that doesn't deal with the problem. To put this right, I need to know who I can trust.'

'I go down the line with you, Caddy. You know that.'

'Let me make it easy on you. Gordon Dulles, right?'

The curt nod from Kuhfuss was all he needed.

A smile of supreme confidence never left Dulles' face as he swung to and fro in the chair behind his large desk. He pushed his finger behind his eye-patch and scratched the empty socket. Caddy had known him raise the patch and reveal the socket in order to disarm antagonists.

130

'Jesus, Caddy, grain margins are that thin, I'll be lucky to make a bonus this year. This way we all make something extra!'

'By stealing from the poor,' he said, raising his voice, wanting everybody to know his brother-in-law for a thief. This despite his telling Kuhfuss that they should go on hiding the short-loaded wheat.

'What is this shit?' Dulles demanded. 'We steal from everybody. We just don't get to steal so much from ships bound for modern ports. Everyone does it. International Grain have made it the state of the art.'

'Then go steal for them,' he advised.

'What?' The old pirate smile vanished as he rose out of his chair, an impressive six-four with shoulders like a football player. 'You don't mean that. I'm family.' He was less than impressive then.

'You're not my family,' he told him. 'I can't rely on a thief. Today you steal from anybody, tomorrow you steal from me. You're through, Gordon. Clear your desk.'

With that he turned out of the office. In the ante-room the three secretaries suddenly became very busy as he stepped through, pursued by his brother-in-law.

'You self-righteous prick,' Dulles said. 'International Grain have been begging me to go work for them.'

'Fine. You'll be right at home among thieves!'

'My information will hurt you real bad, Caddy.'

Caddy stopped and turned. 'Give that thief one thing that damages Hirshorn, I'll bury you both in the same hole. You're through here, now clear your office or I'll have security do it.'

He watched with interest the reverberation of shock this sacking sent through the company. Suddenly no one's job was safe if his brother-in-law could get canned for such a minor oversight. People started to believe that maybe the rumours about his health were true after all.

He smiled when he heard how hard Oscar Hartmine pursued his brother-in-law to join International Grain, and at what he had to pay to get him. In the right circumstances Gordon Dulles was worth $900,000 a year plus bonuses, but these weren't them. He smiled again, figuring how they deserved each other.

131

11

ROCK CREEK PARK WAS THE ONLY serious place where a marathon runner could run in Washington DC without going around in circles or taking to the streets. Jak Redford's daily ten-mile circuit never took him farther north than the Army Medical Center in Maryland, or farther south than 29th and K, where he got off.

An equally serious runner, and one who was passing him this morning, was Rory Spelman. He was lean and sinewy and had a long stride that made the work seem effortless. That had always got to him when they ran together – Rory's seemingly limitless stamina. Rory always laughed about that and claimed it was his pure lifestyle or his pure vegetarian diet. When he ran the marathon he ate only potatoes. But whatever it was, Rory was real competition, as a runner and in most other areas too. At thirty-nine, he was younger, while his striking, dark good looks had gotten ladies of all ages falling in love with him while he was at the seminary. Probably they still did after he quit Christ for law.

They went into a dip on the oil track alongside the creek, and as they reached the rise, Jak found his breathing getting more difficult and didn't immediately realize why. Rory had increased the pace! But on the home stretch Jak matched him, knowing he had enough left to take him. A terrier had lain in wait for him on the first couple of mornings he was out. He had outrun the dog, as he would Rory. They were neck and neck, going hard, causing the heads of the sedan-seated joggers to turn. Sensing his rival peak, he reached for the little extra

132

he had held back. He turned and forced a smile, like he had no problems as Rory came in hard to the gate, fighting for breath.

'How do you stay in shape?' Rory asked, sucking in air.

'You get canned, what else is there to do?'

They walked onto R Street, slowly recovering.

'But you've got pretty good facilities out at Maryland.'

'No serious funding for research. I may as well stay home and read the journals.'

'That's what it's like for us the whole while, Jak.'

Rory was one of the eight lawyers who worked at the Christic Institute out on North Capitol.

'We discussed Mrs Chance's case,' he said. 'The decision to help her was unanimous. We don't get too many like that.'

At Christic, Jak knew, most questions of litigation were democratically discussed by the staff as they all worked for salaries below the national average and way below the commercial rates and therefore had a stake in what they were subsidizing.

'She hasn't got any money, Rory,' he said.

'Nor have we. Can she get over here from England?'

'Will you be handling this?'

That was what he wanted. He had known Rory Spelman from their days at Columbia and trusted him.

'Do we have to race?' Rory furrowed his brow. 'We've got some starts on pesticide poisoning. There's a doctor down in Mexico who'll be pretty helpful – if she lives long enough. Could Mrs Chance do her own legwork? You say she's pretty bright.'

'No. I said she's very bright, and very pretty.'

Rory looked at him and smiled. 'Is this a little human feeling I detect creeping in here, Joshua, my boy?'

'Shit, I haven't looked outside my laboratory in years. What would I know about such things? Dinosaurs could have replaced cabs on the capital's streets.' He wondered if he was talking too much.

'Have you taken a cab since you've been back?'

'I'll call her with the good news.' He took off along the street.

133

'It ain't all that good, Jak!' Rory called after him.

'What time is it in England, Willard?' he asked as he hung onto the phone, getting an unanswered tone on Grace's number.

Checking his multi-function watch, his lab assistant said, 'Twenty-three and forty seconds after four in the afternoon.'

'Are you sure?' he said.

The lab assistant didn't appear to get the joke. There wasn't a lot of banter between them. Possibly both were too serious for their own good. He knew he was, often getting submerged in his work to the exclusion of all else, including relationships.

With Maryland not having a department of biogenetics as such, more a commitment in the mind of the dean to starting one up, he didn't have a great deal of work beyond a little teaching and research from other people's published findings. Willard helped him assemble those. With time on his hands to reflect, he began to hope he wasn't as humourless as his assistant. Such thoughts were the means of avoiding admitting how much he was missing Grace.

He disconnected the call and dialled Crocker-Giant's number in Kansas. On returning to Washington he had talked to the seed company's chief breeder, telling him he was planning a new course, and had gotten all kinds of information on patented seed which incorporated genetic material, along with samples. None of them when grown in the controlled environment cabinets were shown to contain the same DNA nuclei of bacterium gene that was in the wheat from Shearing's field.

'How can I help you further, sir?' the chief breeder asked.

'I saw a batch of your seed that was planted in England. Prairie Red.'

'I sent you samples of that seed.'

'You sent some seed labelled Prairie Red. I don't believe it was what I saw in England. There was new genetic

134

material in that seed, none of it's present in the one you sent me.'

There was silence down the line. He wondered if he had said too much to this man, and if as a result information would now get blocked somehow.

'What is it you're saying, Dr Redford?' the chief breeder asked. 'We have one Prairie Red. You didn't get the samples mixed, sir?'

'It has been known.' He decided not to pursue this tack.

If there was a connection between that call and the burglars he found at his Georgetown house a couple of evenings later, he was slow to make it.

As he turned his latch key in the door, two men burst out and mugged him right there on his own stoop. They took off along the street with his attaché case.

'Hey, what the hell?'

Almost by a reflex action he went after them and easily caught them before they had got the length of the block.

'That's my briefcase,' he said.

'Hey, what shit is this? What the fuck –'

The burglar was clearly angry at being pursued by his victim.

'That's my case you've got there. It's mine.'

The second burglar came back and shoved him. 'Take a walk, asshole.'

They turned away, leaving him shaking with rage. Mostly he was angry with himself for being so helpless.

He needed to talk to someone about this, but felt too ashamed. The obvious people were the police, who only made him feel worse. Plus the fact that they didn't believe him. He wanted to ask them why they thought he would make such a thing up. But didn't. Instead he wanted to be rid of Washington's finest as quickly as possible. When they were gone he tried Grace's number. Still she wasn't home, so he called Rory.

Straightaway the lawyer assumed this burglary was connected to their move against American Chemicals. 'I can't see it any other way – in view of your past relationship with that company.'

135

He didn't dwell on that, but said, 'You feel such a damn fool. Those guys work like it's a regular job.'

'It is,' Rory told him. 'The police gave you a hard time?'

'Like it makes me feel a whole lot better to know they treat the guys who do all the mugging and burglary so decently.'

He decided he would have to be in a lot of trouble before he'd be in any hurry to call the cops again. Maybe not even then.

Getting to work the next morning presented him with another surprise. A new lab assistant was working on a project that didn't look like anything of his.

'Did I get the wrong room?' He opened the door again and checked the number. 'This lab was assigned to me.'

'I got assigned this room by the dean. Talk with him.'

A feeling of unease crept over him. He knew there wasn't a mistake as he pursued Bill Heinz, the dean of the faculty.

'I've got a lecture right now, Jak,' the dean said. He looked like a TV evangelist in a pale blue suit, a silver necktie and a fifty dollar haircut.

'You re-assign my laboratory – you don't call me?'

'I've been calling since around six this morning. Take one of these with you running, for Christsake.' Heinz waved his mobile phone. 'I figured you were going to do serious work on gene expression – put us right on the map.'

'I need funding. I can't do squat writing lecture papers.'

'You're here two weeks and I'm getting leaned on already.'

'What?' That stopped him cold. A shudder ran through him as connections he had so far kept separate began to fuse.

'You're jeopardizing funding from a major commercial concern.'

'American Chemicals? How are they involved?' – making that jump.

'If they are, I don't know how. The call came from Alex Flint of First National.'

That muddied the water some more.

'How does the bank figure in all this?'

136

'All what? What the hell is going on?' Heinz was getting mad. 'I shouldn't have mentioned the bank's vice-president. Just forget that, will you?'

'There's something pretty fundamental at stake here, Bill. Friendship, integrity, honour, are no minor items in a working relationship.'

'Nothing's as fundamental as funding. Try running a goddamn department without guys like Flint. You learn to parley principles a little. I didn't know just who you were drawing down on, Jak – but it isn't anything to do with the college, and this isn't open to negotiation.'

The encounter with the dean took his breath clear away. He felt like he was in a large tank that he couldn't escape from, while the air was gradually being sucked out. He knew he had to take action before he and the academic world he knew and felt safe in disappeared completely. What kind of action was open to him he didn't immediately know.

Calling the bank vice-president wasn't it. Alex Flint wouldn't take his call and didn't return it. After the third call he decided to go to the bank headquarters building and confront him, regardless of what it might do to his relationship with the dean and faculty.

He got as far as the ante-room to Flint's office where a secretary asked if he had an appointment.

'I can't even get the guy to pick up the phone. How can I get an appointment?'

'I'm afraid Mr Flint has left for the day,' she said.

'It's two-thirty. What kind of job does he have?'

'I must ask you to leave, sir, or I'll call security.'

'Inevitably.'

He tried to think out his next move when fate took a hand. Oblivious to what was happening in the ante-room, Flint stepped out of his office. The panic in the secretary's eyes told him who this was.

'Mr Flint,' he said, stepping around the tightly attired young woman. 'I need to talk with you.'

'Who are you?'

'What the hell did you say to Bill Heinz out at Maryland that they dumped me?'

'I have nothing to say to you. I suggest you leave.' He turned back into his office.

Once past that oak door he knew the vice-president would be unassailable and so made a lunge and grabbed his coat.

'Talk to me. I want to know what you know.'

Flint, who was about five years older, fifty pounds heavier and soft-looking, retreated in panic and slipped and crashed to the floor.

'Call the cops, Miss Addison, call the cops.'

She was already doing that.

Jak retreated at a run. He had had enough of cops after yesterday's experience and they sure weren't going to help him unravel this. As he got to the lobby he saw two security guards heading into one of the express elevators. He expected them to turn right after him, but guessed he looked not very different from most other men going in and out of the building. It didn't occur to him then that Flint might not want him pursued once he thought about the situation.

Still, quite what he was getting into he wasn't sure. A small voice inside him said he was better off not knowing, that he should keep on running. Logic told him that if he ran far enough finally he'd come right back to where he started out from. He was someplace close to that right now and facing his past.

The only way out that he could see was to get further in. That scared him, remembering what had happened to his wife and child when he had asked troublesome questions once before. He stopped himself thinking about that. Nothing had been proven. He wondered why these kinds of problems surfaced around him; other scientists got their funding, steadfastly did their work, never deviating, never having their facilities pulled. Although he put a lot into his science, he allowed distractions to affect him: those children dying in the fields of Mexico – a minor item! Grace's daughter dying in East Anglia – another minor item! The smart guys were purposely unaware of such things. He had yet to learn that trick. Maybe he should call Rory, tell him he wasn't able to contact Grace, that he couldn't help further anyhow. He was ready to make the call, but stopped to wonder what would result from it. Would his place of work suddenly be open to him again both here and at Cambridge? It was unlikely. Not immediately. First word would have to filter through to those people in powerful offices, people driven only by profit. They would know almost as soon as he made his decision. Getting some order in his life and stability in his work was a powerful reason for quitting. Against what if he chose not to?

He reminded himself how he didn't like quitting anything before all the answers were in. But on something like this all the answers were rarely if ever reachable. He thought about the possibility of being a little in love with Grace, and what this would mean. Very little. He was no place he wanted to be with her that such a decision could make any difference to; but he cared more than a little about what was happening to science as it scrabbled for funding from any vested interest regardless of cost or consequences. He could never separate himself from the consequences of his work – until now that was. That had been the cause of most of his problems, and would inevitably continue to dog him unless he learned detachment. It was tough, but he was determined. That only left the question of getting up the right smoke-signal to those guys who made major decisions about funding.

Before that happened he ran into Steven Ashurst, a Jesuit priest who was part of the campus.

'Jak! How are you? I heard you were among us,' the berobed priest said, towering a full head above him despite his stoop. Jak was loading books into the trunk of his car on the university parking lot.

'Among you, but not of you, it seems, Steven,' he said and slammed the lid. 'Do you have any contacts at First National?' – here was maybe the instrument of his deliverance. He knew Steven Ashurst was no regular priest, but one who successfully ministered to mammon.

'Bankers like scientists don't have souls.' Ashurst laughed. 'Checking out?'

He shrugged. 'That's not what I had in mind.'

139

'You've been working on cereals, Jak. Has there been some development that might dramatically change what'll happen to wheat next fall?'

'Your department might give you a better picture. Are you still speculating on commodities?'

'It's a science, not a faith.' There was irritation in his voice. 'All the indicators suggest selling wheat, and that's what most of the county elevator operators are doing. Only somebody seems to be buying.'

Suddenly his interest came alive, and he was sucked right back into the possible conspiracy.

'In any quantity?' he asked.

'For every buyer there has to be a seller – that's how the market operates.'

'What does this mean, Steven? Is somebody trying to get a corner or something?'

The priest considered the scientist. 'What do you know, Jak?'

He glanced away, trying to decide if he did maybe know something. He wanted to find out. Maybe he should try and get a few more answers before he quit.

'The Commodity Futures Trading Commission's enforcement division is there to stop that happening. Big purchases get reported to CTFC. Along with open interest.' Jak offered a blank look. 'Someone buys what someone sells. The one automatically cancels out the other. That way the Board of Trade that operates the market doesn't have to deliver what comes due on delivery date. The open interest is what dealers take home. They might hang in there and wait for the price to move, they could even take delivery, it has been known. There's too much wheat around for anyone to be thinking like that – unless you know something.' He waited. 'Jak?'

There was expectancy in the air.

'Can we find out who it is buying wheat?'

'Shit – is there something? Speak to me, Jak. Speak to me.' And when he still got no response – 'It'll mean a trip to Kansas City. I know a floor trader – his son was at the seminary with me.'

On the plane Jak began to get depressed at being so

140

easily drawn back into something over which he had so little control, and would lead he didn't know where, apart from almost certainly blocking his access to any scientific research post.

Seeing the way this man of God operated made him think he was in the wrong line of business. At the airport Ashurst showed no mercy as he beat the cab driver down to twenty dollars for a flat fare downtown. Whether the woman had had a bad day or was looking for an easy path to heaven, she didn't grumble.

In the gallery overlooking the trading pits the priest explained how things worked. His knowledge was extensive.

'The people in the coloured coats trade by open outcry and handsignals in the pit. The step they stand on indicates the month they're trading. All transactions are recorded by the single Clearing Corporation – that's how we know the volume of business.'

A clerk came into the gallery and handed Ashurst a note.

'My friend's invited us onto the floor.'

The view was better from the gallery, Jak found, and easier to follow. Sam Trump, the priest's friend, was in the pit watching a trader from Continental signalling 120 contracts of July wheat he was looking to be short in.

There was activity, but no stampede. Someone finally went long when the price dropped a tick. 'A little speculation,' Ashurst explained.

Before he could find out why, he saw a pink-coated trader take the other hundred contracts.

Sam Trump returned to the desk and tossed his unfulfilled order to his floor clerk.

'Who's buying wheat, Sam?' the priest asked.

'I was trying to. It was a kill or fill at the client's price.'

'Who got that?'

'Hirshorn. They buy one day and sell the next.'

'At a profit?' he asked.

'Well, they sure stay in business, son,' the trader said. He shook his hand when they were introduced.

'Who's pushing the price up, Sam?' the priest asked.

141

'Well, Hirshorn are taking a shot,' Trump said. He thought about that as he watched the large electronic price board overhead and slowly nodded his large head. 'There are two rumours. One says Caddy Hirshorn – the big boss who runs just about everything in that outfit – has cancer, that the drugs he's taking are screwing up his judgement. You want my opinion, that's what most traders believe. That's why they aren't following him. Believe me, people watch and follow Hirshorn's moves pretty damn close – excuse me, father. Hirshorn was a man who knew grain like nobody knew grain. The second rumour is that they're in there buying on behalf of Argentina – to get the price up. Argentine wheat's ready first – at these prices they'd be giving it away.'

'What do you think, Sam?'

Trump paused, like he enjoyed being asked his opinion.

'There's another rumour, father, that Argentina's wheat's in a bigger mess than the Russians'. That they won't have any to bring to market come May. If they do there'll be bread riots down there.' He shrugged. 'Me? I figure Hirshorn's going to get a cold. Caddy Hirshorn's a sick man, no one else would be long in this market.'

'Why don't you guys stop buying?'

'We're grain traders, Jak. We do business by doing business. We're dumping on Hirshorn, and making a little profit while we can. When the boss gets too sick to go on, someone else'll take over, sort out the mess. Hirshorn'll put the wheat back on the market. The price'll come down. Just recently he publicly sacked his brother-in-law for stealing. That's added to the rumours about his health. You got to be crazy to damage yourself like that. There are gonna be law suits following.'

'But there's still an awful lot of wheat out there, Sam.'

'There sure is. I can't see Hirshorn keeping the price up forever, father. I hear tell Caddy Hirshorn's a deeply religious man – maybe he heard ahead of everyone else there's going to be a drought or something.'

'Or that a lot of wheat might fail someplace,' Jak said.

'Did you get the inside track on that from your boss, father?' the trader said.

'It's a science, for Christsake, Sam.'

The floor clerk put the phone down, stamped an order and handed it to Trump.

'Here's a sell order,' he said glancing at the ticket. 'I guess we can dump this one onto Hirshorn.'

Out on Main Street where the wind had the sharpness of a knife blade, Jak's head buzzed with questions he had no answers to.

'What would make a serious speculator buy in this market, Steven?'

'A real good hunch mostly. Forward knowledge about what's going to happen to a commodity. What's on your mind, Jak?'

'Maybe I'm getting paranoid. Maybe it's all coincidences. But here we have a lot of buying – more than the market suggests there should be. While in England a lot of wheat failed, then somebody tries to stop me asking questions.'

'Where do you figure pressure is coming from? The seed company, or the chemical outfit?'

'The way multinationals are interrelated – they could be the same people. Somebody's buying wheat, Steven. The price's going up.'

'That could be like Sam said, the guy running Hirshorn being sick and losing his judgement. Rumours around these markets are usually pretty accurate.'

'But supposing for a moment someone has a different story about just how much wheat there's going to be around.'

'Like who, Jak?'

Right then he wanted to say how he didn't know and didn't care. Instead he said, 'That's what I aim to find out.'

Getting started wasn't easy. He was a scientist not a streetwise detective, and although he could organize evidence, the serious problem lay in gathering this kind of evidence. Approaching the seed company to find out how the genetic material came to be in their seed hadn't gotten him far. The next obvious tack was the scientists working in this field, as he assumed that some of them had done

143

the work. The possibility that whoever it was might not want to talk about it never occurred to him. The scientific establishment almost always wanted to publish its results as soon as they were proven. Some of them did so before they were proven.

The response to his calls to people working in this area caused his paranoia to recur. He found their answers unhelpful and decided it meant that they were either covering up something, or were afraid, in case talking to him resulted in their funding disappearing.

One plant geneticist happy to talk to him was Herman Solkoff, who was trying to unlock the genetic code that would lead to rice fixing its own nitrogen. Chemical fertilizer leaching into the water aquifers was a particular problem when it was poured into the paddy fields.

Solkoff was in Washington addressing a US Rice Growers' Association seminar. They met at his hotel on DuPont Circle. There delegates socialized at the cocktail buffet in the lobby around six o'clock.

'I read your paper on genetic dissection,' he told Solkoff as he drew him aside away from the piano player. He didn't say it had been stolen with his attaché case.

'Did you learn anything new?' the moonfaced Solkoff asked.

'We've had lots of problems with chromosome mutation resulting from segment transplants.'

'We've taken the wrong approach to mutagenesis. If they're repeatable they could be seen as the desired result.'

'Do you figure that's how the bacterium gene came to be in wheat, Herman?'

'It's a truly fascinating possibility,' Dr Solkoff said, removing his spectacles and dabbing a handkerchief to his eyes. 'It means someone's found a method of crossing the gene species barrier. It's not nitrogen fixed from the atmosphere, but it's a big step in that direction.'

'Or the destruction of the whole wheat crop,' he said.

'Arnold Sanson was working on wheat genes to resist Take-all up in Ontario. He got real edgy when I talked with him. What's happening, Jak?'

144

'I figure this mutant gene's not the problem, Herman, but the solution.'

'That's crazy.'

'That's what I keep telling myself. But I come right back to where I started every time.'

'Why don't *you* try talking to Sanson, Jak?'

'I will. But weird things are happening around me.'

That got no response from Solkoff.

Arnold Sanson was away in Mexico for the Christmas recess and hadn't left a number where he could be reached. This merely delayed him, but he saw nothing alarming in it. He went to the Library of Congress and read anything Sanson had recently published. There wasn't much. Certainly nothing touching on the bacterium genes designed to attract Take-all. Sanson had a reputation for not organizing his research notes, and even if he had, maybe this wouldn't be something he'd want to publish.

Holding a prominent position in his specialized field, Jak had access to most published and unpublished papers concerning wheat genetics, and particularly mutagenesis, and was never short of reading material. Frequently he would find himself waking stiff and cold at three and four in the morning, having fallen asleep in his study. None of his reading brought him closer to the answers he was seeking. He was sure they lay in the material Grace had promised to ship over. He would have Solkoff grow the seed to see if he could reproduce his earlier result. Having unsuccessfully tried calling Grace on a number of occasions, he was beginning to wonder if something had happened to her, along with his papers and samples. It wasn't possible that she had simply been out the whole while.

He glanced at the phone on the floor and thought about calling her again. When it started to ring – instantly he fantasized about it being Grace, that she was here in Washington. Papers slid from his lap as he reached out to get the call. It wasn't Grace but Rory Spelman.

Imagining him in his tiny overfilled office in one of several rundown houses the Christic Institute used, he wondered why he did what he did under such conditions.

'Jak? I had a call from my doctor friend in Mexico.

145

Things are hotting up. A lot of field-workers have recently gotten sick from the new round of spraying. Did you reach Mrs Chance? Do you think she could head on down there and talk with Alicia Huerta? Someone has to.'

'I'm having a real problem reaching her. Nor did I get the research material she was planning on shipping over.'

'The problem in Mexico's not going to disappear. But Alicia might. She's getting a lot of hassle. They bury doctors who help the field hands down there.'

That didn't sound like Rory Spelman, he thought as he rang off. This was a guy who was ordinarily full of optimism about changing the world and all the people in it.

He called his former research assistant in Cambridge, and asked her to drive out to Grace's farm. He couldn't get anyplace without either Grace or his research data. If he didn't reach her soon, he would find a way of getting back into England himself. He had a clear idea about how.

The US District Court on 3rd and Constitution, situated behind Capitol Hill, was an imposing white stone building. He had never been inside the court house before in all his time in Washington. Rory, who had asked him to meet him down here, was waiting outside court ten, on the third floor. He ended his conversation with another man who went into the courtroom.

'Sorry to bring you down here,' the lawyer said as he approached. 'Our case against the utilities for dumping toxic waste was brought forward.'

'This is quite some building,' he said.

'Don't be fooled by appearances, Jak. It's more impressive than some of the rulings that get handed out down here.' Rory removed some papers from his briefcase. 'I need Mrs Chance's signature on these before we can get a date for a hearing.'

'I've located her, but it doesn't help much. She's in a psychiatric hospital. My research assistant found her. She couldn't find out why she's there.'

146

Rory nodded. Nothing seemed to faze him. He glanced around, then drew Jak away to a vending machine on the corridor. 'Did you trace the source of your pressure?'

'Grace was trying to get that – maybe that's why she's in a psychiatric hospital.'

'One of our people had a run-in with American Chemicals when she was in private practice in Pennsylvania. She figured they poisoned her dog.' He gave him a long look. 'Sound familiar, Jak?'

Anxiety crept up on him along with echoes from the past.

'I don't want to get back into all that.'

'You are getting back into it.'

'No – it's gone. There's not a thing I can do about it.'

'You can try dealing with your feelings,' Rory said.

'When I want your goddamn advice on my feelings, counsellor, I'll ask for it.'

He was getting ready to run from the anger. His anxiety increased as he was forced to think about the kind of people they could be dealing with. They likely hadn't changed any, but still he was allowing himself to get drawn back. Pacing up and down with his arms folded over his head was a nervous habit he had in tough situations. Finally he got to it.

'This is crazy. I'm not getting one bit of work done. I figure I can't go any farther with this.' He saw Rory's look which he believed was judging him. 'What is it you want me to do? Get myself killed?'

'I can see it would be a problem going back, maybe facing down American Chemicals.'

'Life is really easy for you, Rory. Sure you don't make too much goddamn money, but all you need do is come down here and argue with civilized reasoning people. No one came after your wife and child.'

If Rory had given him an argument he told himself he would have felt better. He knew this lawyer had had his life seriously threatened on many occasions, but rarely spoke about them. Maybe he was too scared to.

'If I could make that different for you, Jak, I would. Say the word and Christic will go after those people. Nail

147

them right to the floor for Marge and Pete. We'd have a pretty good try.'

'Forget it. I need to get back to my real work.'

He strode away to the elevator and punched the call button, sensing Rory watching him the whole while. He didn't look round. The car arrived and the doors opened but he didn't get in. He couldn't. The gates closed. Finally he turned back, knowing this was madness, and that he'd come to regret it.

'You figure American Chemicals know who you are?' Rory asked.

'Maybe I imagined the whole damn thing.'

'You didn't imagine Marge and Pete dying.' He waited. 'I need depositions from Mrs Chance. You planning on going back to England to find out what happened?'

'I'm working on it,' he said.

He drove out to Bethesda Naval Hospital where a security guard offered him directions. He didn't often come to see his brother here, but remembered where his office was located.

Paul Redford, a senior psychiatrist on staff, was three years older than Jak, slightly heavier and a little grayer and around the same height. There were strong family resemblances. These were what he hoped would get him back into England, assuming Paul went along with his plan.

'You're looking in great shape, Josh,' he said. 'I figured all that running would kill you. Sorry I couldn't invite you out to the house for dinner. But the divorce is getting messy.'

'Is it irreconcilable?' he asked. He liked Paul's wife and their two children.

'I've found someone else. She's a lot younger than Fran. Hell, let's talk about your problems. I played golf with Bill Heinz – he didn't say who was leaning on them, but someone is. The money they get via First National is no small item, Josh – going after Alex Flint like that, Jesus Christ . . . If you'd been smart you'd have gotten into virology when you quit chemical pathology. That's where all the money is going right now.'

'I guess I never was that smart,' he said.

'Does that stir up bad memories, Josh?'

His brother's question sounded professional. He dismissed it with a shake of his head.

'Right now I need help getting back to England.'

'I know people in the State Department – you meet someone at a cocktail party in this town. You stay in touch. They're useful contacts.'

'I had it in mind to borrow your passport.'

Paul looked at him for a long moment before responding. 'That's a federal offence. What about my AMA accreditation. You want that too? Why not my credit cards? What kind of dumb move is this, Josh?'

'Paul, things are happening that I don't understand. I need to visit a friend in England who maybe has the key.'

'Is she pretty?' Paul smiled. It said that made all the difference.

'Unless I get this worked out, I couldn't make it parking cars on campus.'

The fear that had kept him running was now touching his brother.

'What the hell have you gotten mixed up in, Josh? – Shit, it's better I don't know.'

From a drawer in his desk he removed his passport and glanced across at his brother, comparing him to the photograph. 'I look five years younger, but I guess you might get by.' He put the passport back into the drawer along with his American Medical Association card, his American Express card and driver's licence. He looked at Jak and nodded solemnly. 'Don't spend too much of my money. Divorce is expensive. I'll get us some coffee.'

Jak didn't wait for coffee, but took the passport and cards and left.

Driving off the parking lot, he noticed the auto parked three down in the row as it started. The black driver looked vaguely familiar but he attached no importance to the observation. Right then he was thinking about taking a flight to England and finding some way of getting Grace out of that psychiatric hospital.

THERE WAS NO TROUBLE COMING into London Heathrow. The immigration official glanced over his entry card and his brother's photograph and didn't even ask the purpose of his visit. There was a problem at the car rental desk. Hertz had screwed up his reservation from Washington on Paul's American Express Card. They didn't have a compact available. After protesting not too loudly they offered him a Ford Granada at the same rate.

Trouble found him as soon as he reached the psychiatric hospital in Bury St Edmunds. The car he saw pull onto the parking lot close to his was one he had seen earlier. He believed it had tailed him – all the way from his hotel in Russell Square. He watched the driver get out and lock the doors. Then go round and check them. Then unlock the driver's door, and relock and check it again. That kind of behaviour convinced him that this man had moved too soon and was trying to delay himself, waiting to see what he did next.

Leaping from his car, Jak approached, startling the driver.

'Are you tailing me?'

The man, who was fifty, bald and wore glasses, recovered himself, then unlocked the driver's door yet again, this time to reach out for his briefcase.

'Are you a patient at this hospital?' he demanded.

'The hell I am! I figure you've been following me.'

'I suggest you might see someone. I'm Dr Rowberry, a consultant psychiatrist. I assume this is a mistake,' the doctor said with an air of menace, before he walked with a stiff gait into the administration block.

The encounter left him feeling stupid, and wondering if it might cause problems when he tried to spring Grace. Maybe they'd think paranoia was normal in a shrink. Dr Rowberry sure seemed paranoid.

The law of perversity guaranteed Grace would be Dr Rowberry's patient. Jak's heart sank when the receptionist said she would have to contact the consultant to clear his seeing her.

'I just got through talking with him on the parking lot,' he explained. 'I'll just go and take a look at Mrs Chance. I'll see Dr Rowberry afterward to discuss the case.'

'Of course, doctor,' the woman said, not challenging that kind of authority. 'I'll tell Dr Hollick you're on your way – he's the registrar.'

He was directed to a single-storey building with four wings off a central lobby. Faced with a choice of four corridors he hesitated. A woman approached, wearing jeans and a sweater. Her name tag said she was a nurse.

'Where can I locate Mrs Chance?'

'Are you a relative?'

Relative to what? he wanted to ask back.

'A relation? I'm Dr Paul Redford, a visiting psychiatrist.'

'Does Dr Rowberry know you're here?'

'I talked with him a short while ago.'

A young man with a beard and wearing an Aran sweater approached. 'Dr Redford – I'm Dr Hollick. You want to take a dekko at Mrs Chance. That's okay, Barbara. I'll find her,' he said. 'I think she's in the TV room.'

They went off along one of the corridors.

'Why are you looking at Mrs Chance?' the young doctor asked. 'She's not particularly interesting.'

'She isn't? A friend asked me to take a dekko – I'm over here on vacation.' He hoped that made him sound sufficiently disinterested.

Grace was in pyjamas and a tired-looking robe. She showed him no recognition and seemed to have little

151

awareness of anything but what was on TV. He wondered if it was the same woman who he imagined he was a little bit in love with. Maybe he wasn't after all.

'She displayed irrational, threatening behaviour when she was brought in three weeks ago. She's on a mild tranquillizer.'

'Can I take a look?' He took the medical record from the young doctor and saw straightaway that Grace was also being given what he knew was a strong sedative.

'Dr Rowberry prescribed that to help her over her bereavement – she'd recently lost her daughter.' He checked his watch and glanced about at three other patients who were staring at the TV. 'Our ward round's about to start. Sing out if you want me.'

He collected the other patients and departed.

Jak turned off the TV and came back to Grace.

'Grace, do you know who I am?'

A vacant, mechanical smile appeared back before her gaze returned to the blank TV screen.

'I can't remember why I'm here,' she said. 'It was to do with why Rose died.'

'Did you find out something, Grace?'

She blinked like memory was seeping through the fog in her brain but wouldn't connect to any words. Maybe he was being too hopeful.

'You were looking for evidence. Did you find some?'

She blinked again. He felt her struggling for something beyond her immediate grasp. He felt frustrated, wanting to put words into her mouth, but didn't know what words.

Another out-of-uniform nurse came in. 'Ah, Grace. The ward round has started.'

'I'm Dr Redford – I'm talking with Grace right now.'

'Oh, but Dr Rowberry's taking the ward round this morning.'

'We'll be right there.' He offered his friendliest smile.

The nurse looked uncertain. Finally she went out.

Although the hospital wasn't locked, he could see from Grace's medical file that being here was still a heavy number. Her drug regime was holding her pretty secure. If he was to get her out he knew he had to move fast as he didn't rate very highly his chances of persuading Dr Rowberry to release her into his charge.

'We're getting out of here,' he said.

'Leave . . .?' Her response was frightened.

'My car's right outside. We'll walk clear out of here, Grace.'

One by one he unclasped her fingers from the wooden arms of the chair and helped her up. He stopped at the door and peered out.

Dr Rowberry was along the corridor talking with the nurse who had come to collect Grace. He then glanced toward the TV room and said something else to the nurse, as he started in their direction.

Right then Jak had no option but to step out and head him off. But the young doctor in the Aran sweater did just that, calling from a doorway down the corridor that they were waiting for him. Rowberry hesitated, then changed course and disappeared into the room.

As he steered Grace across the lobby toward the exit, a woman hurried past, reminding her yet again about Rowberry's meeting. He said she'd be right there, but kept on going, out of the door. He resisted the inclination to hurry. It was a struggle he quickly felt himself losing.

The walk to the car seemed like ten miles, and at any moment he expected the alarm would be raised or someone would come running after them. As if becoming aware of that possibility also Grace glanced round and quickened her stride.

'Walk, don't run,' he told her. 'We're almost there.'

The nearer they got to the car the stronger his inclination to run became. He heard someone call out, 'Stop her, stop her!' Panic seized him and he turned as the shrill cry was heard again. Grace heard it too.

'Stop her! Stop her!'

An old man was waggling a crooked finger in their direction. Jak was about to run when he realized it was a cat he wanted caught. No one went to his aid.

'Take it easy, Grace. No one's going to get stopped.'

They reached the car, where panic wracked at him again as he searched for the key. He figured he had somehow dropped it in the TV room and that he'd have to go back for it. He felt sick.

'It's in the ignition,' Grace said. 'The key.'

Relief swept in. He started to laugh. The engine fired and the car roared away. Only at the last moment did he remember to check if any car came out of the hospital after them. He couldn't tell, so figured none did.

Paranoia began to seep through his elation, and by the time they reached the farm he had twice identified a car that he was convinced was tailing them. Then seeing it pass the gateway and head along the lane he knew for sure. He jumped from his car and ran back out of the farmyard without explanation to Grace.

The auto was parked in a gateway to a field along the lane. The bald driver, who was standing on the door sill, jumped behind the wheel when he saw him and the car accelerated away. By sprinting Jak managed to grab the doorhandle until forced to let go or get dragged along.

He said nothing to Grace when he returned.

'Is it open? I guess not.'

He broke a window and climbed through and unlocked the door. Grace smiled as she reoriented herself in the kitchen, picking up a photo of Rose and holding it close to herself like it was the child. He wanted to hurry her, worried now about what action the driver of that car might take.

'Grace, you'd better get some outdoor clothes on.'

'They'll take me back,' she said. 'The police will take me.'

'Sure, if we're dumb enough to stick around here.'

'I don't want to go back.'

Anxiety made him impatient. 'Get your clothes together, for Christsake.'

She looked like she was about to cry.

'I'm sorry. I didn't mean to yell. Come on.'

He led her up to the bedroom and began opening drawers and taking out some of her things. He hesitated over her underwear. They were plain, simple cotton garments. He preferred elaborate underwear, yet still found himself getting excited. Among papers and letters was her passport. He slipped it into his pocket. When he turned Grace hadn't moved from the edge of the bed.

'Grace, somebody could show up anytime. Get dressed.'

She didn't resist him as he removed her robe and pyjama top. He noticed her round breasts, her slender hips and the thick triangle of pubic hair when she was completely naked. She seemed unaware of the effect she was having on him. How long had it been . . . He pushed his thoughts away as she spoke.

'Can I take a shower? You couldn't always get one when you wanted at the hospital.'

He wanted to say no, but couldn't. Instead he packed her bag while he waited for her. Not quite sure what he should pack he put in some of everything. Next he got the Safeway bags from the roofspace and carried them to the car. She was in the bedroom drying herself when he returned. His eyes embraced her naked body, and his erection came right back up. She stood for a long moment with the towel away from herself looking at him like she was waiting for him to make some move.

'The water was cold,' she said.

He helped her to dress.

He thought about taking a cold shower himself.

Driving along the motorway towards London, he explored what had happened to her, but got no clear answers. He wasn't surprised that Grace had existed in a fog after the medication she had received.

'Could I shower at the hotel?' she said after a long silence. 'You couldn't always get one in the hospital.'

'You took a shower already, Grace.'

'It was cold. I've always liked showering. I couldn't bear starting the day without one. I wanted to wash the day off me at night in the hospital. I don't know what they thought we'd do in the shower. I always felt the same at the farm. To wash away all that I was involved with – am I talking too much?'

'You're doing real fine.' He smiled.

At the hotel she emerged from the bathroom wearing his robe with a towel around her head.

'A farmer's wife told me how her husband had bought some unlabelled fungicide,' she said. 'It was from a supplier in Bury St Edmunds – I had been talking to her about the problems with our cows. The fungicide had got into their cattle's water and several died with respiratory problems . . . that was why I was taken to hospital, I think.'

'How's that, Grace?'

'I tried to buy some Resolution, that's what it was,' she explained. 'The supplier said I had to keep quiet about it as it hadn't got a product licence yet. Then I did something really silly. I asked if Shearing had bought any. He denied knowing who Shearing was. Then of course said he didn't have any Resolution for sale. He'd never had it for sale.'

'Did he call the police?'

'No, I think it must have been Shearing – after I went there and accused him of murdering Rose. I think I hit him. I completely lost control – God, I wanted to kill him. I remember that. I just couldn't calm down. The more I was restrained the worse it was. I attacked the police as well.'

'Good for you!' he said. He wanted to embrace her, but was uncertain of the response he'd get. 'Why don't I go talk to this supplier?'

The farm supplier's vast warehouse was stacked to the roof with everything from rolls of plastic pipe to half-ton sacks of fertilizer, plus every kind of pesticide. There was no shortage of customers, and he had to wait to get help. It gave him time to check out some of the drums.

'Is Charlie around?' he asked when the counterhand finally got to him. 'I need twenty ten-litre drums of Resolution. Walter Shearing said to see Charlie.'

Charlie, who ran the office, said, 'It's getting to be a serious problem finding a fungicide that stays effective these days. I suppose Mr Shearing told you we shouldn't be putting it on sale yet.'

'Yes he did. I have to be careful. No problem?'

As they headed toward the back of the store, Charlie said, 'Where is it you farm?'

156

Whatever it was that had aroused this man's suspicion, Jak wasn't ready for the question and didn't give the right answer; so he didn't get to make his illicit purchase.

The only move left to them now was to approach Shearing.

He was less than pleased to see them.

'Get out of here. Get out before I throw you out,' he ordered, driving them from his farm office. 'And take that mad woman with you . . . she's persecuting me.'

'Call the cops,' Jak challenged, not knowing how he'd handle it if Shearing did just that. 'Let's have them take a real close look at what unlicensed chemicals you've been using.'

Shearing stepped back and looked at Grace, then quickly looked away.

'Yes, we were spraying Resolution,' he said. 'It's perfectly safe, I can assure you. The Ministry is about to grant its product licence. I know that for a fact.'

'Supposing there's a hitch because they find it's causing fatal respiratory problems?'

'Fungal growth in cereals becomes resistant to pesticides so quickly,' he explained, 'we need new products to stay on top of the problem. Resolution is effective. Aggrow Chemicals are three hundred per cent confident of its licence coming through.'

'Nine years ago the Environmental Protection Agency stopped American Chemicals selling it Stateside. That's why they're pushing it everyplace else. Take a look at what it's doing to farm workers down in Mexico and Chile. Sure it stopped fungal growth, and everybody it gets on.'

A hard set came over Shearing's face. 'The Pesticide Advisory Committee here is passing it. Their scrutiny is very thorough. They wouldn't let it through if it weren't safe.'

'That committee's made up of people with a vested interest in the agricultural industry,' Grace said shimmering with conviction.

'Take my advice, Mrs Chance,' Shearing said, clearly resenting her accusations, 'accept Aggrow's compensation and let the matter drop.'

157

That was his last word on the subject.

'I have no intention of letting the matter drop,' Grace stated. She looked at Jak. He nodded. Confirming that. Right then he'd have walked through fire for her.

'From what I can see, Grace, the way ahead of us won't be easy,' he warned as they drove back to London.

'But we will go on – we must. We can get those details now.'

'Sure we can.' He didn't speculate about how the opposition might feel about that.

In the parking lot under the hotel, he waited a few moments, searching around for signs of that familiar car.

'Is there something wrong?' Grace asked.

'I figure you'd better know someone's been following us, Grace. They may be here.'

'The police?'

He shook his head. 'Maybe I'm just getting paranoid.'

'Shall I collect the key?' she offered.

Up in his bedroom, she said, 'Two men called earlier to see you. The woman on the reception desk didn't know who they were. If it's not the police, surely that means someone thinks we really are on to something.'

He watched her pace the room, tossing her thick red hair back over her shoulder. She was excited, and probably a little scared. He was scared, but excited also. He wanted to make love to her more than anything right then, but that scared him too.

'Who are they?' she said.

'Why stick around to find out? We'll hightail it to Washington, talk to the lawyer, fight these guys on firmer ground. You'll like Rory, he's great.'

'Washington?' Grace said, apparently flustered. 'I can't . . . I haven't . . . I mean I can't just go and leave everything.'

'What are you leaving, Grace? Rose is dead, Colin's gone, the farm's gone – those assholes are closing in on us.'

Tears suddenly welled up in Grace's eyes. Instinctively he put his arms around her and held her close and she sobbed against his chest. He had wanted to hold her in his arms for a long while. Even in these circumstances he took pleasure in the contact.

'I can't go. I haven't got my passport or anything.'

'That's taken care of. All we got to do is get out of here.'

He had Grace walk out with their baggage, while he rang the front desk for a five o'clock wake-up call to get an eight a.m. flight. He hung out the 'do not disturb' sign and slipped away, himself. He planned on taking a cab to the airport and telling Hertz to collect the car at the hotel.

Grace grew increasingly anxious as she waited in her seat on the plane, thinking maybe she had misunderstood him over the flight details – despite her ticket being at the reservation desk. Was this the right thing to do? She didn't want to return to that hospital. Anything was better than that. Maybe Jak was getting a different flight. But she was almost certain that wasn't what he had said. The plane was only a third full, but the passengers settled ready for departure. This was one occasion when she hoped there'd be some sort of delay. She glanced at the empty seat next to her as if expecting Jak to miraculously appear, and wondered about getting off herself. Then again about what she was doing here anyway? How could she simply go to America? It was madness. Perhaps she was mad after all. But she knew that staying would mean having to return to the psychiatric unit and being given more drugs. If Jak had been detained at the check-in desk it would only be a matter of time before they came for her. Then she would have to suffer the indignity of being led off the plane like a criminal. She had to get off herself. Now. Soon it would be too late; cabin staff were making their final checks to see if seat belts were fastened and luggage was properly stowed. Any minute they would close the door and start the safety procedure prior to take off. Did that happen before the door was closed? She couldn't remember. She tried to get out of her seat as the stewardess came along the aisle. In panic she struggled against the seat belt.

'Can you remain seated, please, we're about to depart.'

'I have to get off.' She saw the door being closed. 'I can't go.'

Finally she freed the belt and was up out of her seat. The stewardess took fright at her agitation and as she watched her hurrying back to speak to the flight attendant, she thought perhaps they would call the airport security. The flight attendant picked up the phone by the door. This was it. They talked in urgent whispers as she approached. The attention of the entire cabin was on her now. The situation was getting out of control and she could feel her skin prickle with embarrassment.

'If you're quick,' she heard the flight attendant say into the phone, eyeing her uneasily. 'We have a passenger disembarking.' He replaced the phone.

'Did you check any baggage, mam?'

She didn't manage to answer as the doors swung open and she saw Jak running awkwardly along the approach tunnel under the weight of the Safeway bags.

'Are you getting off, mam?' the flight attendant said.

Tears streamed down her face as Jak caught hold of her with one of his laden arms and steered her along to their seats. She had never been more pleased to see anyone.

'Boy, that was close,' he said to a stewardess.

The woman smiled tightly and glanced quickly away from Grace.

13

ANTICIPATING EVERY DETAIL ON A deal this far ahead, when any error could cost him everything, was part of the excitement of business. It got him up at five o'clock each morning. Nothing was random or left to chance. Even the Soviet Union getting turned on its head he could handle, figuring it would be years before their command economy could be turned into a true market economy. But any miscalculation could rupture his plan. Such as that Cambridge professor who had stumbled upon their wheat seed, Prairie Red.

The farmer who had accidentally planted the seed could also prove dangerous if he decided the compensation he had received wasn't sufficient. Caddy was a long way from concluding his wheat deal, and might not come close unless such problems were taken care of. He decided to send Shapiro to England to deal with the farmer; the scientist, being wholly dependent on project funding, would be less of a problem. Unless he somehow got lucky and made the right connections . . . If he then talked to the wrong people and the Russians failed to plant the 300,000 tons of seed they'd agreed to buy . . . The new contract Hirshorn was negotiating with the Seamen's Union would be a stone tied to their ankles as they tried to swim clear . . . He didn't know what was prompting these doubts. He glanced at his assistant who was getting more coffee, noticing his suit. It was immaculate. Clearly Shapiro paid more for his suits than he ever had done on his government salary.

Coming back to a comfortable armchair in the office, Shapiro said, 'You know we don't need to give the Seamen a thing, Caddy.'

It was late. He had returned to work after dinner. He often did. On those occasions his assistant got a sandwich from the machine in the cafeteria.

'We'll give them close to what they're asking, Pat. But we'll make it look like a real fight. I don't want the union seeing what's at stake.'

Hirshorn owned twenty-eight ocean-going bulk carriers of over twenty thousand tons, all of which still flew under the American flag. Patriotism was costly, but the flag was a matter of pride to him. On any given day these ships were hauling Chilean wine to California to blend with the local higher priced wines, or Californian soya beans to the Far East, or Greek bauxite into Houston. He had never regretted holding onto this fleet through the lean seventies and he didn't now want to risk it because of some overlooked detail.

'How much wheat have we got, Pat?' It was always one of the last pieces of information he required at the end of the workday.

'Seven point five million tons of number two,' Shapiro said, rising to the computer and getting the figures on the monitor.

He turned. 'What's the price?'

'A little off $108 a ton.'

He nodded, calculating that at 815 million dollars' worth of wheat. That was a figure he could comfortably sleep on. 'The price is going to rise by forty or fifty, maybe even sixty dollars a ton when the Russians come to the market to buy.' He looked at his aide. 'They will come.' He thought about the wheat Armand Bequai had optioned for him personally. No one other than Gordon Dulles knew about that 1.2 million tons, and now Bequai had warned him the regulatory body were sniffing around.

Another anxiety arose in his mind. He sowed some seeds.

'Can we entirely trust Pierre d'Estaing, Pat?' he asked.

162

'I know the Frenchman has been handling the sale of certain grain parcels for Hirshorn both openly and in secret for many years, but if that seed doesn't get to the Russians like it's meant to, not even I will be able to dump those futures contracts at a profit.'

With a scheme clearly etched out for making serious money of his own for the first time in his life, Shapiro almost didn't touch down when the American jet brought him into Heathrow.

He felt like he was still flying when he checked into the ivy-clad Angel Hotel in historic Bury St Edmunds. There was no time to explore the town's history, not even the ruined abbey opposite his hotel. If he had time he planned to stop over in London and maybe indulge himself for one night. No more. This was something he was reluctant to do in Oklahoma in case his sexual preferences got back to his Christian boss.

As he dressed for dinner he wondered what Walter Shearing truly made of his invitation and why he had accepted it so readily. His assessment of the man based on both the financial and character profile Hirshorn had commissioned was that of a risk-taker, someone who enjoyed money. That wasn't all it told him about the unmarried farmer. Informing Shearing that this meeting would be to his financial advantage had been enough for him. He'd have gone in similar circumstances, he told himself.

Instinct told him who his guest was the moment he entered the restaurant. He waved to the tall, slightly stooped man in the pale gray suit and rose to shake his hand. Shearing was lean and attractive, but nothing about his appearances or manner would have immediately alerted Shapiro as to his being gay. But the report they had on him said he was, that he had once been arrested for assaulting a cop in a gay club.

They were from cultures so many light years apart they may not have used the same language. They basically had nothing to say to each other, but exchanged pleasantries over drinks and while ordering dinner. Then silence fell across the table. Anxiety about the one thing they had in common kept them apart. Shearing gave no hint. Nor did Shapiro. He was afraid to. He wondered how he could send up a smoke signal without putting himself at risk. The firm of enquiry agents they regularly used in England didn't make mistakes about the kind of personal habits that ordinarily would have stopped Caddy doing business with a body. They had confirmed what Shearing was when he had called them to make doubly sure.

Shearing finally said, 'Your phone call intrigued me, Mr Shapiro. What is this about?'

'A simple proposition. Hirshorn want to buy the five hundred acres of wheat you had fail.'

'That wouldn't cost them much,' Shearing said. 'This is a bad joke . . . I've ploughed it in. It wasn't doing me one bit of good.'

'You got seventy-six thousand dollars compensation from Spinetti. Right?'

'Almost right. Sixty-seven thousand pounds.'

'I figure you're short two, three hundred thousand?' He paused. 'We're prepared to pay you the difference.'

That made Shearing sit up and Shapiro smile. He enjoyed this man's response. He was someone who appeared to be in complete control.

'I'm going to be up front with you, Walter – can I call you Walter?' He waited, feeling the tension build. Enjoying this momentary uncertainty. He decided to gamble on his own instincts being entirely right about him. 'The money's to stop you looking at why our wheat seed failed – even though you wouldn't know what it is my boss is afraid you'll find.'

Shearing said, 'A genetically engineered bacterium gene.'

'Jesus Christ!' His smile completely disappeared. Then came rushing back. He felt excited.

'I wasn't about to believe it until now.'

'Believe it, Walter. It's one hell of a story.' He laughed. 'Clearly you're not going to settle for compensation now, not even at this raised level. What I plan on offering you is the means of making one hell of a lot more money besides.'

164

Up in his suite with a bottle of five star brandy, he sat on the opposite end of the sofa from his guest and slipped off his shoes and tucked one foot under himself. He saw Shearing's look and held it for a moment. 'You owe the bank a lot of money, Walter,' he said.

Surprise shot across Shearing's face. 'My land's worth four million. Maybe more.'

'I figure you're good for your note at the bank.'

'You seem to know a lot about me. What's on your mind, Pat?'

Shapiro set his glass down and rubbed his hands along his thighs to disguise a tremor of anxiety. Someone up there had truly taken care of his interests the day he'd resisted stealing the two and a half million dollars he brought out of West Africa for Hirshorn. Had he taken that money, he wouldn't now be in a position to get seriously rich. Two and a half million wasn't any longer that. Here he was at the point of no return. But the big difference between then and now was that his boss would never know about this. Yet still he hesitated, wondering if there was any way Hirshorn could learn of this. He didn't want his boss's disapproval in any way. But there would never be a better opportunity for him with less risk than this. Either he was going to become seriously rich or remain a wage-slave for the rest of his life.

'How would you like to clear your mortgage, Walter? Maybe collect two or three times that amount besides?'

'Is it criminal?' Shearing said.

He smiled, knowing he had crossed the line. Not only didn't he feel any different, he told himself but Caddy Hirshorn would probably approve of what he was doing, for its daringness, its imagination, its initiative, being a man never to let go of an opportunity himself.

'It's not even morally wrong, that I can see. Maybe the way your wheat failed. Maybe that. You had no part in that. But what it set in train is a series of events that'll make my boss a whole pile richer. We could become seriously rich and still only pick up crumbs from Hirshorn's table. You want me to go on?'

Shearing reached past him for the bottle, his hand

165

brushing his shoulder briefly. Then he pulled back and listened without interruption.

As the brandy had more and more effect on him, he wondered about just reaching out and touching his visitor. Would he still take him seriously? The prospect of making two or three million pounds from wheat futures was exciting the farmer. He knew he hadn't made any kind of mistake in his choice of business partner and didn't want to blow it by reaching for something else right then. The excitement his ideas generated in Shearing infected him, also increasing the need he felt for physical contact. The secret nature of their relationship added to that pressure. He was safely thousands of miles from home. To avoid accidental discovery he only ever made sexual contact when he was in other cities of a foreign country.

'It's getting harder than ever for a farmer to make a living these days with all the EEC red tape. We're coming under increasing pressure from the ecology lobby. I suspect all that militates against my ability to maintain my mortgage. Current farming methods are like musical chairs, Pat. While the music is playing everything is fine. It's quite likely the subsidies will stop – your government is pushing for that. There'll be demands to farm less intensively also.'

'It sounds like I got my timing pretty good.'

'You put a lot of trust in me. I could get my friends in the City to grab wheat futures before the price goes through the roof.'

Reaching out he gripped Shearing's shoulder, feeling it was hard and muscular beneath his coat. 'I'm a pretty good judge of where a guy's at, Walter. You'll make a lot more my way, believe me. If we quietly put together a large parcel without spooking the price, we'll make a lot of bucks. You maybe wouldn't get anyone to listen to your story anyhow.'

'Someone might listen to that wretched Cambridge scientist,' Shearing cautioned. 'Your wonderful scheme would produce nothing then.'

'Don't worry about him. He's taken care of.'

'This really is going to work, Pat. I know it.'

'You bet. Caddy Hirshorn is so smart,' he said. 'The only thing he knows more about than wheat is how to make money. The Russians have been stung. They are desperate for that hybrid vigour wheat seed – I guess they figure it'll solve all their problems.'

That caused Shearing to laugh out loud. Too loud. Shapiro detected nervousness in the laugh that wasn't related to his getting seriously-rich-plan.

'They could be short how much wheat do you estimate?'

'Left to their own devices? Who the hell knows. The whole system is in chaos. Caddy figures they'll need around thirty million tons of milling wheat when their crop goes down. If we can put together a mere three hundred thousand tons at something around $130 – the world price jumps to $170 for May wheat – we'd be looking at twelve million profit.'

'Then we would simply liquidate and take our profit?'

'Sure, if we figure that's the best way to go. But Hirshorn plans on taking delivery – Caddy figures there's more profit that way. We should maybe do the same.'

'No way! Christ, Pat, we don't want to get stuck and take delivery of that wheat.'

'I don't see any problems there,' he said. 'I've an agent who can sell our wheat to the Russians – Pierre d'Estaing. He's the guy who sold the hybrid vigour wheat seed to the Russians in the first place. He's the best there is. That's why Hirshorn are using him. Bottom line we can always liquidate and run.'

'Provided we're on a bull market.'

'We will be. The price is going to be jumping. Caddy won't stop buying, no matter what pressure he gets. That's the way he operates. Our biggest problem will come from going over the three million bushel speculative limit. We'll need a number of accounts to avoid that. You've got some people in the City who'll want a piece of this?'

'Better than that,' Shearing said. 'My banker. He's a gambler who, I suspect, has bet with other people's money and lost. Fortunately his losses are small, he's been able to cover them by adding them to clients' loans, or inventing new loan accounts. I'm sure he'll know other bankers who'll run the margin accounts.'

Without warning Shearing's hand dropped on his thigh, surprising him. It remained there. What a really cool customer.

Seizing the initiative back, he said, 'Would you like to stay the night, Walter?'

'I can't stay the whole night,' Shearing told him.

The bank manager Shapiro met over lunch the next day acted like he had been given the winning ticket in the New York lottery. His food grew cold, as he went over the details in hushed excited tones.

'It sounds too good to be true, Pat. The Kansas Board of Trade requires only a deposit of $750 per five thousand bushel contract. That's less than five per cent. It's a wonderful opportunity. The scheme seems absolutely foolproof, notwithstanding the fact that we'd be entering into a slightly unethical arrangement to secure the finance.'

'It's more creative,' Shearing said.

'What we need, Dick,' Shapiro told him, 'is provision for any losses should the market move against us. We have to meet all and any losses at the close of each day of trading. If we don't' – he drew his finger across his throat.

'But with Hirshorn buying wheat futures, surely the market can go only one way?' Richards said. 'That's what I told my colleagues in the other two banks. They're of the same view. That's why they're going to provide some of the funds.'

When Shearing had told him about this bank manager he hadn't guessed the guy would need so little persuading. He was now slightly alarmed by his unquestioning enthusiasm.

'That's the way I figure it will happen, Dick. But we must consider the downside too. There might be any kind of hiccup.'

'I just don't see how. Not if we hold tightly to Hirshorn's shirttails. With you advising us of their every move, Pat, it can't go wrong.'

'I guess I know how it will come out finally. If your three banks continue to maintain that speculative margin, come what may, there'll be no problem. But Kansas will sell us out the day you fail to meet it.'

'We'll meet it, of course. We're revaluing Walter's farm – so he can have drawing facilities for a million against the collateral at each of the banks. Three million pounds will be enough, Pat.'

He nodded, not having dreamed of securing such a line in credit so easily. 'Depending how Hirshorn manage the price of wheat from here on, we could maybe pick up contracts for four hundred thousand tons or more, and still meet all of our margin commitments.' He was afraid to speculate what kind of earnings that might give them, like to do so was a bad omen.

'We don't want any kind of investigation getting started,' he cautioned. 'So nothing illegal, Dick. Not a single thing.'

'One wouldn't dream of it, old chap.' The bank manager glanced at Shearing. 'Rest assured your assets won't be called in, Walter. I'll make sure of that. No one at the bank will ever know. There'll be no breath of scandal.'

Shearing raised his glass. 'To six million dollars.'

A shiver ran through Shapiro. He wanted to call the figure back, pretend that it hadn't been spoken.

'Oh, you're being over-cautious, Walter. We can do better, much better, can't we, Pat. Let's aim for ten or twelve million at least.' Richards beamed from behind his spectacles. 'Those who don't speculate can't expect to accumulate.'

They had both spoken figures that for some inexplicable reason he believed would come to haunt them. He felt uneasy. Now was the time to cut his losses and pull out. Maybe it was just a general anxiety he had about going back to the US leaving Shearing behind. But what he felt now, he had never experienced with any other man he had slept with. But then he had never entered into any kind of relationship where so much was at stake. He was afraid to quit, now that he had crossed

169

that line into the territory of potential serious richness. Here everything seemed exactly the same, yet . . . All he hoped was that Caddy Hirshorn never noticed anything was different about him.

Stopping over in Washington DC on his way back to Oklahoma, Shapiro took a meeting with Wilf Fear, and felt a wave of nostalgia at being back in the West Executive building. The security it represented. Jet-lag, combined with the scheme he had secretly embarked upon, was making him feel vulnerable, he told himself.

They walked out of the gates and across the street onto the Ellipse, the thirty-six acres of grass at the back of the White House where every kind of activity took place, but where lately the increasing legions of homeless gathered. Lines of police sawhorses prevented them sleeping too close to the White House. As he idled at Fear's painful, lurching place, he thought how incongruous it was that there in the most wealthy country in the world, that which still provided the most opportunities, there were people who couldn't get it together to get a roof over their head. A lot of people.

'How real is your anxiety about the West Exec Offices being bugged, Wilf?'

A deep wide smile cut across Fear's mouth, showing even white caps. The VC had started his dental work when he had been shot down over Vietnam. Rumour had it that he was so badly injured his mouth was the only place they were able to inflict noticeable pain.

'Why the hell we couldn't go someplace else away from the teeming poor?' Wilf Fear took his lunch out into the gardens, but fed most of the sandwich to the pigeons.

'It kind of does the soul good to see what's at stake every once in a while, Pat.' He smiled again. 'How much do you figure Redford has?'

'Don't your people have those kind of answers?'

'We turned the gas up under him,' Fear said. 'Those research types can be pretty stubborn. They stick at things reasonable people would quit.'

The CIA man stretched his neck out of his coat and

closed his eyes, letting the wintry sun fall on his leathery face.

'Can you spare any change?' a panhandler said, his dirt-encrusted hand outstretched, palm upward.

'That's pretty much the cry anyplace you go nowadays.'

Fear put his brown bag in the guy's hand and lurched away.

'You have a nice day, asshole,' – came after them.

'You have a nice day too, asshole. Are all your ends closed off, Pat? The last thing we want is some loose detail kicking us in the ass.'

'We won't get any trouble from the farmer. He's a pretty neat guy.'

'What about the seed company? Will they stay closed up? Redford has been trying to reach them. And the scientists who did the original work?'

He wasn't sure what this former colleague was saying to him. 'Maybe it's time you took the corner clear away from Dr Redford. Someone should.'

The look Wilf Fear gave him wasn't too friendly. He remembered the CIA man's reluctance to get involved in this at the start. And still he wasn't sure why he had introduced him to Gordon Dulles like he had, knowing like he did that Dulles would bring it and him to Hirshorn. He reasoned pure profit like everyone else.

'I'll let you know,' Fear said and unhooked his two sticks from over his arm and lurched away.

He watched as Fear headed straight back through the homeless, ignoring their outstretched hands. This meeting had in no way reassured him. He thought about taking a cab downtown to a piano bar on 2nd where contact was easy and anonymous, but decided not to push his luck. His boss was expecting him.

His first meeting back in Oklahoma City the following morning gave him a shock. He thought straightaway of Walter Shearing and how he had maybe led him into something he couldn't control and whether he'd lose everything as a result. When he entered the office Caddy was on a call with the commodity broker, Armand Bequai, telling him to dump wheat. Out of the phone he could hear

171

Bequai cautioning him that the price would collapse.

He felt sick, seeing his own vehicle for getting rich now crashing in flames without any kind of warning.

'Are we getting out of wheat?' – immediately the call ended, trying not to betray his sense of panic.

'We got a problem, Pat. The Commission's enforcement division is leaning on Bequai's operation. I'm only letting go those wheat futures I bought personally through Bequai's nominees. I'm having Hirshorn pick up everything Armand dumps. Your holding's pretty safe.'

That was like a knife in his stomach. He knows! Somehow he knows. How? He was a devil with powers to divine things ordinary mortals never could.

'My holding, Caddy?' – the breath suddenly disappearing from his lungs. He tried to speak calmly, evenly. 'I don't have one – apart from that three million bushels I bought for the company.'

Like a large number of employees, he was holding his speculative limit of wheat futures for Hirshorn. When the time was right he would either liquidate the contracts or take delivery directly to a nominated customer.

'I appreciate your loyalty. Was that business settled in England?'

'It was expensive, Caddy,' – starting to breathe again. 'But Shearing won't make any noise. My assessment of him is that of a decent, hardworking farmer trying to make a living. Our compensation saved him a lot of worry. He was grateful for that.'

'Good. We're flying to Washington. That salmonella problem in our chicken plants won't lie down. I'm taking care of it personally.'

'The Public Health Committee don't buy our plan to clean up the chickens?'

'Newberg says it's cosmetic. He's a conscientious bureaucrat. Senator Harvey has fixed a meeting with him and Betty Shorr.'

'We could blow Newberg away over his relationship with Betty Shorr.'

Caddy nodded. 'We certainly will, but not before we've avoided all that bad press headed our way.'

Dinner in a private room of a dining club in Georgetown was hosted by Senator Charles Harvey. In this situation the senator was playing the honest broker but Shapiro guessed he'd have no problem letting Hirshorn get the tab.

'That looks good, Felix,' Caddy said to the black waiter who was serving chicken to him and Senator Harvey.

'It's good, Mr Hirshorn. Corn fed, less than two months old. Enjoy, sir.'

The waiter left. A bell would summon him when needed.

'He's pretty sold on your chicken,' Joe Newberg said. He and Mrs Shorr were having a vegetable entrée. Shapiro had asked for a fruit plate. His bowel was inflamed. It always got that way after flying.

'Joe, Hirshorn chicken plants employ around five thousand workers in South Carolina,' Senator Harvey said suddenly, forgetting he was the honest broker when it came to his home state. Also Shapiro knew he was up for re-election next year. 'With the navy being the only people hiring, we can't afford to lose those jobs.'

'That's why we didn't go for an injunctive action, Charles.'

'Hirshorn have made costly improvements around their plants,' Shapiro said. 'Caddy ordered this done world-wide, Joe.'

'The jury's still out,' Newberg said. He glanced at Betty Shorr.

Caddy said, 'I share your concern, Mr Newberg. I'd close plants immediately rather than have people get sick.'

'People don't get sick,' the honest broker put in. 'That is a fact.'

'The fact is, Senator, we have a salmonella epidemic,' Mrs Shorr said, 'I'm not even certain that irradiating the chickens would solve this kind of problem either.'

'No one's irradiating my chicken, Mrs Shorr. The public associates that with dirty food. The new bacteria our scientists are introducing into the chickens' gut via feed is taking care of salmonella. They're good bugs.'

173

'I read the report on the process. It depends heavily on antibiotics. The FDA is worried that they could damage the human immune system, Mr Hirshorn.'

'What is it you want from us?' Caddy said.

'A moratorium on chicken production. I guess you'd come at us with a lawsuit if we went that route?'

Shapiro glanced sideways across the table at Newberg, realizing how insecure and vacillating he was. He wondered why Caddy was bothering like this, when he plainly disliked these two adulterers. He should simply publish the details of their sexual relationship. That would finish them.

'I'll make a deal with you. Hold off publishing your report until we get done testing this new gut bacteria. If it doesn't bring salmonella down to tolerable levels, and without any kind of damage to the immune system, you get your moratorium. Whatever it costs us.'

'That couldn't be fairer, Betty,' the Senator said.

'We'd get as much as if we went to court.'

Caddy looked at Mrs Shorr for a long moment. Shapiro waited, expecting him to let her have it, hoping he would.

'This way we won't put people out of work.'

Newberg considered the proposal. The Senator held his breath.

'We'd need to take it to Mrs Shorr's committee. Have them discuss it.'

Caddy smiled, and ate some of his chicken.

After dinner, as they walked to the Hirshorn limousine, Senator Harvey said, 'It's a crying shame we can't make those jobs safe for good and all, Caddy.'

'The trouble with bureaucracy, is that it doesn't get touched by the real world,' Shapiro said from the heart.

'After we get their committee to agree holding off publishing their report, blow Newberg and Mrs Shorr clear away for the adulterers they are,' Caddy said.

Shapiro smiled, enjoying that.

Intelligence, information and analysis were the oxygen that kept life in any company. Hirshorn was no exception. Caddy gave intelligence gathering a high priority when he first took control, and spent a lot of money on the right sort of information, whether from the Kansas City Board of Trade which was the prime marketplace for trading hard red winter wheat, and where the world price was made, or from the US spy satellite that orbited the globe sending back details on crops that were planted, soils that were eroding, weather patterns that were changing and destroying crops. The whole of this intelligence got analysed, assessed and passed to those divisions of the company that needed it. The communications and analysis centre at the Oklahoma headquarters was like the Foreign Office of a government. *Time* once described Hirshorn as part of the government's foreign policy-making machine. Caddy was constantly in touch with his offices abroad, assessing political and economic developments that might affect the company's profitability or investment policy.

Knowing the particular interest he took in wheat, analysts paid close attention to getting the latest information onto the electronic board in his office at the earliest possible moment. Wheat prices moved in ticks, which were ¼c. Not one of them was missed. There were monitors everywhere it was useful to have them in the Hirshorn building.

Rarely was information unwelcome to him. He always worked on the belief that it was better to know than not to know however unpleasant the knowledge was. The report he had just received from the enquiry agents in England who had earlier been asked to draw a profile on Walter Shearing was unwelcome. But he knew he couldn't unreceive it.

Sitting at the small bleached oak desk in his office, he re-read the report. Clearly he understood now what his unease was about his assistant. His only surprise was that it had taken him so long to get to it. Mere suspicions of dishonesty was something he could deal with, but he was homosexual. That was an ungodly act. One that denied life. He had no doubt in his mind about that, or what he felt about those who practised sodomy. But this didn't help him one bit with the dilemma this information

175

caused him. Shapiro clearly had mixed loyalty, having spent the night with Shearing. He spared himself the graphic details of the state of the bed linen at the hotel. Ordinarily he would have had no hesitation in easing Shapiro out, only he knew that if he moved too soon the man would do him a great deal of harm. For now he would have to treat him like nothing had changed between them. That was going to be difficult for he believed such a person polluted the atmosphere with his dishonesty and immorality.

After carefully folding the report away in a desk drawer and locking it, he said a prayer as he often did for the success of his scheme, and to find a way of justly punishing Shapiro when the time was right.

'Mrs Fitzgibbon,' he said as he went through his ante-room, 'when Dr Blumenthal calls, I'll take it in the boardroom.'

The four members of his board were present, along with Shapiro, whom he avoided looking at. He was sharing a joke with Jack Devine, who had a young family he doted on.

This was a scheduled daily meeting. The worry that was dominating everyone's thinking concerned the amount of wheat they were buying and the trouble that was headed their way from the Commodities Futures Trading Commission. The price was going up. But other traders weren't getting hurt, not yet, because most of them were still buying then selling and taking their profit. With so much wheat around, only fools held what they had bought. Customers needing physicals could get all they needed and cheaper in the spot market.

He knew that the underlying worry for most of the board concerned his judgement. Shapiro had told him so. Even though they were family they still only had it as rumour that he had cancer and was having treatment. The volume of wheat they were secretly amassing could prove a disastrously expensive error, while every other trader made moderate gains by selling to them.

'Wheat's up eight and a half cents a bushel,' he said, as if to relieve some of their anxiety.

176

'How much longer can we keep the lid on this, Caddy?' Herb Fixx said. 'With all this wheat we've got, the CFTC is leaning on brokers for the names behind those nominees.'

'I talked to Kansas earlier. A lot of buying's got started from London. Do we know who it is?'

'It's not the Russians. But somebody's picking up wheat, Caddy.'

'Could we speculate about who that is?' he said, glancing across at Shapiro. 'Do you figure someone knows about our moves?'

'Gordon Dulles took a lot of valuable information with him to International Grain,' Shapiro said, without showing any kind of emotion.

'Gordon's still family.'

'It's a big strain on family loyalty,' Shapiro pointed out. 'Oscar Hartmine would expect performance for the kind of money he's paying him.'

He nodded slowly. 'You're not a family man.'

'I like to think of Hirshorn as my family,' Shapiro was saying. 'The only one I've got.'

'I appreciate that.' In other circumstances that statement might have moved him. He wondered if he was wrong about his aide. He knew he had a mother and sister someplace, whom he wasn't in contact with. That told him most of what he needed to know about him. Any man who didn't cherish his family wasn't reliable. 'Gordon Dulles is married to my sister. They have a good marriage; five beautiful children; we still see them in church. I rely on him not to betray us.'

'He knows why we are getting so many wheat futures.'

'Pat could be right,' Michael Whiteman said. 'We've used all kinds of rumours to depress the market. Someone starts buying like they know something is going to push up the price.'

The call came through from his physician, who wanted him to come into hospital overnight for more tests.

'You think it is cancer, Kurt?' he said letting his eyes run over the faces around the table. There was concern, alarm; most avoided his look like they couldn't face the possibility.

177

The physician sounded even less comfortable with the prospect. 'Let's wait and see what we find,' he said.

'Fine, Kurt. It'll have to be after Christmas now.' He wouldn't miss Christmas with his children for anything.

'Whenever you're ready, Caddy,' the physician said.

'Talk to Mrs Fitzgibbon. She'll give you a time.'

He ended the call. No one spoke. It was like they hadn't heard a thing.

'We can add that to the rumours about my health. It'll help keep the price of wheat down. Let everybody dump on us.' He smiled. 'Find out who's buying wheat in England, Pat. Then we'll see about sidetracking them. We'll hit them so hard . . . Are we getting problems with lawsuits over Gordon Dulles' short-loading?'

'The Indian government's filed for thirty million dollars. The US government figures we robbed PL480 programme of about the same amount,' Jack Devine, the lawyer, informed the meeting.

'Those figures are off the wall,' Herb Fixx said. 'So far government audits haven't turned up any grain that can't be accounted for. I figure if any suits get settled, it'll be for pennies on the dollar.'

'I'd say any settlements are going to be Gordon Dulles' problem.'

'Do we have a problem, OH?' Gordon Dulles said, when he found his boss in the dining-room.

'You and me? What the hell are you talking about?'

'I'm getting a kind of feeling you don't trust me.'

'I don't trust anyone, Gordon. I don't pay you the kind of money I pay you because I don't trust you.'

'You keep the goddamn door open between our offices the whole while. I just caught your secretary going through my desk, for Christsake.'

'You did? I guess I'm going to have to fire her.'

'This is pretty serious, OH.'

'Sure. I check everyone out from time to time. Makes me feel safe.'

'You mean I got a clean bill of health?'

'Get some lunch.'

Dulles smiled his one-eyed pirate smile. He suspected his honeymoon period at International was over, and that Oscar might no longer treat him like his personal talisman. Since his arrival, OH, as Hartmine was familiarly known, didn't make a single decision unless he touched base first with him, then with Peter Richmond, his chief analyst, a bright kid who was wedded to his computer console. The problem he had with OH keeping the interconnecting door of their adjacent offices open the whole while was that he had to listen to him at his desk blowing out one end or the other. Sometimes both at once. This wasn't a happy arrangement. And he wasn't convinced that some lack of trust hadn't crept in between them.

One of the perks of his job was the food that was laid out each day in the sumptuous dining-room of this ornate Federal House headquarters outside Dallas. Dulles regretted not being a glutton each time he saw the buffet. He took a mixture of hors d'oeuvres. Heavy lunches finished him for the day, and he was also vain enough to care about his shape. OH took twice the amount of food that he did and followed him to the linen-covered table.

'Hirshorn are still buying wheat?' OH said.

He suspected OH had other spies at Hirshorn who provided daily reports on both the company's activities and Caddy's health. These he helped him to interpret and assess.

'Maybe we should start buying, Gordon.'

'Why not,' he said. 'But our research department is saying something else. It was the last I talked to them.'

'But Hirshorn are buying, goddamnit, Gordon. My gut says buy too.'

'Have you got cancer of the gut?' OH looked at him.

'You want to bet on Caddy's judgement rather than his health. Go right ahead. Close the research department. You'd save a lot of money.'

OH gave an uncertain look as he pushed beef-wrapped shrimp into his mouth, chewed it twice, then swallowed it with a mouthful of beer. He ate like that the whole while and remained as thin as a Kentucky string bean, only ever suffering with heartburn.

179

'Caddy's got too much wheat. He's mostly selling and buying back the same contracts to inflate the price. He's doing pretty good. The Spot's moving up.'

'It sure is. That's why I figured maybe we should hedge.'

'Hirshorn have a pile of trouble with lawsuits; the USDA's coming after them over those chicken plants. Caddy's gambling on making a lot of money on wheat. If he doesn't he's in real trouble. You get in, OH, make sure you get out a shave ahead of Caddy or you're stuck.'

'That's the trick, Gordon. That's always the goddamn trick. We'll talk to the analysts after lunch.'

OH pushed another beef and shrimp roll into his mouth. Four more followed almost without chewing. That was lunch. Dulles knew he was ready to talk to the research department. He put his own plate aside unfinished.

Like many wildcat oilmen Oscar Hartmine had prospered and gone broke and prospered again by letting his gut instinct guide him. But the more analysts he employed – young men fresh from college with no experience of anything but the program that went into a computer – the less he relied on his gut. Even in the short while he had been with the company Gordon Dulles could see his boss losing his grip. That suited him fine.

Pete Richmond, their chief analyst, rarely moved away from the computer console, not even for lunch. He had a plate sent over from the dining-room. Dulles admired his cocky, self-assured manner, but didn't trust him. He was a person out of touch with anything but the soul of a machine; he fell easy prey to charismatic personality. First OH. Now him – his influence, he guessed, was the result of having caught him stealing in the second week of going to work for International. He could have made a name for himself with OH by turning the kid in, but had another use for him. The more he saw of him the less he trusted him, even though he did exactly his bidding. But he would dump him the moment he was done with International, figuring a guy who would steal from his current employer would steal from his next. That wasn't going to be him.

'July through Sept's going to show too much wheat

around for prices to hold, OH,' Richmond was saying, looking at his monitor. 'The USDA tell us fifteen per cent less wheat got planted but a lot of it was higher yielding hybrids. We analysed nitrogen sales across the midwest. They're up some twenty per cent. This pretty accurately mirrors the Department's figures for wheat returns, assuming we get some spring rain. The situation is going to be aggravated by the government auctioning its wheat stocks. You could go long but you'd be smart to stay short as far forward as September. You'll get all you need on the Spot, as you need it.'

'What happens when the Russians come up thirty or forty million tons short, Pete?' Dulles threw in for the hell of it. When the world was collapsing around him, Hartmine wouldn't be able to say that the Russians were never part of the equation.

'Is that going to happen, Gordon? Gee, they didn't tell me. The information I got is that they have a lot of good wheat seed and a lot of good fertilizer.'

'Sure. Hirshorn sold them most of it,' Dulles said. 'That's the craziest move yet in this kind of plan.'

'I got that piece of information too. The way things are under Gorbachev they're set to become net exporters.'

'The price is going up, Pete,' OH pointed out, 'despite this computer bullshit.'

'A temporary blip. Come the new year the bills will be back in their pens. Stay short.' His fingers danced across the keyboard. 'You should get out of soy beans too. If the USDA forces chicken producers to shut down over this salmonella problem, the floor will disappear.'

'Caddy's going to beat that,' Dulles said. 'He's going to bury Joe Newberg and Betty Shorr. The whole thing will disappear.'

'Around here we're betting on the USDA, Gordon,' Richmond said. 'That's the only smart move. There's gonna be a lot of soy beans around.'

Dulles conceded. The analyst made it sound like he had the inside track.

'Sell soy beans,' OH said. 'If it puts Caddy in a tighter corner, great. Jesus, wouldn't it be something to see him without cabfare?' He smiled, showing a mouthful of gold dental work.

In his desire to scare off Hirshorn, OH couldn't see the wall he was headed into. Dulles helped keep him on course. He glanced at Pete Richmond and smiled. The young man was good. He was making sure OH hit that wall.

July wheat climbed rapidly to $123 a ton in Kansas; someone bought a lot of contracts from Europe, and Shapiro lied about not yet getting word on who it was.

That was how Caddy read the situation. Even without confirmation of this he would have guessed his assistant had some kind of angle for himself, and paradoxically would have seen him as a fool if he hadn't. His real concern right then was that this might somehow jeopardize his own wheat deal, proving that random detail that got overlooked. He wouldn't hold back information from Shapiro, that would only have alerted him. Shapiro was close enough to him and smart enough to notice any major shift in attitude and maybe take damage limitation action. But continuing like nothing was wrong between them was difficult. Especially as he felt unclean around his assistant now. He truly regretted that Shapiro came out this way, because he earned his salary, doing a job he was ideally suited for.

Although his scheme for what would be the biggest grain coup ever demanded more and more of his time, their fight with the USDA over the closure of their salmonella-infected chicken plants was becoming pressing. Exposing the relationship between Joe Newberg and the chairwoman of the Public Health Committee hadn't worked. The news media made much of it, but the adulterers refused to resign. Worse, because of media exposure they were more determined in their action, as if to vindicate themselves.

'If the fools truly want to fight, Carl,' he said to his senior lawyer, 'they've got one.'

He met Flint's cold dead eyes across the boardroom table. He had been with the company since graduating law school and was now a non-executive member of the board. Caddy knew him to be vain, and enjoy his own opinion, but smart enough to know when to call in outside help. That was why he trusted the lawyer's judgements.

Flint cleared his throat and said, 'They plan on going before a federal judge to ask him to shut plants where salmonella is carried by seventy per cent or more chickens, Caddy.'

He nodded. 'How are we responding, Herb?'

'By cleaning up our plants. Maximum effort there.'

'As Pat has pointed out,' Flint said, 'the target levels reflect badly on the USDA inspection service. If they had been doing their job efficiently the problem would never have gotten this bad.'

'Have there been kick-backs to the inspectors?'

There was a brief silence around the table.

'Those plants are run fairly autonomously, Caddy,' Shapiro said. 'The managers are all looking to meet their production targets.'

'Sure,' he said. He didn't need to add: look what it got us.

'The feed additive which is putting a new strain of bacteria in the chicken gut looks set to eliminate all salmonella sero-types, including the virulent strain of enteritis,' Herb Fixx explained. 'But its use has got to go hand in hand with good hygiene practices.'

'What's the downside?'

'The FDA's worried that antibiotics associated with that process compromise the human immune system,' Jack Devine explained. 'We could get hit with a lot of law suits.'

'Our independent labs are running tests on rats. They show no damage from antibiotics to the immune system.'

'How about in humans?'

'They extrapolate those results to humans, Caddy.'

'All public health benchmarks are from animal testing,' Flint reminded him. 'The federal courts will accept those.'

'Are we ready to go to court?'

'As soon as our labs come up with their conclusions. I aim to bring in an outside firm of lawyers, Caddy. I had in

183

mind Katz, Moncton and Sher here in Washington. I talked with Bill Moncton. He's had a lot experience in similar cases.'

'When we get the hearing scheduled, take a close look at the judge. Let's pick up some kind of insurance.' He looked over at Shapiro.

There were but two certainties in all this. One, Hirshorn had to win; two, if anything went wrong with buying the judge, Shapiro would take the rap.

14

' A MERICAN CHEMICALS WON'T RUN, GRACE, not from a fight like this,' Rory Spelman said across the table in Nathan's on the corner of M Street and Wisconsin Avenue. 'They can't afford to. They'll come out gouging and biting and kicking like the most squalid street fighter. But don't worry about it. It means we know exactly where they stand when we take them apart. Boy, will we take them apart. Piece by piece.'

The air vibrated as he spoke, yet his words showed no trace of anger. Until then she had never known anyone who seemed so free of anger. Most world-changers she had met were driven by anger most of the time, or the need for attention.

Rory's stillness made Grace concentrate, compelling her to listen, to lean in closer to hear what he was saying. Despite his compassion she began to get angry as he talked about what was happening to migrant farm workers in Mexico, the fact that the government there encouraged the levels of intensive farming that damaged these people, and that the American government did nothing to stop the tide of poison that got exported from the US.

'How do you stay so calm?' she said. 'I get so angry and upset just hearing about it.'

'It's pretty hard to take at times, Grace,' Rory said. 'But then there's so much suffering and injustice, you don't have enough anger for it all. And it doesn't get us any place we need to be.'

'I just envy anyone who can stay calm, but still feel

185

something for those people.' She knew many doctors and lawyers who lacked empathy, having learned to distance themselves as a defence mechanism. Empathy was what set this man apart from other lawyers. Aside from the fact that Rory didn't even dress like a lawyer, in a worn sports jacket, a sweatshirt and jeans.

From the first moment she saw the Christic Institute lawyer, something started happening. Something physical, and emotional, and possibly even spiritual. Never before had she had such an experience. When her daughter died a part of her did too; not only was this almost indefinable area of her dead, but sealed in a lead-lined cask. Rory Spelman hadn't suddenly resurrected those feelings, but the electricity she felt when he shook her hand gave her quite a jolt. What he did immediately was help strip off some of her confusion, especially about coming to America and being plunged into a campaign against a major US chemical corporation. The questions that had hitherto troubled her – Why had she really come? What would she do or hope to achieve? How long could she stay? What would happen when she returned to England? – seemed less important. Here everything was achievable. They would prove how Rose died to the satisfaction of a federal judge, then make American Chemicals pay. It was all so straightforward. She even believed they could make the company stop what they were doing.

From the start she knew that Rory felt something too. She wondered if Jak had noticed, what it would mean to their relationship. She was increasingly aware of what he felt for her, and was touched by his concern, but regretted the sexual emotions that always intruded to prevent men and women simply being friends. That was what she wanted with Jak, but at once knew that was deceitful. It would be so convenient if he wanted nothing but to support her. She sensed him watching her now, his look at once demanding and hurt. She refused to meet it.

'Won't American Chemicals claim they didn't know the pesticide was being sold in the UK?' Jak said, like he was levering himself between her and Rory.

186

'Sure,' Rory said. 'It won't get them anyplace. They allowed their subsidiary to manufacture and store the chemical, despite the EPA ban on the product. They were clearly negligent for failing to keep it off the market.'

He smiled and reached over and clasped Grace's hands.

She withdrew instinctively like from an electric shock, then regretted her response, in case he thought she was rejecting him. Also it made her seem like she wasn't in control. She wasn't. She wanted to put her hands back in his, but was too self-conscious to do so. She heard almost nothing of what he said for worrying about what he was thinking of her. Then with what she decided was clear insight into his character she knew that he didn't care what anyone thought about him.

'Will a judge here give a damn about Hispanic kids?' Jak asked.

'You'd be surprised about some judges, Jak. They can be almost human; halfway decent. A hell of a lot more of them are inclined to support vested interest. We can show American supermarkets getting produce trucked across the border with illegal pesticide residues on it. The produce is not getting properly inspected by the USDA, it's damaging kids here. It's like a circle of poison.'

'What can we do to help, Rory?'

'You guys can do the legwork – we can't afford to employ researchers to dig out information.'

'No problem – now I don't have any real job.'

Feeling to blame for that, she put her hand on Jak's and smiled. When he brought his other hand over hers, she felt a sense of panic. He was making a statement about their relationship. She glanced at Rory, anxious about what he would now think, wanting somehow to convey that they didn't have that sort of relationship. She wanted to know if there was anyone special in Rory's life or if he just treated everybody as special.

'We've a pile of information from Alicia Huerta. And a bunch from the United Farm Workers. You need to run through it, narrow down the evidence to pesticides similar to that which killed Rose. It's a lot of work, but people sure want to help, Grace.'

187

She smiled and looked away.

The dilemma she felt over her relationship with Jak surfaced when the check was presented. Financially she was totally dependent on him, and feared that might lead to a situation she didn't want. Right then she wanted to pay her way, show Rory that she had some independence. That made her feel worse about Jak.

Outside the restaurant Rory unlocked his bicycle. 'I'll get copies of the information we have sent right over, so that you folks can go to work.'

She wanted to collect it from Christic, but was afraid to offer.

'It's going to be great working with you, Grace. We're sure going to do it to American Chemicals – in the best possible way!'

His smile was so inviting that when he put his hand out to shake hers, she couldn't stop herself leaning forward and kissing him. Panic assailed her, confusion followed. She hurried off along M Street, wanting to retreat from this. In many ways life was easier back in the psychiatric hospital in Bury St Edmunds, blown from her skull on drugs.

'Grace! Grace!' She heard her name being called by Jak.

Catching her up, he said, 'He's quite a guy.'

She stared silently at the sidewalk, not trusting herself to say anything.

'What's the problem, Grace?'

'I don't know. I feel strange. I don't know what I'm doing here. If I should be doing this.'

'I can't figure who better to do it.'

She looked at him, suspecting he was simply avoiding the problem by taking action. Perhaps Rory was the same, and she was letting some kind of chemistry distort reality.

'Rory makes all things seem possible while you're with him. He's very positive. You start to believe that we can make a difference. Then when you think about what's ahead . . .'

'Great marathon runners never think about what's

ahead,' he said. 'They just go for it. He trained for the priesthood, but he quit and became a lawyer. What I'm saying here is, he's not pure faith. He's kind of practical too. He's got a good record going against major polluters.'

There were all sorts of questions she wanted to ask about Rory, but feared Jak would misinterpret her interest.

'I guess this is stirring thoughts about Rose. It's stirring up quite a lot of the past for me too.'

'I'm sorry. I was so relieved to get away from that hospital, I just didn't think this through. I can't even buy myself a pair of tights.'

'Hey Grace,' he said, 'do you need some tights?'

'No. No, not right now, I don't.' She laughed. Men were often not very practical, but Jak, she felt, was back beyond even that point.

'I don't understand,' he said.

'Oh, it doesn't matter.'

'I have a little money put aside. That will keep us going. When you win your case, you'll be in real good shape.'

She was touched by this, but still she wasn't sure.

'I can't even get a job.'

'Nor can I, Grace, unless we stop what's going down. I guess I'll apply for food stamps – if there are still food stamps.'

She took his arm as a gesture of appreciation, but knew it was a mistake. He clasped her hand, locking her arm through his. Why couldn't men have plain unencumbered friendships with women?

'I got myself into this, Grace. It was something I should have got done long ago. But I'm a scientist. I guess I don't believe a thing unless I can prove it. I don't have Rory's clear faith. But then someone comes into your life at a given time for a purpose, and still you don't immediately recognize what's staring you in the face – we'll get this done, Grace.'

They walked in silence for a while, through the cold, damp air. She wasn't sure what he was talking about, but he gave no sign of explaining further.

189

'Why aren't you married with a family, Jak?' she asked. Nothing at his house indicated he was.

'I was once,' he said, but stopped like he was on the edge of an abyss. 'You shoot for glittering prizes – you tend to miss what's important, I guess.'

Grace wanted to press for more information directly, but something said he was very vulnerable, so she didn't.

'Did you get your prize?'

'I changed direction at a critical time.'

'Did someone come into your life?' she asked.

He shook his head and kicked a heap of snow on the sidewalk.

'Does it keep you awake at night?' – a reckless question.

He said, 'There's a way to find out,' – and laughed.

'Jak . . .' feeling uncertain. 'I'm so dependent on you right now. I don't know if I can cope with becoming emotionally dependent too.'

He simply nodded and let go her arm. To her surprise, she felt let down.

The genetically engineered wheat investigation that he was pursuing in tandem with Grace's pesticide case was taking Jak no place, and he didn't know how long he could go on with it. The time would come when he'd need to get back to work or go crazy. He was calling people and either getting the same negative response, or being steered in the direction of Arnold Sanson, who was still away on vacation. Then he got a call from Herman Solkoff.

'Jak, I just got through talking to Bob Bauman – he's Sanson's chief assistant out at Guelph University.'

'Is Sanson back from Mexico?'

'No, Jak. He's dead. His car went off the road outside Durango. They don't know how it happened.'

A cold hand from his past reached out and touched him and he shivered. He saw the charred bodies of his wife and son in the morgue. Cars ran off the road and for all kinds of reasons, he told himself. There's no connection. But why Sanson? Why now?

190

'Jak? You still there? Bob Bauman said Fort Detrick took over that project a while back.'

'The army research station right here on our doorstep? Why the hell are the spooks looking at wheat?' Suddenly he didn't want to go on with this.

'You go ask them, Jak,' Solkoff said. 'I can't help on this any more.'

'What are you saying Herman?' There was silence down the phone. 'Herman?'

'I gotta call about the questions I was asking. It wasn't friendly.'

'Who was it?' He knew without Solkoff saying.

'The caller didn't give his name – figure the CIA. I don't know what's going on, Jak, but count me out.'

There was always someone somewhere who would object to questions about things done in secret. Life seemed easier for not asking about such things, but it took a certain type of person to live in that kind of ignorance. He didn't consider himself brave, or heroic; at best he was determined. If somehow he got offered enough funding to work without interference, he guessed he would stop asking questions. But not only wasn't that happening, he knew he had to go on with this if he was ever to get back to the work he wanted to do.

That was how he found himself at the gates of Fort Detrick getting checked in to visit Dr Paul Spicer, the deputy director.

He thought about Grace alone in the city, making other enquiries, if she was safe. All she was doing was taking the metro to Capitol South to the Library of Congress to check some facts on wheat genetics at Fort Detrick. With that they would file for more details under the Freedom of Information Act. The amount that got censored would tell them a lot about what was going down here. He thought about Grace scuffling around with Rory, deciding she was more at risk there. She was impressionable, and he was impressive. Maybe she was falling in love with Rory and that was why their own relationship was going no place he wanted it to. She had talked about him a lot, saying he was like safe anchorage in a storm. Maybe that

191

had been to reassure him. Jak didn't want to think about that.

Dr Spicer bought him coffee and a doughnut in the first floor cafeteria, where he avoided most of his questions. But telling him nothing usable was in itself revealing. They were both scientists and ordinarily would exchange ideas and benchmarks. Fort Detrick was an army medical research centre specializing in virology, working on every kind of viral contaminant known to man, and a lot that weren't. They had a whole department that dealt with viruses in plants.

'We need to know what the worst is an enemy can do to our food, Jak. That's the only reason we looked at this grain.'

'Who isolated the bacterium gene that attracts Take-all to wheat?' Jak said.

Dr Spicer stopped eating his doughnut. 'That's classified.'

'Guess my feeling when that gene showed up at Cambridge. Jesus, it's three jumps ahead of me. Big jumps.'

'Sanson got the gene to express itself out at Guelph. You heard about his death? We gave him a little funding, then took over his work – the problem was he didn't keep proper research notes.'

'Why develop a wheat that attracts Take-all? That doesn't feed one single soldier, or anybody else.'

'We do it because we can.' Spicer smiled.

'Funding's under pressure, Paul. Even for the army. Nothing gets done for nothing. Research has to be linked to purpose.'

'Our only purpose would be defence, Jak. Knowing how to protect our crops from any kind of viral attack.'

'Is that what you expect to happen?'

Spicer didn't answer.

'Why was it planted commercially in England?'

'I understand how you feel about someone ahead of you. But there's nothing to this, Jak. That's all I can say.'

The meeting was over, leaving him with an uneasy feeling. A small voice inside again said quit right here. He ignored it.

'I have a lot of questions that still need answers, Paul.'

'Jak, do you need me to go with you today?' Grace said as she entered the kitchen. He was eating oatmeal at the bench and glancing across the science pages of the *Washington Post*.

She was feeling cheerful and tried to ignore the frustration he expressed in all kinds of petty and belittling ways whenever Rory got mentioned. She wanted to confide to him plans for going after American Chemicals, but found herself getting more defensive and secretive about them. Rory was in love with her, she was certain of that, but he seemed no closer to saying anything to her than Jak was.

'That's an eight hour drive to Guelph,' he said.

'Rory wants to go through some things on the case.'

'He doesn't need to talk to me? – there *are* things I know. Right.'

She felt guilty and so avoided looking at him. 'I thought you could pursue the wheat thing – while I go on with my case.' It all seemed so logical when she had devised the means of spending the day alone with Rory.

'Somewhere along the line the two connect, Grace. You through in the bathroom?'

He got up and went out, not saying that she shouldn't see Rory, or that she needn't make the drive to Ontario with him. She assumed their plan to go to Guelph would stand. Bob Bauman had offered to show them all Sanson had discovered before the CIA took over the project.

During the early part of the drive north into Canada, Grace remained quiet, making it clear she didn't want to go. She thought about Rory, the disappointment in his voice when she told him. She was angry at the reasonable way he accepted the situation. Why didn't he say what he wanted to happen between them? Then she faced the possibility that she had misread him entirely and felt foolish.

Guelph University was a spread-out arrangement of low buildings and a lot of greenhouses, about fifty miles west of Toronto. It looked to Grace unexciting, a place where nothing happened. She was wrong.

Bob Bauman hurried into the reception hall to meet them. A short, overweight man full of regret.

'We got broken into last night. A whole pile of records were destroyed,' he explained, mopping sweat from his forehead. 'I tried calling you. I guess you were on the road.'

Jak glanced at her, and she saw disbelief in his face. Possibly Bauman saw it too.

'Gee, I know how this looks, Jak. I was real happy to show you guys Arnold's work.'

'Is there nothing left?'

'A lot of debris.'

Bauman took them up to the office and labs on the second floor. Even the short walk to the elevator made him sweat.

'Have you any idea who did it?' Grace asked. Some of the broken glass had been cleared but everything was still a mess.

'We could take a couple of guesses, Grace. I figure somebody must be checking your moves for some reason. Why else would they wait until now to move in on us? Hell, our findings have been known about a while.'

Jak folded his arms across the top of his head and walked up and down, scrunching glass underfoot. His anxiety was almost palpable, and she could see he was not a little afraid. She wished Rory were here as he seemed to meet this kind of problem the whole while. He would know how to handle it.

She said, 'This is stupid. A thing like this is only going to make Jak pursue it harder. Whoever it is doesn't know Jak if they believe otherwise.'

'Grace – what are you saying?'

She wondered what her expectations really were of him, and if he could come anyplace near to fulfilling them. The question of who might be watching them wasn't something she readily wanted to think about. Being watched or pursued wasn't quite real for her.

'Arnold Sanson was notorious for not keeping proper records,' Bauman said. 'I worked with him on

194

translocating the bacterium gene that attracted Take-all. There had been no record of a foreign gene expressing itself in wheat until then. I've managed to find some slides of the chromosome that caused the break in the wheat's resistance.'

He showed them the agar slide under the microscope.

When Jak stepped up to the microscope and adjusted the eyepieces it was like he was at once transported to a world light years away. He didn't speak or move for a long while.

She looked at Bauman, who simply smiled. 'It kind of takes you like that.'

'Grace.' Jak straightened up and offered her a look through the eyepieces. 'Translocated with that pair of chromosomes on the right of the slide – this is what sucks up both nutrient and the Take-all virus from the soil.' He turned back to Bauman. 'Why didn't you replace the segment of the gene that attracted the virus? It would have made you famous. We may have had a Take-all resistant wheat.'

'That was the object, Jak. Until Arnold talked to the people who were funding the project. They got pretty excited.'

'Was that the CIA?' she asked.

'That's it. Science rarely questions the paymaster,' Bauman said. 'Getting a seed that totally depleted the soil and left it loaded with the Take-all virus was like some kind of bonus to them. It's crazy. I told Arnold we should destroy what we'd found. He figured we couldn't undo it. It was on the ether. Someone else would get to it soon also.'

'What I don't understand,' Grace said, 'is if the wheat attracts Take-all and doesn't mature, how do you get seed?'

'Only the second generation seed responds that way,' Jak explained. 'Grace's neighbour back in England lost five hundred acres to Take-all.'

'He planted seed we helped develop? Gee, I didn't know Crocker-Giant grew that amount. They shipped it to England? That's a mite unfriendly.'

195

'I guess they were making sure it would fail wherever it was sown,' Jak said. 'How were Crocker involved?'

'They were brought onto the project to grow the seed.' Bauman switched off the microscope and headed out of the lab, becoming curiously animated. Grace sensed he was scared. 'We heard you'd broken the code for fixing nitrogen in wheat. That you quit the programme at Cambridge because they wanted to hand over the patent to the company funding research.'

'In the field of science, I guess rumours are as ill-founded as in any other human endeavour. I wish I had cracked that code. Who cares who owns it? Who can I talk to at Crocker?'

'I don't know. I'm not sure I want to, Jak. You need to talk to someone at the CIA. Maybe the guy who came out here to talk to Arnold – Wilf Fear.'

'Wilf Fear!' Jak whispered. 'A guy with a deeply lined face, walks badly on two sticks?'

She noticed he had turned white.

'That's him,' Bauman said.

He gave them some coffee from the machine outside his office and questioned Jak closely about his own research. It was like a trade-off of information, she noticed, and as Jak talked about the work he had been pursuing the colour returned to his face and it was as if he had forgotten why they were there or what the danger might be.

When they were headed for their car, Grace said, 'Gosh, you really are famous. I hadn't realized quite how famous.'

'Does that mean you'll go to bed with me, Grace?' he asked.

His response surprised her. She knew something like that was bound to come up again unless she somehow slammed the door, denying the possibility. She closed her eyes, hoping the problem would go away. It never did. The increasing sexual tension she felt around Jak made her uncomfortable. She could only ignore it all the while she wasn't directly challenged.

'I'm not really ready for that,' she said. She was scared

that if she was blunt with him he might not go on, and didn't like the conclusion she drew about herself from that. 'I haven't met anyone nicer than you, Jak.'

He came right back with, 'How about Rory?'

'I've hardly noticed him.'

'The way the guy looks at you,' he said, his mood lightening. 'Gosh, has he noticed you. You didn't notice?'

She shook her head, feeling deceitful and resentful that he so circumscribed her feelings that she had to lie.

'I'm going to have to run a marathon,' he said. 'Every day.'

'Could I run the marathon?' she asked, to avoid talking about them.

'Grace, you could do anything you set your mind to. You're that determined. Real marathon material. You want to drive out to talk with Crocker-Giant?'

'Oh, not the CIA?' she joked.

'I saw Wilf Fear in London. He was at the American Embassy when I protested about getting deported.'

She found that shocking. 'Are you sure?'

She knew he was.

Where this would all end worried Grace during the long drive on Route 20 through Indiana and into Illinois. They seemed to be up against something much bigger than American Chemicals, even though she had no real conception of how big they were. It began to feel as though they were wrestling not with a human problem but a totally faceless corporation fuelled only by a need for more profit, a need she didn't understand and couldn't control – that was how Rory had talked about it. Because she couldn't understand what drove such people – even people like her neighbour Walter Shearing who forever wanted more land – she couldn't see an argument or line of reasoning that would stop them. That made her more scared.

They had dinner at a 76 Autostop on Route 70. It looked clean but soulless, like eating in an operating theatre. Checking out the menu, she said, 'If Rory's right about banned pesticides coming back over the border on produce, I'm not sure I want to eat anything.'

197

He looked at her for a long moment and she had to turn away.

'It's a real problem,' he said.

She smiled, and wondered if Rory was having a similar influence on Jak as he now was on her, in the moral choices she was prepared to make, about what she ate. She ordered vegetarian pizza.

'Just how toxic is the produce in the stores?'

'It varies. The problem is pesticide binds chemically on certain foods, cereals in particular. When that happens it gets impossible to detect. That means the maximum permitted safe residue levels set by the USDA get broken the whole while. No one truly knows how safe safe is. The pesticide that killed Rose wouldn't necessarily kill you or me.'

That grabbed her without warning and threw her right back to the farm in East Anglia. She was already feeling vulnerable and images of Rose brought tears to her eyes. She hardly noticed Jak reach over and take her hand. He said something about finding a motel for the night.

The meal was an awkward affair. He guessed Grace was either thinking about her dead child or the motel room he might be trying to head her into. The pizza wasn't any recommendation to vegetarianism. After getting the check, he went out to the rest rooms. His eyes were tired and he needed to splash cold water into them. It was a real restorative and he did it frequently during long bouts of work.

Two men came in wearing suits. Catching sight of them through the mirror, he paid them no heed. Until one of them stepped right behind him and grabbed him by the hair and cracked his head on the basin. He was helpless to do anything other than flail around in panic as his face was pushed under the water. He had no opportunity to gulp in any air and knew his thrashing around was wasting oxygen, but nobody behaved logically in such circumstances. When he felt them lift his wallet he was curiously relieved. This was only a mugging!

Suddenly he was free and on the floor coughing. He

didn't hear the men walk out, but after a short while someone came in with a child.

'Hey, you okay, fella?' He got him up and summoned help.

The cops weren't impressed with his story of muggers in suits. There were no witnesses.

'I don't think they believe me,' he said to Grace as they waited in the restaurant lobby.

Customers and staff looked pissed off at this interruption.

'What the hell are they looking at? This is America for Christsake; three muggings happen every seven seconds!' – plucking the figure at random from the air.

Grace smiled, and took his hand.

The two cops returned from the parking lot. 'Muggers in suits, right?' one said.

'I didn't imagine this,' – pointing to his head. 'They stole my wallet. All my money.'

The cop produced the wallet. All the money was intact.

'It was picked up by your car, sir.'

He glanced at Grace. 'That's crazy. It makes no sense.' He could see even she was beginning to have doubts.

Back on the road, with Grace driving, a thunderbolt hit him. 'I wasn't the victim of two sloppy muggers, Grace, I couldn't have been. Hell, I used my wallet to get the check. From there I went directly to the men's room. Shit. Oh shit.'

Grace reached for his hand. 'How dangerous might this get?'

He closed his eyes and shook his head.

'If it's the CIA,' she said, 'there's no one we can turn to for help.'

He didn't enjoy that. 'Hey, Grace, come on, what are you saying? This is America. There're all kinds of places we can get help.' He didn't sound convincing. He saw her look. 'Our courts for one. Yeah, our courts. They're entirely independent of the Executive. If the spooks are doing something they shouldn't, a Federal judge'll cut them right down to size.'

'And if they don't let us get to court?'

199

'We're both tired. This thing's getting to us. Pull in at the next motel.'

That feeling of unease left neither one of them, not even in the brightly lit motel lobby. Before they reached the desk he caught her arm.

'Look, it'll be a hell of a lot safer if we share the same room.' It sounded like a line, and he held his breath.

'That's fine,' she said.

Nothing happened to either one of them in the night, or between them. The following morning he panicked when he saw her bed empty. He found her in the restaurant eating breakfast.

'I figured you'd been kidnapped.'

'I went for a run. Then I took a swim – they have a heated pool. It's great. I swam in my bra and pants. There wasn't anyone else in it. How's your head?'

'What if we are being tailed – that's real dumb, Grace.'

'Lying in bed's not going to solve a single problem,' she snapped. 'Look, Crocker-Giant will know who you are. Going there won't get us a thing.'

'It won't?' He resented her taking over like this, and worried in case it was because he wasn't being sexually decisive. Maybe he should have tried something last night.

'If they are a part of this, why should they help us?'

'So what do you figure we should do?'

They went to the State House in Kansas City Kansas, to find out from the corporate division if Crocker-Giant were related to American Chemicals.

'How do you know to make these kind of checks?' he asked as they waited for the clerk to find the information.

'Rory told me how to look up company details.'

The thought that occurred to him right then was that Rory was homosexual. He had never known him have a relationship with a girl, despite all the offers he had got when they were room-mates at Columbia. He thought about suggesting that to Grace, but knew it could backfire.

'Crocker-Giant. They were incorporated in 1865 by Ward Anson. Owned by the Anson family until three years ago when Hirshorn Grain bought them,' the clerk read from the screen in front of him.

'Who owns Hirshorn Grain?' Grace asked.

'Mam, you gotta go to Oklahoma to get that. That's where it looks like Hirshorn are incorporated. Crocker here bought out a couple of other seed companies before they got bought. There's one down in Mexico. I can get you those details.'

Coming down the wide steps of the State House, with a sense that Grace was still leading him, he said, 'We headed for Oklahoma?'

'That's another long drive, Jak. Maybe we can get all the information we need on the take-over from the financial papers.'

He felt annoyed that he hadn't second-guessed her.

The information was carried by the *Wall Street Journal* held on microfilm in the library. Decatur Seeds, a grain specialist, had been taken over by Crocker-Giant in the same week as Red Bean Agriculture of Mexico. Two weeks later there was a heavily leveraged management buyout supported by International Grain, but Hirshorn had got control of the company in a counterbid. All this had been thirty-nine months ago.

'Could anyone develop a spring wheat in that time?' Grace asked.

'Usually you figure somewhere around four or five years minimum. But if someone had a head start, and maybe utilized the different growing seasons between here and Mexico. I guess that could be why the Mexican seed company got taken over. With the early season there and the late one here, they could grow two generations of wheat in one year. None of this connects with American Chemicals,' he pointed out.

'Maybe they aren't the problem, Jak,' she said. 'The time scale for developing the wheat could fit quite neatly with the evidence we seem to have of Hirshorn's involvement. Everything seems to suggest that company could somehow be involved. Supposing it's not the government organizing the wheat conspiracy, not any government, not here, not in England, but Hirshorn

201

Grain – they'd be big enough to undertake such an enterprise, wouldn't they?'

'I guess. But that doesn't explain how the government agencies got involved.'

He was doubtful, but for the wrong reasons. He was a scientist who dealt in fact, and although imaginative leaps were fine, human emotions such as jealousy didn't help solve a thing.

'Maybe their acquisitive activity was in order to help develop the Take-all attracting wheat,' he said, 'or at least to ensure complete control at the end result.'

'Supposing it's Hirshorn Grain who're buying all the wheat futures?' she said. 'You said they were buying a lot of wheat to get Argentina's wheat price up.'

'It's not possible, Grace. The broker I talked with figured the guy running Hirshorn was off beam. He's sick.'

'Well, just supposing he's not,' she said, her excitement running over. 'But they're maybe buying wheat to get the price up for a killing of some kind. Just supposing they are. How much would be involved? Money I mean?'

'Who'd ever know. It could be a hell of a lot. It would depend on how much seed got planted to fail.'

'I expect it's a lot more than the five hundred acres my neighbour planted.'

'I guess.' Reluctantly he found himself getting caught up in the excitement of her brainstorming. 'Maybe we should take a look at that grain store where your neighbour's seed came from. It was out on the Gulf at Galveston. If these people are planning to ship genetically programmed seed around the world, it has to be stored someplace.'

'Is it possible, Jak, or are we just imagining this?'

'It's possible, but that doesn't make it real, Grace. Not until we prove it's happening.'

15

'YOU CAN'T JUST WALK IN on those guys and start asking questions,' Rory said. 'They're not going to allow that. You folks will have problems aplenty in Mexico, but at least there you've got one very streetwise lady in Alicia Huerta. People are getting killed down there and not just from pesticide poisoning. Isn't that enough danger to be going on with?'

Jak nodded slowly, clearly not heeding this advice. In fact the more Rory cautioned him about what they were planning on doing, the more headstrong Jak became about it. Grace knew why. They were out at National Airport *en route* to Mexico, with a stopover at Galveston to try to learn what they could at the Hirshorn elevator plant.

'I have to tell you, these are not nice people you'll be dealing with. If what you suspect about this wheat conspiracy is true, I figure the danger there could be even greater. We had some truck with the Hirshorn people when I was with the Security Exchange Commission. We had been trying to make a case against Hirshorn over irregularities in their take-over of Crocker-Giant. Everyone directly involved got some kind of pressure.'

'What happened?' she asked.

'Nothing,' Rory said. 'Nothing at all. They somehow got to the Commissioner, is how I figure it. He ordered me to back off. That's when I quit. It was a long time afterwards that I learned Hirshorn had information on the Commissioner that should have meant him resigning – sure, he should have resigned. It's easy to make that kind of judgement. These people play to win. Grace, you don't have to do this.'

'But isn't Galveston in a direct line to Mexico, Rory?' she said. Nobody laughed. 'We're getting quite good at asking questions – and Jak's head has healed nicely.' Nobody laughed at that either.

She glanced at Jak, hoping she was wrong about why he was being so stubborn about this dangerous excursion, that it was for something other than the attention it was getting him.

'I'm sure it will be all right, Rory,' she said.

'I'd be a lot happier if you were going directly to Mexico to get Alicia's patients to be a party to the Class Action against American Chemicals.'

She smiled and took Jak's arm in the Continental departure lounge, then avoided his eyes. They were like strangers with nothing to say to each other. Jak remained silent. Something was worrying him besides their stopover at Galveston. Maybe it had something to do with Mexico. She glanced back at Rory, who seemed to sense her concern.

'You okay, Jak?' he asked.

'I was wondering about my real work, when I'm going to get back to it.'

'I guess you have to go with this first. Right?'

Jak nodded. 'I don't think there's any danger waiting at the grain elevator plant. I could be wrong – who knows for sure.'

'You could be right,' Rory said.

'Find out if Hirshorn has any tie up with American Chemicals. Can you?'

'They do. American Chemicals' stockholders' listings show Hirshorn holding six per cent.'

'Isn't that quite a big holding?' Grace said.

'Pretty big. I don't know how significant this is in itself. A company like Hirshorn would hold a whole bag of corporate stock. That's a company with earnings of maybe two billion dollars. If it is them at the back of something, you've taken on a real biggy. Hirshorn, you figure, wins the whole time.'

Silence fell between them. She glanced at Jak.

'Maybe we should think again about stopping off at Galveston,' she said.

Folding his arms across his head, Jak walked up and down. She noticed how he did that when he was worried. A part of her wanted to step right up to him and say it didn't matter about going there. Another part of her said, 'I'm sure we can get what we need at Galveston.'

'We can beat the pants off American Chemicals – in court,' Rory told them. 'If you are right about Hirshorn, could be they won't let it get to court.'

Jak nodded, like he knew all that. The Houston flight started to board.

'It's the only way I can get back to work from what I see.'

'Maybe.'

He shook Rory's hand and turned away.

As she watched him approach the gate, she wondered if this was the right move. She'd have been happier had Rory been going too.

'Why don't you get on the plane and go with us?' she said.

'Wow, wouldn't that be something,' he said, and took hold of her and held her at arm's length.

'I understand why you can't, of course – you've many other clients.' She tried not to feel disappointed.

'I wish you weren't getting on that plane,' he said. 'I do wish that. Call me soon. Promise.'

Finding herself fighting back tears, suddenly thinking she might never see him again, she moved forward past the barrier of his stiff arms and kissed him, feeling a surge of electricity. With great effort she hurried away to catch Jak. Another moment and she would not have gone. For that reason she avoided looking back. She knew Rory was still watching, and felt a buzz of excitement about that for a long while after.

There was nothing sinister-looking about the Hirshorn complex, apart from an environmental point of view – a lot of dust coming off a ship being loaded. The sun was

205

shining; familiar objects like Japanese autos and freight cars moved around the railyards; there were guys in hard hats, mostly with regular features.

'It doesn't exactly look like Gotham City.'

Grace was sitting next to Jak in a compact Ford rental car, across the railroad tracks on 37th Street.

'You don't want to head back to the airport?' he said.

Right then Rory's caution seemed foolish, and she wondered about it.

'Jak, this is America,' – like she believed it truly was the land of the free. 'It's broad daylight. These are just working men doing their job. Nothing's going to happen. Is it.'

He smiled and started the car.

They weren't challenged as they crossed the rusting tracks and drove in through the main entrance. The guard in the office glanced up at them and went back to his magazine.

She looked at Jak and they both began laughing. Could these folks have anything to hide if they were this open? She felt relieved.

On the dock by the 300-foot-long dilapidated terminal buildings they still went unchallenged, and when they approached the ship and started up its steep ladder. The air over the holds was full of dust and noise. Grain was rattling from the eighteen inch conveyor funnels that were high off the holds. The man on the crane gantry was getting directions by radio from the two stevedores on the deck.

Jak shouted, 'You shipping wheat?'

There was no reply. The man had cans on and made no attempt to remove them, but watched Jak scoop up some spilled grains.

'I guess you are at that.'

'You shouldn't be up here without a hard hat.'

'We wanted to ask about some wheat seed.'

'Get the hell outta here.'

That was a conversation stopper.

'Friendly soul,' Grace said, descending the ship's steep ladder.

A feeling of unease crept over her as they walked through the plant. This was intrusive, she thought, and these people had a right to be angry with them for coming here asking questions on little more than a suspicion. She put herself in their position, then finally told herself there'd be no problem if there was nothing to hide.

Alongside the silos, which at a distance belied their size, they met a yardworker, who wasn't any more friendly.

'Where's seed stored for Crocker-Giant?' she asked with a smile.

The man looked at her, then at Jak, and back to her.

'Seed grain? Mostly in the bagging sheds, I guess.' He pointed off to some sheds on the other side of the railroad tracks. 'D'you talk to the people in the office about being down here?'

'We'll get to that,' she said, trying to sound tough.

As they moved away, she sensed the yardworker watching and glanced around. The stevedore approached and spoke to the yardworker, who pulled a mobile phone from his pants pocket.

'Do you think he's calling their security?' she asked.

'Maybe.' Jak quickened his pace.

The bagging shed would have comfortably accommodated a jumbo jet, without displacing any of the grain there. The floor between the railroad tracks through the centre was made up of open steel decking with shutters beneath which were chutes onto the conveyors. These carried grain up into the giant hoppers ranged along either wall. Each bin had a card in its pocket saying what was being bagged. They couldn't find any Prairie Red spring wheat as they checked out the bins, nor did they know how they would get to it if they did.

They could hear a Cat at work behind one of the mountains of grain heaped on the ground. It was mere background noise, until the machine came around a wheat pile straight at them.

The driver blasted the horn but didn't stop.

They scrambled beneath a hopper as it went past.

'Was he trying to run us down?' she said.

Suddenly grain flooded out of the hopper. Jak pulled her free as wheat surged then eddied around their ankles before seeping away through the floor grilles.

'We could've gotten buried under that.'

The Cat came back, a half ton bag of seed swinging on its hook.

'Let's get out of here,' Grace said.

They ran painfully, their shoes full of grain. Fleeing into the safety of bright sunlight, they stopped to empty their shoes. A rock bunced off the metal side of the building nearby, startling them. Some of the yardworkers were headed alongside of the shed. Someone threw another rock.

'What the hell is this?' Jak protested. 'We only want to ask . . .'

'Jak . . .!'

She knew a mob when she saw one. These people weren't about to listen to an argument, no matter how well reasoned. She grabbed his arm and they ran. Hard. Easily putting distance between themselves and the rock-throwers. As they rounded the end of the shed they met the barrels of two .38s.

'Hold it right there.'

The two security guards looked like they had regularly pistol-whipped suspects before getting themselves thrown out of the police department. She thought then about Rory's advice and felt curiously reassured.

She was taken with Jak to the security office, where on establishing their identity the guards became confused. The plant manager was called.

Jak's story that they were collecting data for a wheat project didn't seem to convince Mark Kuhfuss. He had worry written all over his face.

'Snooping around here,' he said, giving them back their ID, 'you could have an accident. You don't have hard hats.'

'Your people are none too friendly.'

'They figured you were the FBI investigating short-loading. They've had it up to here,' – indicating the gills.

'You could have a lot worse problems, Mr Kuhfuss.

Somebody's developed a wheat seed that attracts Take-all virus in the soil. We think maybe it was shipped from here.'

Jak told him their theory briefly; Kuhfuss listened; the guards looked blank. One picked his nose.

Afterwards there was a long moment before Kuhfuss responded. Grace glanced at Jak, wondering if he sensed what she did about this man, that he knew something and maybe wanted to tell them but couldn't for some reason. Maybe she was being fanciful, she thought.

'Thanks, Saul,' Kuhfuss said to the guard. 'I'll see they get back to their transport.' He pointed them out of the office, but said nothing until they approached the parking lot.

'You getting close to fixing nitrogen in wheat, Dr Redford?'

'You know about that?' Jak's tail went up like a peacock's. 'I maybe expect scientists working in my field to know about my work, no one else.'

'I've read some of your papers. It could bring more problems.'

'For the chemical companies, sure.'

'The world's got more wheat than it can sell.'

'That makes our conspiracy theory more feasible,' Grace argued, 'not less.'

'You got a couple of problems – more than a couple. You'd never keep a thing like that quiet – too many people would need to be in on it. The Commodity Futures Trading Commission wouldn't let anyone get that many futures. Not enough to make the difference. You don't have a whole lot that will stand up.'

'I saw five hundred acres of spring wheat fail in England, Mr Kuhfuss,' she said. 'For no logical reason at all.'

'Wheat sometimes just doesn't respond to logic, Mrs Chance. I don't know why you figure it was shipped from here.'

'Because that's where the seed merchant in England said it came from.'

Kuhfuss looked at her but didn't reply.

209

'Are you shipping that wheat seed?' Jak asked. 'Your people sure as hell act like you are.'

'Being an academic I guess might excuse your blunt approach, Dr Redford. We've all been under suspicion for a while, we're a mite touchy.'

Kuhfuss looked across at those towering blocks of silos. Grace followed his gaze. It had gone there several times. She wondered if that was where the wheat seed was.

'You make money in this business by having a good reputation,' Kuhfuss said. 'You can't make a nickel from wheat seed that fails – unless you were out to destroy . . .'

'Then what would you do, Mr Kuhfuss?' Jak asked. 'Buy futures? Corner the market?'

Kuhfuss laughed. 'No way. There's a three million bushel ceiling. The Commodity Futures Trading Commission police that level of trading. Three million bushels is a lot of wheat, but it's not a corner. The US grows around 2.3 billion bushels. That's a lot of wheat. You'd need to grab a whole big chunk of it to call it a corner.'

'Someone is buying a lot of wheat, Mr Kuhfuss,' she said, growing impatient. 'The price is climbing.'

'Sure, Hirshorn are buying. We're one of the major players. We buy all the time and a hell of a lot more wheat than three million bushels. What you can be sure of is a customer's name is on every lot. You can be equally sure that all those customers will take delivery.'

It was like a rehearsed speech, she thought.

'Do you think we're crazy?'

Kuhfuss hesitated, then smiled politely.

'You figure you've got something, talk to the CFTC,' he said. 'Jimmy Keiller's the guy who runs their enforcement division. He will put together an investigation. But you'd better get it right first time. He won't go round twice with you.'

'Do you get seed here from Mexico?'

'They grow great hybrid vigours. The Russians are crazy for that seed –' Kuhfuss stopped abruptly.

'Is Red Bean Agriculture one of the growers?' Jak asked. And when Kuhfuss didn't answer, – 'Do we keep looking, Mr Kuhfuss? Do we?'

'I've got to get back to work. I have a plant to run here,' Kuhfuss was growing agitated. He started away across the parking lot, then turned back suddenly. 'Give me a number where I can reach you, if I hear anything.'

As they drove away from the grain elevator, Grace said, 'I think he was trying to tell us something.'

'Something seemed to be troubling the guy.'

'Could the Russians be getting that wheat seed, Jak?'

'He did bring up the Russians. And for no reason I could tell.'

'If the CIA funded development of that seed, that's like the government. Why would they choose to do that to the Russians? That would get all kinds of world opinion against them, wouldn't it?'

'The CIA isn't the government, Grace,' he said. 'Sure it's a government agency, but it's not subject to public control – talk to Rory about that. They start projects without any meaningful oversight from any elected representatives.'

'If the Russian wheat harvest failed, it would mean them coming here to buy it from whoever holds the most wheat. Hirshorn's wheat may have been earmarked for customers, but if the Russians came along with a bigger price. Should we talk to that man at the CFTC, Jak?'

'What do we use for evidence, Grace?'

In an instant she could see the whole devastating wheat conspiracy. 'I know we're missing some of the details to support our theory, but it is happening, Jak. I know it is. If we do nothing it will happen. We could at least talk to this man Keiller.'

'Kuhfuss said we'd only get one shot with the people at the CFTC. If we talk with them we'd better make it good.'

'Well, what can we do to make it any better than it is now?'

'I don't know,' he said.

'If we wait it could be too late.'

'I think we should head down to Mexico. Maybe we can find out how Red Bean Agriculture fits in with this.'

Despite Rory's warning about the danger they would

likely meet here, they had stepped from the belly of the monster unscathed. That made Grace feel confident. She wasn't sure about going to Mexico right now. Whatever was here seemed more urgent. She wondered if Jak was going in that direction simply because he could.

The tiredness Mark Kuhfuss felt had little to do with being fifty-seven or working long hours, or that grain trading, even at his end of the business, needed split-second judgement to make the difference. He could handle that. What he couldn't easily deal with, was where he suspected Hirshorn were now at with wheat. Sure the world was currently awash with grain, but too much or too little had always been a problem. Hirshorn traded better than most and stayed profitable, so he couldn't figure why they would get into a deal that would wreck prime wheat-growing land. If it had been Gordon Dulles behind this . . . But he had departed. Caddy had to be in on it, and that worried him more. He had delayed on taking any kind of action, instead denying to himself it was happening, or figuring there was nothing he could do anyhow. Now there was a way to get this stopped. With a little help Dr Redford and Mrs Chance might find a chink in the mighty Hirshorn armour. With something as big and complex as a deal like this had to be, some detail always got overlooked. But if they managed to blow this apart, how much damage might get done to Hirshorn? Would they survive? Sure they would, he reasoned, Hirshorn were lucky, and had God on their side. Earnings would dip, but the company was big enough to sustain any damage. That risk was to be set against the whole of the Russian spring wheat getting wiped.

He rose from his desk and went to the computer console and tapped in the entry code and accessed all those customers scheduled for wheat delivery. A flour mill belonging to Hirshorn were set to take 200,000 tons of No 2 hard red. He checked their purchases over the past three years. They were forty-six, forty-eight and forty-seven thousand tons respectively processed. Hirshorn would have a lot of grain on their hands if their plan went wrong. Maybe they couldn't survive after all, especially if Caddy truly had cancer.

What made him more tired was there was nobody to talk this out with. Again he tried convincing himself that he had imagined the whole thing, that there was no problem with the seed wheat the Russians had got, that Hirshorn was instead helping them. But he couldn't. The wheat seed had been sold via Pierre d'Estaing, like Hirshorn weren't involved. It made no sense.

The intercom buzzed and he reached out and pressed the line button, noticing then that his fingernail was chewed and ragged.

'Mr Shapiro,' his secretary said, 'I have Mark Kuhfuss on the line. He wants to talk to Mr Hirshorn.'

What about? was his immediate thought. But he didn't imagine the Galveston plant manager would tell him the purpose of the call, even if he asked him directly.

'Say Caddy's not available and put the call through here.'

Clearly from his tone Kuhfuss was disappointed at getting him instead of the big boss. Pleasantries were exchanged, a patently thin slick of oil over a sea of hostility. Then Kuhfuss said, 'The FBI are about done with their investigation. Am I glad about that. Kind of wears a body down after a while.'

'What's their story, Mark?'

Kuhfuss hesitated.

'They found we had overshipped by four hundred tons instead of hiding the balance of any underloaded grain. Federal Inspection buys that.'

The elation he felt right then was there in his voice. He couldn't keep it out. 'I guess the boss will stop those losses out of your bonuses, Mark!' He laughed.

'I could live with that,' Kuhfuss said. 'Adjusting those computer records was no minor item, no sir.'

'Mark, –' What was he saying over a phone for Christsake.

'It involved the computer going down for six hours,' Kuhfuss continued. 'That caused all kinds of problems.

213

But I managed to lose a whole boatload of wheat. That's how come I'm showing four hundred tons overshipped. That was a real risk. The FBI could have challenged that. Instead they were plain embarrassed when they reported their finding.'

'Mark?' He felt uneasy. This was like talking to a crazy man who had saved their life. 'The government will have to back off suing us now, and the Indian government,' he said. 'Great, Mark. You got everybody's ass out of a sling.'

'I couldn't see Mr Hirshorn with that kind of trouble,' Kuhfuss said. 'Will you tell him, or will I?'

'I'll tell him. But I guess he'll want to call and thank you himself, Mark.' He'd make sure of it.

'I need to talk to him. Something else came up. I think Mr Hirshorn should know about it.'

'It did, Mark? Can I tell him what it is?' There was a long pause.

'A couple of flakes came out here saying we've shipped wheat seed carrying a Take-all attracting gene.'

'What's that, Mark?' He sat forward in alarm, knowing at once who he was talking about.

'It's connected with some wheat that failed in England. If that's the case, Pat, the Russians are gonna have a lot of wheat fail. That was from the same wheat seed they got.'

Following that call, he sat on the edge of his chair feeling exposed and vulnerable. Something needed to be done about Kuhfuss or everything could be at risk. He pressed the intercom. 'Ruth – is he free?' He needed to talk to the boss. Only lately he was acting kind of strange, like he didn't want to be near him.

'Who are these people?' Caddy asked.

He watched his boss pause from putting papers into his attaché case, uncertain now. 'I figure it's Kuhfuss we got to worry about, sir. What he might do.'

'He did it. He tried to call me.'

'It's that plant geneticist from Cambridge,' he said. 'He figures something's happening to the Russian wheat.'

Caddy nodded slowly. There was disapproval in that gesture.

'We dispose of governments when they try to stop us; we squash the opposition like some kind of bug – we'll lick this problem in our chicken processing plants. How come we don't deal with a couple of amateurs? This guy was supposed to have been taken care of back in England. What is he doing showing up in Galveston? You're not paying attention to details.'

He smarted at that, not enjoying his boss's censure.

'We have to think about someone being behind him,' he said. 'Could be International Grain sent these people.'

The look Caddy fixed him with forced him to glance away. Suddenly he capitulated, surprising him.

'You could be right about my brother-in-law. Maybe he's not as honourable as I had hoped.'

'Who's to say, Caddy.' He appeared embarrassed. 'I don't want a single thing to go wrong, sir.'

'Then do something about these people. Before they become a major item on our agenda.'

'I called Wilf Fear. The CIA can handle them.'

'Every man has his weakness. Find theirs, exploit it.'

With tension creeping into his chest and almost stopping his breathing, he said, 'I'd like to know yours, Caddy.'

In the silence that followed he was left wondering if he'd misjudged the moment to try and win back the friendship, the feeling that had passed for intimacy in their relationship. He was afraid his boss would completely reject him, leaving him resentful.

'Vanity,' Caddy said at last. 'That's why God has burdened me with skin cancer. Everything is for a purpose. But I have to confess I'm coming to no clear conclusion about God's purpose in this. My kids are waiting for me to help paint our church.' He started out, but turned back. 'Deal with these people, Pat, any way you have to.'

That left him wanting to do anything he could to please his boss.

16

O**N DRIVING NORTH FROM CULIACÁN** in a fairly old
rented Chevrolet that didn't seem very reliable, all
Grace could see was a dispirited human existence clinging
to an inhospitable landscape. Miles of cultivated land
spread in from the coast like a disease. She tried to ignore
her first impression of Mexico. Somewhere she hoped to
see a more optimistic way of life. The Best Western hotel
on the outskirts of town seemed to be it. All the roads off
the main highway were unpaved, which explained why
the car's suspension among other things was wrecked.
Groups of disorganized farm workers were camped on the
margins of the highway with placards. Grace made Jak
stop. Her Spanish was rusty, but she managed roughly.

'They are protesting that they have no work and no
homes, and their children are hungry and without shoes,'
she translated.

'Welcome to Mexico,' Jak said. 'You'll see worse than
this.'

Grace thought about staying cocooned in the hotel,
until she found she was sharing her bathroom with
six-inch lizards.

Dr Alicia Huerta hadn't been at the airport to meet
them as arranged. That was worrying. Her office, which
sat among a collection of dusty adobe houses outside of
Guasave, was deserted. They left a note under the door.
But she didn't get in touch that first evening.

The next morning she still didn't get in touch, which
suggested something sinister may have happened to her.

'Can a doctor just disappear?' she said, when Jak

returned to the restaurant from calling her office and home again.

'Rory said she was in a dangerous profession. Maybe he underestimated how dangerous.' He glanced at her and added, 'I guess he loses touch with reality.'

She smiled, noticing he had made several such observations.

'What shall we do?'

'We can't get anyplace unless we make contact.'

They went out to her office again. It was still locked tight, along with the *farmacia* that was attached to it.

Grace stared at the dusty uncared-for buildings, thinking about the people who lived here. There was a point at which people became paralysed by the hopelessness of unending poverty. These people seemed to have reached that point, where even picking up and burying the festering, flyblown dog she saw along the street wasn't possible. Her only comparable experience was the numbing depression she had known after Rose's death.

An ancient VW Beetle arrived in a cloud of dust. A woman in her forties got out to unlock the *farmacia*. Jak approached and asked if she was Dr Huerta in slow, over-articulated English.

'The doctor no come today.' The woman looked worried.

'She was supposed to meet us at the airport yesterday.'

Suddenly she brightened. 'Si. You are the Dr Chance?'

'I'm Redford. She's Grace Chance. Where is the doctor?'

'The police take her. When she go to the airport.'

'Where did they take her?'

She was at the police station, a smart white marble and stone building with a dusty, rutted road in front of it. They spent a long while trying to get a response from the officials in their tan uniforms. No one spoke English, and Grace found the local Spanish dialect made communication tortuous. But clearly the cops knew who they were seeking.

After about two hours of waiting, a police lieutenant

217

showed up and asked in English to see their passports, and driver's licences, wanting to know why they were in Mexico. Jak offered his without hesitation.

'You're holding Dr Huerta,' he said.

'We throw away the key this time,' the lieutenant said. Everything on him was gleaming from his hair to his boots. 'Why you want Dr Huerta?'

'We need to ask her some questions.'

'You ill? There is a fine hospital in Culiacán.' He looked at Grace and smiled. 'Dr Huerta is a communist. She causes big trouble for the farmers. We ask questions. She don't answer.'

'Can we put up bail?' Jak offered.

'Sure. You got a million dollars?'

'A million! Are you serious?'

'You ain't got the money,' the police lieutenant said and smiled at Grace again.

'What is Dr Huerta supposed to have done?' she asked.

'She kill a lot of people.'

'I don't believe it,' she protested.

'Don't argue with these people, Grace,' Jak said.

The lieutenant looked at him and handed back the passports. 'You are nice people. So I release her.'

Law enforcement here seemed more capricious than dangerous, and she didn't understand Jak's nervousness.

Dr Alicia Huerta was small and energetic and looked about sixty, but was in fact forty. She emerged through the station, haranguing the police, then greeted Grace and Jak like her liberators.

'The charge is false,' she told them as they left under the gaze of policemen on the station veranda. 'This is why they let me go.'

'They said you killed some of your patients,' Grace explained.

'The growers here give the police many bribes. They arrest me often, but we never go to court – maybe one day.'

'Will your patients go to court on our case in America?' It occurred to her then that they might not want to.

'Rory asks this many times. These people understand only courts that send loved ones to prison.'

'All they have to do is give us their evidence,' Jak said.

'Against the people they work for. It's the only work they have.'

'Pesticides have been killing and injuring them.' Jak sounded like they were doing these people a favour.

'Si,' Dr Huerta said, and glanced at Grace, who understood at once what she was saying.

'It's a bit like when you're depressed, Jak. You just can't do anything but passively accept the situation as part of the way of life.'

'These are Mexican Indians, they have no rights,' Dr Huerta told them. 'They are encouraged to migrate from the interior with their families because they are cheaper than the Mexican farm workers you see picketing outside the town. They cannot return, there is nowhere for them to return to. They do not work, their families starve. The growers say the sprays will not harm them. Come.'

At her sparsely equipped office, which was a barefoot medical practice, she moved the worn examination couch and lifted the rug. From beneath a trapdoor in the floor she removed some box files.

'The police take my records often. They do not return them.'

'Don't you protest about that?' Jak asked.

'Si – Rory say you want people poisoned with Americano Chemical Company pesticide. We have many. These records I keep hidden all the while.'

'A product used in England has the active ingredient dichlorpronine,' Grace said. It meant nothing to the doctor until she described how it affected the breathing.

'We find many such cases here. Then we talk to the *campesanos*.'

The detailed records she kept on everyone treated for suspected pesticide poisoning were written in English. The medical records were part of her campaign to have the appalling conditions for farm workers ended by legislation.

The extent of those conditions weren't something she could imagine from the day and a half she spent with Alicia Huerta going through the records. Not until they

219

were taken to where these people lived and worked did she begin to comprehend how blighted their lives were. Initially she felt numbed by the misery and squalor.

'I don't remember anything as bad as this ten years ago when I was last here on a research project,' Jak said.

'Where was that?' Alicia asked. 'Maybe they were Spanish Mexicans working in the fields, not Indians.'

Jak didn't reply. Grace watched him closely, curious to know why this affected him so badly. There was a sensitivity about him she hadn't hitherto suspected.

'Are you okay?' she asked.

He smiled and shook his head and walked away.

On the margins of the vast cultivated tracts, where winter fruit and vegetables grew, whole families dwelt in the flimsiest of shacks. Their shanty dwellings, huddled on the narrow strip of land between the highway and the irrigation ditches alongside of the crops, were made from any scraps of rubbish; flattened cardboard cartons, tar-paper, the odd piece of corrugated tin, oil drums – some serving as structural supports – plastic bags, woven palm fronds. Their resourcefulness was amazing, while attempts to claim some privacy were touching where consumer debris was passed into service as picket fences to demarcate boundaries. There were some tents patched with plastic bags, and an old trailer which was long past travelling.

With no sanitation the camp had the rank smell of human detritus hanging over it. A dead dog lay near the irrigation ditch, a rib poking through the dried-out carcass, its teeth shining incongruously with the whiteness of pearls in its open mouth.

As they stood talking to the occupier of a shack, Grace's gaze sought the dead dog to avoid staring at these dwellings for fear of being intrusive or crying with pity. These people didn't even have the right to call these places their own, but paid rent, she learned, to the landowner for the dubious privilege to squat here.

One woman they visited told how several members of her family had difficulty breathing after getting sprayed with pesticide. As she talked to Alicia small children

220

clung to her skirts – children too young to work, and with no school to go to. Grace smiled and crouched down to them. There was no communication. The watchful children simply turned away behind their mothers' skirts. She was uncomfortable smiling here, knowing that she would walk away, back to the sanitary hotel, to America, to England, to hope, while these people seemed to have none.

'The father of her seven children got sick in the fields,' Alicia told them. 'Two of her children got sick yesterday when they pick tomatoes. They could not breathe.'

'Could we talk to her husband?' she asked.

'He died. Like someone suffocated him.'

Rose crowded her thoughts and she turned away, tears staining her eyes. She heard Alicia asking about the chemicals used.

The Indian woman stooped through the doorway of her camphouse and reappeared immediately with a blue plastic drum. The top was cut off and wire pushed through two holes for use as a water pail. It bore the faint lettering Smartkill. Grace clearly understood what the doctor said next, even in the rapid, unfamiliar Spanish.

Alicia was exasperated. 'Empty drums are not thrown away. They use them to hold water for the family,' she explained.

Jak folded his arms over his head. 'Don't they know how toxic this stuff is?'

Grace looked at him, wondering what he was feeling right then.

'These people cannot read,' Alicia said. 'Not in Spanish. Sometimes the label is in English.'

She turned back and shook her head at the makeshift pail as the Indian woman reached for it.

'But what point I tell them this when they get their water here?' – pointing to the irrigation ditch, which held four inches of oily grey water, the run-off from the fields.

Grace wasn't sure if she could go on with this. And but for Alicia she would have fled. This woman was pure inspiration.

The more she saw of her the more determined she

became to help her to make things better for these people. With clear insight she knew that she had so little to give and to deny even that would be to deny a part of herself and what had happened to Rose.

The next family they visited had lost a son whose trachea had completely closed following a spraying accident. His uncle who was involved in the same incident, had had an emergency tracheotomy performed by Dr Huerta, but not before permanent brain damage resulted from his oxygen supply being stopped. The family had three other workers and when they returned from the fields they invited them to sit with them, and offered them bottles of Coke. Grace was grateful for even that slightly warm sticky drink out of a bottle, then realized that it cost so much relative to their three-dollars-a-day wages.

Two women were cooking over an open fire in the yard, and nine children watched with grave expressions as Alicia explained why they were there. Her words were met with slow head-shaking, and uncertain glances at Grace and Jak.

'The growers threaten them if they make trouble. They take away the work. Then they cannot live here.'

Grace nodded, not caring to push these people.

'But your kids are getting sick,' Jak said. 'We want to stop the growers making you sick.' He spoke slowly, as if trying to help them understand both his foreign language and aspirations.

Alicia translated, but the head-shaking continued.

Summoning the most appropriate words she could find in her limited Spanish, Grace said, 'My daughter died because of this pesticide. We want to stop these terrible things happening to your children.' She turned to Alicia. 'Do they understand?'

The doctor nodded, but the expressions of the *campesanos* didn't change.

The response was the same everywhere along the fields.

'Employers pay thousands of dollars for this kind of loyalty,' Jak said. 'I don't understand why these people won't take our help.'

222

'They're frightened of the growers,' Grace said. 'Everything they've got could be taken from them.'

'But they haven't got anything, for Christsake.'

She turned away. 'Why won't the government here protect them, Alicia? There must have been calls for tighter controls on pesticides. These people are Mexicans too, after all.'

'This is part of our economy, yours also,' Alicia said. 'Our government would have to provide alternative housing, sanitation. They cannot. There are enquiries and health inspections; still the spray planes come, still the pesticides run into the irrigation ditches, still people take that water for cooking and for washing clothes.'

'Carrying it in old pesticide drums,' Grace said.

'It looks hopeless, no? In three years the land becomes a salt desert. First the irrigation water is taken from the aquifers, then the sea water seeps in. Then the growers move on, abandon the land.'

'Meanwhile scientists are developing salt-resistant plants,' Jak said.

Without any warning, a plane appeared over the horizon and began dropping a miasma of chemicals over the ripening tomatoes in the field.

From the margin land Grace saw pickers getting drenched also. What was happening was outside her experience, yet at once painfully familiar. The smell of the chemical on the air brought her daughter sharply into focus. Pickers scrambled away as the plane circled.

'Jesus Christ! Don't they get a warning?' Jak was saying.

'Sometimes they blow the whistle. But it causes delay.'

'What are they spraying during picking? They must know that is in direct contravention of the pesticide manufacturers' code.'

'Fungicide – tomatoes they reach the supermarket in good condition when they go to America.'

She felt the same helplessness she had experienced at the hospital when Rose died. She heard her daughter screaming now and wanted to block her ears. As the drone of the aircraft faded she realized the screams were from a child in the field. A mother was running and scooping a girl into her arms and rushing her to the irrigation ditch. Instinctively Grace ran forward then, as the mother moistened the end of her skirt.

Reaching out to stop her, she said, 'No. You will make it worse. Worse.' She searched round for practical help, not knowing if her Spanish was understood. Then remembering the bottle of water in their car, she grabbed the child and hurried back along the track.

While Alicia explained to the mother about not using the ditch water, Grace wondered what the point was as there was no clean water for such emergencies. She bathed the child's eyes.

Pickers fleeing the field now began to gather at the car, as the spray plane made another run. They watched Alicia closely as she examined the child's eyes.

'The packing station is along the highway,' she told Grace. 'They have a shower there to wash off the chemicals. They threaten me not to go there.'

Without any hesitation, Jak climbed behind the wheel of the Chevy as Grace got into the back with the child. She beckoned to the mother, who went with them with some uncertainty.

'These are not good people,' Alicia warned. 'Be careful, si.'

The car seemed badly affected by the sprays too, and refused to start, then stalled. Grace was ready to run there with the child.

The packing station was right by the highway, its long, low sheds and thousands upon thousands of packing crates stacked around the yard were covered in dust.

No one challenged her as she marched the Indian woman and her daughter into the small washroom. The place was hot under the corrugated tin roof and smelt of drains. The water didn't run out through the hole which served as a toilet also, but poured across the floor and under the door. She smiled as she watched them stand fully clothed beneath the stream of water. It was like a new experience for them. The girl stopped crying and soon began to laugh excitedly.

The mutual pleasure was shortlived when raised voices reached them from outside. Grace found Jak arguing with someone she took to be the manager. He had two men with him, both carried long sticks.

'He says we shouldn't be here with these people,' Jak told her. 'He's telling me the pesticides do no harm.'

She wheeled on the man in a sudden rage. 'That's nonsense. Children are getting sick. Some are dying.'

'No, *señora*' The station manager had a disarming smile. 'The chemicals make them strong teeth and bones.'

'Don't be stupid. They're toxic.'

He looked puzzled. 'Why you in Mexico?' – the smile returning.

For a moment she thought perhaps this man really didn't understand about these chemicals and believed them harmless.

'We're looking at the damage the pesticides are doing to field-workers,' she said.

'Ah, si.' His smile broadened. 'You the good friend of my Dr Huerta. Where you stay? With Alicia?'

His smile was so precipitous she imagined she could even like this man.

As they drove out he said, 'You come and use the shower any time you want. You very welcome, *señora*.'

The *campesanos* seemed amazed that they all returned safely. They examined the mother and child in disbelief, thinking them something special for having survived this; Grace extra special for having organized it. She and Jak were invited to eat supper with them. It was an offer they couldn't refuse, but she faced it with trepidation.

The meal of vegetables from the fields and highly spiced tortillas had to be full of pesticides and certainly prepared in insanitary conditions, but besides giving offence there was nothing she could do. The more they ate the more they were offered. The guarded watchfulness of the Indians gradually disappeared during the evening, and they became curious, asking her and Jak questions which in the First World nobody asked, but here they found themselves answering. They forgot about the possibility of food poisoning, and ever so briefly the plight of these people. Her mood lightened and she began to enjoy herself.

Walking across the parking lot back at their hotel, Jak put his arm around her shoulder. She leant her head on him like it was the most natural thing to do, feeling unconcerned about what it might lead to right then. It no longer mattered. For the first time in a long while she had a very clear sense of what she aimed to do with her life: to help these people get a better deal.

On the open corridor which overlooked the pool, she allowed Jak to steer her to his room. She offered no resistance as he found his key and unlocked the door. The lights in the room didn't work. There were several lights off in the corridor, she noticed. The surprise was that anything like electricity worked at all down here.

'Perhaps the fuse has blown, I'll try mine,' she said, stepping through the dark room. She stopped suddenly, seeing the outline of a man by the door of their adjoining rooms. 'Jak,' she said in alarm, 'there's someone here . . .' She shrieked as the man grabbed her.

'Grace . . .?' She heard Jak groan on an intake of breath. She turned back as he crashed against a table, tipping it up as he hit the floor.

She didn't see where her attacker came from, but someone hit her with something dull and heavy. Her thoughts swam, while any physical protests grew less effective as she tried to pull herself through cottonwool. Finally the attack ended, but she was scared to move in case these people were still there. Her muscles ached and she badly wanted Jak to hold her and tell her everything was all right. Some voice deep inside told her things were far from all right. After a while she was aware of her own breathing, and a whimpering sound that was coming from deep within her. She felt embarrassed. The only other sound was of crickets outside. She closed her mouth and forced air through her nostrils into her lungs to try and stop the sound she was making. It worked. But still she was scared, too scared to find out what had happened to Jak. She feared he was dead.

Crawling painfully across the floor, calling his name in a

226

whisper at first, she began to panic when there was no reply. Each thought brought a worse conclusion, but none suggested why those people had been waiting for them. Only that it must have been a mistake.

Jak was on the floor, his eyes open staring at the ceiling. He groaned when she reached her hand under his head.

'Are you all right, Jak? I was scared you were dead.'

'Are you sure I'm not? Jesus, it feels like the roof came down.'

'What are you doing?' she said, suddenly angry that he hadn't come to check if she was all right. She started crying again, and hated herself for being so weak.

'Grace? Are you hurt?'

He got to it at last, but the belated concern didn't help.

'How can people be so wicked, doing what they're doing, especially to those children? It is wicked. It's murder.'

'Is that what this is about?' he said. 'I figure it was robbery.'

'It can't be – what have they robbed?'

There was nothing missing that they could tell. But still Jak was reluctant to accept what was behind this, despite Alicia's warnings. Grace wondered why.

'Jak, we've got to do something to stop what's happening here. We've got to.'

'Sure, that's why we're here,' he said. 'But first we gotta call the police.'

She wasn't sure if that was the right thing to do, but didn't want to row with him, so ignored her anxiety as he made the call.

17

THE PRELIMINARY HEARING ON NARCOTICS charges wasn't held in a courtroom. Grace was brought from her separate prison cell to appear with Jak before the *procuraduria de justicia*, whose job it was to listen to possible evidence and then make compromise proposals. From what she understood of this process, the result would mean a reduced sentence. However, a prerequisite was their admission of guilt. That wasn't something she was about to agree to. She wasn't sure how Jak felt about it.

Their arrest had been like something from a bad dream. The police had arrived very quickly with pistols drawn, and with a lot of shouting and threatening body language that needed no translating. They had been thrown to the floor with their hands behind their heads and their legs spread. One policeman had beaten Jak when he didn't respond fast enough; then her when she protested.

Being arrested, charged and held in a cell for two days was frightening, uncomfortable and interesting in that order, she found. The police didn't like drug dealers, especially not foreign dealers who vehemently maintained their innocence. The police held all the trump cards and the guns, while disappearing into the bowels of the police station felt as though it could last forever. The Mexican jail was hot, dirty, smelly and overcrowded. She was in a cell with fifteen other women and no toilet, only an open drain beneath a tap, where the women would squat and relieve themselves and where finally she was forced to also. The tap was for washing, drinking and flushing what, at times, was reluctant to be flushed down that drain. There were benches around the wall where most of the women slept, but some had to sleep on the floor. After her initial shock, she began to get interested in these women and how they survived, a number of them were only girls.

A camaraderie sprang from their curiousity about her, an Englishwoman, here. She told them something of her life in England, and why she was in Mexico. None of them believed she was a drugs dealer, and readily accepted that the police had framed her. Two of the girls were dealers, while the majority were prostitutes who couldn't afford to bribe the police. One thirteen-year-old was the most curious of all, and asked many questions about her life, some of which she didn't understand because of the dialect. With her own halting Spanish she learned that the girl had no family and virtually no schooling, and that she would be sent to an orphanage, which she said was worse than prison. The girl had been working as a prostitute. Grace told her how children in England were made by law to attend school, how many of them didn't want to and dropped out. After a while she realized this was making little sense to the girl, who had been on the streets since she was nine, encouraged by her brother after her mother had died. Here she realized how fortunate the circumstances of her own life were in comparison.

Often in that cell with its fetid smells from unwashed bodies and human faeces, she thought about Jak, if conditions were any better for him, and how he might be coping. Some of the women said there were many gang rapes in the men's jail, which alarmed her. She tried to speak to the guards to get information about Jak. Only after the thirteen-year-old whispered to her that the women exaggerated to frighten her did she feel less anxious. She wondered if his demands to see the American Consul had produced anything more than brutal responses, and if he persisted in the face of them. One of the block guards who appeared at night was more sympathetic when she sought news of Jak's well-being.

229

He smiled and said he would find out for her. She clung hopefully to this human response, ignoring the women who told her the guard would do nothing, or if he did how it would cost her plenty. Later that night he came and told her Jak was okay. He unlocked the cell door and told her he would take her to him. Her spirit suddenly soared, less at seeing Jak than finding someone so decent among her captors.

'You should not go with him,' the thirteen-year-old girl whispered.

'What?' Grace said, confused now. One or two of the other women were awake on their pieces of bench, watching.

'Come,' the guard said, beckoning her with a smile.

She didn't want to affront his kindness with mistrust, so she went.

He led her along the unlit corridor that was open to the yard and where some older women slept. They turned into a cell.

'Come,' he said.

Grace stepped inside and he shut the door.

Stupid. How stupidly naive, realizing then at once that this man, feeling he had helped her, now wanted rewarding.

'No,' she protested. 'No. I don't want this.' She pushed him off as he thrust his dark unshaven face in hers and tried to kiss her, his hands pulling roughly at her breasts like he was trying to tear them from her chest. She screamed and lashed out at him, catching him a blow across the cheek. He surged at her and punched her. She grabbed his hair and pulled it until he shouted in anger and pain, but inflicted more pain on her from a series of blows. She fell back to the dusty earth floor and felt him on top of her at once, his hand scrabbling under her dress, trying to pull her pants down. A part of her mind said this wasn't happening, it couldn't be. A part of her spirit said to give up, there was no point in struggling. It was like drowning, she decided, when you simply lost the will to drag yourself to the surface one more time to fill your lungs. But somehow she managed to fill her lungs and

230

screamed and screamed, clawing, tearing with her nails, getting purchase on any part of this man she could, biting him also. She became aware then of other noises, apart from the raucous, laboured breathing from the guard. It was a noise from beyond this cell and it was growing and spreading along the corridor and across the yard. Other women were calling out in a rhythmic chant, 'Rape, rape, rape.' Whatever the intention or the desires of the guard, clearly he couldn't carry them through in these circumstances. He left quickly, slamming and locking the door after himself.

Grace sat up and caught her breath and began to shake, but was determined not to cry. She pressed herself back against the wall and hugged her knees, drawing them tightly into her chest. More than frightened now she was angry with herself for being so stupid. Her cheek was stinging she noticed, and she felt tacky from having that man's hands and thoughts all over her. But she also felt a glow of well-being then, and knew it was because of what these women had done. Despite the meanness of their own circumstances they had demonstrated that they could care what happened to another human being whose only connection with them was that she was a woman. That was sustaining, she found, and provided enough encouragement to go on.

Her thoughts sought Rory, and she sensed he would have been less bothered by the deprivation of their situation than either she or Jak were. She decided she would tell no one what had happened – nothing had happened.

The worst thing for Jak in this situation was clearly his inability to communicate. This was obvious in the office of the *procuraduria de justicia* where Grace was taken the following day. As she sat with Alicia and the lawyer she had got for them, they heard Jak protesting as he was brought along the corridor. 'I'm an American,' he was saying. 'You can't keep me here. I demand the American Consul – don't you understand, goddamn you.'

In the office the guards removed his handcuffs. His slept-in face, with two days' beard growth, crumpled as

231

she rose to greet him. They embraced awkwardly at first, then he clung to her like she was the last refuge.

'What the sweet Jesus is going down, Grace?' he asked. 'Can you make sense of this?'

'The women in my cell say it's to stop us going on.'

'The women . . . What the hell do they know?'

'Si,' Alicia said. 'The growers have done this thing, Jak. This is Arturo Garcia, a lawyer. He will help you.'

Garcia rose from the seat. He had a medallion around his neck and a pot belly as tight as an unripe watermelon straining against his shirt buttons.

'Serious charges are made against you, *señor*.'

Jak started to shake. 'That's crazy. We got beaten up in our hotel room. We called the cops, but they hauled us off to jail. I've been here two days, for Christsake. I want the American Consul.'

'Jak,' Grace said, and glanced at the lawyer who, Alicia had told her, was often at risk doing the kind of work he did. 'Some people have been here for months –'

'Americans?' he said, refusing to be placated.

'I told Grace, the police charge you with drug dealing, which means you could go to prison. They arrested two men who say they were making a deal, but you tried to double-cross them.'

'That's a lie – we weren't dealing a damned thing.'

'I explained exactly what happened, Jak.'

'We know this is not so. Meanwhile your work it stops.'

'You're damn right it does,' Jak said. 'It stopped the moment I got into this shit.'

Tears moistened Grace's eyes. She was aware of Alicia watching her and knew she understood what was going on. If she looked at her she would cry. She hoped Jak would have been more resolute. So easily he seemed to forget the terrible suffering around him, while people like Alicia and Arturo went on day after day in the face of such adversity, refusing to think about their own safety or comfort. She thought about the closeness she and Jak had earlier found, how they were certain to have drifted into a physical relationsip. His reaction here would have been a greater shock to her had that happened.

'We have good news, Jak,' Alicia said. 'After you help the child of Chauta Zapaldo, some field-workers will help you.'

'Great, Alicia. We're in jail, goddamn it,' Jak said.

Without needing to ask, Grace knew that he would want to accept the deal the arbitrator had so far outlined.

'Jak, we can't just walk away. We have to stay and fight.'

Surprise came over Jak. 'You mean there's an option?'

'Si,' Garcia said. 'Because some rules may have been broken –'

'Some!' Jak interjected.

'They didn't get you an interpreter; they didn't inform your consulate of your arrest – we can do a deal here.' He glanced at *Señor* Mendoza, the arbitrator, who waited with ring-laden hands folded across his stomach. 'Maybe you can go free on condition you leave Mexico.'

'Jesus Christ,' Jak wailed, 'on the first plane.'

'Jak, I said I wouldn't agree. I won't go.'

'What? Are you crazy? Do you know about Mexican *prisons* – you've only been in jail so far. That psychiatric hospital you were in would seem like the Holiday Inn. Only you won't get the sedative. You want to risk that?'

He looked at Alicia, then the lawyer. They said nothing.

'Grace, this is real heavy. It could be for a long time.'

'We didn't do anything, Jak.'

'Sure we didn't. That's why they're prepared to let us walk.'

'That's the whole point. These people doing this, it must mean they're afraid of something. Jak, I started on this to find out about why Rose died, to have somebody accept responsibility.'

'You did it, Grace. You nailed those bastards.'

She shook her head, knowing what she was doing was right. 'They won't stop for a moment. I can't walk away. What happened to Rose is happening to so many of the children here. It doesn't matter whose children they are.'

'You won't do a thing for them from a Mexican prison, Grace.' Suddenly he stopped and looked between her and

Garcia, then let out a low groan. 'It's both of us or none, that's the deal? Right?'

'I'm sorry, Jak. I have to try.' She held him, but his body was stiff and unresponsive.

'You are very brave,' Alicia said, touching her face and smiling. 'Arturo will not let you go to prison.'

Jak clearly had no belief in that statement.

Arturo Garcia seemed less than certain too.

Although *Señor* Mendoza, the arbitrator, had no English, he got the drift of what was happening. He rose to leave, angrily pointing out the possible bad consequences.

'I don't want to go back to that jail,' Jak said. 'Call the American consulate, tell them what's happening.'

'They did, Jak,' Grace told him. 'No one there is exactly rushing to help save an American drugs dealer.'

'Jesus, Grace,' he wailed. 'What have you got us into here?'

'I'm sorry. I couldn't have got this far without you.' But now she regretted he was involved against his will.

'I'll talk to the arbitrator. I insist a judge hears your case today. Or you are given bail. It could mean a long wait, but I will talk with him, Grace.'

'Thank you.'

Garcia went out. She went and sat on a bench against the wall with Alicia and held her hands. She got a lot of strength from her. Jak paced around.

'Don't you have patients to see, Alicia?' she asked.

'I will leave when you are free.'

They waited four hours before finally getting to a judge. But then she didn't think it boded well when they were put back into handcuffs. These implied both danger from them, and guilt. She couldn't follow what was said as Arturo argued with the prosecutor and the judge in front of his bench. They spoke heatedly and rapidly and frequently all at once. When the judge at last turned on the prosecutor, telling him, as far as Grace could understand, that he should get his act together, she foresaw a long wait back in jail. She wondered how Jak would manage. That was all she could think about. Had she agreed to the arbitrator's deal they might be on their way home by now. His home, not hers. She had no home. Maybe that fact was clouding her judgement. Suddenly she felt depressed, and the judge rising and striding out only brought her down further.

Then Arturo was standing before her, smiling, helping her up; then shaking Jak's hand. Alicia embraced her, telling her she was free. This had been like a bad dream. Now people were telling her that it was over, but she couldn't quite believe she was awake.

Emerging into the afternoon sunlight spilling across the courtyard around which the palace of justice and offices were built, she noticed a pile of broken furniture, an old cooker and sink unit, a wardrobe and a mattress. It seemed incongruous sitting there, but somehow summed up the process of justice: what it lacked in formality it made up for in humanity.

'That judge was great,' Jak said, bouncing around, punching the air. 'Boy, wasn't he something, doing it to the prosecutor like that?'

'Without witnesses the judge he refuses to hear the case,' Arturo said. 'The police failed to bring to court the two men who say you had double-crossed. This judge makes trouble for the police.'

'Will they come after us again, Arturo?' Jak asked.

'This is possible. You should leave here soon.'

'No, Jak,' she told him on the way back to their hotel. 'I'm more determined than ever to get this done. You go if you have to.'

After showering and eating they went directly to the fields, Jak still protesting that this was a dumb move. The reception there was enough to change his mind. These people ascribed some magic to them for having defied the growers, and shown themselves even more powerful than the courts.

Field-workers approached and touched them and quickly withdrew, the more brave shook their hands. The sun was getting low over the sea now, bathing everything with a warm orange, and although there was another couple of hours of light in which to pick tomatoes, no one

235

was interested in working.

Someone arrived by truck from the packing station to check out the problem that had caused the stoppage, but turned right round and went back.

The next day, with little Pina Zapaldo dogging her every step, Grace went with Jak, Alicia and Arturo to collect depositions from field-workers who had become sick from contact with pesticides. In answer to her questions about the chemical's identity they were shown the pesticides dump close to the packing station. Here spraying machines, the size of which she had never seen before, with huge wheels on stalk-like hydraulic legs for straddling the vines, waited alongside stacks of fungicide drums bearing the name Smartkill.

Grace tried to remain detached about this to prevent herself crying. But tears slid silently from her eyes. She wondered when she would have cried enough, or if any amount of tears could wash away the suffering all this was causing to so many. Behind this detachment she found Rose.

'Will these people go home, Alicia, when Grace helps them get some compensation?' Jak asked.

'It is not that simple. They have no home other than this, or where the next crop is. The growers will punish them for helping you.'

'You should get that judge down here.'

'Ah si,' Alicia said.

Grace looked at her, knowing she was accepting that he didn't understand. He wanted simple solutions to infinitely complex problems, not just for dealing with migrant Indians but the whole of life so geared to profit that it displaced life itself.

When they returned to Alicia's clinic to collate the depositions, there were many patients waiting. One was Cesar Martinez, whose relative affluence set him apart. He had information on Red Bean Agriculture, which Jak had now started asking about, trying to further the wheat conspiracy investigation.

'They use much of your pesticide on the wheat, *señor*,' Martinez said like he believed the two lines of inquiry were connected.

236

'What kind of wheat is it, Cesar?' Jak asked.

'Very special, *señor*. My cousin has a very important job.'

'Can we talk to your cousin?'

Jak's interest suddenly seemed to come alive.

The possibility that there was something wrong about Martinez only occurred to Jak after they had been clunking eastward through wheatlands for about forty minutes. He didn't know why that was, and certainly it wasn't anything he could have stopped the car for, or suddenly announced that he wasn't going on. Not without looking crazy. Better crazy than dead, he thought. But still he didn't turn around. Martinez was in the seat next to him, guiding him. Grace and Pina were in the back of the Chevy as it lurched and heaved along the dusty track. The car was unhappy too. Dust was getting into the carburettor and it felt like it was about to quit. This was not the place, he silently told it. The arid landscape with its ocean of wheat reminded him of Kansas only here there were mountains. If they were headed into a trap he didn't know what the hell he could do about it anyway.

'Just whereabouts is your cousin, Cesar?' he said, seeing a speck on the horizon, which he believed was a combine. He felt better for seeing that.

'Cerra Blanco, si,' Martinez said and banged the padded dashboard, pointing up ahead.

'How much wheat do they grow here?'

'Much wheat, *señor*. Is ten thousand acres. Much seed.'

'It all goes up to Kansas to Crocker-Giant? You know that for a fact?'

'Is a fact, *señor*.'

The feeling he had about this man right then was that he was telling him anything he wanted to hear.

'This all goes to make the good old American wheaten loaf. Right?'

Martinez looked at him and smiled.

The combine was getting closer, but he couldn't figure out what it was doing. He looked at it a long while before he realized it wasn't cutting wheat.

Without warning Martinez slapped the dashboard, indicating for him to stop the car.

'We get out here and talk to my cousin, si.'

'I thought your cousin was in Cerra Blanco?' he challenged.

'He's on the combine. You come, si.' He smiled and beckoned to Grace as he slid from the car.

'What is it, Jak? What's going on?' she asked.

'I don't know. Something doesn't feel right here.' He looked about, trying to make up his mind what to do. The combine was about two hundred yards away and coming toward them.

He got out of the car and started to follow Martinez. He glanced back as Grace emerged with the child. He wanted to tell her to get back into the car and keep the engine running, but didn't want to alarm her. He waited for them to catch up.

Then he had it. He knew it was a set up. For as Martinez signalled to the man on the combine his shirt caught on the breeze. There, sticking in the back of his belt, was a gun. Pina pointed to it.

'Run! Get in the car.' As he said it he ran forward, not knowing why or how until he kicked Martinez in the back, sending him sprawling. He started back to the car, helping Grace get the girl in.

Now wasn't the time for the car to quit on them. Inevitably it did. He hit the gas pedal too soon and only succeeded in flooding the engine in his panic. The starter turned over and over but it wouldn't fire the engine. The points were dirty or full of dust.

'Jak!' Grace said, sounding the alarm.

The combine was right ahead of them now and showed no sign of slowing down. Martinez was running alongside, his gun drawn.

Then he found himself saying a prayer out loud, a relic from childhood buried deep in his psyche. The car started and suddenly shot forward.

Martinez fired at them and he instinctively swerved the car off the track through the short, sparsely planted wheat. A hummock of rock came up and hit the engine pan with a loud bang that made Grace jump. The engine stalled like it had been concussed.

The combine swung round less than elegantly and bore down on them as he tried turning the engine again and again. He thought about their chances of outrunning the combine on foot. They weren't good with the child, not over the kind of distance involved and with no place to hide.

He closed his eyes and prayed again. Silently this time. The motor fired and he stepped on the gas pedal without looking at where either Martinez or the combine were. The car shot away and onto the track.

Grace looked back. 'You did it, you did it!' She threw her arms about him and kissed him. 'You were great.'

Pina was less impressed. On the way back she fell asleep in Grace's arms and so stayed with them at the hotel. What worried Jak was that no one on their side seemed surprised at what had happened, or shared any concern about doing anything about it.

Alicia said, 'Make sure you lock your bedroom door.'

He wasn't about to call the cops, but did think the incident was somehow worth more than a footnote.

He suggested they sleep in the same room that night. And Grace had no objections to sharing the large bed. She was completely wrapped up in Pina.

'It's like having Rose in bed,' she said. 'I don't know how I'll ever hand her back to her mother tomorrow when we leave.'

He looked at her in the fading evening light. Her thoughts were transparent. She was thinking about not leaving.

'Staying's not really possible, Grace, with no money and no residence status.'

'Oh, I was only thinking about it.'

He smiled and looked at her lying beside the child softly stroking her face. He turned away, thoughts crowding in on him. Most of them unpleasant.

In Alicia's office the following morning they packed the depositions into plastic bags for travelling. No one but Jak seemed to want to get to the point of departure. He had a feeling something might crop up and stop them yet.

'I will keep copies in case something happens,' Alicia said. Clearly she didn't want Grace to leave. He thought that maybe these two women had had some kind of conversation earlier about Grace staying on.

'Nothing's going to happen, Alicia,' he said.

'We will say a prayer. No?'

'Well, they have been known to work.' He extended his hand. 'It's been a real experience, Alicia.' They were finally on their way.

Then Grace did it to him. 'I can't go, Jak. Not yet. Not without saying goodbye to the people who helped us.'

'Grace! Let Alicia say goodbye when she takes Pina back.'

'I have to, Jak. You go if you want to.' She left the office quickly.

No way could he leave without her. But his foreboding increased as he went after her and got heavier when, failing to turn her around, he drove her out to the growing fields.

Anxiety gnawed at him as he stood by the auto and watched Grace wandering among her new-found friends saying goodbye. She was a big hit with them and they were as unhappy for her to go. They approached and followed her like she was a talisman of some kind, while she behaved like she had all the time in the world.

'Come on, Grace,' he said, tapping his watch. 'We'll miss the goddamn plane.'

Grace smiled, then went on her rounds, saying that she would soon return. Pina, who was holding her hand, was smiling the whole while. He had never noticed a child smile like she did. Certainly she and Grace had something special going.

The truck he saw kicking up a storm of dust along the track fulfilled all his worst fears. From where he stood he could see it was loaded with men. The Mexican version of strike-breakers.

'Grace! Let's get the hell out of here. Grace! Get going.'

He ran along the track, grabbing her as a dozen or

more goons poured off the truck bringing their hickory axe handles. The station manager screamed at field-workers to get back to work. One of the stickmen then made the mistake of taking a swing at Alicia. Grace flew at him, punching him squarely in the face. The surprise of her blow sent him reeling.

'I told you to stay away from here,' the station manager said, turning to Alicia.

'These people are getting sick,' she said, pushing Grace in the general direction of the Chevy.

'I take care of them good,' the manager said.

'You spray them with poisonous pesticides,' Grace said, turning back at him as she reached the car.

'Is good – I fix you.' He cracked Grace's head against the car roof. Jak tried to prevent him from doing it again, but some stickmen jumped him. That brought Grace wading back in, ignoring Alicia's pleas to get into the car.

Field hands, who had started drifting back to work stopped. Then they started out of the field, at first in ones and twos. One encouraged another, then another, until they were all, men, women and children, headed back to the margin land, some picking up hoes and stakes and rocks as they went. Walking at first, then more quickly, then running.

The station manager ordered them back to work, but they kept coming. Like a swarm of angry hornets they turned after the stickmen, raining blows on them. The manager and his goons were easily outnumbered and fled. The truck circled and roared away, stranding stickmen, who chased after it. Field hands chased them, vanquishing them totally.

'Finally these people have stopped accepting their lot in life, and have taken action. Action always makes people feel better,' Grace said. She was exhilarated.

Alicia said, 'This is a very good thing.'

The high they left on had evaporated when they were in the car and driving toward Culiácan. Grace was silent in her seat, staring out of the window at the litter on the margin of the highway. He didn't risk asking her what she was thinking about. What they had witnessed in Sinaloa

241

was but a speck in the catalogue of iniquities all over the world, and he knew there wasn't a thing he could do that would make any difference. If he said that to her he guessed she wouldn't speak to him again, and might not even leave Mexico, just to prove him wrong. If he did speak of it he knew he could easily find himself on the edge of the abyss.

Stopping at the sign of a soft drink vendor on the dusty track at the side of the road was a mistake, he realized too late. There were three kids running the stall, twelve-year-olds. Certainly none of them were any older than those kids that had been stood in a field down here ten years ago and sprayed with Smartkill. He almost drove right out again.

When he brought the squeezed orange drink with chunks of watermelon back to the car, Grace was staring directly ahead through the windshield. He stood and watched her a while unnoticed, thinking how beautiful she was. The sun had brought more freckles out on her face and arms. He thought about what might have been for them down here in other circumstances.

'You've done more than enough, Grace,' he said, giving her the drink. 'There can be no doubt about that,' – trying to get her attention.

Still she refused to look at him.

'What's enough? Us stopping eating produce with pesticides on it? Well I suppose it's something – if there's enough of us. I'm going to go back afterwards. To help Alicia.'

'Why? As some kind of atonement for Rose's death?' He hadn't intended it to sound as unfeeling as he guessed it did, and wanted to somehow call the words back. Maybe he was projecting onto her the guilt he felt over what had happened to his own child, and those Mexican kids they had purposely sprayed with pesticide. All he knew was that he wanted to be anyplace but here right now in his relationship with Grace, but didn't know how to get himself there.

'Don't you feel anything, Jak?'

What he felt then was more uncertain than at any time,

and more than a little afraid. Perhaps he was incapable of feeling any longer.

'Grace . . .' he began, 'I shut down my feelings long ago. They scared me. I reasoned how I had to get in control and decided shut-down was it. Since meeting you I'm relearning about feelings. I've been where you are, I guess.'

He paused for a long while, not knowing if he could go on. His uncertainty ebbed, then rushed back leaving him paralysed. He didn't know what to do, but knew he had to give something.

'I was involved in those experiments. We stood kids in fields out here and sprayed them with Smartkill. I was a chemical pathologist then. Eleven- and twelve-year-olds. Like those.' He glanced at the three soft drinks vendors who were playing football with a can. 'They're the most vulnerable.'

He couldn't look at her for fear of what he would see, but could almost feel her disbelief.

'I couldn't believe it either. Looking back now . . . Jesus, I can't believe it still. Afterwards, after I got done with American Chemicals, I wanted to come out here, maybe pay something back. I couldn't face it . . . I changed my job instead. I figured I'd make produce grow without chemicals. The best thing anyone can do is what they're good at. Go after American Chemicals, or Hirshorn. That helps these people most.'

Standing there at the side of the car, remembering those kids, thinking about his own wife and child, he had to fight back tears. He was trying hard not to cry. He hardly noticed Grace slide from the car until she put her arms around him and held him close to her. The pain was unbearable. Then he cried.

He couldn't tell her what he suspected American Chemicals did to him, to his wife and son. He could live with Grace's rebuke as he had lived a long while with self-rebuke, but he couldn't take her pity.

18

A FEELING OF EXPECTATION RAN through Grace as she dressed in her tiny bedroom in Jak's house. She chose her prettiest dress which she remembered buying in celebration of getting accepted back into college. All that seemed like it belonged to another person in another life. Then she remembered the dress she had bought at the same time for her daughter, could see it so clearly. Splashes of bright colour from an artist's brush on a brilliant pink canvas. She had taken a long time choosing it. The dress had been similar to one Rose had seen a girl wearing in a children's serial on TV. She had wanted one like it so much, but had never got to wear it. A great dark cloud descended on her, tears started and wouldn't stop. Oh Rose, where were you now? Why did you have to leave? She sat on the edge of the bed and drew her fingers across her eyes to try and wipe away tears that couldn't be wiped away. She had talked about her death to Rory, who believed that a child's passing almost certainly meant some kind of kharmic or past life debt, and through the work she was now doing she was helping pay off the debt. Hadn't Rose paid? What more could be paid? But it seemed if the debt was big enough the soul paid again in the next incarnation. She had never considered such a philosophy before, accepting it in the absence of any other explanation, but still finding it so unfair that Rose had to die.

What was she doing now, getting excited about seeing Rory? What right did she have ever to be happy or excited again? She felt herself slipping back further and further and was helpless to do anything.

Someone was calling her name, she realized. Then there was a hammering on the door. 'Grace. Grace, are you okay? Grace?' Jak came into the room. 'We're going to be late for lunch. What's the problem? Tough being back, is it?'

She summoned a smile in response. It took great effort, but somehow seemed easier than trying to explain to Jak what was going on.

Throughout lunch she almost didn't hear Jak as he recounted what had happened to them in Mexico, but knew he was telling it substantially differently from how he had obviously felt at the time. Rory seemed to make an effort to listen, even though he had heard most of it from her straight. With the three of them at the round table in Nathan's, she was able to watch how Rory was with Jak, trying to read a meaning in every look or gesture that came her way.

She thought about her call when they had got back into Washington last night. She had over-apologized for it being so late, despite him telling her that one a.m. wasn't late for him, that he had fallen asleep reading background material on a case. He had seemed nervous and talked a lot. She found it easy talking to him and had stayed on the phone for more than an hour, while Jak had wandered restlessly around the house. Prickles of conscience made her uncomfortable about Jak, knowing she was deceiving him, even though she hadn't promised him a thing. Staying with him, having him help her, blighting his own career, fostered expectation. She should have killed that expectation long before. Now she could only hurt him. He had been badly hurt in the past, and mostly because he was a man he couldn't let feelings surface and be dealt with. Still she didn't know how to reconcile the awfulness of what he had done ten years ago to children down in Mexico. The easiest thing would have been to walk away, but he needed as much help to come to terms with it as she did. She wanted to talk to Rory about that, but couldn't get an opportunity with Jak around the whole time.

245

On the phone last night she had been certain of Rory's feelings about her, and what hers were about him. She didn't know if either would ever do anything about them. If they dared to, or even if it mattered. Today there was no hint of sexual chemistry, nor any exchange of emotions. Today he wasn't interested in justice for Rose alone, but for everyone being damaged by pesticides; Grace wanted to be that generous. He had no interest in getting even; she would like to have been so balanced. She didn't know what kept him going in his constant struggle against enormous odds, but wanted to be with him in it, only couldn't. She needed contact on a more human level in order to survive.

'Are you okay, Grace?' Rory said, taking her hand.

It occurred to her then that he thought that she and Jak were lovers. She flushed involuntarily and wished she behaved less like an adolescent. She wanted to run, but felt trapped.

'Grace was great,' Jak said, taking her other hand, causing Rory to withdraw.

'When those cops came down on us for dealing, man was that heavy. Twenty years in a Mexican prison staring you in the face is no minor item. Grace really let them have it.' He glanced at her.

What was he saying? What was he implying about them? Rory's eyes were on her now, demanding the sort of signal that she couldn't give.

'American Chemicals will keep up the same kind of pressure here,' Rory said. 'We've got to expect some real tricky moves against us.'

Last night she had heard a tone in his voice that wasn't here today. She wondered if she had imagined it, or if he was just playing games behind Jak's back.

'You did a fine job getting those depositions. They should really do it for us,' he said.

'How long will their lawyers try to keep us out of court?' – it wasn't what she wanted to say right then.

'I'll move for an early hearing on account of the continuing suffering, I figure we might get a hearing before the summer recess.'

'Summer?' Could she maintain this unnatural situation with Jak that long. And she worried how he might react, if they got a lot of pressure now. 'The suffering those people are being put through is unbelievable, isn't it, Jak?'

'It sure is. And for crummy subsistence pay.'

'It's appalling even if the wages were liveable,' she said.

'Grace,' Rory said, 'the court action won't change that.'

'That's what's so depressing. Nothing seems to change.'

'Economic growth won't change things. That means more pollution; alienations; ill-health; war, exposing us to the terrible potentiality for more evil. Exploitation simply feeds itself. Somewhere down the line we're going to run into a lot of trouble, ravaging disease, starvation, a cataclysm of some kind for sure. I guess I sound like some Old Testament prophet.' Grace followed his gaze which fell upon the next table where plates of half-eaten food were wasted with cigarette butts ground out on them. 'It doesn't seem reasonable that this level of consumption can continue while people starve in our own backyard.'

'It could come pretty soon,' Jak said, 'if that wheat seed has been sown. There could be real problems this year.'

Rory looked at his watch. 'I need to be at my next meeting,' he said, but didn't move. 'How is that investigation looking?'

Jak shrugged. 'There's a missing link. But hell, I'm not sure if I'm the right man to find it anymore. This isn't the kind of investigation I should be conducting. We know the seed was developed; it was grown and has failed; there's motive. But pulling all this together, that's something else.'

'That would be a great court case,' Rory said. 'Show Hirshorn manipulating food commodities while half the world is hungry. Their PR machine would never lift them off their ass.'

'You want to take it over?' Jak offered, glancing at Grace.

Was he she wondered testing her response? Maybe she didn't understand the demands his work made on him, but this investigation seemed more important.

'It would really be somethig to get those guys into court.

247

Between Hirshorn and American Chemicals, we'd turn agriculture around. Do you want *me* to talk to Jimmy Keiller at the CFTC?'

Jak hesitated. He glanced at Grace again.

'Mark Kuhfuss said we only get one chance there,' she said.

'Sure. Jimmy never did tolerate fools.'

'Oh, you know him, Rory?'

'Sure, I had some dealings with him when I was with the Securities Exchange Commission. You have to get your facts right. He's a pretty straight guy.'

'We don't have too many facts. That's the problem.'

'That's how it was when we went after Hirshorn at the SEC. Everyone had a real strong feeling about those guys doing things they shouldn't during their take-over of Crocker-Giant. Hirshorn found all kinds of ways to stop us.'

'What are you saying, Rory?'

'If we'd have nailed them maybe there wouldn't be this problem with wheat. If you don't do it there'll be a lot of people in the world going hungry because of inflated food prices.'

'But even if we got it right about the wheat scam,' Jak said, 'we still don't know for sure they're behind it.'

Time ran out for Rory, he had to get to his next meeting. An awkward silence fell between them like each of them were aware of him wanting to say something that wasn't on the agenda. He didn't and Grace felt let down.

In the street before he climbed onto his bicycle Rory embraced her. He was so close she could smell the warmth of his body, carrying some faint trace of perfume that reminded her of Rose. This was a human response and she didn't want him to let her go or leave her.

'Grace, what you got done in Mexico makes me real proud.'

'Hey, what about me, Rory?'

'Sure, I'm real proud of you too.' He kissed Jak.

After Rory had departed she was confused. Physical contact with him only added to that confusion. She was left with Jak and feared she would somehow stay trapped in this relationship out of gratitude.

Jak was silent as they walked back to the house, pulled deep into his coat against the cold, damp day. She got a strange feeling off him, and thought perhaps he had recognized something going on between Rory and her that she had yet to see herself. Possibly it was that which prompted his next move.

'I've been thinking about quitting the wheat conspiracy investigation,' he said. 'Forgetting the whole thing. Maybe you and Rory can get to concentrate on the pesticide case better.'

She wanted to say that's a great idea, but found herself saying, 'That's crazy, Jak. Why would you want to do that after all that's happened?'

'Maybe for that very reason.'

'You can't just quit. You can't. You know how important it could be. No one else can unscramble this.'

Maybe that did it for him, or maybe it was the message from Kuhfuss on the answerphone that pulled him back.

The grain elevator manager was in Washington for a grain shipping conference and wanted to meet. When Jak called the number he'd left, Kuhfuss invited them both to the National Grain and Feed Association headquarters on 15th Street at conference end. He wouldn't say what he wanted to meet about.

'It can only be about the wheat scam, Jak. It has to be important for him to call you.'

'Then you go,' he said.

'I can't go on my own. He'll want to talk to you.'

Jak paced about the room. 'Jesus Christ, I've got to be crazy getting sucked back into this.'

She watched him grow more agitated as he continued to pace. Finally she said, 'What's the real problem, Jak?'

'Don't you know?' he began. 'Jesus, don't you really know?'

She closed her eyes, not wanting to hear.

'I take my work pretty seriously. Hell, maybe I pay it too much attention. Maybe I figure it's too important to notice anybody around me too much. But I've noticed you, Grace. I think about you a lot. Most of the time.

249

Living here with you like this, well . . . Jesus, I'm not doing too great at this.'

Closing the gap between them, she put her arms around him and kissed him on the cheek. Suspecting this moment was coming and dreading it, she was now surprised at how easily she was able to take control of the situation.

'Jak, I don't know what I would have done without you. I'm very fond of you, you're such a kind man – allowing me space as you have. Without it I don't know where I'd be. Let's go on being good friends, and see what happens.'

Clearly he was disappointed, and for a moment she wasn't sure how he was going to respond. Then he gave a tight smile.

'At least you didn't run over my feelings, Grace, or slam the door. I guess we might find something together at some time.'

She said nothing, but knew she had simply avoided the problem.

'I've got to start putting in a lot more roadwork.'

It was ironical that Colin, her absent husband, should turn up then. That was her first thought, not how he knew where she was. She'd had no contact with him since that night when he collected his belongings from the farm.

There was a long moment of non-recognition when the familiar man in the dark grey business suit came into the room. He had put on weight and had grown a moustache. It rather suited him. Colin smiled, and extended his hand. A total stranger.

She had nothing to say to him so an awkward silence filled the space between them. She glanced at Jak who looked like an intruder in his own house as he watched them, shifting his weight from foot to foot. Why didn't Jak make some small talk? Was he enjoying her discomfort?

Her mind moved on to why Colin was here.

'Life looks good for you,' Jak said, giving a friendly smile.

'I fell on my feet. I'm doing all right.'

'How did you find me?' she wanted to know.

'Oh that,' Colin said. 'It doesn't really matter. There are things we have to talk over.'

'Such as?' she said.

Colin glanced at Jak, then back at her.

'Can we go out somewhere and talk? It's important.'

'Stay,' Jak offered. 'I'll go and meet Mark Kuhfuss. Good to see you again.' He shook Colin's hand.

'Jak . . .?' She pursued him to the door, embarrassed by the situation. She whispered, 'I don't know what he wants.'

'Talk with him. Find out.'

He smiled and went, leaving her stranded.

Back in the sitting-room she found Colin searching through papers, and resented his intrusion more.

'You shouldn't be looking at those,' – grabbing the papers.

'Are they secret?' he asked.

She didn't like this new-found confidence; he'd become as arrogant as he was distant. But then she was no longer that person whom he had helped escape from a smothering father.

'Can we go out?' Colin said. 'Out of your lover's house.'

'We're not lovers.'

'After your trip to Mexico, who are you kidding?' he said, smiling the whole while. 'Not that I care. I don't. Look Grace, I don't want to row. Let me take you out to dinner.'

Her thoughts were in a turmoil. She realized then that Rory couldn't but think she was sleeping with Jak. It was an obvious conclusion. That was why he held back from expressing a clear intention.

'How do you know so much about my movements?'

'You didn't make any secret of it, Grace. I hired a private detective. They call them skiptraces here.'

'I didn't skip anywhere. You're the one who disappeared without a word.'

'I really don't want to argue. Let's go and eat.'

She couldn't think of a logical reason for not going.

'Can you afford this?' she said as they waited to be

251

seated in Clyde's on M Street. Dinner cost $60 for two without the Guinness they served.

Colin became irritated. 'I don't need to count every penny like we did back in our marriage.'

'Well, aren't you the lucky one. I don't have any money at all.'

'You could have. Shearing bought our thirty acres, by the way. And the rest of the farm. His kind always win.'

'How much for?' She felt no sense of loss.

'Twenty-nine thousand. He must have had some sort of crooked deal with the bank. We still owe them thirty-six thousand pounds, even after the milk quota was sold.'

'That hardly seems fair.'

'Nothing is, Grace. You grab what you can, when you can, any way you can. That's what you do if you want to survive. I've got the things from the house if you want any of it. It's not worth much.'

Those relics of their past held no appeal for her.

'Aggrow Chemicals substantially increased their compensation offer – after a bit of persuading. To twenty thousand. I'm going to accept.'

'But we're suing the parent company, American Chemicals.'

'It's a waste of time. You won't win. Not against them.'

'We've depositions from people who lost their children, their husbands, mothers. It was the same poison that killed Rose.'

'You're being irrational. I've seen the work-up sheets on that pesticide, all there is. You won't win. That stuff from Culiácan won't help.'

'How the bloody hell do you know all this?' She was furious, yet a cold glaze fell across her eyes. 'You seem to know so much, you must know I won't give up.'

When he wouldn't answer she turned and started out of the restaurant, but blundered into one of the dining areas instead, becoming confused and thrashing about until she found the exit.

'Grace, stop being so stupid,' he said in the street. 'I'm accepting the compensation.'

'You can't.' She was shocked. 'You can't.'

252

'I'll tell the Immigration people how you escaped from a psychiatric hospital, that you're living with the man who helped you. They're all born-again Christians, the people down at Immigration. They'll kick you out of the country.'

He laughed as she tried to break his grip. People in the street were looking. Next a cop could appear. She wondered what would happen then.

'I need the money, Grace – for the chemical distribution business I've started. You're wrong about Aggrow Chemicals. They help grow better crops for all the hungry people.'

Breaking free, she ran from him then as she would from a madman.

She didn't have her latchkey, so sat on the stoop and wept, feeling sorry for herself, for the years she had spent with such a stranger. She wanted to go to Rory's house and talk to him about how she should handle this, and also to explain about Jak and herself, but wasn't sure if she could just walk in on him, assuming he was home anyway. But after reasoning that he wouldn't live according to rigid social rules like needing a phone call before anybody visited him, she ran all the way to the brown stone house with its timber stoop on Swann Street.

'Grace.' Rory was surprised. He threw the house door open wider to let her in.

She hesitated for only a moment.

She wasn't certain who moved first. Her arms went around him and he lifted his arms to match her embrace. They came together hard and tight in the hall with the street door still open. They kissed. Her hands travelled over his body. She had wanted them there a long while.

'I can't tell you how much I wanted to see you,' he said. 'It seemed like I could never find a moment with you on my own.'

'I know. I wanted you to touch me so much.'

He moved his mouth closer to her and their lips touched again. She felt like she couldn't breathe but she didn't care. Someone appeared down the stairs and went out the door saying something that neither one of them heard.

They went up to his one-roomed apartment, where

books and papers sat around in heaps looking for permanent space. Even the bed was thick with them. The combined anxiety and eagerness that Rory displayed made her smile. Holding him close she looked down his body from over his shoulder, then let her hands go where only her eyes had been, slowly, uncertain at first, then more desperate as the pressure inside her increased, her gentle touch yielding to firmly palming him. But he didn't do anything, and she began to get scared in case something was wrong.

'I know what I want to do,' he said, 'but I don't know how to do it. Do we need to talk about what is happening?'

She kissed him hard, then slowly shook her head as she stepped back from him. 'It'll just happen, I promise.'

With trembling hands she began tearing at his shirt, her fingers not managing to undo the buttons fast enough, wanting to tear them off.

'I've no experience at all of this kind of relationship. I've never made love before.'

The statement didn't mean anything to her, it certainly didn't matter. She guided his hands onto her breasts and he began to gently knead them like it was second nature to him.

'I can feel you against me,' she said. 'It's wonderful. I want you so much, Rory. I want to feel you inside me so much.'

As his confidence grew his hands found a will of their own and moved down her thighs and came right back up, drawing her skirt up ahead of them. Feeling his hands on her bare thighs made her shimmer with excitement. She moaned now into his neck as he became bolder. Her hands moved below and began unfastening his belt.

'Oh, Grace, Grace,' he whispered as her hands held him now. 'I love you so much. I want it to be so perfect.'

'Rory, when you feel this way it's absolutely perfect.'

Lifting her from her buttocks with his hands inside her panties he carried her to the bed. She clung to him like she was drowning.

None of the books or papers got moved from the bed, but all ended up on the floor.

254

Afterwards Rory strode around the apartment, springing up on every step.

'Grace, I can't tell you the feelings and sensations that happened to me. I didn't know feelings like that existed. Grace, it was wonderful. I can't tell you how wonderful that was.'

She smiled and put her arms around him and noticed him get hard against her again, while she felt herself starting to get excited. They made love once more with all the feelings and sensations swamping her like before. Never before had she achieved orgasm on the first occasion with a man, and never twice with her husband.

'Do you think it weird,' Rory said afterwards, 'getting to be thirty-nine before ever making love?'

'I think it's wonderful, Rory. It couldn't be more perfect.'

Jak entered her thoughts for the first time. How would she tell him what had happened? That was something neither of them was sure of doing. Rory offered to speak with him. That seemed like the easy way out, but she couldn't take it.

'No, I'll tell him,' she said. She didn't know how or when, all she knew was that she didn't want to sneak around, pretending this hadn't happened.

She told Rory about Colin's earlier visit and what she believed he might do.

'Unless you're completely crazy, Grace, under our constitution a husband can't sign away his wife's rights. He can take whatever he likes from Aggrow Chemicals. Unless he can prove you were a willing party, our courts will ignore the fact. We'll sue the bastards down to their shorts.'

That made her feel good. She laughed. The feelings of guilt she had about Jak changed the moment she started talking about his relationship with American Chemicals and what he had done to those children down in Mexico. However, the guilt soon flooded back when Rory explained some of what had happened to him subsequently.

255

'Jak knew he was wrong to do what he did down there, right after he'd taken part in those tests. He quit his job and started protesting about what had happened. He did actually go a long way to getting that kind of testing stopped. But then his wife and his son died. Some thugs working for the company burned his house down. Neither Marge nor Pete got out alive.'

'Oh dear God, I don't believe it. The poor man. American Chemicals did that?'

'That was the best guess anyone could come up with. Whether they had planned it that way . . . Nothing was proven. But there was no one else around who'd want to do that.'

She felt sick as the whole ground she found herself on changed, along with the rules, bringing an entirely new perspective on Jak. She couldn't speak for a moment.

'Some things don't need proving,' Rory said. 'You could understand a body running and hiding. I was real surprised when he came back here and started looking at some of that stuff again with you. He's got to be opening up a lot of old wounds.'

'Why didn't he say? You never know what Jak is feeling.'

'He's pretty buttoned down. We're ready to fight that one with him at Christic. He's only got to say the word.'

'Does he never talk about what happened?'

'I've tried talking with him,' Rory said. 'That was a pretty heavy thing to have happen. Maybe he'll talk to you.'

'Not now. I don't think he will.'

'Grace, you'll do whatever is right. You have a good instinct for that. What you can't do is live Jak's problem. None of us can. All we can do is be there to support him when he's ready to take it on.'

She put her arms around him and held him for a long while without saying anything, drawing on his strength just like she was plugged in.

'I'll walk you back. Help you talk with Jak. I'd like to.'

'No.' She smiled. 'It's okay. I'd rather go on my own. I love you, Rory. I love you so much. Do you love me? Do

256

you? Tell me again.'

'I love you, Grace. I love you. I love you. I love you. I don't want you to leave. Not ever. Just move right in here, why don't you? I can't bear the thought of you not being here all the while.'

She smiled again and finally managed to kiss him goodbye.

Back at the house she watched Jak pace agitatedly as she told him what had happened with Colin and why she had gone to Rory's. But right then she couldn't bring herself to speak of what had happened between them. She knew it was a mistake, dishonest of her. She would tell him when the moment was right and she didn't judge it to be so then. Something was troubling him. He knew about them somehow. Perhaps he had detected some change in her that she wasn't seeing. The longer she put it off the bigger an obstacle he would become. But still she couldn't speak about the love affair, not then.

'What's wrong, Jak?'

'Nothing – I'm pissed off at missing Kuhfuss. The guy leaving the conference early like that. He didn't even leave a message about why he had changed his mind about talking to us.'

'Maybe someone changed it for him,' she speculated. 'Jak, Rory said what happened to your family – why didn't you tell me?'

'Jesus Christ!' Without any warning anger exploded out of him. 'He's such a bleeding heart, that guy. He likes to make everyone out a cripple.'

'He wants to help. I want to help. You want to know what that is?'

'Don't pity me, Grace. I don't want that. It was all a long while ago. Forget it.'

'It looks to me like you haven't even begun grieving.'

'Jesus Christ! All I need around here is a little space to myself to do some work – so I can make some money . . .'

Seeing that as some kind of criticism of her, she stepped back. Shocked. Hurt. Knowing she had to tell Jak what had happened right then. As the words formed in her mind, he reached for the phone that started ringing.

257

Rory was on the line. He said in response to Jak's brusque tone, 'I'm sorry, Jak – these things happen, I guess.'

'What the hell are you talking about, Rory – well I don't need your pity. I'll work out what happened to Marge and Pete my own way.'

There was silence between them.

'What is it you want, Rory?'

'Look, I called Jimmy Keiller. Can you two guys be around at the Commodity Futures Trading Commission for eleven tomorrow morning? I've fixed for you to meet with them.'

'You figure we've got something to tell him?'

'The Enforcement Division's been hearing rumours about Hirshorn buying a lot of wheat. He'll listen.'

'Fine,' Jak said, 'but will he take action without evidence?'

'Maybe Kuhfuss will supply the missing link. The CFTC are taking a serious look at Hirshorn. Any help you give them.'

Jak managed to reach Mark Kuhfuss as he arrived at his office in Galveston the following morning.

'Grace and I have a meeting this morning with Jimmy Keiller,' he told him. 'I figured you'd fill in some holes, Mr Kuhfuss.'

'I'm not sure how, Dr Redford,' Kuhfuss said. 'If there was anything to this wheat conspiracy theory of yours, I'm sure Hirshorn would be glad to help in any way they could.'

'Then talk to us. Tell us about those shipments.'

There was silence from down the phone.

'What do I tell those guys, Mr Kuhfuss? Have we got something to run with?' Jak waited. 'Mr Kuhfuss?'

'Hirshorn's delivery manifests are three and four times oversubscribed,' Kuhfuss said.

'What does that mean?'

'Customers have more wheat ordered than they'll take delivery of . . . Look, I'm sorry about yesterday. I got to thinking about the situation some. I don't want to do anything to hurt Caddy Hirshorn. Why don't you come out here, maybe we can figure someway to go on this – let me check my diary.'

He suggested them meeting Wednesday morning, but refused to say anything until then, not even when Jak pushed him.

'Do you really think he's got something?'

'The hell do I know? The smart thing to do, Grace, is to put off this meeting we have at the CFTC. Until we see what Kuhfuss comes up with.'

'What if he doesn't come up with anything more than we have now? What if he's just trying to find out what we've got?'

'Then I guess that would be as good a jumping off point as any. If the Enforcement Division turn us down, we've got to figure that's it, Grace.'

She said nothing, knowing the one thing that would keep him running was the one thing she couldn't give him now.

The office Jimmy Keiller occupied on the sixth floor of the building on K Street was spartan. There wasn't one personal item around the place, not a photo, a certificate, a baseball glove. Nor was there one single comfortable chair in the room. The room disturbed Grace. Why would anyone live like this? This level of self-denial was some kind of sickness, she felt. Keiller himself was living denial; his short, intense body was as stripped-down as his office; he wore a dark green utilitarian cotton suit that looked like it would wash and tumble dry. His hands were the only things not buttoned down. As he listened to their story, with only occasional interruptions for clarification, he made cat's cradles with a large rubber band. Every now and again his glance settled on Grace, making her feel uncomfortable.

Story's end left him clearly unimpressed. 'My training as a lawyer tells me that no matter how good the tale is, it's nowhere without evidence. I understand from Rory your track record in your own particular field of research is one hundred per cent, sir. But here you're kind of short on evidence. The kind that I can act on.'

'Someone is buying a lot of wheat futures,' Grace said.

She had sensed from the moment they walked into his room that he wouldn't believe them.

'The weather's been harming grain production some. Unless they get rain in the Midwest, it'll hurt more. The large-trader reports filed with us don't indicate any kind of corner, by Hirshorn or anybody else. Do you know how much wheat is needed to take a corner, Mrs Chance? You're talking fifteen, maybe twenty million tons. You got to be some kind of magician to sneak that on by.'

'We're not crazy,' Jak said, pacing now with frustration. 'Sure we don't have hard evidence. That's why Rory sent us down here. He told us you could put together an investigation.'

'What is it we investigate, Dr Redford? Your story is pretty fantastic. Hirshorn's market manoeuvring is enough for us to start asking some questions maybe. But genetically engineered wheat being sold to the Russians doesn't make me pause. How the hell would they buy wheat nowadays? I figure Rory was more than a mite pissed off about missing Hirshorn while he was with the SEC. I can see why he'd believe there was some substance to this story of yours, why he'd call me. But for us to go full tilt at Hirshorn, we'd need to be two hundred per cent certain and have a locker full of evidence. Those people buy political and judicial favour like ordinary folk buy shirts.'

Keiller put his rubber band aside and rose, indicating the meeting was over. 'Why don't you talk to Kuhfuss, see if he holds any kind of key to this. I feel I should encourage you – who knows, you could get lucky. But you'd need to come back here with just a smidgen of evidence at least. Call me.' He gave them his card.

Riding down in the elevator Jak folded his arms over the top of his head and leant against the wall.

'I guess this is too imaginative for bureaucrats like these.'

Grace mistakenly read his mood for disappointment.

'We can push on with it, Jak,' she said.

'I don't know. Maybe I did make a mistake.'

'What's really getting to you?' What had happened last night popped up in her mind, and she wished now that she

260

had told him for she didn't judge this the right moment.

'Withdrawal symptoms. I feel kind of relieved. Like now I can quit. I need to get back to work, to constructing a wheat that will benefit everybody.'

'So that people like Hirshorn can manipulate it in the marketplace for more profit while half the world goes hungry.'

'Grace, you're getting to sound a mite like Rory – it's boring.' His statement surprised them both. 'There's not too much we scientists can do about the marketplace.'

She clenched her fists into tight balls, wanting to hit him. 'I'll go with it, if that's okay. Maybe boring Rory will help too.'

'Shit!' Jak tried to force open the doors as the car arrived in the lobby. 'The whole thing'll get to become some kind of moral crusade against the evil empire of profit – there's nothing wrong with profit. That's how most science gets funded.'

'Well, what's it to be, Jak? Do you want to go on with this, or do you want me to go on alone with Rory? I will, happily.'

'Look, I'll give it one more shot with Kuhfuss. If he comes through – if not, you'd better make do with what you got on those pesticides. But I've got to tell you, I don't feel good about it. It feels to me like I'm making a big mistake here.'

Grace smiled, believing he was just looking for excuses.

'Are the CFTC running a full-scale investigation on us?' Caddy Hirshorn asked, sitting on the edge of his hospital bed. 'Or is that just rumour?'

'The head of the Enforcement Division talked with Margaret Meredith. She gave the go ahead for a full-scale investigation,' Shapiro said. He watched his boss stand unsteadily and turn towards the electrically operated recliner, wondering if he should offer to help him, call a nurse or leave him to his own devices. A couple of times recently when he had offered to help Caddy he'd been curtly brushed aside. He didn't know why he was getting that kind of treatment, but he reasoned that maybe it was

261

nothing to do with him, but the state of Caddy's health. If there had been some other kind of problem he was sure he'd have heard. He got to hear about most things that happened around the grain division, along with all kinds of other things outside that could affect the company. Like the decision made by the CFTC Commissioner to investigate Hirshorn. That was passed to Shapiro from a friend working on the security floor at the Commission.

Although this move could potentially cause them a lot of problems, Caddy didn't seem unduly worried. He wasn't sure why, unless it was that his boss believed the scheme they had set in train was politically unstoppable. But then he didn't think Caddy could either be that arrogant or so badly underestimate the power of either the Commission or the Boards of Trade to make a trader divest part or the whole of his holding. There were many details to attend to still if they were to bring this off, and dealing with them from his room at the Hirshorn Memorial Hospital, even one as luxurious as this, wasn't the best place. He figured his boss was worrying more about his health than he pretended to.

'The liver has eighty-five per cent over-capacity,' Caddy said, lowering himelf onto his recliner and tilting it back. 'After those cancerous nodules were removed, I'm down to around eighty-four per cent over-capacity. I can live a long while with that kind of safety margin, especially with the signals it's continuing to send the market. That's the minimum I want for Hirshorn on this deal. The very minimum – eighty-four per cent overkill.'

'I figure we've got it. Every bushel of wheat we've optioned is clearly assigned to a customer.'

Caddy flicked his hand dismissively. There was no strength there. 'We've had the CFTC policemen sniffing around before.'

'What concerns me is Margaret Meredith getting excited about that plant geneticist's speculations.'

'So it should. You haven't taken those two people seriously enough,' Caddy said, fixing him with his round, pale blue eyes.

That stung him. He could have kept back the

information about the Commission, held off warning of the danger he saw in Mark Kuhfuss. The problem he saw here was Caddy's arrogant attachment to his own unswerving belief in the loyalty of his employees, regardless of circumstances. That prevented him responding to these dangers. Now he was unfairly blaming him. He showed none of his feelings, for he knew one day soon he too would be rich. Not Caddy's kind of rich, but enough to compensate for the stinging he suffered.

'You'd better get those people headed off someplace, and fast. Do it before they reduce our margin of safety. You've had enough warnings about them.'

Finding this criticism life-threatening, he began sucking in air through his teeth, trying to stop himself suffocating. He knew who he'd have to go to to get this done, but wasn't sure any longer if it was such a good idea.

With one leg a full inch shorter than the other, Wilf Fear was better adapted physically than most people to golf, and far better adapted mentally, Shapiro found. They were playing nine holes before breakfast on Hains Point Course in East Potomac Park. Although this was a more discreet meeting place than his West Executive Building office, it wasn't so discreet that stopping for a leak on the fairway whenever the need took him passed unnoticed. Washingtonians were sensitive to people pissing in public.

Two properly attired players scurried past with their trolleys, glancing back at Wilf Fear leaking into the wind.

When he had finished he lurched back over to tee off.

'We figured you were going to do something about Redford and his lady, Wilf. They're getting more troublesome.'

'Doing *something* is real easy. Doing something that doesn't rebound and knock us on our ass is something else.' He took a practice swing while waiting for the two players who had overhauled them to get clear.

'How long do we wait? Till they blow the whole goddamn scheme?'

'You're in such a big hurry, hire some *pistoleros*.'

'I figured that's what you were, buddy.'

263

Wilf Fear hit his ball squarely, lifting it three hundred yards, adequately expressing his feeling.

'I've got to tell you, *buddy*,' he said, 'the sands have shifted so far we can no longer even recognize the line that most suits your outfit in this deal. When this had got started, there still existed an old Evil Empire. But it's disappeared so fast that the whole of the State Department went into tailspin. Being good old Americans we are opening our billfolds. Of course this action had gotten buoyed by the popular groundswell for every new landmark in Russian affairs. What happened back then was the reactionary hawks in the government and Pentagon had run for cover. No one wanted to listen to their alarm calls. But I've got to tell you, Pat, those guys regrouped, they found themselves a new strategy, and are quietly promoting it behind the scenes. The spectre of fascism is rising out of the chaos. They are drawing influential figures into their powerful orbit. There is no political posturing or sabre rattling that anyone wants to support publicly. But they are ready to make their moves, guys in the CIA, in the Pentagon, on some of the most powerful committees in both the Senate and the House. These are the kind of people who form powerful cabals that devise policy entirely separate from that of the elected government, and having devised it, advise the President. They don't plan on losing that power. Their advice is to put on the brakes, close the chequebook. They are saying all the struggling for national identity within the independent Russian states is going to lead to a massive conflagration in Eastern Europe. So be prepared. This cabal doesn't give a shit how much money Hirshorn was going to make as a result of Russia's misfortune. But with the seeds of Russia's imminent agricultural misfortune sown, they might see more to be gained from the Russians learning about it.'

'Jesus Christ!' Shapiro said, his breathing becoming laboured. His knuckles were white on his club handle. 'What do they aim to do?'

'Maybe nothing just yet. Not before your company makes its killing in the markets anyhow.' He waited.

264

'If they do inform the Russians, Hirshorn will be flat on its ass.'

'I'm a policy advisor, Pat, not a policy maker. I'm a facilitator not an innovator. I don't have any instruction about the problems the Ukrainian and Georgian states are going to have with their wheat harvests. Officially no one in the State Department or anyplace else knows about that. All I'm trying to do here is alert to these shifts in the political climate. I'm talking to you like this because I don't want to see you blown off course.'

He took a deep slow breath in through his teeth. Then another. He decided to adopt Caddy Hirshorn's bold position, wanting to believe it. 'There ain't a thing to be done to change this now, Wilf. In a month or so the Russians will know their wheat's failed. They won't need the Pentagon or the CIA to tell them. Then they'll start looking to buy.'

'I guess it's all a question of timing – whether you guys at Hirshorn are rich assholes or flat busted assholes.'

'I figure we could all live with being rich,' he said. 'This is only an assessment of the situation?'

'You bet.'

Shapiro nodded. 'You meanwhile had better get something done about Redford and his lady.'

He was headed right back to Oklahoma to talk with Caddy. He thought about talking to his partners in England first, but finally decided not to call Shearing, as much as he would have liked that. If Fear's warning was valid and the hawks moved ahead of them and the Russians retaliated by not purchasing wheat in the US, they'd still need to get it someplace. That might put him and his partners in a stronger position.

19

'TWO SLEEPLESS NIGHTS AND TWO pretty miserable days, and I tell you folks, I'm no nearer to resolving the dilemma I find myself in. It's a bitch,' Mark Kuhfuss told them.

Grace could see clearly that he was troubled. He had taken on a grey, worn look; there was helplessness in his eyes.

'I would have liked to have talked with Caddy Hirshorn to try turning him around before I talked with you. But he's in hospital. You know he's got some kind of cancer. I guess there is no one else – apart from that guy you saw at the Commission, Jimmy Keiller. But that would be to strike directly against Hirshorn. I figure there was no way for you not to arrive out here. You're like death and taxes. I guess the outcome could be just as tough. But Christ, I've got to do something or we're going to get to a point where there is no turning back. Maybe we got there already.'

All the while he was talking Grace could barely contain her impatience, it was leaving her breathless. She realized this man was about to open a door that revealed everything, and she wanted him to go right to the door. But she was afraid in case he suddenly took fright at the consequences for his company and backed off.

'I don't know if it was smart bringing you out here,' he said, slowly shaking his head. He got up from his desk and went to feel the coffee jug on the electric stand. He took some cups from a deep drawer, poured them some coffee and brought it to them, then went back behind his desk, sat and remained silent.

266

'What is on your mind, Mr Kuhfuss?' Jak asked.

Kuhfuss looked across at him, then at Grace. She smiled encouragingly.

'It's not safe for you to go on with your inquiries, not the way you're going about it.'

'Is there some other way to go?'

The plant manager didn't answer.

'What happens if we do?' She didn't think there could be so much worse than what happened to them in Mexico.

Kuhfuss suddenly became animated. He said, 'You come out here poking around, picking up all kinds of dumb shit. A rumour here, maybe half a rumour there, like you don't know squat. Have you got any idea what's going down on this deal? Billions of dollars. Think of the pressure that puts on people.'

Jak nodded slowly. 'Someone might kill us to stop us.'

The casual way in which Jak said that, impressed her. Such realities might have been his daily stock in trade. But then she thought about how someone killing them was a real possibility, and she got scared.

'The people I work for don't ordinarily conduct business like that. But with this kind of money involved, who knows what might happen. Turn right around, and head back to Washington. Forget the whole thing. That's my advice.'

The statement created a moment between her and Jak. It confirmed that there was a wheat conspiracy, even if they didn't have the evidence to satisfy the CFTC. Maybe they'd never get that.

'You had us come all this way to hear that, Mr Kuhfuss?'

There was a long silence. Kuhfuss went back to the coffee machine and switched it off, then switched it on again. He walked to the computer console and made exactly the same move. He picked up a rubber band and stretched it over his big hands until it broke. All displacement activity.

'I've been trading grain good years and bad years ever since I hauled a trailer load off my Daddy's farm when the bank closed us out. I remember those times with a deep sense of shame and injustice. That members of your own

267

species could do that to you, much less Americans. My folks had worked themselves into the ground to meet the note on that land only to see their sorghum and corn shrivel on the stalk for want of water two years in a row. There was no cushion to fall back on. It was a hard business then – it still is a hard business. In a good year you make a penny on a bushel. It's an unforgiving business; you've got to best everybody who's trying his damnest to shaft you. You bring off a big deal, you live with your enemies. Other times you try not to get caught short in a rising market. It kinda makes life interesting, that's why you do it, I guess. Hirshorn survives because it knows its business.

'I don't mind the Russians getting screwed – they know how the game gets played. They beat our farmers near to death back in the seventies. They picked up so much cheap wheat here they re-exported some of it at a profit. But what's about to happen to them now is something else. The poor bastards just about learn how to farm so it can work for them, so they'll be able to have enough in a moderately good year, then . . . They're not only going to be short a whole pile of wheat, but they'll get mashed when they come here to buy. They're not going to be able to sneak in here like they did in '72. No way. Hirshorn are gonna be waiting.'

'Your boss has bought all of the wheat.'

'He sure is trying. Do you know what that'll do to the Spot – the cash market for wheat? There won't be a bushel to be had anyhow. Prices'll go crazy.'

He stopped at the computer where his thick fingers dropped onto the keys. A set of figures appeared on the monitor.

'We got companies down here to take every bushel of the twenty million tons we got control of. Millers, feed processors, even feed lots for Christsake! – feed lots, can you believe, buying up Number two hard red. My guess is not a quarter of it will get to those customers.'

'It's all headed for Russia instead?'

'Mrs Chance, it'll head out to whoever's got the biggest need and the best price. Russia, if they can ante up. The

Russians'll try to get some from Hungary or France, even India. They'll pick up a little grain from old friends. But with the volume they'll need, and the price wheat will make on the world market, there'll be but one place they can buy from.'

He paused. Grace found herself holding her breath in case he decided to stop now.

He didn't. 'Hirshorn has a new contract in place with the Seamen's Union. It allows for Soviet shipping to carry fifty per cent of any grain they purchase. We had to give a lot away to get that. The seamen got guarantees that the US fleet would get to haul twelve million tons of grain minimum, of all we export. I figure we expect to get a hell of a lot more back.'

'Let's go back a piece,' Jak said. 'How was that seed got to Russia?'

'Through a French grain dealer Hirshorn sometimes use – he sold them three hundred thousand tons . . .'

'Three hundred . . .? That's fifteen million tons off the field,' she said, instantly doing a rough calculation in her head. She was always good at arithmetic.

'The Russians'll be looking for maybe twenty-five million. This was a hybrid vigour yielding around five tons an acre. Come May, they will be in deep, deep shit. That's without any regular grain failure.' He got some more figures up on the monitor. 'May hard red is now standing at $138 a ton. When the Russians get here they could be looking at around $180. Maybe more. Who the hell knows.'

'That's four and a half billion dollars' worth of wheat.' Jak glanced at Grace.

She found herself still calculating.

'Can you imagine four and a half billion dollars? Can anybody? You read those figures in the financial pages, that kind of money keeps Poland afloat.'

She thought about the sums involved. She could not imagine what one billion dollars would buy, nor what space it would fill, much less four and a half billion.

'Help us to stop them,' she said, like that was a reasonable request and a possible goal.

Kuhfuss's laughter was neither mocking nor mirthful.

269

'A deal with that kind of tab, Mrs Chance? Jesus. I keep thinking about those poor bastards in Russia working all year only to see their crops fail. Just like my own folks, broken-backed and broken-hearted, the dun at the door.'

'It's an act of war, destroying a country's harvest,' Jak said. 'The Russians will get pretty steamed.'

'They'll be pretty mad, sure. You figure they can go to war? They'd have to borrow the money first. Who'd lend it? You figure our people didn't work that out when they got this started? Anyhow, the Russians bought the seed from a Frenchman, Pierre d'Estaing.'

'Was he in on the deal?' she asked.

'I don't know. I guess he had to be.'

Jak summarized the situation: 'Hirshorn are buying wheat futures well in excess of real sales. They plan on taking delivery. Hirshorn bought Crocker-Giant, the seed company, then financed the development of a hybrid wheat seed that attracts the Take-all virus. They sold it to the Frenchman for the Russians . . .'

'D'you get that from Crocker?' Kuhfuss asked. Then stopped and looked between them. 'Jesus, you people haven't got anything more than the kind of speculation I've been making.'

'We know the work was done. The seed got sold to Russia.'

'When I called you,' Kuhfuss said, 'I figured you had something more than a string of coincidences to excite Jimmy Keiller with. When Hirshorn's domestic customers are delivered short and surplus gets sold to Russia, who do you figure will complain? The Russians won't admit to getting suckered. They're in such a mess they may not even know. Americans will bitch at maybe having to pay five dollars for a loaf of bread. But what the hell. Could be it'll cost more than five dollars – there wasn't much snow in the Midwest this winter.'

She got to it quicker than Jak. 'There won't be much moisture in the ground to swell the wheat.'

'That's right. Underproduction here only needs to combine with maybe flooding in India – which happens

270

more and more as they strip out their trees – along with what you people call a drought in Europe, Mrs Chance. Wheat could make eight or nine dollars a bushel. That would mean a lot more people around the world starving than there are already.'

'While Hirshorn makes a big, fat profit.'

'No argument there.' Kuhfuss picked up his phone that was buzzing like it refused to be ignored.

As he listened he suddenly became agitated.

'What are you telling me? The FBI didn't get done with their investigation? They found how many tons hidden there? No way! Look, I'll be right over.' He snapped the phone back and brushed his forehead like some insect had settled there. He looked at his visitors.

'Is there a problem?' Grace asked. Concern was written on his face.

'I don't know what the hell's going on here. Something is not right.' He glanced at the monitor. 'You know what those figures relate to? They're the over-filled wheat orders Hirshorn have taken. Two, three times more than they ordinarily fill for those customers. I guess the people at the CFTC might make something of those.' He turned away from the screen. 'Something came up. Help yourself to coffee and anything else you need.'

He went out quickly.

'What do you figure that was about?' Jak said.

She shook her head, thinking about the information that was on the VDU.

'Can we stop this happening, Jak?' she said.

'Maybe we're not assembling the details in the right order.'

'This might impress the CFTC – Mr Keiller said if we got some evidence they'd have to take us seriously. We could take a printout of this.'

'Would you know how to?' he asked.

She paused to consider the console, feeling confident from the work she'd done on their farm computer. The printer on the table was a relatively quiet machine, but when it started up it sounded to them like hammers were striking an anvil, alerting everyone to what they were doing.

271

The list of Hirshorn's customers seemed endless. There was page after page of densely packed information. Twenty million tons was a lot of wheat to disperse, even when that was only happening on paper. Finally it stopped and she pulled the folded sheets free. She turned to Jak, who was checking through papers on Kuhfuss's desk.

'Look at this.' He pointed to what looked like computer entry codes in the front of the diary. 'Can you access those shipments of wheat seed?'

All that was required was the right nine digit code. Then as if by magic the details appeared on the screen. But it was meaningless to them. Thousands of tons of wheat had gone out through the terminal, none of it to Russia.

'Ask about Prairie Red Number Two wheat seed,' Jak said.

She accessed the code, then programmed the question. 'Incorrect procedure' came up. In the diary were a whole series of codes. On the fourth attempt information on shipments of Prairie Red came up, giving the shipper, the broker, cost, freight and insurance; 301,209 tons of it on a mixture of Russian and East European ships, booked by a French shipping agent, Charles d'Eon for the purchasing agent Pierre d'Estaing and all bound for Odessa.

'Mr Kuhfuss wouldn't take kindly to that.'

The voice startled them. Kuhfuss's secretary was standing in the doorway.

'No, I guess he wouldn't,' Jak said.

Grace felt little better than a thief, but that didn't stop her tearing the sheets out of the printer.

'He wants you to join him up on silo nine. He'll meet you.'

She gave them directions, saying nothing about the pages as Grace folded them away into the small purse that was across her shoulder.

Taking the tiny elevator to the top of the silos was a nerve-racking experience. The car was an open cage, which made the height more frightening. Anxiety closed off any thoughts Grace might have had about why they were being invited up here.

There was no one to meet them at the top of the series of twenty-seven interconnected concrete silos.

'Gosh, you don't realize how big these are,' she said, feeling no less anxious for being out of the elevator. She hadn't realized before how heights affected her.

An operative in a zip-through coverall and wearing a dust helmet over his face appeared from among the superstructure that carried the conveyor belts.

'Is Mr Kuhfuss around?' Jak asked.

'He sure is. In the silo there,' – pointing with a wrench he was carrying across to the open hatch. He offered the wrench to Jak. 'He needs that.'

It was large and heavy and stained at the business end.

'That looks like blood.' Jak laughed nervously.

'Yep – sure does.'

The operative stepped into the elevator and shut the gate.

Crossing to the steel hatch that was open to the silo, they peered into the arc-lit gloom below. Grace felt suddenly sick. There was a lot of space between the rim of the hatch and the grain a hundred feet below. She had to turn away quickly and gripped one of the steel poles of the large tripod over the hatch.

'There's somebody down there. It looks like Kuhfuss.'

The edge in his voice forced her to turn back and peer over the rim. She took some deep breaths, telling herself not to vomit. As her eyes adjusted to the light she saw him stretched out.

'He looks like he's dead,' Jak said.

As his words faded there was an awful empty silence.

The wind blew through the superstructure. The early afternoon sun had lost all of its heat.

Blood drained from her face.

'Are you sure he's dead, Jak?' she asked.

There was no way anyone could tell from up here, but the way he was lying gave her a strange feeling.

'Hey, buddy,' Jak called, turning back. But the operative had disappeared. Grace screamed as the wrench slipped from Jak's hand causing him to reach over

273

for it. But it plummeted into the gloom, burying itself in the grain far below.

'It's okay,' he said. 'Take it easy.'

The words meant nothing. She was trembling uncontrollably. 'What are we going to do?' she said. Rory popped into her thoughts. She decided he would know what to do. Perhaps Kuhfuss wasn't dead. Maybe that wasn't his blood on the wrench. 'We must try to help him, Jak.'

'What do you mean we have to help him? What do you have in mind for us to do, Grace? Go down there?'

That notion obviously held no more appeal for him than it did her. But she knew that one of them had somehow to climb onto the bosun's chair, which was on the tripod over the hatch, and be lowered into that vast cavern.

Her stomach started to rise in her mouth as she watched Jak reach for the chair and swing himself out onto it. He hung over that empty space but couldn't seem to move. She couldn't make any move to help him. If he asked her to lower the chair she wouldn't be able to. At that moment she despised herself for being like this.

'There's a phone in the elevator,' he told her. 'Get some help up here. Get some help, Grace. Get going.'

She watched him let go the rim of the hatch to lower himself by the electric winch. She shrieked as the drum jolted, almost tipping Jak from the chair.

'Get going,' he called at her. 'Go on. Use the phone.'

Taking some deep breaths, she let go of the tripod leg and started back across the top of the silo.

Wrenching the elevator gate open, she almost tipped headlong into the empty shaft. She screamed and flung herself back, shaking and sobbing. The elevator wasn't there. It didn't occur to her right away that somebody might have tampered with the safety override that should have stopped the gate being opened; she was trying to stop herself shaking.

Slowly she crawled across the deck of the silo and inched her way up the side of the balustrade, but couldn't at first bring herself to look over the side. Finally when she managed to she got dizzy. She didn't know what to do. She told herself over and over again that she was being stupid. That her mind and the demands of the situation could readily overcome this disability. It seemed to work when at last she managed to open her eyes. A yardworker below looked like an ant. She shouted but couldn't get his attention. She would have to try and go down the outside metal staircase at the end of the row. She shouted again but her voice was suddenly drowned by the overhead conveyors starting up, running empty.

Instantly she knew what this meant, and fighting down her panic she ran now, back to the open hatch. There was no time for feeling sick or being afraid. Jak was still on the bosun's chair inching his descent to the grain level. She had to get him out of there quickly.

'Jak!' her voice seemed like a distant croak. 'Jak, get out. Jak. Get out of there. Get out.'

He obviously couldn't hear her. She saw him step off the chair onto the grain and sink into it as he tried to walk across to Kuhfuss. She called again and again, her voice sounded like it was echoing through the deep tube.

Finally he looked up from examining Kuhfuss's body as the first grains of wheat started tipping off the moving conveyor into the silo. More fell, then more and soon there was a stream and then she could no longer see him. Her mind and senses were suddenly assaulted, and through this assault she found herself running along what seemed like the thousand miles of conveyor ducting at the top of the silo, looking for an emergency stop button, knowing there had to be one, and that if she didn't find it Jak would soon be dead. Maybe he was already dead. In her panic she ran right on past the red control box, but something registered and she turned back. The conveyor juddered to a halt the moment she hit the button, and an alarm bell started up. She didn't know whether that meant danger, or that help would soon arrive. How soon she couldn't guess, but decided it wouldn't be soon enough for Jak. A single respirator was hanging inside the control box; the thought that hit her when she saw it made her tremble. But somehow she knew she had to try and go down into the silo to get Jak out.

Dense, oily dust swirled around in the space and she could see nothing as she peered in. The light from the arc lamp came right back at her like headlamps in fog.

'Jak? Jak?' she called. She wanted to cry when there was no response.

Instead she grabbed the auxiliary control panel to the bosun's chair and brought it up fast, praying Jak would somehow be on it. The chair startled her as it burst through the gloom full of wheat. She tipped it out then climbed aboard, pulling on the respirator without even thinking about what was below. Descending was as anxious-making as driving through fog. The impact on the grain below was totally shocking and she was thrown out of the chair. She thrashed about on the wheat, trying to locate Jak. When she couldn't, she believed at once that he was dead. How could anyone possibly have survived in this? Irrationally she felt guilty at that moment for the relationship she had started with Rory. She began to cry. A choking sound stopped her. She turned about, trying to see, trying to touch something other than grain; joy at once rushing at her. Jak was still alive! Was it possible or had she imagined it? She scrabbled forward, listening for another sound. Turning first one way, then another, getting totally disoriented. When the short sound came, a faint cough, it startled her. Jak was right alongside her. She pulled his shoulders clear and removed the respirator and put it on him. Then dug the rest of him clear, the exertion in this atmosphere was exhausting and she started to cough. She felt like she was choking. She tried to get Jak into the chair but couldn't. The effort proved too much for her. Oh dear God, what am I doing so wrong in my life? She tried again, and when finally she managed to push him into the seat and bring the strap over him there wasn't another thing she could do. She collapsed on the grain. She tried to move her hands to find the control box, but every exertion was painful now. Her lungs burned and she coughed, and as she did, so she breathed deeper, which made her lungs hurt more. Take some slow and easy breaths and go to sleep, she could hear a voice saying. She was tired. She wanted to sleep.

276

The grain settled to the contours of her body as she lay on it, packing it down as she vibrated from coughing. If she kept perfectly still she could avoid some of the pain, but she mustn't even breathe.

Jak simply hung there on the seat, a dead weight slumped against the strap. She got a lot of comfort from him being with her. Maybe he was asleep too now.

Unless you move you'll die. The thought jolted her awake. She realized that she had to get the respirator off Jak. That was their only hope. But the effort was proving too much. The image of her out on her first half-marathon with Jak came to her. Her lungs had had the same searing pain then when she thought she was going to die. Only on those runs her mind wouldn't allow her to be defeated. She reached into the same place to get herself through the pain. She knelt and pulled the mask from Jak's face and put it to her own and sucked clean air into her lungs. It made her cough and drop the mask. Panic tried to take the upperhand. She fought it and found the mask at once and strapped it on.

Putting her legs either side of Jak's waist to sit on his lap, she hugged him along with the winch wire as they slowly ascended out of the silo. Grace wrenched off the respirator and sucked in clean air, coughing out what dust she could. When she turned back to Jak he was tipping forward against the strap, dangling over the silo. That sick feeling rose in her again, but she resisted it as she pulled the chair clear and released the strap, spilling him out onto the deck. She cleaned the grain from his mouth and put hers over his and breathed air into his lungs. Almost at once he started to cough and splutter. It was a painful process. She kissed him and held him like she didn't want him to breathe, crying now all the while. Her tears leaving streaks through the dust on his face.

The alarm bell was still going, but no one had responded.

'I thought you were dead,' she said, holding him. 'Oh Jak, I thought you were dead.' She kissed him again, and tried to stop her tears.

'Someone killed Kuhfuss,' he croaked finally in a

277

hoarse whisper. 'Somebody tried to kill us too . . .' His voice disappeared.

The statement made her shake violently, as if realizing for the first time the enormity of what had happened. 'We really did find something.'

'Oh shit,' Jak whispered and began to shake too, then he started to cough.

She held him close to herself and felt better for it. Slowly her breathing recovered to normal, but she couldn't easily adjust to what had happened to them.

The three police cars that eventually swooped across the railroad tracks, klaxons wailing, signalled some kind of help, if not hope. She watched their arrival from the side of the silo. Then slowly her fear-clogged mind came to understand that the six uniformed cops who climbed from the cars and ran toward the silos with drawn pistols weren't about to help them.

'Jak?' Her tone said it all.

'I've got a real bad feeling we've been set up for this killing,' he said.

'That can't happen. It can't!' She was shocked. 'We'll tell them the whole story. Everything.'

'With the kind of money that's involved here, you figure they'll believe us? Our taking the rap for killing Kuhfuss is just perfect. Jesus Christ.' The raw fear in his voice frightened her more. 'My fingerprints are on that wrench. They're all over that wrench, goddamn it.'

The breathless, helpless anxiety that came at her was like that in a familiar dream where she had committed an irreparable crime that took her beyond morality. Only now she wasn't dreaming and hadn't committed any crime, but still she was afraid the record would never be set straight.

'Let's get away from here, Jak. So we can think. Please.'

'I don't know what to do,' he said.

A terrifying thought occurred to her then. They might put her back in hospital, imprison her with drugs. The more you protested the more drugs you were given. 'This won't be like Mexico,' she said, 'where the charges were

278

laughable. Whoever did this really means to stop us. We should get out of here.'

He ran with her to the end of the silos, where the metal staircase took them down to the ground. They hit the bricks and started to run again, but didn't go ten yards before he pulled her up sharply.

'Grace, this is America. We didn't kill anybody.'

'I know,' she said. 'We're just trying to stop someone making four and a half billion dollars.'

'Hold it right there, mister.'

The voice, a rasp on the edge of panic, caused her to half turn. A cop at the end of the silo had a gun levelled at them. The instinct of flight in both of them took over at the exact same instant. A shot rang out as they ran. Grace found that deeply shocking, somehow assuming the policeman wouldn't fire because they were innocent. She wanted to turn back and protest, but Jak tugged her on. Her dust-filled lungs were painful from the exertion, she couldn't imagine how his must be feeling, and wasn't sure if they'd make it to the car.

The Mustang convertible had been the only car Avis had had available at the airport. Jak had argued that it was an unreasonable expense as he wasn't making any money. Now as he floored the gas pedal Grace was glad they hadn't tried another rental company. Maybe Avis wouldn't be quite so glad as the gate barrier ahead of them rolled across their path. The Hirshorn guard, with his pistol drawn, didn't manage to get off a shot as the car hit the gap, snapping its wing-mirrors clear off and taking a gouge out of either side. Almost at once the police klaxons began wailing as those cars came after them.

Voicing what was a mutual doubt, Grace said, 'Can we outrun them?'

'Our best hope is to dump this and run.'

'I don't see how. They'll see us.'

Anger flared from Jak. 'Then you think of something, Grace!' He started to cough.

She closed her eyes almost in prayer, but had no better ideas.

The car raced across the railroad tracks, where the

warning bell and the flashing red lights signalled an approaching freighter bound for the elevator. Clearly the police drivers knew what they were doing, and as they hit Port Boulevard, that ran parallel to the railroad tracks, they put on a lot of speed, closing the distance between them. Soon they would overhaul them. She shouted a warning to Jak over the whine of the engine. For a moment she thought he was letting the car go out of control as he wrenched on the wheel and veered off the highway, buffeting them across the railroad only yards ahead of the freight train. She closed her eyes as the engineer blasted its horn. Somehow they were clear but headed back into the enclosed waterfront area.

The next shock was when they roared along the quay. She was sure the car wouldn't stop. But its brakes held.

'Get out,' Jak bellowed.

She didn't argue. He held his foot on the brake pedal through the open car door, then suddenly released it and leapt clear. The car sailed off the quay and nosedived into the water.

They didn't wait to see it sink, but ran hard back down the wharf and disappeared into the long low terminal building as the first of the wailing police cars made its appearance. She and Jak sprinted like crazy the three hundred yards to the end of the empty building and peered out over the rustling railroad tracks. Here they caught their breath and tried to clean off some of the dust. Jak looked a mess and she assumed she did too and wondered how far they'd get looking like this.

'It doesn't appear very hopeful,' she said.

Then without warning Jak ran out across the tracks, using the stationary freight train for cover. She went hard after him, not thinking from then on. Stepping out from between the huge steel funnel-like grain cars, they headed off along 37th Street.

'Hadn't we better walk?' she said. 'Like normal people.'

She didn't feel like a normal person as they walked unhurriedly into the downtown area in the pale sunshine. She felt very conspicuous, even after they had cleaned up in the washroom in the visitors' centre on the Strand like any of the thousands of visitors to Galveston.

The police sirens were still wailing away over on the Ship Canal as she stepped on the Houston bus with Jak a short while later. The plan was to head out to the airport to pick up another rental car.

'Avis try real hard,' Jak said with a tired smile, 'but I guess we'd better give our business to another rental company.'

There was speculation among the passengers about what had caused all this police activity. Grace smiled and leant her head on Jak's shoulder. Exhaustion overcame her. She wanted to go to sleep. But believing they were now murder suspects, however unjust that was, she knew sleep was a risk she couldn't afford to take yet.

20

'THE SMART THING TO DO, Grace, is turn yourselves in,' Rory said. She pictured him pacing around his tiny office, books and papers falling as he turned. 'I want to see you, Grace, touch you, know you're okay.'

She wondered how much of his advice was based on his own needs. He hadn't said anything about flying out to see her, only that he had six dozen meetings this week, half of them double-booked. Why did he need to keep so busy? The thought surprised her. Maybe because she found herself surviving all that had happened to her, she was becoming more self-sufficient. Maybe her thoughts about Rory might then have something to do with the fact that everything that happened to her, happened with Jak.

'If you decide to go to the cops,' Rory was saying, 'I'll go with you. Nothing bad is going to happen. Trust me.'

'I do, Rory.' She was calling from the phone booth outside a Roy Rogers fast food outlet on Highway 45. Neither she nor Jak knew where they were going as they headed north through Texas. She had insisted on calling Rory, but now wished she hadn't. She had expected him to tell her not to get within a million miles of the police until he had proved them innocent.

'We can't bust this frame with you on the run. It's going to be tough, but I'd expose any kind of injustice to get you free, I promise.

She said nothing but leant her head against the side of the booth on a pole amidst the arid landscape and looked over at Jak. He was sitting against the hood of their

282

rented car, kicking away a piece of sage brush that had blown against it.

After the long silence, Rory said, 'Grace, I love you.'

Why didn't that stir her? she wondered.

'Jak wants to take a look at Crocker-Giant. He thinks we'll find something there. We had all the information out of Hirshorn's computer. We had it all. We could have blown the whistle. You'd think God was on their side or something, wouldn't you.'

'It sometimes looks that way,' Rory said. There was another silence. 'Grace, I know some people out in Kansas if you're headed that way. They operate an organic farming co-operative of some kind – a real seat of the pants outfit. They're friendly folk. I could call them for you. You could stop by there. Maybe rest up. Meanwhile I'll get a chance to find out what happened at Galveston. Grace, we'll get through this, I promise. Everything's going to be okay. Believe me.'

She wanted to believe him. But right then she was feeling tired and vulnerable. She wanted to rest a while, be comfortable and safe. The thought of being with Rory, being held by him, reassured by him almost made her cry. But then she knew that life with Rory would never be comfortable or reassuring in the way she had always viewed such a relationship. He had too many fights to fight. She resigned herself to not being able to relax until she was through with this and had got the answers she wanted.

The prospect of Rory's hippie friends waiting for them in Kansas did nothing to reassure Jak. He questioned if it was the right move throughout the two-day drive across Texas and Oklahoma. Grace found herself getting irritated by his disparaging remarks. 'Do you have a better suggestion?' she demanded. He didn't. Another time she said, 'Why don't you shut up, Jak? We don't have anyplace else to go.'

The thought of hiding on a farm with Jak, not knowing what was happening and with nowhere else to go weighed heavily on her. The situation was pretty stressful for him, she decided and linked her arms through his and leant on his shoulder, feeling real affection for him.

283

'Jak, I start to shake when I think about being in that silo.'

'Don't think about it,' he said. 'I don't want to be reminded.'

He wouldn't talk about that and she suspected he was just storing up trouble by not talking it out.

The sun was getting low when they turned off the Kansas turnpike in Chase County and followed Rory's directions. There in a field stood a neatly lettered billboard proclaiming 'No chemicals since 1972'.

'I guess these are Rory's hippie friends,' Jak said.

'Well they may be hippies,' she replied, cheering a little, 'but that's as good a crop of field beans as you'd see anywhere.'

All she saw were young, vigorous, generally weed-free plants.

Jak started the Budget compact and turned onto the signposted track. They travelled for about half a mile through cultivated land before reaching the farmhouse. The disorganized yard, full of broken-down equipment that was years past its best, reminded Grace of her own farm, and she felt strangely nostalgic.

A head carrying a luxuriant hair braid was bent inside the engine of a half-track. The owner turned as their car arrived and revealed an equally thick beard.

'Wouldn't you know it,' Jak complained. 'Right out of Woodstock.'

She gave him a look as she climbed from the auto.

'Is Milly Gittleman around?' she asked.

'You Rory's friends? I'm Victor.' He wiped his hands down the front of his overall and shook her hand. He glanced at Jak. 'You know about tractors, Jak?'

'They replaced the horse, didn't they.'

Victor laughed. 'When they work. Old machines – you've got to make most things that bust. You can't get spares most times.'

'Why don't you go back to the horse?'

Victor gave him an uncertain look and waited. 'I guess you'd need to get its consent. Milly's around back.'

They followed his directions to the three large plastic

growing tunnels on the packing crate littered land at the back of the house.

'We'll be into dope parties around a camp fire here.'

Getting truly weary of his petulance, Grace said, 'Jak, will you shut the fuck up.' This situation was putting as much strain on her, but her reaction shocked her more than him.

All notions of hippiedom were put to flight by Milly Gittleman. In her billowing bib and brace coverall, she looked like a spare, hardworking farmer struggling to hold on to her land. She was fifty, with a florid smile like a welcoming beacon. She was thinning thousands of tomato seedlings when Grace came along the humid tunnel.

'You must be Grace.' She threw her tanned and freckled arms around her, surprising her. 'Rory described you, and how! He must be in love or something. He's been calling every hour to make sure you got here. You're welcome, honey. Indeed you are.'

She didn't let her go until she noticed Jak.

'You're the infamous Jak Redford. Why don't I give you a hug to show we don't bear no grudge for what you're doing to wheat?'

'It's pretty obvious it's not me Rory's in love with,' Jak said. 'I didn't know he figured I was infamous.'

Milly was naturally hospitable and stopped work to make them feel welcome. Across at the house she offered them coffee and cake, and told them to treat the place like their own.

'Would you prefer tea, Grace?' she said in the big kitchen that was untidy with clothes, magazines and general paraphernalia of family living. A black overweight one-eyed dog wasn't quite so hospitable. She lifted her head to give them a look, but didn't move from in front of the stove.

'Coffee's fine thanks. Do you have some milk?'

'We don't, Grace. We're a pure vegetarian community. We don't use anything from animals.'

'Wasn't that a cow in the yard?' Jak challenged.

'Sure. It has the same status as the dogs and cats around here. They don't get to vote, but they don't get exploited neither. You want soya milk? We pulp our own beans.'

Grace flushed with guilt now as she remembered how they had kept the cows on their farm back in England. Obviously even the old-fashioned way wouldn't have been acceptable here.

'Gee, you've got an ice-box,' Jak said as Milly got a jug of milk from the refrigerator.

'We use appropriate technology.' Milly smiled like she had been through this many times. 'I got to finish up my tomato plants. So enjoy your coffee. Make yourselves right at home. You'll meet everybody at supper.'

'Can we do anything?' Grace offered.

'Sure. We'll get you jobs organized soon enough. Just enjoy.'

After she had gone, Jak said, 'I should call my old pal Rory, find out what the hell he told them about me.'

'Does it matter? They look as if they work hard around here.'

'Sure, pulping all them soya beans, man!'

She smiled, and thought about Jak's world being turned upside down as it had. All things considered he was probably coping a whole lot better than she gave him credit for. Ever since Rose's death her world had been turned upside down too, and every step she had taken toward understanding that, she believed was some sort of progress. A relatively short time ago Jak's life had been settled, the path plainly marked out, his anticipated progress steady and clear. But now each new bend on the way seemed to increase the turmoil. It seemed to her that he would no more readily talk about what was happening to them now than he would about the death of his wife and son. Again when she tried to broach what had happened in Galveston, in the relative security of that kitchen, Jak veered away.

'Forget it, Grace,' he said. 'Let's just forget it.'

'I don't think I can, Jak. I keep seeing us down in that black hole and I start to panic again.'

'It'll pass. It always does.'

Silence followed. A gulf opened up between them. She didn't know how to close it, but wanted to.

286

The bad news that Rory phoned with didn't lessen the pressure on them. They were both being sought by the FBI for murder.

'The Galveston police hauled that Mustang out of the Ship Canal, and they didn't find your bodies like they figured. The FBI got called in because you fled the state. That was confirmed when you were traced renting a Budget compact at Houston Airport.'

This made Grace more uncertain about turning themselves in, and now Rory wasn't so sure it was such a good idea. 'Oh that's great, Rory. What if we'd taken your first lot of advice?'

'I want to get some leverage on the case before I walk into the federal prosecutor's office with you.' That was all he said.

When she relayed what had happened to Jak he paced around the kitchen, his arms folded over his head like he wanted to stop the reality of the situation battering out his brains.

'Jesus, this is something else. Up until now I had kind of half convinced myself that the police would somehow know we didn't kill Kuhfuss. You kind of expect more of those guys for some reason. You see them in movies – they're so goddamn smart at figuring things out.'

Grace put her arms around him, willing away the hurt and confusion he was suffering as she had so often done with Rose. How close to being children men were in certain situations. Always circumstances involving feelings.

'Friend Rory had better come through with something real fast.'

'He will, Jak. And we're safe here. I just know these are people we can trust.'

'How long can this goddamn mess go on for? I was fixing to quit after Galveston. What a mistake. I should have got out long before.'

That made her feel bad, like this was all her fault. She withdrew her arms, but he seemed not to notice.

'My work is getting so far away from me, that's the real problem. I guess I could start a research project on the prison farm.'

Grace laughed too loudly. 'I'm glad you've kept your sense of humour.'

'I'm not kidding,' he said.

Before dusk fell they took a walk around the farm to see what the extent of their prison was. There was a lot of evidence of hard work that went into this sustainable way of life. Jak was impressed. His mood began to lighten.

'We came pretty close back there in Galveston,' he said, taking her completely by surprise. 'I don't know how you got me out of that silo, Grace. I start to sweat thinking about that suffocating grain. My mind went blank with panic, I saw myself getting drowned by all that wheat pouring in. I was suddenly blind, I couldn't move, then when I finally tried I just kept sinking. I knew I had to try and stay on the top of it or get totally buried. The real problem was finding any air to breathe. Look.' He showed her his palms. He had broken out into a sweat just talking about it.

She put her arms around him, seeking as much reassurance as she was trying to give.

'Back home a neighbour and his son died in a grain silo. It happened so quickly.'

'Do you still think of that as back home?' he asked.

She closed her eyes. 'I don't know if I think of anywhere as home right now. It's a nice feeling really, not being tied down.' She glanced at him, knowing he needed a more settled life. She thought about telling him then what had happened with Rory, but still she couldn't.

'Thanks for getting us away from Galveston like you did. I'd had never thought of anything so clever.'

'Those assholes tried to kill us.'

She leaned her head against him as she thought about that.

'Maybe if we somehow let them know we won't go on with this,' she suggested.

'They would have to admit there was something going down. And first we'd need to clearly identify who *they* are. We made it perfect for them, fleeing the state.'

'I'm scared, Jak.'

'Maybe we can live out our days on this hippie farm.'

The two men and the woman who appeared on a tractor and trailer weren't remotely hippieish, nor were their two dogs. There wasn't a braid or a beard or ear-ring between them that Grace noticed.

'Get aboard,' the tractor driver said, 'it's supper-time. I'm Mike Gittleman. This is Nan Penzer, he's Lee Stanford. That's Timmy, she's Truly,' – the last two being a black and white, and a tan dog.

Lee stuttered badly on trying to say hello as he helped her onto the trailer. He couldn't get a single word out. He was around twenty-five and looked at Jak like he was assessing the competition.

'Can you lift a hundred pound sack of beans?' Lee asked, the words suddenly spurting out.

'I doubt if I can even eat a hundred pounds of beans,' was Jak's reply.

Everyone laughed. Everyone except Lee.

Preparing supper was a disorganized arrangement where everyone pitched in. Eating was equally chaotic, and particularly disturbing for Grace were two of the cats that wandered along the large rectangular table trying to eat out of food bowls or off plates. Mike Gittleman allowed one of them to eat from his plate.

When one approached Jak and he lifted it off onto the floor, Mike said, 'Don't you like cats, Jak?'

'They're fine.' There was no enthusiasm in his voice.

'Not everyone takes to animals like we, Mike,' Milly said.

'They sure don't,' Mike said.

'Are your animals pure vegetarian?' Grace asked.

'Don't seem right to kill one animal to feed another.'

'Cats are naturally predatory,' Jak said.

'We try to stop them killing birds or rats.'

'But they must take your crops.'

'Sure. The rats and birds take a little, Grace,' Mike said.

'They drove us mad on our farm back in England.'

'Were you ever rid of them?'

She smiled, conceding the point.

289

'They have their place on this earth, a purpose too. Man's so smart he just hasn't seen it yet. We can get by just fine without interfering too much with anything else.'

Mike broke off a piece of cornbread and fed it to one of the cats that was back on the table, then gave a piece to the one-eyed black dog at his feet. The other dogs rushed up wagging their tails for a piece too.

Grace wondered how long it would take her to get used to animals on the supper table, if she ever would.

'How come you take us in without knowing about us?' Jak asked.

'Are you murderers?' Victor asked.

Jak hesitated and glanced at Grace.

'Rory said you were in trouble,' Milly said. 'We trust him.'

'But you don't even question what kind of trouble.'

'We'd be happy to sit a spell, you've a mind to tell us,' Mike said.

Grace looked at Jak. 'I'd like to tell someone. I would.'

What they had to tell took the best part of two hours. Cats and dogs curled up with them near the fire. The Gittlemans asked only a few questions, and seemed to draw no conclusions when it was time to go to bed.

Their reaction was judging them, Grace assumed. But later when she was helping Milly wash the supper things she changed her mind, deciding it wouldn't matter to them if they had done what they had been accused of. They were judged as they were found. Liking animals was a more important measure of character.

'We really didn't do anything wrong, Milly,' she said.

'I'm sure you didn't, honey. But it still wouldn't matter none. Victor used to work for a meat-packer in Kansas City. That's about as cruel as you can get – the way they treat those steers before they get butchered. I'd say he's healed now. No one has to be what they've been in the past.'

'What those people are doing is wrong,' Grace insisted.

'Couldn't be right letting folk go hungry while they make more money. I daresay those people think it's right.'

In saying that she sounded like Rory, Grace thought.

It was then she began to understand that whoever was behind what had been happening possibly wasn't knowingly wicked. That those people got up in the morning and had breakfast, experienced emotions similar to hers, could possibly be held in the grip of some terror like those she knew. Suddenly her antagonists were given human perspective; her own fear that had cried out for support started to ease back.

A difficult situation arose for her as a result of not being truthful with Jak about what had happened between her and Rory. With quilt and sheets they climbed the narrow flight of stairs to a room in the roof. Mike reassured them that nobody would find them out here. There was only one room and one bed.

'Eh, Mike,' she began, more embarrassed that they weren't a couple than that Mike thought they were. 'We're not, eh . . .'

'It gets real cold, Grace. A body could freeze.' He smiled, and reminded them that they all rose at five-thirty.

The silence between them found her on the verge of telling Jak, but finally she said, 'I'm so tired I don't care.'

The way it came out was her in bed with a sheet and blanket, and Jak on the floor with the quilt. One cold, the other uncomfortable. Finally she sat up and put on the light.

'Jak, look, we are adult. Surely we can share the bed without expecting anything to happen . . . You know,' – then why was she concerned that that may have sounded like an invitation?

'We can?' Jak said. Then – 'Oh we can.' Doubt seemed to creep in. 'Can we?' He started to the bed, forgetting his quilt.

'Jak – bring the duvet.'

She noticed how he used the quilt to cover what was happening to him physically, but decided she couldn't suddenly change her mind and send him back to the floor. Despite herself the situation made her a little excited. As she adjusted the bedding, she turned and accidentally touched him.

'Oh – oh my God.' She giggled nervously.

291

'I'm sorry . . . sorry,' – like caught with a dirty thought.

They wrenched away from each other so violently that Jak ended up on the floor. Then as he stood up she saw his erection was jammed against the inside of his shorts.

'I'm sorry. I don't have any . . .' He gingerly got back into bed.

She felt like laughing, and could feel bubbles of laughter trying to creep out of her. Suppressing it made it sound like hiccoughs. Rory slipped into her thoughts as if a buffer to Jak, but those thoughts were like tissue paper. She was cold and would have enjoyed physical contact for warmth, but knew what other meanings that would have. What would she do if Jak simply turned around and offered himself to her? The idea tantalized and excited her. She knew they would never be physically closer together than this or emotionally closer after their ordeal.

'Jak?' she said after a while, wondering if he had gone to sleep. 'What are you thinking?'

'Work . . .' he croaked. 'About getting back to work.'

'Ah,' she said, 'I keep thinking how I might help those people in Mexico.'

'Oh . . . I see. One of the charitable trusts might help.'

'I'll use any money I get from American Chemicals.' She couldn't believe they were having this conversation here.

'Lobby Congress to stop the export of toxic chemicals,' he suggested.

'Jak, do you miss your wife still?'

There was a long silence. Finally he turned.

'Jak?' she said, and reached out to hold him like it was the most natural thing to do.

He moved into her. She reached down for his shorts, while his hand scrambled to get her pants over her buttocks.

Then they were together, truly together. Grace clung to him, needing this physical contact so much. Rory slid in and right out of her thoughts again. She cried. They weren't sad tears.

By the third day at the farm, Jak found himself so relaxing into the routine around the place, early morning starts, hard work and sweet nights with Grace that he began to think of himself as a normal human being. Most of the pressure of the past months had left him and he didn't even want to think about returning. That morning they were getting involved in a gleaning operation on a neighbouring farm. Everyone went to help harvest the field of rutabagas, including Timmy and Truly – only the black, one-eyed Bella refused to go.

'The Gleaners' was a name frequently heard around the Gittleman's farm.

'We're a loose-knit kind of organization,' Milly explained. 'Most of us are farmers – but we're getting a lot of city folk joining in nowadays. What we aim to do is glean some of the six hundred million tons of substandard produce that gets ploughed in on American farms every year. We distribute it among the poor. Can you believe six hundred million tons? That's what the estimates are. Sometimes it ain't even substandard, just a heck too much of it to be profitable. We collected up forty-five thousand tons last year. A fly speck by comparison. But I can tell you, those folk who get it lifted feel pretty good about doing something constructive rather than just sitting back complaining about poverty, or leaving the problem to government agencies.

'The neighbour we're picking up from still farms with chemicals. In the early days we had all kinds of problems with spray drift,' Milly said. 'He hadn't believed we were serious farmers. I guess he figured we were just a bunch of hippies. We were pretty hippieish in those days, with our radical ideas and way-out clothes. The farm was a haven for draft dodgers. But those boys certainly weren't work-dodgers.'

Jak glanced at Grace and smiled.

'More than a smidge of that peace and love culture stayed around, Milly,' Jak said.

'We sure hope that had a lasting effect. It don't stop a body being a good farmer.'

'Maybe it makes for better farmers,' Grace said. 'More like stewards of the land.'

'That's exactly right, honey,' Milly said.

Out in the field, moving behind a harvester belonging to Alan Banion, a bigger farmer in the co-operative, Jak said, 'What's wrong with these turnips?'

'Frost damage,' Victor told him. 'It causes the skin to break and later heal in a rough ridge. The supermarkets want produce like it's out of a factory. Apples and tomatoes have got to be the right shape: no blemishes on the squash; no specky potatoes. Toyota should be out here farming.'

The three large harvesters the gleaners had brought in moved steadily along the field, with string bags coming off the back, which other helpers boosted onto the trailers and trucks. Still more hands and some children followed through bagging those vegetables that got missed.

Following behind Banion's machine, Jak was determined to pace Victor, who had a similar build to his own but with hard, stringy sinews clearly used to this work. He could feel the fifty pound sacks pulling on his arms, while Victor seemed not to notice the weight as he stooped, seized the sack, boosted it and moved on. He hadn't done any running lately and knew he needed to when some kind of competitive madness made him quicken the pace. He got to the next sack ahead of Victor, then the next. Victor increased his pace also, effortlessly, it seemed.

'Hell, this beats working!' Jak said, running for the next sack. They were getting ahead of the trailer so the driver increased his speed, closing the gap between them and the harvester. Soon both of them were running, then racing each other. Other gleaners stopped work and watched them run themselves right out of a job.

A false sense of security was being created for them staying at the Gittlemans', but there were moments when he imagined himself settling into this life, leaving the cares of the world far behind. He was pretty sure Grace was enjoying it as much. He thought about this type of sustainable farming in relation to both his own work and what Grace planned on going after. In some ways it provided answers, but it failed to satisfy their separate needs: hers to find justice for her daughter, his to become the genius who transferred the Nif genes *en bloc* to make wheat fix its own nitrogen. There were probably as many obstacles in the way of this radical change in the use of farmlands as there were to him easily achieving his goal. Chemical companies wouldn't want this safe, alternative system, where green manure such as ladino clover got used, not here, not in Mexico, nor the Third World where they saw new markets opening up. Despite his love affair with Grace, which was dominating his waking and sleeping and colouring the horizon, he knew his thoughts had to struggle back to what was happening outside. Rory wasn't making too much progress, and whenever Grace spoke with him she became increasingly snappish and irritable. At first he put it down to disappointment in Rory not finding a way to lever them out of this frame, but then he began to think there was maybe something else going on between them. Was he getting jealous?

'Do you have any dealings with the Crocker-Giant outfit?' he asked when they were all cleaning down packing-cases one wet afternoon.

'You don't farm long these days before you meet Crocker,' Milly said. 'Why they even sell organic lines.'

'We wondered when you'd get back to that,' Mike said.

Jak looked across at Grace. 'We can't stay here all our lives.'

'Sure you can,' Lee stuttered. 'Can't they, Milly. They can.'

'Nobody around here's raising any objection.'

Lee Stanford had fallen in love with Grace for everyone to see. He tried to relieve her of every job. He had even asked Jak if he planned to marry her. He had avoided answering by saying she already had a husband.

'People in the co-op likely grew some of that seed you're chasing,' Mike told him. 'Alan Banion, I'd guess.'

'Alan grows wheat seed under contract to Crocker every year,' Milly said. 'They think a lot of the fact we don't use chemicals.'

Anxiety suddenly made his throat dry. He looked over at Grace to assess how reaching to the outside again would affect them. What he saw almost stopped him saying,

'Would he talk to me?'

'I can't think why he wouldn't,' Mike said. 'It's his daughter's wedding this weekend. You won't get a bit of sense out of him before then.'

'Why can't we let it be for a while?' Grace said in bed that night. 'Maybe they'll forget all about us?'

'You know that's not going to happen,' he told her.

She turned away from him.

'Grace?' he said. But she didn't respond. If this was the price of their relationship he thought perhaps it was too high.

As part of the Gittlemans' household, he and Grace were also invited to the wedding at the Banions'. After the ceremony guests packed into their large wood-framed barn, which was bedecked with bunting and flowers. Alan Banion, dressed in bib and brace coveralls and a plaid shirt like so many of his guests, was splashing punch into any glass that passed in front of him.

'Congratulations, Alan,' Milly said, giving him a hug.

'It is quite something to get a homely daughter off my hands,' he said.

'Ah come on, she ain't but a mite homely,' Milly said.

They watched the pretty bride dancing with her new husband. She was in a white wedding dress, he was in jeans.

'You still racing Victor?' Banion asked.

'I'd've been beaten good if we hadn't run out of field.'

Alan said, 'You want to know about Crocker – they are mean sons of bitches, I can tell you. They hit you with all kinds of penalties to avoid paying on time.'

'Where do they grow their wheat seed?'

'I know where three hundred acres of it gets grown. More punch, Lee?'

Lee extended his cup automatically. He was looking at Grace and having trouble getting his words to come out.

Banion filled the glass, but Lee didn't remove it.

'I can't get any more in it, Lee.'

Lee finally said, 'Will you dance with me, Grace?'

'It doesn't seem like anyone else is going to ask me, Lee.'

'He sure is moonstruck,' Banion said as they went onto the boarded-out dance square.

'Ain't he just,' Milly said.

'Stop by tomorrow, Jak. I'll show you where we grow for Crocker. I might even have some of their seed.'

'You mean you saved some of it?' he said.

'Crocker'd be pretty pissed if they knew.'

'Do you always keep back seed?'

'Half bag or so. Always have. Come by tomorrow. Enjoy now.' He turned away to some other guests.

Jak's gaze sought out Grace.

'He ain't a serious rival, Jak,' Milly said.

A smile crossed his face. 'Oh, I wasn't thinking about that at all, Milly. I was thinking about the evidence Alan Banion may have, and where it might lead us. How it might keep us out of prison. I've been thinking about my work some. Life out here is leading me to reconsider my approach. Till now I've been trying to get the gene that makes the bean harbour rhizobia bacteria do the same for wheat. I figure maybe I can adapt the method by which the bacterium gene was transferred into Prairie Red to attract the Take-all virus. The more I think about the possibilities the more frustrated I get at not being able to go to it.'

'Why do you need to, Jak?' Milly asked.

The question startled him. 'To help feed the world more efficiently.'

'But the world's already got more food than we can use. All we got to do is stop feeding it so wastefully through livestock to make animal proteins that the body can't get rid of anyhow.'

He looked at her. He hadn't got an argument, but wasn't about to tell her that maybe she was right.

'Come on, let's dance.'

The only real difference between the aftermath of a party in a barn and one in a house, he found when he drove across to Banion's place the following day, was that a mess in a barn could be lived with.

'You'd be out of the wheat business a long while if you'd planted this,' he said, plunging his hand into the bag of seed harvested last season for Crocker-Giant.

297

'It looks like any other prime seed,' Banion said. 'You reckon it's programmed to fail?'

From the way Banion asked, he could tell he didn't believe it. The seed looked so good, that illogically he had his own doubts about this being part of the batch that had been sold to Russia.

'Can you get me into Crocker?'

'You give me a real good reason,' Banion said. 'Maybe not then. I do a lot of business with those people.'

'How much did Mike tell you?' he asked, deciding then to risk telling him everything.

Retelling what had happened made it easier, faster, with more detail in the right order. What he clearly had in his favour was this man's dislike of the business practices of Crocker-Giant, whom he believed capable of most things. Against this was the fact that they provided a substantial part of his income. Banion wasn't going to blow that away without a lot of consideration.

The jury was still out as far as he was concerned.

Meanwhile Jak had a little more evidence in the physical seed, but no controlled environment cabinet to grow it in or lab to check if it had that same bacterium gene.

When he arrived back at the Gittlemans', Mike said, 'You get clear of that murder charge, Jak – Budget'll murder you over their charges on this.'

'If we return the car, the FBI will jump us.'

'Victor and Nan are driving into Kansas City tomorrow. They could dump it on a Budget lot.'

He wasn't sure. 'What if they get picked up?'

'The turnpike's pretty quiet. The alternative would be to burn it. But you ain't done nothing criminal, Jak. Why start?'

He needed no more persuasion.

There was no problem dropping the car off at the Budget lot in Kansas City. But the next evening when everyone was finishing up the chores before supper, apparently the same car came right back along the track. No one moved as it stopped in the yard. The driver didn't get out.

Jak glanced about, ready to run, wondering if this was a trap and how far he'd get.

Finally Milly let out a surprised holler and stepped forward.

'Rory. Rory Spelman.' She hugged him out of the auto. 'Why didn't you let us know? You scared us half to death.'

'I figured you weren't going anyplace.'

'I hope you've got some good news,' Jak said.

'I guess the news doesn't amount to more than a short phone call. But no way could I have made this trip if I had risked making the call.' He looked around at the faces in the yard. 'The FBI listen to our calls at Christic. I may as well have mailed them your address.' He searched around again. 'Is Grace off someplace?'

'She's inside starting supper.'

He watched closely as Rory entered the large kitchen. Grace looked flustered when she saw him. She hadn't showered or changed when she'd got in from planting cabbages earlier. She pulled at her clothes trying to tidy them. Her gestures had an odd familiarity to them, and Jak realized why. What they didn't tell him, the electricity sparking between those two as she ran across to him, did. Everybody noticed it and seemed awkward. He felt suddenly angry, no longer able to deny what had been niggling at him a while now. Lee ran off, headed for the cellar. Jak felt like joining him to take his hurt out on a sack of potatoes.

'I can't believe how good you people look,' Rory said, aware that he was the centre of attention.

'You folks have a lot to talk about,' Milly said.

She took over Grace's supper preparations.

The news Rory brought could not have been designed to make Jak feel worse. The FBI had dropped the murder charge against Grace, but were still seeking him. If it was a means of dividing them, it was succeeding, despite Grace reaching across the table and squeezing his hand. He withdrew it. The gesture was petulant, but he refused to help how he felt right then. His thoughts grappled with Rory. Where was he going to stay tonight? And how long did he plan on being around – rather than what else he had to say.

'I figured how we can move on this,' Rory was saying. 'When I was with the SEC I had some dealings with Oscar Hartmine who runs International Grain. This is a deeply unpleasant man, but he's got a real grudge with Hirshorn. According to the *Wall Street Journal*, International are short of wheat. They're gouging out their organs to try and meet their commitments. If it is Hirshorn behind this, Hartmine would do anything that would have the Commodities Futures Trading Commission force them to divest and get the price of wheat down. Jak –'

'*If* it is them,' he challenged. 'We still don't have any kind of evidence. It won't work. The CFTC wouldn't go for it before.'

'But you're not a major player,' Rory pointed out. 'Hartmine could prove your white knight.'

Grace avoided looking at him when she said, 'It's worth a try, Jak. We've got nothing to lose.'

'*You* haven't. A while ago you wanted to stay put and hope they would forget about us,' he reminded her. 'If he's wrong about this guy and he calls the cops, I get to lose my liberty.'

Rory said, 'I'm ready to go to court with you on that. This way we could get ourselves some leverage.'

'Are you ready to go to jail instead of me if we don't?' he wanted to know.

'I could meet them,' Grace suggested. 'But I know Jak won't allow that. It would have been daft anyway as his word carries such authority.'

Jak got up from the table and paced around.

'Can you set a meeting at a safe venue?' Grace asked.

'I figured we'd do it in Kansas City.'

'Will they meet us?'

'They've got everything to gain, Grace.' Rory smiled. 'You will pull clear of this mess, Jak.'

'I just wish I felt a hell of a lot better about it.' He folded his arms over his head. Finally he nodded. 'You'd better set up the meeting.'

'I'll get right to it. We had a real break on the pesticide

case,' Rory said.

That sounded like more good news for Grace alone, and Jak regretted not being able to feel wholly pleased for her.

'We located the data American Chemicals submitted to the EPA when they got Smartkill licensed. It's as phoney as a two dollar bill. Their data from animal testing is false.'

'How?' Grace said. 'The EPA gave their approval.'

'EPA scientists run tests based on the evidence submitted to them. Rarely do they start back at first base.'

The rush of emotion through Grace was almost palpable. Jak watched her leap up and throw her arms about the lawyer.

'That's wonderful, wonderful news. Does it mean we get American Chemicals into court sooner?'

'Maybe. Could even mean we'll get the EPA to fight it for us. What it will mean for sure is that American Chemicals will come out gouging. They'll start to get really mean. Right, Jak?'

Jak nodded.

What the hell kind of friend was Rory anyway?

It didn't occur to him that Rory might feel the same way about him when he learned what had happened here between Grace and him. But he felt he had first claim to her. What worried him was how Grace felt about that. He wanted to step right up and stake his claim, but rose instead and went out into the yard and felt the cool evening air on his face and arms. It felt clean and good. There he found his wife Marge, along with their son, Pete. Both were so close he could almost touch them. That had never happened before and he wondered why now. 'I'm sorry Marge,' he said quietly. 'If only I had known then what I know now.' There followed a litany of regret and self-recrimination. He wondered, paradoxically, if it was some kind of progress getting thrown back ten years like this. All he knew was that it was a whole lot less painful to draw a shutter through his mind.

After a while he was aware of someone joining him, and for a moment thought it was his dead wife again. But

301

a physical hand gripped his shoulder and without turning he knew it was Rory.

'I should be real pleased about what has happened to Grace. I am, I guess. It kind of leaves me isolated.'

'Maybe,' Rory said. 'It doesn't make a bit of difference to her case. The new evidence. It won't make too much difference to American Chemicals. Their earnings will dip a piece if they pay compensation on any scale.'

'But no one will give a damn about what's happening. Not here, or in Mexico or England or anyplace else. Right?'

'Some people do, Jak. The real problem is, most of us can't relate our day to day struggle to the world and how that's being harmed. We're all that disconnected.'

'So we win something maybe, but win nothing at all.'

'Maybe we win more than we know, Jak. One person starts to care who didn't care yesterday. It takes a pretty imaginative leap to understand that the movement of your hand affects the farthest star. People won't accept that on trust and without absolute proof. That's where science has taken us. What your side fails to understand is that your faith, the kind you call science, is in the end less powerful, less effective than anyone else's.'

'You're the guy who lost Jesus and dropped out of the seminary,' Jak said, feeling mean for saying it; then angry that Rory simply nodded. 'Don't you ever get mad, for Christsake? I feel like I want to take a swing at you,' – not really believing these kinds of feelings were happening to him.

'You know your problem, Jak, you don't have any vision. All you do is go for detail. Develop a new kind of wheat to feed the world. It won't happen. There's a real paradox in that no one person can change the world, but with his thoughts one person can change the world.'

'Didn't you hear what I said?' he demanded.

'I heard you. Do it if you've got to.'

He looked at the lawyer, wondering what it would take to provoke him. 'Rory, you're full of shit.'

'Grace told me about you and her,' he said.

302

'She did? What did she say?' – anxiety grabbing him.

'You've been through a lot together,' Rory said.

'That's all she said?'

'I understand how these things get started. I love her, Jak.'

'What does Grace feel about that?' he asked.

'She feels the same way.'

That did it. He flew at Rory, trying to punch him. The blow caught him on the shoulder. Rory grabbed him around the neck and Jak lashed out with his elbows, stabbing away at him, until he let go. He got another punch in, stinging his hand, before Rory managed to get his arms around him and pin his arms to his side. Frustration burst out of him, in a fury. He wriggled and thrashed and finally got free and tried to hit again, but found himself punching air as Rory scrabbled away, got to his feet and ran. Jak ran after him, straight out through the field of tomatoes and into the acres of cabbage beyond. There he pulled him down, but neither of them had much fight in them. The emotional discharge had left them exhausted. He tried to hit Rory again, but couldn't when he did nothing to avoid the blow.

Sitting among the young cabbage plants, Jak folded his arms over his head holding in his pain and anger and disappointment; his hand hurt too.

'Did she say she loved you?' he asked.

'That's what she told me from the start.'

In the face of this declaration he refused to believe all he had had with Grace meant nothing. He refused to roll over and die. With his career now in ruins Grace was all he had.

'Why the hell would she have a love affair with me?' he demanded. 'What does she plan on doing? Going between the two of us?'

'She talked about that with Milly, who told her that first of all she should find herself, be herself, please herself, then these things would have a way of working out. Grace wants to go back to Mexico when she gets this done. Would you go there with her?'

Jak didn't want to think about that. He said, 'I'm not giving her up, Rory. I'll fight you again if I need to. I'm not letting go of her.'

That was his last word on the matter.

The fact that Rory said nothing worried him.

21

FINALLY OSCAR HARTMINE'S STOMACH WAS telling him what Gordon Dulles had known for weeks, that he was in deep trouble. For weeks OH had been saying that the problem was indigestion. But no amount of seltzer changed the fact International Grain Traders were short a lot of wheat. Nor did it stop him farting like a Gatling gun all day long. Many times he had told his boss he ate too fast, and without chewing properly – 'Eating's a waste of time, Gordon, unless you're making a deal over the lunch table,' OH had said. 'I encourage all our executives to operate that way. Fast eater, fast thinker.' Dulles resisted eating the way OH ate. He'd sooner not eat. If OH had taken more time with everything, eating included, he might have seen some of the pitfalls and might not have this pain in his gut. His biggest problem right now was cashflow. The market was moving relentlessly against him. The Board of Trade was increasing the margins on his trading accounts. He was selling assets to meet his losses as lines of credit with his banks dried up. Dulles didn't feel one bit sorry for this crashing ego.

'How big's the trouble we've got, Gordon?' OH said, stepping from the elevator in the Federal House headquarters.

'We're short a lot of wheat, OH. That's for sure.' He scratched his empty eye-socket behind his eye-patch. 'Pete Richmond's been sending instructions to our representatives in the pits to sell. The analysis looks right. It's the market that looks wrong.'

He almost laughed at the frenzy his boss was getting

305

into, but was finding his volatility harder and harder to take. His own anxiety had something to do with that. OH was as likely as not to fire everybody, living by his credo of gut response.

'What's the bottom line, have we figured it?'

'Unless the price eases, we're looking at one-eighty to one-eighty-five million dollars on the downside.'

'Goddamn computers! Those goddamn analysts can't do a thing that's practical. A trader listening to his gut'd know better.'

He crashed through the double doors into the computer room where twenty-year-olds were reading the screens like runes.

'What's your computer saying we do now, Pete? Run up a rat's ass?'

'We're making the right moves,' Richmond responded in the aggressive fashion OH expected from bankers and the Board of Trade.

'I pay you six hundred K to second-guess. Your goddamn computer strategy's worth jackshit. We sold wheat we don't own for prices that look real sick now.'

Richmond shook his head. 'Stay short, OH. The market's going to find you. There's too much wheat out there.' He glanced at Dulles, who looked away.

What the kid didn't understand was the kind of problem OH was having meeting the margins. If he could have hung on and met those calls the price would eventually turn down, but he was out of time and money.

Safeguarding his own credibility, he said, 'Have you any notion what's happening out there, son? May wheat's near five dollars a bushel. There may be a lot out there someplace, but the market's acting like it doesn't believe it.'

'Shit, Gordon,' Richmond said. 'There's nothing to believe. I'm saying hang short, that's the smart thing to do. We did our homework, OH. The wheat's out there. The price will ease.'

OH's guts obviously told him something different. 'We'd better buy some wheat and damn quick.'

The 'U' turn surprised Dulles, but he figured it was too

little too late. With his credit lines being squeezed OH couldn't any easier go long than he could stay short, but if he took a long position he wouldn't need to meet his margin commitments on a daily basis all the while wheat was climbing. He figured the price could go to five and a half or six dollars a bushel. If it did OH would get wiped out by holding to his present short position.

'Buy wheat,' OH said. 'The way out of this kind of trouble is to take action. Jesus, anything is better than getting squeezed to death. That's what my gut says to me, son.'

OH's pain had all but disappeared completely when he took the call from Rory Spelman. A least he was growling less. 'I remember this guy,' he said. 'I can't think of one good thing about him. He's a trouble-maker. But if he wants to make trouble for your brother-in-law, Gordon, that's got to be worth listening to. He says he has information that can turn the market around.'

'You believe him, OH?'

'Sure I believe him. Why not? The only thing you can be certain about with this guy is that he won't have an angle or be looking to make money for himself from it.'

They had agreed to meet at the Alameda Plaza, Kansas City Missouri, which was around the corner from the Board of Trade. OH said, 'Have someone book a suite, Gordon. I guess we can still afford that.' He smiled for the first time in a while and his gold mouth lit up the office.

The news they received *en route* to Kansas City wasn't so good. Two of the banks that were their biggest creditors were foreclosing. They were owed eighty million dollars between them. OH called them from their hotel and told them he was about to turn the market around.

'Christ, Oscar, you're going long now!' the banker yelled.

'Damn right. It's giving me some room here. The market moved up eight cents. I need till tomorrow, Frank. Let's meet and talk about it over lunch.'

He secured a twenty-four-hour stay of foreclosure.

'This had better be good,' OH told the lawyer who

307

arrived on his own at the $490-a-day suite. 'We're in deep shit and I'm in no mood to get jerked off.'

They watched him smile, then pour himself some mineral water from the icebox. 'Can I get you gentlemen something?' Rory offered.

The question surprised them.

OH sank into a chair and said, 'Give me one of those,' like a guest who wasn't about to hurry his host.

Bringing the Perrier water across the large sitting-room, the lawyer, who looked to Dulles like he needed a couple of good breakfasts, took a chair opposite OH. He spoke in a quiet voice that caused OH to strain forward and brought Dulles in closer. As Dulles listened to him outline the wheat conspiracy that threatened the existence of International he felt his anxiety increase. Here was someone – a random factor – who was about to blow everything. He reached into his vest pocket for one of the beta-blocking tablets he always carried with him. Swallowing it with some water didn't lessen the danger this lawyer represented now, but it made him better able to deal with the problem calmly.

'Have you got any evidence to prove any of this, son?' OH asked, extending his glass for more mineral water.

'Jak Redford and Grace Chance are right down in the lobby,' Rory said. 'They'll confirm all I've said.'

'Get them up here.' A vein of excitement seized OH now. 'I want to believe that this is all possible. Jesus Christ, wouldn't that be something.'

The woman and the plant scientist arrived, had a drink, told their story eagerly, tripping each other at times. Dulles found them singularly unimpressive. The woman was attractive, but looked like a fresh-faced hill-billy. He had somehow expected more from all he'd heard about them. They were over-anxious, but that didn't mean they weren't dangerous.

'What do you think, Gordon?' OH asked.

'It would explain a lot of what's happening to wheat, why Caddy's buying so much. But it all looks too simple. Where's the evidence?'

Maybe it was the effect of the beta-blocker, but he felt

his own anxiety start to ease considerably. 'Having all kinds of smart theories is fine. Producing hard evidence to prove whatever happened is something else.' In the face of this all Jak Redford could do was offer more technical detail. He knew his boss wasn't interested. He never was in details. Finally Dulles didn't disguise his disbelief.

'I figure these guys're jerking our wire, OH. Sure the market's gone crazy, but wheat could as easily have followed your lead with dealers selling and driving the price down.'

'But it didn't, Gordon, did it?'

'If Crocker-Giant somehow fixed a gene to screw the Russian wheat harvest that'd mean the end of trading as we know it. You won't buy wheat at any price.'

'But it all fits, Gordon – way back when Hirshorn beat me to buying that seed company. Why they tried so hard.'

'Did they fix the weather too?' He directed the question at Redford. 'There has barely been enough snow in the Midwest this winter. How did they organize that?'

'I know about biogenetics,' Jak said. He pulled an envelope of wheat seed from his coat pocket. 'Have a bio-engineer raise this in a controlled environment cabinet. Then look at the new bacterium gene that repeats itself in every plant.'

'If Caddy is gambling on anything, I figure it's on there not being enough rain this spring. Wrecking Russian wheat – Jesus Christ, not even Caddy Hirshorn would do that,' he said. 'What we should do here, OH, is call the police. These guys are wanted for murder. I guess that's what this whole fantasy is about.'

'Hirshorn set up that killing,' Jak said. 'Only he stood to lose from what Mark Kuhfuss had to tell.'

'Caddy Hirshorn? Many things he is capable of – maybe even murder if he was in a real tight spot. But he looked upon Mark Kuhfuss like a brother. He had him killed to frame you? Why not kill you instead?'

'Someone tried to, Mr Dulles,' Grace said. 'But that wouldn't necessarily have stopped Mr Kuhfuss. I know Jak didn't kill him. Why would he? Mr Kuhfuss was the key to proving all this. He gave us those dummy sales orders Hirshorn have in their computer to lower their excess wheat positions.'

'Have you got copies of those orders?' Dulles asked.

'We lost them in the silo.'

'You bet. Pretty damned convenient, Mrs Chance.'

'Have the people at the CFTC get a warrant to look inside the Hirshorn computer, you'll see it's true.'

OH stopped pacing across the thick rug and turned to Dulles, wanting a response. He got only his disbelief.

'Jesus, Gordon, it's crazy, but it's worth a shot. If we could get the CFTC to buy this, and take a look at Hirshorn's holding. If those sales are badly padded they'll force them to divest. The price of wheat would head south and turn us the right way round.'

'Sure, we'd better take a crack at them, OH,' he said. 'But I figure spring rain might be a surer bet.'

'I'll talk to Margaret Meredith at the Commission. If anybody runs with this, that lady will. Give us any kind of evidence you've got, along with all your best guesses. We'll sink that bastard yet.'

That prospect visibly buoyed OH. 'I figure all we need is for Margaret Meredith to run, the banks to reschedule our debts, and the market to plunge.'

His gold smile glistened in the afternoon sun as Dulles' anxiety seeped back. Maybe OH could just bring this off. He was an old wildcat oilman, and sometimes no one got more lucky.

For the first time since getting out of the silo in Galveston Grace began to believe this might all come out as she had hoped. The meeting left her feeling positively cheerful as she drove back to the farm with Jak. He was in a good mood too, but she suspected that might be because he was returning with her, while Rory was heading back to Washington. Whether Jak realized it or not, they couldn't go back to the way things had been then. That would hardly have been fair in the circumstances. She loved both men for their very different qualities, but was prepared to live without either one of them, as clearly she couldn't have both. She wasn't even sure that she wanted them both. So perhaps she didn't want either. Through her initial confusion she had clung to Milly's advice, that she should try to find her own true centre, from where things had a way of working out. Everything else created some kind of distortion as you tried to please somebody or everybody.

The feeling of optimism vanished the moment they arrived back and Lee Stanford rushed to meet them. Babbling incoherently. He was pretty upset.

'Lee? What's happened?' Grace asked. 'What on earth's wrong?'

The young man was white and shaking. He tried and tried but couldn't get the words out. Alarm rose in Grace. Something was seriously wrong.

Jak searched around the yard for hidden dangers. Everything looked the same.

'G . . . Grace . . .' he managed at last. 'I done something really dumb. Jesus, I'm sorry . . . I'm really sorry . . .' He couldn't look at her. 'I called the FBI on Jak.'

'Lee, no! You stupid, stupid . . .' Anger flared in her and she wanted to grab him and shake him and make him tell her it wasn't true.

But Lee turned and fled, rushing across the field in front of the house and not stopping.

Panic caused Jak to leave straight after him, but not in the same direction. She had no option but to go with him. They went across to hide at the Banions' farm and await word of the FBI's arrival at the Gittlemans'. Word didn't come. Nerves tightened as tension mounted during the evening. Night fell and still the FBI hadn't shown up.

'Do you figure he called them, Grace?' Banion said.

'He called them.' She was quite certain about that. What she was less certain of was why. The sense of despair that settled over Jak expressed itself in self pity, and she felt irritated by it.

'We can't stay around here,' he said. 'I'm not sure that we could survive on the road now – you don't have to, Grace. I don't think I want to. I'm ready to turn myself in – maybe I should talk to Rory.'

'I'd better take you guys on in to Crocker-Giant come the morning,' Banion said. 'Maybe you can get the evidence you need.'

'But you might lose their business,' Grace said.

'Would that be something! Hell, all kinds of people want quality organic wheat these days. Don't worry about it none, Grace.'

No one challenged them as Banion headed his pick-up into Crocker-Giant. The morning was bright, clear and fresh after the recent rains, and the growing plots on the farm outside of Emporia looked vibrant with life.

A security guard was reading a book in the entrance of a large old farmhouse that served as the offices. He glanced up at the visitors.

'Morning, Pete,' Banion said. 'Feels like a hot one.'

'Bet you been praying,' – was his response.

'The rain sure helped. We're going up to see Jerry Wasko. Is he around yet?'

'Sure. He's up there someplace.'

They had to wait to see the contracts manager, but got coffee from the vending machine in the open-plan office that was a modern extension back off the house. People greeted Banion with something to say about the weather or farming. The normality of this worried Grace. These were obviously decent people, doing a job they plainly enjoyed. Could they be involved in something as dark and sinister as they suspected? She stopped herself. The wheat conspiracy had gotten started. Somebody was behind it, had engineered the wheat to fail. Decent, ordinary people sometimes got caught up in things they didn't know they were caught up in, she told herself.

Jerry Wasko was big and friendly, the kind of person who didn't look at all deceitful, she decided instantly. But she remembered Alan Banion's complaints about the way this company did business. Someone had to effect that policy. Wasko got some coffee and listened to Banion's difficulties with his bank simply because he hadn't seen a contract yet.

'They're late going out,' Wasko explained. 'I'll try and spring yours. Or I could call the bank for you.'

She was impressed by that. No one had done that for her at her bank.

'Sounds good. This is Jak and Grace Larcom.' Banion lied easily. 'They're starting a farm back east and want to talk about some organic lines.'

'That's where smart farmers are now.' He shook their hands and smiled at Grace until she found she had to look away. 'If Crocker can help you folks.'

'We plan on growing spring wheat – hybrid vigours.'

'You're talking to the right people – absolutely.'

'We saw one Alan grew for you – Prairie Red.'

Wasko looked at Banion and nodded. His body language changed, Grace noticed. It became stiffer, more alert.

'That's a possibility. A vigorous wheat. Stands well.'

Banion shifted uneasily, and finally made his excuses and went to get his contract sorted out.

The doubt about this man's involvement in anything wrong deepened when Jak asked for any data that was available on Crocker wheats. Jerry Wasko offered them a tour of the operation. A company with so much to hide wouldn't let them around the growing plots, through the work-up sheds, where they had controlled environment cabinets, with explanations of how they logged the progress and categorized every seed according to its genetic makeup. Crooks didn't behave like that.

'Is that for future patenting?' Jak wanted to know.

'Sure. The guy with the most patents controls the market. Hirshorn, Shell, Union Carbide. They're all scrambling for patents. What it does is ensure quality.'

'Won't weakness be bred into the seeds too?' Grace asked.

Wasko smiled at her. 'I love your Englishness, Grace. It's real charming. What we're out to do here, is improve on the original. Farmers saving seed from previous crops cause most problems with diseases carrying over. Wheat streak mosaic is our current headache. We'll get to a wheat that resists it eventually – like most other diseases.'

'What are the problems with Prairie Red?' Jack asked. 'We heard it was susceptible to Take-all.'

313

'We produced around one hundred and thirty thousand tons. We didn't see that kind of problem.' Wasko paused and looked between the two of them before shaking his head. 'No, sir, we did not.' Alarm bells started in Grace as she sensed this man knew who they were. That wasn't really reasonable, she told herself, but that didn't stop her panic or her desire to run. 'We've got all the Prairie Red details here on the computer.' He stepped up to the terminal on a bench in the shed and accessed the information.

Instantly Grace tried memorizing the access code, but was having difficulty concentrating. She glanced at Jak who was reading the information coming up on the green screen. Every stage of the seed's development was there.

'Why was the genetic material inserted into the plant so many times?' Jak asked.

'The code on the screen reading "GM 112" indicates genetic material for the hundred and twelfth time,' Wasko explained. 'We have tried more frequently to get plants to express themselves with foreign genetic material.'

'Was it attracting gaeumannomyces graminis or was it a process of resisting the Take-all virus?'

Wasko smiled. 'We did have some problem in the early trials with the seed attracting Take-all. Every bit of it we grew folded on us. That was such a damn shame after the promise it showed.' He checked his watch, then said, 'Look, you folks will have to excuse me. I've got some calls to make. But stick around, and I'll get back to you.'

He strode away along the shed and went out.

The urge to run came at Grace again. 'He suspects something,' she said. 'I just know he does.'

'That's crazy, Grace. How could he? It's here, the whole programme, everything we guessed. He wouldn't have gone off like that if he suspected anything.'

That seemed to make sense, but her anxiety wouldn't leave her. 'Maybe he wants us to reach for it just to be certain.'

'Well, his wish has come true. If we get this to Jimmy Keiller – Jesus.'

'They might kill us, Jak.'

314

That stopped him. He looked along the shed at the technicians. 'These are regular Americans with problems like you and me. That's sunlight outside. We can walk right out through those open doors.'

In these circumstances she wondered if what she suggested was possible. But someone had tried to stop them.

'He wouldn't be dumb enough to leave us here with this information if he figured we were some kind of danger.'

'It could be his phone call is going to make sure we're not,' she said. 'There's a phone right there on the wall.'

Jak looked at the phone, then at the technicians again. 'I don't want to believe this, Grace. I know some strange things have happened. But we came here to get hard evidence. Can we get this information out of the computer?'

With trembling fingers she tried the code she had memorized. Some part of it was wrong and she got 'error' on the screen. She tried again, reversing the last two digits. But then she didn't know how to get it onto the printer. In attempting to she repeatedly got 'bad command' up on the screen. Jak right alongside twitching with nervous tension, only made her more anxious and prone to error. 'I can't do it,' she said.

She tried again as he strode along the shed to one of the technicians.

'What is the printout command on the computer?' he asked.

'Didn't Jerry give it to you?' the man responded. 'Gee, I guess you should check back with him.'

'I forgot it – it's no big deal, –'

'Jak!' Grace called as the printer suddenly started. He came running back and gave her a hug. The technician picked up the phone and punched out a number. She saw Jak's look. 'I can't make it go any faster,' she said. 'I can't.'

'You remember the growing plots Wasko took us through. The grid references. Here.' He pointed to them on the printout. 'They last planted this seed in March in sections P2, P3 and P7. Look.'

'It should still be growing,' she said.

Grabbing the printed record the moment the machine

315

stopped, Jak flew out of the shed. 'Come on.'

She ran hard after him along the service road, checking off the plots which were each about a quarter of an acre. P-block was a half-mile from the building. They headed down the track between O-block and P-block. P2 and P3 had young spring wheat growing, both plots looked pretty healthy. On P7 was a miserable stand of stunted wheat that had been planted three weeks earlier. It looked exactly like she remembered the wheat Shearing had had fail back in England, and momentarily she felt sorry for him for accidentally getting caught up in something that he could have had no control over.

'The Russian wheat will look like that pretty soon.'

Grace became mesmerized with the image of millions of acres of wheat withering on the stalk. She found no difficulty imagining fields that stretched from one horizon to the next. She had seen Shearing's prairie-like wheatfield wither as though sprayed with herbicide, but despite everything she still couldn't quite believe that the Russian wheat was going the same way.

'We should get some of this to the CFTC,' Jak said, taking a knife and a plastic bag from his pocket.

'Will they really do anything, Jak?'

'I don't even want to think about that.' He plunged into the field and began digging up wheat plants.

She joined him and held the bag. The roots of the first plant they dug up were black and rotten.

'Regular Take-all couldn't ordinarily get so advanced in spring wheat this young.'

Panic caused Grace to leap up like a startled jack-rabbit. 'Let's get out of here. Please, Jak, now. Before something awful happens.'

'We've waited a long while for this. It's the evidence we need at last. We're sure not going to get back for more.'

Jak dug up another plant.

Without warning a strange bird appeared. An angel of death. She recognized it at once. It came in silently at first, headed directly for them. She watched, unable to move, unable to say a thing. Finally Jak heard it and rose.

'Grace!' he shouted, breaking her spell.

They took off across the field like sprinters, running directly beneath the plane, as it began descending. Their move was unexpected and the plane overshot them. Grace heard it bank again but kept running after Jak. The stand of trees they were headed for seemed too far to reach before they were overhauled.

She glanced round and saw the plane level off as it made its final run in on them.

Turning caused her to stumble and she cried as she fell. She saw Jak look back, then beyond her to the plane. There was only a moment's indecision before he turned and ran.

What his thinking was then she couldn't guess. She was too busy feeling deserted and hurt. She started to get upset. But then immediately stopped herself, refusing to allow herself to be disappointed in the actions of others. Back on her feet she ran hard, veering off to the left, trying to avoid the plane as it came in only yards above her head. It dumped the contents of its spray tanks, drenching her.

The shock caused the breath to go out of her and she stuttered forward, trying to protest through her breathlessness. She fell to the ground, gasping for air, drawing the pesticide into her lungs. The choking miasma enveloped her, filling the space between her and Jak, linking them in its sticky web. She coughed, feeling her lungs on fire. Her trachea began closing, while her rising panic shut out more air from her lungs.

The fact that she didn't die wasn't enough to convince her that she and Jak had only been sprayed with water, and that her suffocating reaction was emotion-induced hysteria. That made her feel worse. But she accepted it was so when she survived the showers inside the Crocker-Giant building, and afterwards was given a white zip-through paper coverall to put on. Her lungs stopped burning and she was able to breathe okay now. She just felt angry.

One of the two FBI agents who had been waiting for them when they were brought in off the field was talking on the phone to someone as she emerged from the shower

317

room. With his sombre nod into the phone and glances across at her and Jak, she assumed they were in more trouble than she had bargained for. Jak would go to prison. She would be deported, if not worse.

Finally the FBI agent hung up the phone and came across to them. His look measured her. She was naked beneath the paper suit and was made uncomfortable by that look.

'Are you okay now, mam?' he said.

'No, I'm bloody well not. What they did to us was . . . It was so irresponsible,' – using anger to mask her embarrassment.

'Sure,' he agreed. 'These folks were pretty mad at you for coming in here like this. But they don't plan on pressing charges.' He turned to Jak. 'It seems your work back in Washington is pretty important to someone, Dr Redford.'

'Great!' Jak mocked. 'Maybe the FBI can talk to someone about funding that – I'll just head back to Washington without a word of complaint.'

'I guess all you need is the right attitude, sir.'

'Aren't the FBI just amazing,' Jak said.

Grace began to think so too as uncertainty crept up on her. The FBI agent ignored the put down. 'I guess some wrong conclusions were jumped to back in Galveston.'

'You mean we're free to go?' She was almost afraid to ask.

'It's not that easy, mam. You've got a problem with Immigration. But I guess if your lawyer explains about the case you're taking through the Federal court, they'll give you a sympathetic hearing.' He smiled.

That smile disturbed her more deeply than anything that had happened recently and she was worried but didn't immediately know why. As they rode back to the Gittleman farm in uneasy silence, as though they had nothing to say to each other, she thought that maybe in her emotional hysteria, when she believed she was reliving Rose's death, she had stirred up other emotions that left her feeling this way. But for that FBI man's smile she might have shared Jak's unquestioning relief. Then suddenly she had the answer: someone somewhere had decided they were no longer dangerous rather than that they were innocent. They could be allowed to return home without any risk. She found that devastating.

'You okay, Grace?' Mike asked.

She nodded, holding back tears of disappointment that threatened to wash them all away.

'We're sure gonna miss you guys around the place.'

That made it harder for her to avoid the tears. 'I can't believe the FBI passing on us like they did.'

'On me!' Jak said. 'I figure they did a real fine job.'

After a moment she said, 'Jak, someone called them off. And we no longer have Crocker-Giant's printout on that wheat.'

'Grace, I don't give a damn. I'm not going on trial for murder. That feels pretty good to me. You bet.'

Glancing round at him, she realized this wasn't the man she had started out with. There was a mile-wide chasm between them. She knew it would get wider.

'Going on trial for murder might have been a very small price to pay in the circumstances.'

22

'NOWHERE DO I FEEL AS safe talking to you these days as I do in here,' his brother-in-law said as he settled in the sauna room. These days Gordon Dulles rarely paid them visits to the house with his wife and three of his kids. Caddy Hirshorn missed that. He especially liked seeing the kids. They got on well with his own.

'You've lost a lot of weight,' Dulles said. 'You're looking in great shape, Caddy. I need to dump some weight. I work out regularly, but this roll around my waist doesn't want to leave me.'

Caddy was propped on the slatted bench against the wall. He leaned forward to scoop some more water on the stones to get the heat up. He had lost weight but it hadn't been sweated away in the sauna. They didn't talk directly about the cancer he had had removed, or what the real prognosis was. The ploy to confuse the market with disinformation about the state of his health confused his brother-in-law too, he guessed.

'Caroline said you quit your physician. Is that smart, Caddy? The guy could tell the world you're not really sick.'

'I'm feeling pretty good, Gordon,' he replied. 'I'd bury him.' He laughed, enjoying this deception. It brought added excitement to his market manoeuvres that his health might otherwise have robbed him of.

'I've found a truly gifted homoeopath. Chinese. He cured Jake Rubin's brain tumour.' Such a wildly divergent change of course alarmed those around him as much as it had his physician. He suspected Gordon Dulles' problem was that he feared he truly was losing control.

'As long as he gets it right, Caddy.'

'You pay attention to detail, the right action follows. The same as in business. I should maybe get mad at Pat Shapiro. He hasn't been giving Hirshorn his best lately – a lot on his mind.'

'The guy wants to get rich.'

'I can't see any argument with that, Gordon. It's how he figures on going about it. Our lawyers found a way to deal with Dr Redford and his lady friend – finally.'

'What if they talk to the Commission and they decide to go after us?'

'Redford? No. He had too much to lose. Margaret Meredith wants to make a name for herself at the CFTC. She's making the worst kind of mistake tying in with OH. They had an affair a while back. We're filing a complaint to the chairman of the Commission, citing her for prejudicial behaviour. How bad is it looking for Oscar?'

'The Board of Trade have increased the maintenance on his speculative margins again. As of yesterday he can't settle his losses. He's still trying to go long, but the banks won't meet him. They've given him till Tuesday or they close him out. We're all looking for alternative sources of finance. There aren't too many options.'

'Wheat will make six dollars a bushel even *before* the market gets to hear about the Russians coming in short.'

'Are the Russians going to have anything to come with? Our friends on Capitol Hill will need a lot of persuading to lend them that kind of money,' Dulles cautioned.

Caddy nodded. 'They'll get the money. They'll come. We'll get some rain out here, Gordon. We'll sell some wheat. Get the price down – we might even pick up a little more wheat before the Russians get to town.'

He rose slowly and threw a whole pitcher of water over the hot stones, making clouds of steam. He could tolerate the kind of heat that sent most people heading for the exit.

'Steer Oscar to the Toronto bankers James and Howell. They'll lend him twenty million dollars on his elevator out on the lake.'

321

'It's worth three or four times that.'

'Sure. But his bankers here will grab it without giving him another dime. James and Howell will close him out just the same, but they'll sell us his elevator. I guess Oscar won't be paying your bonus, Gordon.'

'I'll pass on suing him.' Dulles gave him his old pirate smile even without his eye-patch on. 'We'd better not underestimate the CFTC, Caddy. They could still have us divest our holding. We'd have a lot of problems if they move for a one hundred per cent margin call. They might go for that option with Margaret Meredith pushing.'

'It won't happen. We'd fight all the way, Gordon.' He laughed. It was a good feeling.

The laughter from Gordon Dulles sounded hollow.

He wondered if his brother-in-law's nerve was beginning to crack. Now wasn't the time.

With their relationship being that of banker and favoured client, past meetings he had had with Dick Richards had been gentlemanly affairs, usually conducted over an indifferent lunch in a local hotel in Bury St Edmunds. But since the change in their relationship to something bordering criminal, signals to meet tended to be more urgent. The latest demand by Richards followed notification he had received from the regional bank about an inspection he was getting next week of clients' accounts with large and persistent indebtedness.

'Isn't this a routine procedure to make sure there's sufficient security against loans?' Walter Shearing said. 'There is, Dick, more than enough. I don't think we're going to cause the bank long-term liquidity problems.'

Richards continually wiped imaginary dirt from the edge of his desk with his finger. 'This inspection couldn't be coming at a worse time. Alarm bells might sound if the collateral you've put up is inspected too closely.'

'I can't see why that would happen. This is a *routine* inspection. I know enough about banking to recognize that. If it wasn't they'd descend without warning.'

'Wheat's at $5.010 a bushel in Chicago,' Richards pointed out. 'We should liquidate.'

He was not pleased by this panic summons. Less pleased to be told to sell his investment short. He knew that whatever problem Richards phoned with it meant the same thing, loss of nerve. He thought about the other two bank managers who were involved, neither presented any kind of problem. The documentation they had for collateral sat in their vaults and they issued money to buy wheat futures as if there were no question as to its probity. At their meeting to review the situation they ascertained future requirements in a manner that suggested this was regular business, taking the dips and rises in the market with the same equilibrium.

'You can't be serious about liquidating. I want to be further ahead than $1,800,000 before we do.'

'But I'm calling on more and more funds as we buy more wheat contracts. Another two hundred and seventy-five today. That's $348.562 needed for the margin. I think we should call a halt, Walter, while we're ahead.'

'I think not.' Shearing calculated what 1.375 million bushels would earn them if wheat went to six dollars as Pat Shapiro's boss was convinced it would. 'Just draw down more money from my loan account to meet the margin call.'

'I'm not sure if I can – not with Region's inspectors coming. If they discover the deeds to your property are photocopies I'm dead. I'd like to get out now and take our profit.'

'Absolutely not,' Shearing said. 'You might be satisfied with a few thousand pounds to supplement your tacky little gambling habit. I'm more ambitious. If you sell us short now, I guarantee your career with this bank or any other bank will be finished.'

A low cry was emitted from the bank manager.

'Every day the market trades we win – ignoring the dips. All you have to do is keep your nerve.'

'God, if this goes wrong,' Richards whined, 'I don't know what I'll do.'

'You'll jump under a bus, like the rest of us. Everything's working exactly as Shapiro said. In five or six weeks, we'll see five million pounds plus profit. Think about a million pounds of your own, earning you ten per cent for your retirement. Meet those margin calls. You know you can.'

Richards closed his eyes.

For a moment Shearing thought he was about to cry.

'It is all possible if you keep your nerve.'

'But I know what Region will say if I allow more to be drawn against your loan account. They will scrutinize your affairs closely. They will, I promise you.'

'Then find another way.'

Richards buried his face in his hands. After a moment he said, 'There is a way. There are a lot of securities belonging to another customer, Mrs Kettley. She's getting quite old. They're in the vault. Negotiable bonds. She never disturbs them from one year to the next. I suppose one could simply lodge those with the broker to satisfy the margin.'

'Are you sure they won't be missed?'

'I can't think that they would be. She hasn't touched that paper in years. They would go back immediately after we liquidate our position. Neither Mrs Kettley nor anyone need ever know.' He swallowed hard. 'I can't see any other way of meeting the margin calls.'

'Then do it,' Shearing said, ignoring the illegality of the move.

Rain was falling in sheets out at National Airport as he waited for Hirshorn's Lear jet to taxi in. Pat Shapiro stepped onto the disembarkation lot from the stretch limo and held a large umbrella over his boss as he came off the plane. Along with Carl Flint the lawyer, they were headed in to a meeting with Commissioner Margaret Meredith at the CFTC. The rain had fallen steadily for two days, and following so close after the huge batch of wheat Hirshorn had sold, it had helped bring the price of wheat down a whopping forty-eight cents a bushel. None of it did Hirshorn any harm, but paradoxically did a lot of short-term damage to Oscar Hartmine, who got badly squeezed on the margins with contracts he had gone long on. How had Caddy got to know so much about

324

International? He assumed from his brother-in-law. Shapiro suspected he was being kept out of things more and more. That worried him, especially as he didn't know why.

'How much does the CFTC have?' Caddy asked as they headed in across the Potomac.

'Mrs Kuhfuss may have talked to them about Mark's holding. I guess we can't blame her for that,' he said, choosing not to think one unkind thought about Kuhfuss now in case it came back on him. 'Those enforcement dicks were practically camped in her back yard.'

'We tried to stop them harassing her,' the lawyer explained. 'The judge denied us.'

'Judge Parker?' Caddy said. 'The judge who is trying the case against our chicken plants?'

'Unfortunately we couldn't reach Judge Parker,' Flint said.

'What the hell do you mean, unfortunately, Carl?' Caddy snapped. 'Are these things left to chance? We've got a judge whose political ambitions coincide with our desired result, and we don't get him in on this business? Did he refuse to help us here?'

'No. He was out of town.'

Seeing Caddy in such a bad mood Shapiro was reluctant to be the bearer of yet more bad news. But he knew he had to tell him.

'My informant says the Commission had a pretty comprehensive list of Hirshorn employees holding wheat for us. The good news is they can't get anybody to talk.'

Caddy simply nodded, and looked askance at Shapiro, causing panic to settle over him. Slowly, he sucked in air through his teeth, trying to get control of his breathing.

The elegant Margaret Meredith, the CFTC Commissioner with investigations oversight, knew how to use her considerable charm. But her soft, feminine image was deceptive, and belied a hard edge which he suspected had cleaved many an unsuspecting male ego. Shapiro not only was unmoved, but took an instant dislike to her. Her office was overstuffed with antique furnishings which bore out his friend's information about how she skilfully made the bureaucracy work for her. She got the chairman to support her in any direction she chose to go. She had been known to approach the House Agricultural Committee in Congress directly, and without getting her chairman mad at her.

Caddy was impervious to her charm also, and blocked every avenue she tried to open up. Shapiro enjoyed that. But this was a lady who was used to scheming, and he could almost hear the movements of her mind as she tried to manoeuvre around yet another blocked response.

'I plan on picking up *more* wheat, Margaret,' Caddy told her in the face of the suggestion that he divest his holding in wheat of his own free will. 'The price is easing now the Midwest has had some rain. It makes sense to pick up more wheat.'

'The Commission can't allow that, Caddy.' Her tone took on a threatening note. 'You recently sold a million tons of wheat. That helped the price some.'

'I merely took a little profit to purchase an elevator up on the lake – that must have helped out Oscar Hartmine even if the easing wheat price didn't.' Caddy offered a tired kind of smile.

'You bought International's lakeside elevator?' Commissioner Meredith seemed surprised. 'I haven't seen that reported, only that OH was in trouble.' She looked at Jimmy Keiller who plainly didn't have that information either.

'It belonged to the Canadian bankers James and Howell. Some prior arrangements they had with Oscar.' Caddy shrugged.

'Mrs Meredith,' Flint said, 'Hirshorn had legitimate title to every bushel of the wheat it sold. We didn't infringe the rules.'

'It's not the wheat futures Hirshorn holds in its own name that concerns us, Mr Flint,' the Commissioner said, 'but those you are speculating in through nominee accounts with the intention of manipulating the market.'

'Come on, Margaret,' Shapiro said, 'you'd be between a rock and a hard place proving that.'

'You've a speculative position of ten million tons that

you effected in tandem with employees, sir,' Keiller said. 'Contrary to the maximum three million bushel net long or net short position.'

'We've optioned a lot of wheat to fill a lot of customers' orders. Good customers. American customers. People we don't plan to let down.'

'Customers owned by your company, Caddy, all with three and four times what they regularly buy.'

'Not a single bushel of that won't get delivered,' Shapiro said.

'Sure.' Margaret Meredith smiled, showing her evenly capped teeth. 'Why are so many of your employees holding wheat contracts, if not pursuant to a clear concert of action?'

'The last I heard I was a market leader,' Caddy said. 'I make a move, folks follow. The wheat contracts I hold are in strict compliance with the rules, Margaret.' It was Caddy's standard answer.

Margaret Meredith smiled again when she said, 'I figure you will try and make us eat dirt over this, Caddy. But we can live with that. Jimmy's made over a hundred employees each holding three million bushels.'

'Has a single one of them admitted that?' Shapiro said.

'Most of them would die for Caddy. In fact we figure one of them did. We talked with Mrs Kuhfuss. She knows her husband was killed because he talked to us.'

'If you're peddling that story,' Caddy said, 'you'd better have some hard evidence to support it, Margaret, or I might start getting mad.'

'She's waiting to hear from you because she doesn't know what to do with all those contracts Kuhfuss was holding.'

'I'll call her,' Caddy said. 'Give her the benefit of my experience.'

'We're getting pressure from other traders,' she said.

She stared across her large desk at Caddy. Shapiro felt she was defying him to challenge her previous relationship with Oscar Hartmine, the main complainant. He glanced at his boss, thinking for a moment that he might bring it up. He was disappointed that he didn't.

'I had hoped to *persuade* you to liquidate your position, Caddy. So what I plan on doing is asking the Kansas City Board of Trade to impose a hundred per cent margin call on all wheat contracts. You might find it cheaper to liquidate your position.'

'Do that and you'll put every other trader out of business. There'll be all kinds of shortages – nobody will sell physicals. I'll be the only player left in the game. How would Oscar Hartmine meet those kinds of margin calls?'

An almost imperceptible smile slid across Shapiro's face. He waited, closely watching Margaret Meredith. She didn't miss a beat.

'Then I'll have the KC District Court order you to liquidate down to three million bushels,' she said.

Caddy rose. 'Margaret, I'll see you in court.'

Going down to the elevator, Caddy said, 'You figure anybody other than Oscar Hartmine is calling foul here?'

'A lot of people are getting hurt,' Shapiro said. 'But Hartmine's the only one making any real noise, I guess.'

'A lot of the other traders will support our position. We've got to do some work on that,' Caddy said. 'How did Oscar get our delivery figures?'

'I figure Kuhfuss gave them to Redford and Mrs Chance.'

The elevator arrived at the lobby and Flint held the doors open. But Caddy didn't step out for a moment.

Shapiro waited as his boss's look slowly rounded on him. His breathing started getting difficult.

'Is that why they killed him?' The words were cold and smashed open his mind like Caddy was using an ice-pick on him. 'It makes no sense. It was a dumb move to try and lay blame for his death on those two. It was certain to rebound on us with the two fugitives proving they weren't killers.'

He shook his head, stepped out across the lobby, leaving Shapiro feeling isolated and sick at his stomach, like that whole problem was going to come right back at him.

As a communicator Commissioner Meredith used every resource at her disposal. She was a surprising lady too, calling a press conference as she had to announce her moves against him. Despite the problems that might cause him, Caddy admired her steely nerves. When the time was right he planned to offer her a job with Hirshorn, one she wouldn't be able to refuse. He wasn't concerned what her past relationship with Oscar Hartmine had been. At her press conference she proved articulate, accessible and charming. Watching her on the TV screen in his study, he recognized a personality that attracted men and one that would have women believing every word she said. Here she had cast herself as the bulwark against rising food prices, while he was a pirate who would hold the consumer to ransom with bread at five dollars plus a loaf. She was good. If Hartmine had managed to keep this lady on his board he might not have his current trouble, and they might not have been able to insinuate Gordon Dulles into his company. But as effective as she was, he knew how vulnerable she was through Hartmine.

Outside the Commission building on K Street the *Eyewitness* reporter summarized the story like nobody could possibly have understood what Margaret Meredith had said, explaining how the CFTC were asking the District Court to liquidate Hirshorn's excessive holdings. Caddy only half listened to the reporter, thinking instead of how the *Wall Street Journal* would treat the story, putting it into context with some serious analysis of the crisis in farming and the knock-on effect for banks carrying such large farm debt. Shapiro had spoken to a contact there, giving Hirshorn's case. Carl Flint was preparing a general response for the media.

Randomly now his thoughts moved on to his health. He sensed it failing and was afraid his economic power would go with it. He wondered if what was happening on the business front was part of the pathology the homoeopath had spoken of to him over the phone. Why with all his wealth, enough to literally move mountains, was this such highly recommended Chinese physician proving so inaccessible? There could be few clients able to pay him more. He might die before the man scheduled a meeting with him.

The phone started ringing on his private line that only a small number of people had.

Armand Bequai, the Wall Street broker, was calling about *Eyewitness* News.

'I didn't figure she would talk to the press,' Caddy said. 'But I do admire the nerve of that lady for doing so.'

'Cite her for prejudicial behaviour,' Bequai said. 'She once sat on Hartmine's board – on his cock too, according to gossip.'

Caddy felt embarrassed. He didn't enjoy the earthy language that most men used to discuss sex. 'She's an attractive lady, Armand,' he replied. 'But Shapiro's working on that angle.'

'When the markets open tomorrow wheat'll go down again with this on the streets. Dealers are figuring you'll have to divest. There was heavy selling at close today. It could open down limit, somewhere around four-point-six dollars. I've started buying.'

'Keep right on buying wheat. All you can get.'

A few minutes later Flint called to read his press release.

Caddy listened to the carefully worded statement, and made minor adjustments. 'Unethical, Carl, not unprecedented, for government officials to break confidentiality. The rest is good. Shapiro's getting information on the lady's relationship with Hartmine. Add that to the statement. How is it looking for us legally?'

'Unless some of our employees talk, the Commission can only assume we're in concert. But their administrative judge could lock up our futures contracts way past delivery anyway, Caddy.'

'That would cost us a lot more,' he said. 'If we were to short the market with these wheat contracts we would make a good profit. Not as much as I planned on making by taking delivery and selling to the Russians. Getting this wheat locked up is how big a gamble?'

'They'd need good cause,' Flint told him. 'The appellate court might see it different. What we need to reduce the risk is some political help.'

He nodded slowly to himself, knowing just where to get it from.

330

'I'm not giving up a single bushel, Carl – add that to the press release. I'll talk to Deke Turetsky at the White House to make sure I don't have to liquidate.'

Forgetting to set the brake and seeing the car roll away and come to a halt against a huge tractor tyre in his farm yard, indicated to Walter Shearing the sort of mental state Richards was getting into. He wasn't sure how the man had driven here like this. Death on the road might have released him from the terror which had increased its grip on him ever since the price of wheat had started to fall. His death would certainly have brought added complications, like someone from Region closely scrutinizing the collateral the bank held against his loans. These were undeniably dangerous times with bigger and bigger margin calls being made daily by the brokers.

'I daren't talk to you from the bank, I daren't,' the manager whined as Shearing quickly led him away from a fertilizer truck that was being unloaded. 'Did you see the price of wheat this morning?'

'Yes, I saw it. Of course I did,' he snapped.

'It's disastrous – we should have sold when I said. It's a disaster.'

'Shut up. It'll rise again. Hirshorn are still buying – I talked to Shapiro, he says we've got to keep on buying.'

'Shapiro says! Shapiro says,' Richards echoed like a taunting child. 'Don't you realize we've lost nearly four million dollars over this past week – we've had to find that to settle the brokers. They want yesterday's trading losses, and they're increasing our margin.'

'Give it to them,' Shearing said. 'Pay them, for Christsake.'

'I can't, Walter. I've already used Mrs Kettley's securities. Right at this moment I see no way of getting them back. If she were to call for them now, we'd go to prison.'

'You bloody fool – if we don't meet the margin they'll sell us out – I'll lose everything. How will you get them back then?'

'I should never have got into this,' Richards said. 'I never should have let it get started.'

'You're in whether you like it or not. So stop whining like a bloody old woman and think of some practical solution.'

Clearly Richards had none.

In his office he stopped pacing, his face turning white with anger. He knew what he had to do, that it was useless relying on this partner to do it. Then he decided that when he managed to pull them all clear of this crisis Richards would no longer be his partner, he wouldn't get a penny share in the profits.

'Which of the three banks has the original deeds to my property?' he said. 'I'll use them as security and raise the money we need in the City.'

It was nine years since he had practised law but he had kept up friendships with the senior partners of his old law firm. Tim Wheeler-Penrose was also on the board of a merchant bank and was happy to talk to him about money.

'I hope you're not being blackmailed, old son,' Wheeler-Penrose said as he glanced over the deeds. He laughed.

Shearing didn't give any explanation of why he wanted to borrow two million pounds against his property.

The banker had dined with him on many occasions at his beautiful Queen Anne house and knew the value of the farm. The title deeds he'd brought to lunch clearly told his former partner the property was unencumbered with any sort of mortgage.

'I can't see any kind of problem at all, Walter. Unless you want to walk out with it in readies.' He laughed again.

Shearing laughed too, as much in fear as relief.

23

OVER THE LAST THREE YEARS Wilf Fear had been little more than a name to Caddy Hirshorn, someone connected with covert activity; possibly the person who engineered Mark Kuhfuss's death; a faceless facilitator without whom democratically elected governments couldn't function – nor autocratically run businesses.

A capable person, was his instant assessment when he met the man who was waiting by his stretch limo at National Airport. He held both his sticks in one hand and shook hands first with him and then with Caroline. A man who was socially adept, but devoid of real emotion, he decided, as they rode into the city. Fear talked knowledgeably to Caroline about couture clothes that were available in Georgetown. A person you wouldn't want working other than on your side, but paradoxically, a person you were almost certain to regret working on your side. Watching him as he massaged one of his damaged legs, which was rested on the adjacent tip-up seat in the back of the car, he was coming to regret this man's involvement without quite knowing why. He wasn't even sure why Fear had met them at the airport. The prime purpose of this trip was his much awaited visit to Wing Lu to get his homoeopathic treatment started. If he was patient and gave nothing, he figured his curiosity about the CIA man would eventually be satisfied.

Nothing was ever free.

That was his first lesson from his Daddy. Any business employing outside agencies, even those belonging to government, eventually had the tab presented. That was

333

what this visit was about. The price. Fear was writing out the tab during this ride in to the White House to see Deke Turetsky, the President's senior advisor. He had known from the start, when Gordon Dulles had first told him of the CIA's involvement with the extraordinary plan to dump the Russian spring wheat that there would be a price. Possibly even a high one. Three and a half years ago when their objectives had been different but compatible, almost any price would have seemed acceptable; but now according to Fear, they were not only different but completely incompatible. Under pressure from the Pentagon, who were having problems with their budget deficits and armament deficits re-emerging with the communist threat from Eastern Europe, the CIA were trying to move the goalposts. Wheat wasn't an object to be bartered with for peace, but the means of reintroducing the cold war.

'No one objects to you making a profit, Caddy,' Fear said. 'You'd still make a handsome profit if you liquidate now.'

'No doubt about that, Wilf,' he said. 'Maybe as much as a billion dollars clear. Who would complain about that?'

Fear laughed like he believed he had his agreement in the bag. 'The Commission would get off your back. You could take the money and run.'

'Your people have that kind of pull with the CFTC?' he asked. 'I guess they do at that. What about the judge who's hearing the case against Hirshorn Chicken? Could you have him accommodate us all the way down the line?'

A smile creased Fear's face and he reached into his coat and removed some folded sheets and handed them to him. 'Judge Westbury Parker hasn't led a blameless life.' He glanced at Caroline.

Caddy glanced at the report on the judge. It looked incriminating. 'Presumably this would do it to the judge. Hirshorn Chicken would have a clean bill of health. Right?'

'This is not just the Pentagon looking for a few more tanks and rocket launchers, sir. But a whole constituency out there that's fed to the back teeth with *glasnost*. No one wants the bad old cold war back, but some people in the Pentagon figure we're being suckered.'

He looked at the CIA man for a long while, realizing his mind was as crippled as his body. He didn't like the route it was attempting to lead him along.

'You guys will need something more to bait the Russian bear than me refusing to sell them my wheat.'

With a nod, Fear said, 'That'll do for a start, Caddy.'

'I need time to think about this,' he said like he was perfectly amenable to the idea of such a prize getting snatched from his grasp. 'It's never the prize that gets me up mornings. God, do I love the thrill of the race. Taking the Russians to the brink over this wheat gets the adrenalin flowing. Let me think about your proposition.'

'Sure, there's time before they come looking for grain.'

'If I buy this, I'd need to handle things my way,' he said looking to gain some time. 'If the market even suspects I'm caving in I'd make less than a great deal of money.'

'Sure. I understand.'

Caddy smiled, wondering who was kidding who. He wasn't about to make any decision before he had his meeting with the President's senior advisor.

'My needs are simple, Deke,' he said from a comfortable armchair in Turetsky's opulent office with its view of the front portal of the White House. 'I want the CFTC off my back.'

'The President knows you for a real friend, Caddy. He'd like to accommodate you, but the Commission is making its noise public. That's why those guys have a mandate – so that everybody gets a fair crack.'

'I have no problem of any kind with that – when the Commission behaves impartially.'

'If a holding as big as yours got sold to the Russians, Caddy,' Turetsky said, 'inflation in the domestic market would cause the President all kinds of problems. We'd lose the beneficial effect a deal this size would have on the deficit.'

'The Russians are going to come looking for wheat, Deke. You can count on it. If they can make my price . . .'

'This whole thing is no longer as simple as saving the farmers' ass, or the banks' ass.'

'You're changing the ground rules. Right?'

'A lot has happened since this got started. Power bases in the Pentagon have regrouped. Those guys are prepared to make relations as cold as is necessary to suit their purpose.'

'Deke, you're a deeply untrustworthy fellow,' he said. 'You came to me looking for help to get the President elected. I kicked in; I liked his free market ideas. Your people came to me to help save the American farmer, and some banks, too, from what I could see. I put my company on the line – sure, I'll make some money.'

'A hell of a lot of money, Caddy.'

'What do you guys figure I'd do with all this wheat?'

'The President can't live with bread at five dollars a loaf.'

'Let him eat cake, like everyone else,' he said.

The presidential advisor didn't get the joke.

'He won't eat dirt, Caddy, that's for sure.'

Caddy looked out over the shaved lawn below the terrace and stretched, running his hands across his springy close-shorn hair. Anxiety that had been creeping over him suddenly left him. He saw a way here to make an even bigger pile of money than he would on the original deal, without being at odds with the President and those power bases in both the Pentagon and on Capitol Hill, but he would need Wilf Fear's help. That he wasn't so sure about, the CIA man not being driven by anything as decent as profit.

'You'd still make big bucks.' Turetsky nodded. 'I'm told you got a hundred employees working in concert and holding close to eight million tons of wheat. The Commissioners did their homework.'

A friendly smile started across Caddy's face.

'Gee, Deke, I'd hate to rely on those guys.' He paused and considered the economist, thinking how he'd hate to have to rely on this man too when the chips were down. All politicians were basically dishonourable; those people who advised them tended to be worse than dishonourable. 'This is a hard business. Sometimes you make a profit by shaving fractions of pennies per bushel; sometimes you bottom out like Oscar Hartmine. But always we feed the world, meet that great human need, Deke, no matter who is president or how long he's there for. The CFTC got their sums wrong. Did they ever. I'm holding nearer to twenty-four million tons of wheat, and I'm still buying all I can get.'

'Half the domestic market? That's not possible, Caddy.'

'The good Lord blesses the harvest, Deke. Look at the open interest in May and July wheat. I've got companies the Commission would never trace to me holding contracts. I haven't been sitting on my butt for three years. The wheat I've cornered would give the world's five hundred million undernourished a hundred loaves each. The US government could provide that, or the Canadian Wheat Board, or the European Community. But they don't. Oh sure, they give them some, a little here, a little there – enough to ensure the Third World stays dependent. Do you know why they don't give the starving enough to live decently? Because we all operate according to market forces, and there is no free lunch.

'I traded on inside information about the Russian wheat harvest taking a nosedive, that was part of the deal – none of us knew what was going to happen in Eastern Europe. When the Russians come to me to buy wheat, if they can make the price they get the goods. That's the way the market operates, that's the direction some of us have been persuading those folk out there to go in. We know the market's the only system that works, Deke. I figure either the Russians get my wheat, or we'll see such turmoil out there the whole of mankind will be on the brink. Keep it in mind when you talk with the President. I'm not divesting, Deke. Not one single bushel will I let go unless it's a physical sale.'

He rose and extended his hand. 'It's always a pleasure, Deke. Now I have another appointment.'

In the corridor Wilf Fear shuffled after him and said, 'Guys in the Pentagon and on the Hill are going to get real mad if it goes through. Your friends in high places will stop taking your calls. Why are you so wedded to this goddamn Russian wheat deal, Caddy?'

'The truth is I'm not.' He paused at the top of the stairs and waited for Fear. 'There is a way that both our objectives can be compatible. I'd need some help from your people.'

'Where does it leave the Russians?' Fear asked.

'No place they'd want to be. But with God's help, and a little more from your people, Wilf, we'll finish exactly where we both have it in mind to finish.'

They started down the stairs together.

'I'm sure the men behind the men with the guns will be real pleased to hear that,' Fear said and smiled with a crease in his face like the Grand Canyon.

In the car as they drove away from the White House down West Exec Caroline asked, 'Do you trust him, Caddy?'

'I'll keep my eyes open,' he said.

On M Street, way above Wisconsin, the chauffeur ignored the impatient honking of cars as he crawled along looking for the address of the homoeopath.

'He'll get it right, Caddy,' Caroline said, taking his hand.

He clearly read her anxiety about his health, knew she was still questioning the wisdom of changing his physician on the sole recommendation of one of their grain brokers whose brain tumour had been cured by this man.

'I don't aim to leave you yet.' He lingered too long over the kiss he gave her to be that convincing.

'Shall I come in and wait?'

'He said the initial examination takes two hours. He'll want to talk to you after. Meet me back here.'

He squeezed her hand as the chauffeur opened the door.

Details of his distant relationships with his parents were dredged from his memory as he sat facing the homoeopath across the polished hardwood bench in Wing Lu's office. The paper blind at the window filtered the sunlight, making the sparsely furnished room restful. He almost drifted off to sleep. The hard, low seat he was on and the anger his memories stirred up kept him awake. With a distance of twenty-two years from his Daddy's death, he had been convinced that they had had a great relationship, one of master and pupil, each having something to teach the other. But that wasn't how it was coming out here. He remembered the humiliation he suffered whenever he got things wrong; he had told himself they were lessons his Daddy needed to teach him in the harsh world of business. But it had got that he was terrified of making a mistake for fear his Daddy would tear into him. He had learned fast and well, and didn't make mistakes, and then had become so powerful that any mistake, however costly, would never be challenged. But he was left with a legacy of anger and hostility that he didn't know he had, until he began opening up to this stranger who clearly wasn't impressed by worldly possessions or power, and didn't appear to be listening anyhow. Glancing across at him and seeing his eyes closed, he wondered why he was letting this pour out. Maybe he was getting angry at Lu for not listening or not telling him what his problem was. Just what it was he expected from this homoeopath, apart from some instant cure, he wasn't sure. He at least expected him to take some notes, or make a physical examination apart from looking at the scars on his back.

Moving forward from those bitter memories to what was going on currently, and making money, made him feel more comfortable, in control.

'This deal is so big. It doesn't bear thinking about. We're talking maybe four billion dollars. The Russians will drive the price sky high. It's been a long time coming, a deal like this. My company does pretty good. I'm pretty rich. According to *Forbes Magazine* I rate among the ten richest people in America. It'll be something to see, dealers and traders and speculators grabbing for wheat when this thing breaks, taking what they can get at any price. Panic and greed is what will drive them. Nothing else. There's never truly any real shortage. I'll be controlling the whole market because I made all the right moves all the way down the line. It takes your breath away just thinking about it.'

Opening his eyes, Caddy looked at the moon-shaped face opposite him. It showed not a single line, even though he guessed the guy was his own age, early fifties.

'Do you want to hear this, Mr Lu?'

339

'You don't wish to tell me, Mr Hirshorn. Why is that?'

'I don't have any kind of problem there.'

'You don't get angry when you talk about your deals.'

'That's because I've got control of everything. Almost everything. There are a couple of details that could get loose.'

Wing Lu nodded slowly. 'The better I know you, the more effective your remedy. Bodily symptoms are only a manifestation of what is inside. Simply removing the symptom as your physician did does not remove the cause.'

'What is the cause?' he wanted to know.

'I have known you only two hours. I'd be a fool to pretend to know,' Lu said as he swayed rhythmically on his seat bones. 'Possibly it relates to your need to make lots of money, which you hang onto, possibly out of fear of poverty.'

'I'm a very rich man. Didn't you hear what I told you about *Forbes Magazine*? I've never been poor.'

'There is not always apparent logic to our fears.'

'I try to be generous,' he said. 'I've always tried to be Christian. Possibly you don't understand the Christian way. I give ten per cent of my personal income – gross. To the Church, to cancer research . . .'

'Why do you do that – why do you give to cancer research?'

'To help those people find a cure for cancer.'

'For you, Mr Hirshorn?' Lu smiled.

'I had it in mind for anybody who gets cancer.'

'But the pathology of each case is uniquely individual. Can there ever be any universal panacea? Only the materialism of our age leads us to expect one. You can only cure yourself of cancer when you realize the cause. All I can do is try to find a remedy that will help this process. Sometimes the remedy succeeds; sometimes the person fails to self-realize.'

'If I gave more of my income away,' Caddy asked, 'would the cancer go?'

'Possibly, if that proves to be the blockage. Money is a form of energy. If you block any flow of energy then problems are created. Scientists develop pills to make you unblocked but it doesn't solve the problem. Part of your pathology is hanging onto food, like money, possibly fearing there will be none tomorrow. Your accumulating more grain than anyone in the history of the world has ever managed to is a symptom of your pathology.'

'That's business,' he protested. 'Clear and simple.'

'But of course. What if you had no grain?'

'I wouldn't have any money – bottom line.'

'Would that be the end of the world?'

'It would be pretty inconvenient.'

Lu closed his eyes and rocked some more, smiling as he did so.

'Are you saying I shouldn't be rich, Mr Lu?'

'I can't judge whether you should be rich or poor. People get diseases because of their own uniquely individual pathology. We must seek a remedy that helps you come to the truth. Why not stay there for a few moments and face your worst fear.'

'I haven't got any fears, Mr Lu,' he said.

'Then you are a fortunate man indeed.'

The homoeopath rose from his woodblock stool and went out.

Immediately Caddy feared that this man wasn't going to treat him, but couldn't bring himself to call him right back and admit that he did have fears. Instead he remained on that solid wooden chair and let his mind drift back to his Daddy, and what had driven that man so relentlessly: fear of God and the business failing after he had managed to pull it back from the brink of disaster. His father's entire life had been business. The work ethic he had instilled in him was born out of the spectre of failing. Caddy had the same kind of drive, but also a determination not to neglect his family in the process of developing his business. He thought about being without help and penniless in the world to test himself. His mind explored the possibility and the more he tried the harder it was to imagine. Because of that he concluded it wasn't a fear he had.

When he dressed and went out to the ante-room he

341

found Caroline talking with the homoeopath. Lu wanted both her and the children to write in as much detail as possible all they observed about him. He wondered what he would have said about his Daddy if he'd been given such an opportunity. Anger surfaced again. He believed his children would deal with him more kindly.

'When do you want to see me again?' he asked.

'Perhaps in three, perhaps six months' time,' Wing Lu said, surprising him. 'It will depend how quickly your remedy helps to bring about change. First I will work on your remedy and send it to you. I would like you to note all changes that start to occur when you take the remedy, mood states, feelings, mind states.'

'Don't I get anything to take now?'

Lu shook his head. 'The sooner I get those details from you and the children, Mrs Hirshorn, the sooner I can complete the remedy. Now I would like one hundred and fifty dollars.'

'Send your bill, for the attention of Mrs Fitzgibbon,' he said. His secretary took care of such matters.

'I don't send bills,' Lu told him. 'Money is an exchange of energy. If this is a problem to you I can live with two-thirds of my fee.'

He laughed out loud, enjoying the feeling. 'I don't have that kind of problem. Do you have any money?'

Caroline shook her head. 'I have maybe ten dollars in my purse. Some credit cards.'

He didn't even carry those.

'A cheque will be fine,' the homoeopath suggested.

A chequebook wasn't something he carried either. How could he fear being without money? he thought, as he went to borrow the $150 from his driver. He never carried money in case he was mugged, but concluded that he wasn't afraid of ever being without money.

342

24

THERE WAS AN UNREALITY ABOUT returning to the house on P Street. Grace couldn't relate to anything there, and couldn't put herself in contact with a single reason for being in Washington. Not even Rory. It was as though suddenly he was potentially no longer a partner for life, and wasn't even in the race, despite his phone calls and desire to meet with her. Life in the city crowded with people and automobiles and buildings seemed such an alien way to live after the Gittlemans' farm. She wanted to get right back on the plane. The most immediate problem was in being here with Jak now they no longer seemed to be going in the same direction. The situation was made more tense because she had ceased sharing the same bed. Jak was forever cornering her, trying to pin her down to see if her plans involved him. He was so pleased to have been wrenched clear of all that chaos, and nothing would make him risk getting plunged back into it. At first she tried to be reasonable, tried not to blame him for wanting to find the threads of his life which involvement with her had badly frayed; but she did blame him, and felt angry with him as she sensed their opportunity to do something slip further away. Jak refused to talk about what might have been, and that frustrated her more and increased the tension between them. The feeling she quickly got at the house as they moved around like strangers with no common language, was that Jak resented her being there now on any other terms than his, and resented supporting her financially. On opening his mail, he complained about bills, with no job and no means of paying them. She wanted to flee. She talked to Immigration about staying on and getting a work permit so that she could keep herself. A meeting was scheduled for later that morning. They were being very sympathetic making life suspiciously easy for her. Immigration, for Christsake! Maybe she was getting more and more paranoid. She decided she would get a job and find her own apartment while she fought the pesticide action. There was no alternative as she didn't have her airfare back to England. She had a lot of sorting out to do and fast, before circumstances dictated all of her moves. Rory called, causing more immediate problems.

'What's wrong, Grace?' he said.

The flatness in her voice said it all, but she said, 'I'm fine, absolutely fine. It's strange being back.' Jak was crashing around and, she suspected, resented her talking to Rory. Maybe she should just hang up and tell him that she felt no more attracted to Rory right then, than she did to him. But she wouldn't give him that satisfaction.

'Look, I've got to be someplace else,' Rory said.

'Of course you have, Rory,' she said.

'Grace?' he said.

Was she being unfair on him, on both of them because of the way she was feeling or because of the demands she felt they both made on their own terms? Why couldn't Rory say I'm going to drop my other meetings? Why was he always so damn busy? It was like he was trying to prove something to himself.

'When I'm through do you want me to stop by for you to go to Immigration?'

There were going to be more problems with him than with Immigration. Glancing at Jak as he searched the bookshelves for published papers that he didn't need right then, she took the line of least resistance. 'I'll meet you at Immigration.'

Jak went out, and returned a short while later and grabbed up another bunch of papers and went out again. Finally she could stand it no more and went to find him in the sitting-room, where he was showing no real concentration or purpose.

344

'Jak? We do have to talk before we have a real problem.'

'The only problem I've got is that I'm not getting to any serious work. So no one's making any money around here.'

'I'd better try to get a job and pay some rent,' – disguising the hurt she felt. She rebuked herself, knowing that was a ridiculous response. Why should she expect him to support her? Even if there were impediments to employment, she could work in the black economy as a waitress or a house cleaner.

'Maybe Rory has some ideas about a job.' She knew that was provocative.

'Not one you could live from, that's for sure – those guys out at Christic don't set much store by making money.'

'I think I'd better find somewhere else to live.'

'With Rory? What is it you figure on doing? Moving in with him? That guy lives in a shoebox – then you know that.'

'Too right I do – he banged my ass against the wall.'

For a moment she wasn't sure if he was going to hit her or cry. Finally he did neither.

'I'll get any kind of job I can find. I'll rent a room at the YWCA.'

'Christ, you can rent a room here if it'll make you feel better – that's not the problem. You know it's not.'

'I don't know a thing because you don't tell me about your feelings.'

'I've been blaming you for things going wrong around here. I wanted to get at you, make you feel bad for dumping me.'

'I'm not dumping you. I want to get my own life sorted out before I make any more commitments.'

'I know my life is in a mess right now. I'm in a corner and can't back out . . .'

Seeing him struggling with his feelings made her feel worse. She reached out and touched him. He turned and was in her arms. She could feel him pressed against her, hard and needing comfort. She remembered similar moments with her husband when making love seemed the easiest course. It provided no sort of answer. It was merely palliation.

'Something will turn up, Jak, it always does. Yesterday you believed you were wanted for murder.' She stepped back from him, finding it quite easy.

He didn't reply, but she could tell how angry he was. He wanted to make love to her, and she got excited by the idea of him taking her by force. And wondered what might bring him to that point.

Something did turn up. His brother Paul came by the house. He had been trying to reach him for days.

'Did Bill Heinz get you? I ran into him at a party. He has some serious funding for your wheat project.'

A cloud visibly lifted from Jak. He said, 'He does? How serious, Paul?'

'Hey Josh, call him up. I just stopped by with the message.'

Grace didn't like brother Paul and wasn't sure why. Maybe it was no more than that he was a psychiatrist and brought bad associations but he had a way of looking at her like she was a sex object that he was assessing the value of. The woman he had left his wife for had recently left him, he told them in a self-pitying way.

When Jak called the dean, he found him downtown in a traffic jam.

'Jesus, Jak, why don't you get a mobile phone? I almost allocated all this money to someone else,' he boomed out of the phone. 'We've got funding for a brand new biotech unit out at Maryland.'

Something was wrong here. It was only a feeling she had and not one she could pin down. She wished she had made love to Jak now so he hadn't opened the door to his brother or heard about this offer.

'We want the number one team there with you leading it, Jak. The Baedeker Trust has committed money for the next ten years' work. The Trust guarantees the programme would continue uninterrupted.'

'Without outside interference?' Jak asked.

'You'd be running the entire shoot, Jak. You'll have

tenure with a chair in biotech. All the Trust wants are the patents on anything you develop. I figure that's reasonable.'

'But these should be for the benefit of mankind, Bill?'

'Of course. No question about that.'

They talked about staffing ratios, the equipment needed, the permanent site the Trust was looking for to house the unit. The downtown traffic remained solid.

Suggestions and proposals bubbled out of Jak as he bounced around the room. He seemed so buoyed by this news that he was in danger of floating away. 'I can't believe this is happening. It's magic, Bill, pure magic. With the right facilities, along with some discoveries I've made recently over what looked like a neat piece of biotech in wheat, I feel very confident that this new approach to fixing nitrogen in wheat will succeed. In fact I'm almost certain it will.'

'I want you to put Maryland University on the map. That's all we want, Jak. Success is the highest prize there is.'

'Bill, can I get a favour?' he asked. 'I need to get a friend on a course. A mature student.'

Grace suddenly felt embarrassed, knowing he was meaning her. She knew he probably meant well for her, but from now on she was making all her own choices, even if they were the wrong ones.

'Jesus Christ!' Jak continued to bounce around the place. 'Jesus Christ, that really saved my ass.'

Grace couldn't help but feel pleased for him, and she didn't protest about the option he'd secured for her, as the whole atmosphere in the house had now lifted. But the feeling she had that something was wrong about this wouldn't leave her.

From that point he hardly noticed she existed as he began calling biotechnicians about joining the team. He didn't even get upset about the time she spent with Rory.

'Taking the place at the university is a great idea,' Rory said. 'You could stay on here after the Class Action was heard against American Chemicals. You get to finish college with a lot of debt is the only problem.'

347

They were running through Rock Creek Park. She preferred not to run on her own.

'But all things being equal, you'll be pretty competitive, well placed for a high-paying job, if that's what you want.'

'I'm not sure if I do. Especially not the debt.' Now the idea had settled on her, there was a lot to think about, mostly what it would mean to her going back to Mexico.

'Have Jak push the college to fund you from one of their bursaries. Do it, Grace. Take the offer.'

'I'd just get more and more indebted to Jak. I'd sooner get a job and pay my own way, if I took the place.'

'Grace, do it any way you can. Don't pass up the opportunity of getting back to college just because you figure it compromises your independence.'

'It doesn't just compromise it,' she said. 'It removes it completely.'

Walking out of the park, he said, 'Who is it funding Jak's programme?'

'A trust called Baedeker,' she told him. 'But I doubt if Jak would care if it were the Devil himself.'

Rory smiled. 'You know it could be at that, Grace.'

That feeling of unease about who was so conveniently providing the finance came right back at her. 'Maybe we should take a look at who Baedeker are. Can we do that?'

He told her how to check out trusts at the Libary of Congress, how to identify the trustees. The first part presented no difficulty, but she ran into a brick wall with the eleven trustees. Most of them were prominent lawyers, half of whom had practices on Wall Street.

'You can't get much tighter than that,' Rory said. 'The only trustee I know personally is Bill Moncton. I could call him. He may tell us something. But probably he won't.'

Moncton was right then appearing at the District Court for Hirshorn, which they found rich with irony. He didn't return Rory's call, nor his second and third call.

'I figure we should just stop by the court to talk with Moncton during the lunch recess. You want to meet me down there, Grace?'

When she met Rory at the court building he was sitting

348

cross-legged on a bench looking pretty pleased with himself.

'Did you win a big case or something?' she asked.

'I figure we could be just about to, Grace. Do you know what's happening down here to Hirshorn?'

'They're getting the pants beaten off them? They're going to go out of business?' she speculated.

'That could be about to happen. Getting beaten. I don't know about going out of business. That would be too much to hope for.'

The idea caught fire in Grace. 'What is happening?'

'The witness currently giving evidence to support Hirshorn's contention that their chicken plants aren't dangerously contaminated is a gift from God. He's the scientist who owns the laboratory that ran so-called independent tests on a new gut bacteria in chickens that is supposed to combine with an antibiotic regime to combat salmonella. Hirshorn have introduced this in their chickens to overcome the problem. But it looks like it might be causing more problems.'

'What has this to do with our action?' she asked.

'Aside from damaging Hirshorn, it could get us a lot of help from the USDA. I talked with Larry Winpisinger, their lawyer. He wants to trade the information we've got – he'll give us any help he can in return.'

'For what? What have we got, Rory?' she said, getting impatient.

'Oh, didn't I mention that. A colleague at Christic has turned up information that'll blow this so-called independent scientist right out of the water. His lab did the original work on the Smartkill assessment. It doesn't add up.'

'You mean, it's false?'

'That's just what I mean.'

She held her breath for a moment, not knowing how to express her excitement. 'Is that for real? You have the evidence?'

Rory passed her the folder from under his arm and rose.

Listening to the proceedings from the public benches in the courtroom, Grace found her excitement retreating in

349

the face of the USDA lawyer's performance. Larry Winpisinger, who she now felt she had a vested interest in, was only passing good. The tail end of Bill Moncton's examination of Dr Sissini, an extremely careful man in everything from what he said to the way he dressed, looked far more impressive. Then Bill Moncton at six feet six with a broad straight back was pretty impressive to look at. Perhaps he alone would win the day in court.

'Following the radical treatment with this new gut bacteria,' Moncton was saying to the head of Blakemore Laboratories, 'has salmonella in chickens been eradicated?'

'The conclusion to our extensive testing,' Dr Sissini replied in a voice that seemed to resonate with integrity, 'is that the remaining three or four per cent will cause nobody any problem.'

She was ready to believe him, and the last of her optimism seeped away.

'We're not headed for an epidemic, like the USDA suggests?'

Dr Sissini laughed. 'If we are, the Department has been deceiving the public for a long time. They have permitted most processing plants to operate with ten times the level of salmonella in chicken to that it can be reduced to with this new process.'

That was all Bill Moncton wanted from this witness. Larry Winpisinger rose, stoop-shouldered, and hesitated for far too long to be convincing. His body language as he walked to the lectern carrying a thick report suggested he had little to say worth hearing. Grace wanted to tell him to straighten his shoulders, confront this witness like he believed in himself.

'Dr Sissini,' he said, offering a friendly smile and a gesture that told everyone he was harmless. 'This report of yours is pretty impressive.' He weighed it theatrically. 'Did it take long to compile?'

'Three months.' Dr Sissini answered.

'All three hundred and ninety-seven pages with such convoluted data, minute detail? It took me nearly that time to read it.'

No one laughed.

'You wrote and compiled this in *just* three months – concluding all the tests that were needed?'

'The matter was urgent, Mr Winpisinger.' Dr Sissini was soft-spoken, of Italian or Jewish extraction, neatly combed and fastidiously manicured. Not a hair was out of place. 'Twenty scientists worked on the project, along with research and secretarial assistants.'

'The principal scientists being as highly qualified as you, sir?' The thrust of the question seemed to challenge those unspecified qualifications. Grace's interest was alerted.

'In their own disciplines some are more qualified.'

'All were dedicated to the same end?'

'Exactly right, sir – getting the truth. Nothing else would do when the stakes are so high.'

'High enough to fudge the report, Dr Sissini?' The lawyer flicked through the pages like he wasn't interested in the answer.

'I object to this line of questioning, your honour.'

'I can see why, Mr Moncton,' the black judge said. 'I'm going to allow it – in the interest of truth.'

Grace felt a surge of warmth for the grey-haired judge.

'I'm not a bacteriologist, Dr Sissini,' the USDA lawyer said, 'but I think I do know a put-up job, even when dressed in technical horse shit.'

With that he tossed the report over his shoulder. It hit the floor, spilling over a wide area. The half-dozen or so spectators spread thinly around the public benches, along with those people serving the court suddenly came alive.

'Dramatic gestures more suited to jury trials, Mr Winpisinger,' the judge told him, 'kind of litters my court.'

'My colleague will trash the report, your honour.'

The assistant lawyer from the USDA's table quickly gathered up the papers, blushing self-consciously as Winpisinger waited at the lectern without either proceeding with the case or offering to help.

'Perhaps you'd tell the court, Dr Sissini,' he said finally, 'how you cut your lab time for proving not one, but two procedures, and their effects on humans who eat chicken

351

– from three years, which the FDA regularly takes, to a *mere* three months.'

'By multicomputer simulation – a technique developed at our labs. One computer extrapolates first the effect of one part of the procedure, and locks it into a program while another does the same; a third computer then extrapolates on the basis of those two results and so forth. That continues until a picture of all contingencies is built up.'

'This is capable of mirroring the long-term effect of this salmonella-destroying gut bacteria on humans? The erosion of the human immune system that results from ingesting unsafe levels of antibiotics?'

'Not only does it do that, sir,' Dr Sissini replied, 'it gives a less distorted picture. If your colleague can find page three-twenty in all that horse shit, you might read the conclusions.'

There was laughter at that. Winpisinger waited for it to fade, then raised his clipboard. 'I held back page three-twenty.'

'This is it, I guess,' Rory whispered in her ear.

'You conclude that the process is safe and effective. How did your client respond to that?'

'They were satisfied,' the witness said.

'I'd guess the client, Hirshorn Chicken, were pretty relieved too – that the public isn't at risk. How would it have been had your computer simulations shown a contrary picture?'

'The question didn't arise.'

Rory smiled and squeezed her hand. She withdrew, her attention fixed on the protagonists.

'Is it in your interest to allow such questions to arise?'

'Objection,' Moncton said, rising. 'Dr Sissini isn't on trial.'

'His lab is billed as independent,' the judge pointed out, 'yet the client pays for the assessment. I'd like to establish right here how independent independent is.'

Moncton glanced around at someone on the public bench closest to his table. His expression showed no flicker of concern. Grace followed his glance to the man, whose round face had recently lost weight. It showed no sign of anxiety, unlike the mobile face of the Jewish-looking younger man next to him. Instinctively she knew she was looking at the boss of Hirshorn, and felt a tremor of excitement mixed with anxiety. She wanted to go over and speak to him, to ask why he was doing what he was, but she was afraid to move. Reasoning deflected any action she might take, and she told herself she was being fanciful. This might not be Caddy Hirshorn at all, but Bill Moncton's bookie.

Dr Sissini was saying, 'Hirshorn would have accepted the findings. That's the only condition under which we conduct this work.'

'And if your findings meant closing chicken plants?'

'I think they'd very urgently seek remedies – as they have been doing.'

'In this case, if the solution proved as bad as the problem, your clients would be prepared to write off hundreds of millions of dollars. Is that what you're telling this court?'

'They share our concern about public safety. They clearly don't want to sell a dirty product.'

'Only if you ignore the reason they're in business – profit,' Winpisinger told him. 'But whatever the client's motivation may be, there is no doubt that *your* number one priority is public safety. No matter how deeply this were to run counter to your client's economic interest?'

Dr Sissini didn't hesitate. 'Number one priority,' he said.

Nodding self-assuredly, like he was enjoying the moment and deciding to share it with the court, Larry Winpisinger walked back to the table and collected a folder.

At this point Rory squeezed her hand again.

Winpisinger opened the folder, then looked directly at the witness.

'Let's go back ten years. Your *independent* lab ran some tests for American Chemicals on a pesticide called Smartkill.'

'That's a long time ago.' Dr Sissini lost eye-contact with the lawyer for the first time.

'I have Blakemore Laboratories' work-up sheets.' He approached the witness. 'Are they your work-up sheets?'

'They certainly look like our work-ups.'

'I offer these as an exhibit, your honour.'

Copies were taken across to the judge by the clerk.

'These tests show – and I'm sure you will explain the chemical pathology for plain lawyers, Dr Sissini – that this pesticide caused major respiratory problems in laboratory rats. If extrapolated to humans it would have caused your clients to abandon costly research and development.'

'Possibly,' the witness said, safeguarding his position. 'But rats don't respond in the same way as humans.'

'Then why use them as experimental models?'

'Because we can't use human models,' Dr Sissini said.

'Despite the fact that they are different from humans,' Winpisinger argued, 'rats are used as models, and based on these findings your clients would have been forced to abandon Smartkill. But what happened was your laboratory became less than independent and changed the result by omitting data.'

'Objection, your honour, counsel is drawing a conclusion from the witness with his conjectural statement.'

'I'll sustain the objection,' the judge said. 'I would appreciate if you'd get a question or two in there, Mr Winpisinger.'

'I'll rephrase. Did Blakemore Laboratories omit details from the Smartkill assessment to support its client's case for a licence from the EPA?'

'No, sir,' Dr Sissini said. 'They did not.'

'Sir, I suggest you are misleading this court. The data shows that your *independent* lab falsified the conclusion. Only the vigilance of the EPA in banning the product prevented major injuries resulting.'

'I'm going to stop you here, Mr Winpisinger, and recess for lunch,' the judge said. 'I want to read what's contained in this report to consider if it's admissible. I would have appreciated your showing me this earlier.'

He rose and went out.

Grace was surprised. She felt cheated, and even a little

disappointed in the judge. It was suddenly like he wasn't interested in seeking justice, but in protecting the status quo.

Bill Moncton nodded slowly and smiled when Grace went over to his table with Rory.

'You can see why I didn't get back to you, Rory,' he said as he rose up out of the chair and shook his hand. 'I'd set aside a week for this case.' He turned his look to Grace and didn't look away. Nor did she, feeling no sense of embarrassment or discomfort, but enjoying his frank appraisal.

'What do you think, Grace? Did Larry Winpisinger do us a lot of damage with those goddamn work-up sheets?'

'He looked fairly impressive, I was surprised.' Grace glanced between the two lawyers and hesitated. Clearly Moncton didn't know how the report had got into Winpisinger's hands, and she wasn't sure she would be able to lie to him if he were to ask her.

'Am I glad we're not before a jury. You called me to present for Grace against American Chemicals.' His smile broadened. 'I figure you'd do better talking to old Larry there.'

Grace said, 'You're on the board of the Baedeker Trust – we're trying to find out whose money's behind it.'

With a low whistle and a smile that followed close behind, Moncton said, 'You sure shoot from the hip, Grace. I like that, especially in a woman – it's not American Chemicals. That's all I can say. You know they've set aside five million to fight, Grace,' – glancing at Rory. 'Those guys are real worried.'

'They'll need a lot more than five for the kind of compensation they'll be paying out,' Rory said.

'Maybe my firm should take it on a contingency. Are you guys free for lunch? Those Hirshorn lawyers drive me nuts.'

Rory said, 'Why don't you go on ahead – I'll catch you up.'

It wasn't until Moncton guided her away to the elevators that Grace realized that he hadn't told Rory what restaurant they were eating at. Then she thought

355

maybe he had no intention of joining them anyway. She assumed he was going to talk to Larry Winpisinger to negotiate the kind of help the USDA were going to give them on their case.

'Is this your first day at this trial, Grace?' Moncton asked as he studied the menu. 'The veal is pretty good here, by the way.'

He saw the face she made.

'I guess you don't want the veal?' he said. 'I just bet you're a vegetarian. I guess that's what comes of hanging around with Rory.'

'It might have something to do with it.'

'They brought on the vice president of the American Vegetarian Society last week. The guy was a nut, but a pretty convincing one. He was a bacteriologist, knew his stuff too. I had a lot of problems taking him apart. I'm not sure if I did. I can tell you I didn't eat meat last week. I'm not sure I will ever eat chicken again.'

'You think the Hirshorn plants are contaminated?' she asked.

'Along with just about every other chicken plant in the country from the evidence I've seen.'

'Then why are you defending them?'

'Because I'm an attorney and they tell me their plants aren't contaminated. If you want a lawyer to make emotional judgement based on political positioning, you couldn't do better than Rory.'

'He's the least judgemental person I know,' she argued.

'Is he the least emotionally involved?'

'That sort of involvement means he has commitment. That doesn't make for a less successful lawyer necessarily.'

'He won't win your case for you, Grace. He's got too long a score to settle with American Chemicals. He'll miss the target for sure.'

She felt angry that he was talking about Rory in this way. She reached out for any ammunition she could find to aim back.

'He's going to get Larry Winpisinger to help.'

'Why would he do that? Where's the percentage for him?'

She bit her tongue at her stupidity. Emotion made her say what she had, but she still wasn't convinced that emotional commitment, even in a lawyer, wasn't the best way.

'I guess that's where Larry got all that shit on Dr Sissini's lab. That's the kind of stuff Christic would have on file. The son of a gun. Am I right?'

She liked this man for his response, he openly admired Rory for finding it in himself to fight that way. He wasn't a bit cross about it.

Over lunch he didn't reveal who it was behind the Baedeker Trust, but suggested she did some research on the name Baedeker.

'Would you have dinner with me one day next week, Grace, or are you committed emotionally to Rory?'

'I'd like to,' she said. 'All you have to do is call me.' She gave him her number. She glanced at her watch. 'I'd better get over to the Library of Congress.'

Moncton smiled. It was warm and generous.

'Caroline Elizabeth Baedeker!' she read over the phone from her notes taken from the *Oklahoma Star* in the Library. 'She married Arkadi Gunston Hirshorn at the Church of All Saints, Oklahoma City, 3 June 1966.'

'Great work!' Rory said in his office. 'Hirshorn. It figures.'

He didn't say anything about her slip to Moncton. She didn't tell him about the dinner invitation.

The more she thought about the Baedeker Trust the more angry she felt about having been tricked. What made her more angry was her fear that Jak might not care.

The new biotech lab that was being equipped at Maryland was bordering on awe-inspiring. The people working there moved around like worshippers before their deity. The whole atmosphere inhibited her and added to her frustration as she pursued Jak, who was being treated by everyone like the high priest.

'Grace, to be perfectly frank,' he said in a desperate whisper, 'I don't give a damn who's funding my work. The money's there. No one interferes with what I do, that's fine.'

357

'A short while ago you were ready to blow Hirshorn apart.'

'We couldn't prove a thing,' he reminded her.

'A couple of lucky breaks, that's all it needs.'

'I got them getting out of that murder charge and getting this unit set up.' His face suddenly came alive. 'All I need here, Grace, is a couple more breaks. We've identified the bacterium that forms the rhizome nodules – we're trying to get this gene to express itself in yeast – if we can, a whole world of possibilities opens up for its expression in wheat.'

'Jak, don't you realize what happened? They bought us. We're theirs. The charges against us are dropped; Immigration gives me a work permit for the asking; Hirshorn funds your research.'

'What I'm doing is working for all those people who can't grow enough food for themselves, Grace. That's pretty fundamental.'

'It's Hirshorn Grain who will be the sole beneficiary.'

'No!' Jak protested.

'I can see you think that's an impediment to the important work you want to get on with. But at least think about it.'

'There is no alternative, Grace. This is all there is. I've got to get it done.'

'Rory said we could try the Russians. Tell them what happened.'

'You figure they'll believe us? With no evidence? They'll take us for a couple of flakes and kick us right out.'

'You could give it a try, Jak.'

He laughed.

That hurt, especially after what they had been through.

'I'm sorry, Grace. There's too much at stake here. Have Rory go down there with you. He's crazy enough.'

That hurt for a different reason.

Without a moment's pause, Rory marched into the Russian Embassy on 15th Street with her and asked to see the agricultural attaché. Grace didn't think him a bit flaky. They were given literature about how Russia was changing, how the economy was changing, about emigration, along with a hundred other cataclysmic changes that were taking place in the twelve Republics. But nothing about how they were going to cut the waiting time at their embassy, which now had a stream of American visitors.

'Do you think they've forgotten us?'

'I don't think so,' Rory said. 'I guess we're not going to get to anyone.'

They waited a while longer, then left. Back on the street, the uniformed secret service officer sitting astride his motor cycle had changed shifts, but he looked just the same as the guy who was there when they went in. He stared at them without blinking as they began laughing.

'Who do you figure he's protecting from whom these days?' Rory said. 'In some ways our administration is taking longer to adjust!'

The secret service man continued to look at them.

'God, have we got this right, do you think, Rory?'

'Maybe we should tie a note to a brick and hurl it through the window.'

She sighed, resigning herself to not getting the information to the Russians this way. What other way could there be?

'Don't give up yet, Grace,' Rory said. 'We haven't even started on Congress. With the spectre of inflation in the supermarket if the price of wheat gets much higher, someone in Congress is going to be sufficiently concerned to lean on the secretary for agriculture – it's worth a shot.'

She put her arm through his and kissed him on the cheek. 'What I love about you, Rory, is your persistent optimism. You never know when to quit.'

At least they were still in the race.

25

'ONE MORE DAY AND I would have been home and dry,' the bank manager said as he lit another cigarette and paced around the hotel room.

Clearly this man had convinced himself of that, Walter Shearing thought, trying to check his frustration. He wanted to stuff his fist down his throat to shut him up.

'Just one more day. Why couldn't the situation at the bank go on undisturbed? It's like fate is conspiring to mock me with the discovery of those missing securities. Why did it have to be now rather than after the wheat had been sold to the Russians? One more day is all we need.'

'Tell me about the visit by the securities under-manager again. He told you Mrs Kettley's securities were missing?'

He would have preferred to keep his mind off the negotiations that were going on in the suite three floors above between Pierre d'Estaing and the Russians. They were undeniably close to a sale of all of their wheat, but not close enough, he feared, to save Richards' skin. They'd need another way.

'I told him I had posted them off to her broker. Lying was the only thing I could do. If I hadn't he'd have presumed them stolen, and Region's investigators would have descended on the bank like a ton of bricks. The police might have been right behind. Then the securities belonging to other customers that I've had to use for our margin commitments would have been discovered missing also.'

'Was the securities under-manager convinced? Was he?'

'Doubt entered Richards' voice when he said, 'He pointed out that I hadn't entered the movement in the book. He was challenging me, that's what it felt like. This move on my part, sending off the securities like that, was unusual enough to arouse suspicion. In retrospect it was a stupid thing to say, but I was so surprised that Mrs Kettley had called for her paper – Damn her! No other excuse would have forestalled an investigation.'

'I told you not to do anything illegal – it's a bloody mess.'

'You kept pressing me to meet those margin commitments. You said we'd all go to prison if I didn't,' Richards whined.

'We might yet,' he reminded him. 'What's this under-manager likely to do with his suspicions?'

'I don't know. Perhaps he'll check the other portfolios in the vault. He might call the manager at Region. He'll certainly telephone Mrs Kettley's broker at some point to see if they have arrived. Why did that stupid old woman suddenly need them? Why is God conspiring to bring me down like this? Is what I'm doing so wrong? Well, is it? What's taking them so long up there? Why can't they just agree a price so we can get it all settled? I don't know if I trust d'Estaing – I feel like I want to run, to get as far away as possible. Do you trust d'Estaing? Do you?'

'Shut up, for Christsake, Dick. Don't talk absolute nonsense. Shapiro says d'Estaing's absolutely the best, that's why Hirshorn use him. He'll get the absolute best price. Get a grip on yourself. You're getting to be an absolute pain in the ass.'

'Don't you realize what it means, those securities being missed? I'll go to prison.'

'Nonsense,' he said, and watched Richards' hand tremble as he lit another cigarette. There were three others already burning in ashtrays. There was no way he could ever rely on this man if the situation came to a police investigation.

He had few worries about anything going wrong at this final stage. He couldn't see that it would for him at all. If it did he intended to deny any knowledge of the bank

361

manager's fraudulent activities. As for the whole less-than-legal scheme that Shapiro had brought him to make money, clearly it wasn't going to make them as much as had originally been envisaged. Certainly not if he had to share with four other partners. He decided then to dump the lot of them. He hesitated about Pat Shapiro, remembering their night at the Bury St Edmunds hotel with fleeting pleasure. But concluded finally he was merely being sentimental. Dealing them out would be an easy enough move to make as all of the money would go from d'Estaing directly into his account. He felt no compunction about keeping it, knowing that he had taken the lion's share of the risks by putting his farm in hock.

'Nothing's going to happen quickly, Dick,' he assured him. 'There'll first be an investigation of the mail. That always takes days. By this evening our deal will be in place. When the banks open tomorrow our pockets will be stuffed. All you'll do is simply discover that you forgot to post the securities. Just rely on d'Estaing, he'll do the deal. Have a drink to calm your nerves, instead of filling this two-hundred-and-twenty-pound-a-day room with cigarette smoke.' They were in the Grosvenor House Hotel. He was using alcohol to calm his nerves. But Richards lit another cigarette and continued to pace.

'It took me a whole year to give up smoking,' he said and laughed. It was gallows laughter.

'Just think about the money, Dick.'

'I can't stop thinking about the bank finding out.'

'Oh for Christsake!' he screamed, no longer disguising his irritation. 'You're like some whining old woman.' This level of anxiety began getting to him, and he wondered if there was any way Richards could possibly suck him into his mess.

'I shouldn't have called in sick. I know I shouldn't. It looks suspicious. What if someone at the bank phones my home? My wife thinks I'm at work.'

'They'll assume you have a girlfriend, Dick.'

'That's the most frequent reason bank managers steal.'

He was relieved when Pierre d'Estaing came in smiling, and poured himself a whisky. The dapper little man was

362

like a dynamo that wouldn't stop running.

'They pay $4.82 a bushel for ten million bushels of Number two hard red.'

'Take it. Take it . . .' Richards said without hesitating.

Using his pocket calculator, Shearing said, 'That's under $180 a ton. We might do better liquidating our position. We expect the price to go higher when news of the Russians' disastrous wheat harvest gets out.'

'If this news gets out, my friend,' d'Estaing said. 'If this thing happens . . .'

Shearing knew they were running against time now with what was happening at the bank. But still he didn't want to settle quickly.

'I squeeze them a little more. Hirshorn will not make them a deal like this. But if they are forced to liquidate, the price could go way down.'

'Take it,' Richards repeated. Stress was producing strangled notes from his larynx. 'Don't lose the deal.'

'You can do better than this, Pierre,' Shearing told him, realizing he was going to make less than even his revised figure. The one person he wouldn't be able to cheat of his five per cent was d'Estaing, as he would have complete control of the wheat once the deal was made. He would collect the money.

'Sure. I squeeze. They cannot go home without wheat.'

'How soon will they pay?' Richards wanted to know.

'Not until the wheat boards their ships. I arrange delivery quick to the Houston public elevator. First they borrow the money.'

That didn't sound like soon enough to save Dick Richards, Shearing thought and almost smiled.

Oscar Hartmine was the first grain trader the head of the Russian Exportkhleb called when he slipped unobtrusively into New York. Their relationship went way back and had been mutually beneficial.

'Jesus Christ,' OH wailed. 'Aleksei Krevenko's coming all this way to see me, and what kind of a position am I in? I can sell them about enough wheat to make a box of goddamn Wheaties. Goddamn it.'

363

'We can get them plenty of wheat, OH,' Dulles told him. 'When we know, a) that they need wheat in volume, b) are willing to meet the price, and c) are *able* to find that kind of money.'

As they rode downtown from the Carlyle on E76th, where OH kept a suite, he knew what was worrying his boss: the possibility that the Russians had already picked up most of their wheat needs and his was a courtesy call. He knew also that wasn't the case, unless Aleksei Krevenko had outfoxed them all, in which case Hirshorn was down the tubes. Krevenko was shrewd and couldn't be underestimated, even if he had little room to manoeuvre. That wasn't what was worrying him right then.

'He's trying to get a little way ahead before the market learns just how bad their wheat position is.'

'Maybe it ain't even half bad. We didn't hear nothing. Their harvests are getting better the whole while.'

That worried Dulles. Maybe Krevenko's trip to the US was to make courtesy calls all round. Or maybe it was to sell wheat.

'How much do you figure they picked up, Gordon?' OH asked as their cab arrived at the Waldorf Tower on E50th. 'Those guys'd never give a straight answer. You figure their wheat's in real bad shape?'

'Relax,' he told him. 'They've hardly had time to unpack.' He got the fare, doubting if OH had enough even for cabs these days.

In the elevator, OH said, 'You figure Hirshorn's sold them wheat?'

'If he had, the price would've jumped and we wouldn't be here, OH. The way I see it is they're looking to us for some kind of fall-back position –'

A despairing growl came out of Hartmine, causing the maroon-coated operator to glance round.

'Jesus Christ – in the seventies I made all the running.'

'A fall-back position to what, Oscar?' The question was starting to give him as bad a stomach as OH's.

'It'll cost us money to sell wheat to the Russians.'

'We can always walk,' he said.

'The hell we can, Gordon.'

The elevator let them off at the twenty-ninth floor. The Russian security men there on the corridor were no less conspicuous for *glasnost*.

'Oscar! My good friend.' Aleksei Krevenko stood at the double doors to the large sitting-room of his suite with its pale green and gold furnishings. 'Your health is good?' He took his hand in both of his and drew him into the room.

'Never better. You know Gordon,' OH said. 'We hear you've got a lot of problems with your wheat harvest.'

'In Russia now we have many, many problems. Few solutions,' Krevenko said. He smiled out of an almost perfectly round face, showing large gaps between his teeth. 'Now we have farmers owning their farms so sometime it will be a little better. Sometime. Farmers they lie about their yields fearing they will have nothing left for tomorrow. But now I'm in New York to ensure tomorrow we will have bread. So there are little distractions here and compensations.'

'That's what keeps you young,' Dulles said and put a friendly arm around his shoulder. Not the easiest of gestures, as Krevenko was about fifteen or so inches shorter. He wore a neat grey suit that obviously wasn't bought in Russia. Nor were his shoes. Rome at a guess. 'You gotta be careful in this town, Aleksei. There's a lot of Aids.'

'In Moscow we have Aids.' He nodded solemnly. 'But little treatment centres.'

Dulles wasn't in any hurry to get down to business. He was prepared to sit and talk, for hours if need be to try to find out what the true position of the expected Russian wheat harvest was.

OH showed no such patience. He said, 'How much wheat are you coming up short?'

'This year our production will be good. We maybe sell you wheat now the price is so high. First we drink, take food, then talk.'

'It sure is high, Aleksei,' OH said. 'It's costing an arm and a leg.'

'Arms and legs we all have. If we need grain I think we

365

are so friendly to the West now we qualify for American aid. Yes?' Krevenko's grin was boyish, despite his being about fifty-five. 'You like my joke, Oscar?' he ushered them into the dining-room. 'Please.'

An aide who had taken a call extended the phone. 'Aleksei Michailovich – the Minister of Agriculture.'

Both Dulles and his boss were more interested in the reason for that call than in the food they were being offered. They stopped in the doorway. Krevenko saw their attention and smiled. 'Please – food, drink.' He pointed to the bedroom for the call to be transferred there.

Dulles wondered right off why the aide had announced the call in English. They didn't need impressing as to how important Krevenko was. The Minister calling like this signalled something important was happening maybe.

'A goddamn lousy half a million bushels,' OH said and punched the side of the elevator as they descended three hours later. It was a different car man, but he looked alarmed just the same at Oscar's outburst.

'At least they bought it, OH. For a while there I figured they were looking to sell,' Dulles said. 'It's early days.'

He felt good. Krevenko's purchases, small as they were, meant they were not only short of wheat, but could find some money to purchase US wheat. The Russian's next stop was Oklahoma. He wished he was going too instead of hanging around New York listening to OH complaining, and waiting for the pieces of the plan to work out. Not knowing if they would work out. Anxiety was making him impatient to get this done then rejoin Hirshorn, maybe as company president if his brother-in-law was as sick as he suspected.

Caddy had planned to make dinner as he sometimes did for special guests, but didn't have the energy and so left the food to his cook. He was distracted at dinner, thinking about the CFTC who were making moves against him in court to have him divest. Those guys didn't know when to quit, and might wreck his plans yet. When his attention returned to the table he saw how accomplished his children were, coping with the three Russian visitors as easily as three class-mates back to eat. They talked about the church they had all recently helped to paint . . . 'Dad could easily afford to hire painters,' Sarah, his eldest daughter, was explaining . . . Maybe she would be the one among his seven children to run the business. She showed the strongest instinct . . . 'But the church is the centre of our community and we have responsibilities towards it. You can't hire someone to take those. If we do we're saying we're above the community and all it stands for, its values. That's when it starts to break down . . .'

She looked in his direction to see how she was doing in explaining his values. He smiled, feeling proud of her.

Caroline, with her infallible instinct for timing, knew when to rise and make her exit, taking the kids with her. Tonight he would have preferred them to stay, not to have to talk business, but he was almost too weary to stop them. Then when Shapiro arrived for the after dinner part of the evening, he didn't attempt to. He wouldn't have his assistant in the same room as his children now, feeling the persuasive corruption that came off him to be too contaminating.

Aleksei Krevenko rose, and kissed Caroline's hand. He had none of the remoteness of bureaucratic Russians of yore, but was a tactile person, always touching and without any self-consciousness. He had five children of his own and nine grandchildren. His two colleagues watched silently and responded politely when providing information, but the same sense of freedom pervaded them.

'Caroline, you take your beautiful children,' Krevenko said. 'This is pity. But so.'

'We'll see you at breakfast,' she told him. She reached over Caddy's shoulder and squeezed his hand. He knew it was her way of saying not to overtire himself. She wouldn't speak of such things in front of guests. Each of the children kissed him goodnight.

'Arkadi,' the Russian said after his family had departed, 'such hospitality. You are Russian at heart. Business is a pleasure, Arkadi, yes.' He was the only person ever to call him Arkadi.

'It sure is,' he agreed, and rose, trying to disguise his stiffness.

He took his guests onto the enclosed terrace where the pool was, to sit at the long marble-topped table amidst the orchids and sweet-smelling jasmine. The Russians politely accepted port and cigars. The maid brought out coffee.

'You see,' Krevenko teased, making an expansive gesture at the surroundings, 'hard work makes many rewards. In Russia, everyone works for rewards now, Arkadi, but still our economy fails.'

'These things take time to get right, Aleksei. You can't shift from a command economy to a market economy overnight and not have problems.' He wasn't sure if they were ever going to get free of their problems.

'But the people they expect there to be none. They look to the West and say this we want now.'

'The people's needs always have to come first. That's the only way a market economy works. Fear of shortage makes it work a little better.'

'When we have shortages now we have riots in the streets. Something is not working.'

'Give them time – they'll learn that the rouble is more powerful than any system of government. There could be shortages here soon. The price of everything will just go up and up. Bread first. We didn't have enough snow in the Midwest. Some of our winter wheat frost-burned. The weather's getting so you can't rely on it anyplace. Grain'll be short all over.'

'At these prices, I think we have some to sell,' Krevenko said.

'If you have grain to sell, you're talking to the right person to buy it.' He watched the Russian closely, but nothing betrayed his true position. He didn't believe they would have a single bushel of wheat for sale.

'But the KGB inform me that you have all the wheat.'

'Somehow I didn't think those people were any longer reliable with their information,' he said. 'Did they tell you the Board of Trade is trying to take it from me?'

'This also. I do not understand why they do this thing?'

'I think it's called democracy,' he said with a smile,

368

'letting the little guy in with a chance.'

'But this is America – we would bring cash to the market.'

'The market's rarely free, Aleksei – not even for cash. Will Russia need wheat this year?'

Krevenko shrugged. 'Maybe not much.'

'You bought a little in London, some more in New York. Prices are already pretty high. If you come looking seriously for wheat they're going to get a lot higher.' He studied the head of Exportkhleb, wondering where Russia would borrow the kind of money required to buy the amount of wheat he anticipated they'd need. Their changing economy was nowhere near sufficiently consumer-led to dictate this man buying wheat at any price. Despite inflation at around 200 per cent, the central body representing the twelve Republics was having talks with the World Bank about further borrowing. The real gamble was whether they would up the ante. 'Take my advice, Aleksei, get what you can as soon as you can before the price goes through the roof.'

'You will sell us this wheat, of course.'

'I can't even think about that,' he said. 'Every bushel of wheat I've got is destined for other customers. I have enough grain to fill those orders. I might be able to find you some.'

Nothing hooked a buyer like the belief that whatever he wanted wasn't available. That was what made a seller's market. The purpose of inviting the head of the Exportkhleb to his house like this wasn't to sell him wheat, but set him up so that what he subsequently managed to buy would be seen as a major achievement. Serious negotiations would eventually take place at their hotel in New York with or without the news of the Russian grain harvest breaking.

'Do you figure they're hooked, Caddy?' Shapiro said as they walked to his car in the warm night air.

'The real question is not how much wheat will they need, but how much can they afford to buy?' He stopped by the Porsche parked on the neatly rolled gravel driveway and watched his aide. More and more lately, the man seemed to be coming apart at the seams. Little things

369

like a sudden loss of concentration betrayed him. As much as he abhorred his company nowadays, Caddy preferred to be close to him to witness this disintegration.

'I'll get back here before breakfast, sir,' Shapiro said.

'You got anything you need to tell me?' he said without warning, surprising himself as well as Shapiro. He believed that confession was good for the soul. He wanted to give him this last opportunity.

'Caddy?' Shapiro questioned.

In this man's face he could see anxiety, which he tried to disguise with a puzzled expression; the fetid smell of deceit was oozing from his pores.

Details of hurts were something he held onto, sometimes for years, awaiting the opportunity to pay back. Shapiro had been given more chances than he chose to take. Maybe he believed too many of the rumours about his health, and thought he truly was losing his grip.

He smiled and shook his head. 'You get a good night's sleep, Pat. There's a lot of work ahead of you.'

'If you bring this deal off the way you figure, domestic wheat will go completely crazy,' Shapiro said.

'The Russians are going to need a lot of wheat. One hell of a lot. Maybe thirty million tons or more.' He made it sound like there could be no doubt.

'Then people will pay any price for what's left. If we could sell the same pile over, we'd join the colossal rich.'

He looked at this smart homosexual Jew trying to figure if he had somehow second-guessed him.

'It's either a genius or a crook who sells the same goods twice,' he said. 'Let's settle for the Russians. Folk here will soon get used to bread at five or six dollars a loaf maybe. They've had unrealistically low food prices for too long. We should let the market make the running. That way everybody gets an even break.'

Watching Shapiro climb into his auto and drive off into the night, again he wondered if somehow this man had second-guessed his plans. And if he had, what he might do. There was no telling when ambition to be rich combined with lack of conscience. With so much at stake now, even he was beginning to feel anxious. In the

370

stillness of the night, he thought about Mr Lu the homoeopath leading him to recognize his obsession with money,
the fear of not having enough, if that could possibly relate
to his cancer and the means of ridding himself of it. There
would be time to attend to his health when he had pulled
off this grain coup. This would be so big that even his
Daddy would have been impressed. He had quadrupled
the size of the company from the time of his father's death,
and increased earnings sixfold, but still he had something
more to prove. This deal would be enough. After this he
could ease up and get well.

With the Russians in town rumours were thick around the
markets. Prices rose and dipped with each new rumour.
Some traders tried to buy wheat in anticipation of the
Russian needs, but there were few sellers. Despite the
absence of market-makers the price edged up as if to
tempt those with long positions to sell. Mostly the
markets watched and waited.

'Are the Russians finding any more wheat?' Caddy
asked in the grain-dealing room at his Oklahoma
headquarters. The thirty or so grain dealers were
responding actively to the hectic input of information via
phone, screen and printer. The atmosphere was electric,
the amounts being transacted exciting. But wheat was like
a becalmed yacht in the middle of the hurricane.

'Their biggest problem is money,' Shapiro replied.
'International Grain went and committed another half
million tons – wheat they can't get. Armand Bequai
figures Hartmine will lose money on that deal.'

He nodded. 'He's losing it every other place.'

He was ready to go to New York to talk wheat prices
with the Russians whenever they wanted to call him to the
table.

'When the market learns just how bad the Russian wheat
harvest is going to be, the kind of pressure to divest we've
seen so far will have been nothing. The Board'll hit us
every which way.'

'Shouldn't we sell to the Russians ahead of this kind of
trouble?'

'Sell them what? They only want to talk with International.'

'This is getting real scary,' Shapiro said.

He looked at him. 'These are exciting times.'

To everybody's surprise the Board of Trade failed in the District Court to get Hirshorn to divest. Ironically, the regulatory body's moves to stop him did more damage to the market. The price of wheat at the exchange rose to its up limit of 25c on the day and didn't move. The Board of Trade responded immediately by issuing an order requiring buyers and sellers with open positions in wheat of more than three million bushels to bring them down to one million by next Tuesday, the May delivery date.

'The real beneficiary of that move is Oscar Hartmine,' Caddy told one of the big traders he called. 'Oscar's got a long-standing relationship with Aleksei Krevenko. He's selling him wheat he can't afford to buy. I figure Margaret Meredith is blatantly attempting to undermine this bastion of the free market in order to help Oscar – they used to be lovers.'

He made sure there wasn't a trader large or small who didn't get that information, and most were infuriated by it. Noises of rebellion were heard. The CFTC came under a lot of pressure to rescind the order to liquidate down to a million bushels.

'No way will we sit still for this, Caddy. We fight for free markets, and when a perfect situation like this comes along these assholes try to restrict us,' the trader said over the phone. 'I'm long in wheat and plan on taking delivery and selling to the Russians or anyone else with the money to buy.'

'I'm taking the same line, Louis. I've got a lot of wheat and no plans to liquidate my position,' he responded. 'I'll go all the way to the Supreme Court on this.'

Nearly every other large trader moved in behind them, taking a similar line, including arch-rivals like Bunge and Cargill. Finally he got an angry call from Commissioner Meredith.

'What the hell are you saying about me, Caddy, that's getting traders so steamed up?'

372

'I'm just telling it like it is, Margaret. You're trying to stop us making a buck the good old American way.'

'All we're trying to do is regulate the market and bring some stability to it.'

'Have you looked at the market lately? Following the Board's declaration, it is totally chaotic. You had traders rushing to liquidate and plunging the price of wheat; – that sent speculators retreating –'

'But with all you major players buying even more wheat the price is up limit again.'

'If you take my advice you'll let the market take care of itself, Margaret.'

'That would mean the big players carving things up between you.'

'Your problem is you have no faith in the system. It works if you leave it alone.'

'We're going to stop you, Caddy.'

'You're trying. But I figure you're going to find the market is bigger than the regulatory authority. Your bias in favour of Hartmine is all too transparent. My advice is to back off while you can.'

'I'm warning you, Caddy, don't make this personal.'

That caused him to smile. This kind of excitement was exhilarating.

The news that broke from Russia on the Friday afternoon following market close, that their spring wheat was failing badly, coupled with their approach to the World Bank for a $4.5 billion loan, caused the situation to get ugly. The big traders felt doubly cheated. They figured the CFTC had inside information about this, knowing they wouldn't be able to cover the demand if those traders with long positions wanted to take delivery instead of liquidating as usual on or before Spot day.

Caddy encountered some traders ready to attack Hirshorn and accuse them of trying to corner the wheat market; but more who were willing to defend them, whether on the record on CBS news and in the *New York Times*, or off the record elsewhere. But most argued that these were the legitimate moves of a free market.

373

'Hirshorn is a large physical user of wheat, they need to hold big inventories,' Armand Bequai told the *Wall Street Journal*. 'They couldn't conduct their business any other way unless they were forever laying off labour and rehiring. These're the kind of problems the Boards of Trade were designed to prevent. Not create with such dumb moves.'

A similar statement to the *Washington Post* came from the president of the Grain and Feed Association.

Through it all, he called to friends on Capitol Hill to take soundings about their support, never once mentioning past services he had rendered them. As the pressures built up, he swam, finding motion through water relaxing.

Gordon Dulles flew in on the weekend to update him on moves by Oscar Hartmine. Caddy clung to the rim of the pool at the deep end and listened with single pointed attention.

'He took two meetings yesterday with Commissioner Meredith. I didn't get invited to either.'

'You figure they were of a romantic nature, Gordon?'

'OH is that worried I'd be figuring he can't even get it up any more. They plan on seeing the Agriculture Secretary today to have him block you, Caddy.'

'That kind of move makes sense.'

'Hal Arndt might just oblige them,' Dulles said, tension showing in his voice.

'D'Estaing called. He has control of the 270,000 tons he sold the Russians for the party in London,' Caddy said. 'At around $179.325 a ton. Shapiro's people losing their nerve looked like it was very timely. The price closed at under $178 a ton yesterday.'

'Well, I tell you, Caddy, my nerves are getting a mite stretched. With Congress leaning on him, Hal Arndt might not take a whole lot of persuading to enforce a wheat embargo on any sales to the Russians.'

'No problem, Gordon. Provided its ceiling is up around twenty-four, twenty-five million tons.'

Dulles snorted down his nose. 'Maybe Shapiro had this from the Agriculture Department ahead of us, that's why they sold early, figuring the price'll take a dive.'

'You credit them with being too smart. They lost their

nerve and sold cheap. Circumstances favour them right now. They won't stay that way. D'Estaing says the party in England is calling him hourly to see if their money is coming from the Russians.'

'I don't know why the hell you're spending so much time getting even with Shapiro,' Dulles snapped. 'If the Department enforces an embargo and we try to liquidate, the price'll go through the floor. It could head south anyhow, there are that many elements we can't control. Forget Shapiro, for Christsake.'

'Is there some evidence that this is costing us our main deal?' he asked.

'It could, Caddy. You left the guy in place too long. Never has so much been riding on a single deal.'

Not often had he seen his brother-in-law lose his nerve. He didn't enjoy the spectacle. Shapiro was a detail he refused to ignore. The man had to be punished. He heaved himself from the pool, purposely making a show of his physical strength. The effort took more out of him than he wanted to admit. A prayer formed in his mind, that he'd have the strength to carry all this through.

'I'll fly to Washington first thing on Monday to meet with Hal Arndt. I'll call on Wilf Fear too – his people can earn their keep.'

'If ever you figure whose side they're on.'

'The guy who snaps his fingers the loudest, I guess.'

When he snapped his fingers, people paid attention. They didn't always like what he had to say, but they concentrated all the same. Rarely did he take his fights into the public arena, then only if whatever argument he put forward was resisted in private. That way he kept his friends both on the Hill and in the Administration.

He knew that Hal Arndt, the Secretary for Agriculture, expected to remain on good terms with him, despite telling him that he would impose an export embargo on any sale of grain to the Russians over five million tons – that figure would let Hartmine off pretty lightly, along with most other grain traders.

As they talked in the Secretary's sumptuous office on the second floor of the USDA Administration Building, he said, 'I plan on selling the Russians twenty-two, twenty-four, maybe even thirty million tons, Hal,' – like this was an everyday trade. What he knew for sure was that this man didn't want him for an enemy.

Until then Hal Arndt clearly hadn't believed Hirshorn had control of such amounts of wheat, and hearing this declaration caused his large square face to throw up an incredulous smile. 'I can't tell you the kind of pressure I'm getting from Congress to stop any such market manoeuvre. If the Administration permitted a sale of that size, Caddy – why that's half the entire domestic market.' The sheer magnitude of the potential sale alarmed him. 'Jesus Christ, Congress'd kick my butt so hard I'd be shitting in next week.'

Instead of rising to meet this challenge, he said to the bespectacled Secretary, 'A sale of that size would be great for American farmers, Hal. We're talking around five billion dollars' worth of wheat.'

'You know what that'll do to the price of bread?'

'The East Europeans have dumped their command economies. Are we going to adopt one? It seems to me that's what the Kansas City Board of Trade is going for. I figure we operate a free market. So do most of the other traders.'

'But you guys step right up for export enhancement subsidies to compete with foreign wheat,' Arndt pointed out.

He smiled. Whenever the Administration started calling a subsidy a subsidy it meant they were on unsure ground. Every government back as far as Roosevelt and his Square Deal for farmers, had invented all kinds of euphemisms to disguise the fact that they were heavily subsidizing farmers.

'Hal, you know I've always supported the campaign to end any kind of subsidy on food.' He waited for the Agriculture Secretary to concede that point. It was a long wait, but finally the man nodded. 'With wheat at around $178 a ton, your department will save $1.650 billion in subsidies over last year's price. And as much again in storage costs. Blocking *any* kind of deal to a foreign buyer makes no sense.'

376

'We'd be glad of the saving, Caddy, if it helps reduce the deficit,' Arndt said like he was in a corner. 'But I can live with the deficit easier than with Congress if we run out of wheat here – that's a real possibility I gotta consider, goddamn it.'

'There are a lot of people who want to see the deficit reduced any way they can, Hal – Hirshorn has a lot of friends in Congress who want that. Worse, you could find yourself toughing it out with the wheat states if the Russians buy from Europe, India and Australia. They've got to get supplied someplace.'

That possibility seemed to worry Arndt. 'But you'd hurt real bad, if that happens, Caddy. All you need do is liquidate.'

'I'm not going to hurt a bit as bad as American farmers, Hal. Back last year I was buying wheat at five cents a bushel below the posted county price. Traders were laughing all the way to the bank when they dumped it on me at those prices. They figured I was sick and had lost my judgement. Wheat's got to go down below $102 a ton before I hurt. You figure the price is ever going to go that low with the Russians sitting in New York? I figure I can undercut the entire domestic market.'

'Caddy, this is mid-term election year. That's a mite unfriendly.'

'And that's emotional blackmail, Hal. I've stood up for this Administration. I now consider your actions hostile. Every bushel of wheat I bought was within the rules of the free market. If you guys try changing those rules mid-game, I'm going to get mad. I've got a lot of domestic customers for delivery. I guarantee I'm going to deliver wheat to all those customers, whatever kind of deal I make with the Russians.'

'You are, Caddy?' He sat forward. 'Then why the hell are we getting so steamed up about the Russians? No one minds wheat going to Russia or anyplace else they gotta need. That's only humane. What we gotta protect is the consumer at home.'

'No, Hal, what we're talking here is the right to operate freely in a free market. Hirshorn can go into the pits and survive, whatever the prevailing market force. But if you hog-tie me with embargoes or restrictive practices, saying who I can or cannot sell to, I'll come out gouging.'

He smiled, like he wanted this to stay friendly.

The Secretary of Agriculture smiled too. He suspected it belied his unease.

'But you are going to supply the domestic customers as a matter of priority?'

'Hirshorn's business practices are the embodiment of everything American; the President fought his election campaign on those same principles. Now you're telling me that this way's the un-American way. That's not right. The American public won't buy that.'

'I've gotta tell you Caddy, some influential people in this Administration would be happy to see the Russians go short, especially with the increasing instability there.'

'Not me, Hal. Those guys are trying to operate a market economy. All it takes to play is money.'

'Did you know they have been talking to the World Bank about a loan to buy grain?'

'I hope they don't impose too many conditions.'

'Give me something, Caddy.'

'I already did. A reduced farm deficit.'

He glanced at his aide, who hadn't said a word throughout the meeting. He guessed why. A grain embargo could hurt him badly, and nothing he had to say would have convinced the Secretary for Agriculture to avoid such a course.

Going down the wide steps onto Jefferson Avenue, Shapiro said, 'What happens if the Russians decide to starve rather than take our deal?'

'Only a fool chooses to starve.' He made it sound like an irrefutable fact. He paused at the open door of his limo. 'I'll look in at the District Court later and catch you there. I've a personal meeting right now.'

'Ah,' it was a note of surprise coming out of Shapiro. 'Right, I'll get a cab.'

Caddy climbed into the car and the chauffeur closed the door. He was meeting Wilf Fear and didn't want to risk Shapiro learning about the help he was seeking. He thought about what his brother-in-law had said about never truly knowing whose side the CIA were on or what their objectives were. But he had no choice but to approach Fear right now.

Something was in the air. The atmosphere on the second floor was electric. It crackled like it was about to catch fire.

Pacing around the washed Chinese rug in his office, Gordon Dulles could barely contain his rising anxiety. It was added to by the door between his own office and OH's having been closed since lunch. He wanted to believe that his boss was ashamed of his belching and farting finally, but that wasn't it. He bunched his knuckles then flexed his fingers like a boxer. He knew he had to take some kind of action. Oscar Hartmine was planning some desperate assault against Hirshorn and Dulles wasn't convinced that his brother-in-law was yet unassailable. He heard the intercom buzz on his boss's desk and OH say, 'Show them up.'

That did it. Stepping across to the door, he pushed into the office and said, 'What the hell's going on, OH?'

'Gordon,' OH said like he was expecting him. His boss was as excited as he was nervous. 'You know Margaret Meredith.' She was sitting on the sofa in a mini skirt with her long, shapely legs crossed. Dulles' eyes went to the short, tense man wearing the drill suit as he paced around. 'This is Jimmy Keiller. He does all the investigating of irregularities for Margaret.'

He took that not to be an accurate job description from the deadly look on Keiller's face.

'We're going to do it to Caddy but good. We got a kid on his way up with his lawyer. He worked for Caddy's Wall Street broker Armand Bequai. They just broke all the rules there were to break. Bequai had this kid buying wheat futures on secret nominee accounts for Hirshorn.'

'Is he going to talk on the record?' he asked.

'He sure is.' OH punched the air in excitement.

His secretary showed in the lawyer who looked barely old enough to have qualified at the New York bar; his client looked fresh out of college. Gordon Dulles felt sick

379

that this treacherous youth might betray such a pillar of the commercial establishment and possibly cause its downfall.

'Mr Westbrook, how long did you work for Armand Bequai?' Keiller said, right after everyone had been introduced. The interview was being openly recorded.

Dulles hated the smart-assed confidence Tom Westbrook and his lawyer showed, and wanted some way to pull them down.

'Just over a year, sir,' Westbrook replied.

'You worked on accounts for Hirshorn Grain?'

'No, sir. The wheat futures I bought were for Mr Hirshorn personally.'

'In his name?'

'No, sir. There were eleven different nominee accounts.'

'Do you have the names of these nominees?'

Westbrook glanced at his lawyer, who snapped open his Gucci attaché case and separated a single page from the sheaf and passed it across the desk.

Right then and without even knowing what evidence it contained, Dulles wanted to grab the bag of papers and run with it to the nearest paper shredder. He knew that wasn't the smart move. The way to help Hirshorn was to sit tight and hear the evidence, and make his move then.

'How much wheat was held by each of these nominees of Mr Hirshorn – to your certain knowledge?'

'They each held open positions of approximately three million bushels.'

'Were there other nominee accounts within the firm?'

'Yes, sir. Controlled by Mr Bequai, and two other brokers there.'

'Mr Westbrook, why did you leave Armand Bequai?'

'My client doesn't need to answer that,' the lawyer said.

'That's okay,' Westbrook said. 'I was fired for talking to one of Mr Hirshorn's rivals.'

There was a silence.

'Oscar,' Dulles suddenly declared, 'you're the guy who used to signal Oscar.'

'How the hell do you know that?'

'I was around Hirshorn when they found him out, for Christsake.'

'Is this true, Mr Westbrook?' Keiller asked, some of his confidence gone now.

'Jesus, Oscar, you try and use this on Caddy, he'll stamp us right into the ground, and legally.'

'That's right. Margaret,' Keiller said. 'Did you know about this?'

'It makes no difference,' she said. 'Go on with the interview.'

'Sure it makes a difference. A jury will believe this is a guy trying to settle old scores.'

'It won't run as far as a jury, Jimmy. We'll hit Hirshorn so hard with this they'll have no option but to divest or we'll have our Administrative judge lock their grain up way past delivery.'

'This is criminal, Margaret,' Jimmy Keiller said as he paced the office, overstretching rubber bands to breaking between his hands. 'If we've got the evidence, we should bust those bastards doing it the right way. It's the only way to go.'

'And who benefits finally from that?' she asked. 'Hirshorn. Gordon's right, they'll stamp us into the ground while we're following correct procedure.'

'That's great. Just great. They break the rules. So we break the rules to stop them from breaking more. Just what the good Jesus are we doing here, Margaret?'

'I sometimes wonder, Jimmy. We try and regulate the market, I have to tell you, with the best means at our disposal. This isn't some penny-ante violator. This is *Hirshorn*. They have too many important friends for us to make our moves too public. If you steal big enough someone will always move the goalposts. You can count on it. We tried, Jimmy and failed your way.'

'If you want to go on with this,' Keiller declared, 'I'll take it to the Chairman.'

'Hey asshole, butt out,' OH said, towering over the CFTC lawyer. 'This kid came all the way from New York to do a public service.'

'I advise you not to go on with this interview, Mr

Westbrook. I advise you to come to my office at the CFTC and continue it there.' With that he snapped off the recorder and removed the cassette and put it in his pocket. 'I don't want to argue with you on the record anymore, Margaret. I'm sorry it came out like this. It really looked like we had Hirshorn there for a while.'

Gordon Dulles said not a word. The silent laughter deep inside his chest made him feel real good right then.

'Caddy Hirshorn is the Prince of Darkness,' Wilf Fear said. 'I have no doubt about that, and believe me I have met some dark spectres during my time working for the government.'

'What can we realistically do to stop him, Mr Fear?' Grace asked.

She and Jak were sitting across from the CIA man and Rory Spelman at the formica-topped table in the cafeteria out at Maryland University. She knew Jak didn't want to be at this meeting and was ready to run. This was a last desperate gamble to stop what was happening.

'Jak's the principal means of stopping the deal going down. Only Jak won't play ball.'

'What the hell difference does it make – the wheat's failed just like we knew it would. If your people were so goddamn concerned why the hell did you let it get sold to Russia in the first place,' Jak was shouting. 'No – in the first place why did you let the seed get developed?'

'You're the scientist, Jak. You know the answer to that better than me.'

There was silence at the table. Everyone's eyes were on Jak, willing him to go along with Fear's plan.

'Jak,' Grace said. 'You know what he's doing can't be right.'

'At this moment Hirshorn is in New York negotiating with the Russians,' Wilf Fear said. 'He'll get a real good price for his wheat too, now he's ruined theirs.'

'I can't stop this happening, Mr Fear.'

'All you have to do is tell the Russians how Hirshorn suckered them with the Take-all-attracting wheat seed.'

382

'I could be wrong about that.' He glanced at Grace again.

She tried not to show her disapproval or her disappointment. Somehow she hoped he'd respond if she brought the CIA man here with his information. Now she was despairing.

'I figure they will find what you have to say irresistible.'

'Why does the CIA want this deal stopped so bad?' Jak asked. 'Isn't selling wheat to the Russians good for American farmers any more?'

'Forget the Russians, Jak,' Rory said, 'and the American farmer. Remember Hirshorn almost had you guys killed. They framed you for murder. How do you figure you pulled clear there? Good fortune? Luck? You think I want to get involved with spooks from the CIA? What I see here is the end objective being more important than the means.'

There was another long silence at the table.

'Jak, this is your last shot at stopping those guys dominating the world wheat trade. Hirshorn will for sure when you find the genetic code for wheat to fix its own nitrogen.'

Jak's silence was paradoxically like a clarion. He rose from the table. 'I don't want to argue this thing further. I know what is important and I don't want to get thrown off course by a sudden sea change at the CIA. You people just can't seem to understand the significance of this work. It matters not who pays for it, the goal belongs to the whole world.'

Grace rose too and went after him. He quickened his pace along the corridor, but she caught him by the arm.

'After all we went through, Jak, you can't let this happen.'

'There's no way I can help, Grace. This is political and it's dirty – it's something I have no control over.'

'It's been like that from the start. What we're trying to do here is gain control. It's the last chance.'

Jak looked at her, and for a moment, she sensed he was about to give in and go along with what Fear had proposed. She could see he was scared, his breathing was tense and shallow. He folded his arms over his head like he was in pain.

'What is it, Jak?' she asked.

'All I want is for these problems to leave me. Why don't you people just butt out of my life?'

Being reduced to 'these people' hurt. She started to turn away.

'Grace, I'm sorry,' he said. 'Look, there is something else involved here. We've made a serious breakthrough. We've got the rhizome nodule-forming genes to express themselves in wheat. Can you believe that? We've switched them on. The yeast cells are more similar to plant cells than they are to the bacterial donor genes. We've actually got them to express themselves.' There was suppressed excitement in his voice waiting to burst out.

She looked at him like he was from another planet, knowing what kind of leap forward this was, and what it meant. Nothing in her armoury would deflect him now. She could even ask him to marry her and he probably wouldn't hear her.

'The genes are expressed. They're producing within the cell the protein for which they are coded. We've repeated the experiment a dozen times, Grace. This doesn't mean we can fix nitrogen in wheat yet, but Jesus I'm closer than ever before.'

For a moment she felt confused. She wanted to rejoice in his success, but couldn't. She saw something altogether more sinister on the horizon.

He was like a child with a long-promised present and here she felt like some wicked stepmother who was about to take it from him. 'Who's going to benefit from this discovery? Don't tell me mankind. Look closely at the contract the university has with the Baedeker Trust. There is nothing in it that says your discoveries must be shared with mankind. Nothing suggests they're striving for the greater good. All of your findings are owned exclusively by the Trust. The Trust is completely in the control of Hirshorn. Not a single ear of wheat resulting from your discovery, whether grown in Kansas or Ethiopia will escape a royalty to Hirshorn.'

'I can't undiscover it, Grace. The idea is on the ether. In time other plant geneticists will get to it.'

'The choice is simple, Jak.' It was the way Wilf Fear had spelt it out. 'Unless we terminally damage Hirshorn, they will dominate the world market – your discovery will only add to that domination. You know how they'll do it – growers will be offered this new miracle seed and then get a period free of royalties. That way Hirshorn will entirely undermine the economic base of all other commercially grown wheat. Then they will just name their price.'

'Jesus Christ, you've got it all worked out!'

She almost smiled at him getting angry. Hopefully she might steer that anger in the right direction.

'Why the hell would the Russians believe me?' he said. 'There's no goddamn evidence of what happened. Their wheat rotting in the fields doesn't prove anyone did it to them. It's Take-all, every wheat grower has that problem from time to time. We're no place on the conspiracy theory, Grace. No place the Russians will want to go. We do not have any evidence. Do you understand, Grace. That's what we'd need.'

After a moment, she said, 'Jak, Mr Fear has copies of Sanson's research from Guelph. Copies of Hirshorn's shipment manifests to d'Estaing, the French grain salesman. He has their bogus customer orders covering their corner in wheat; the work-ups from Crocker-Giant showing how the wheat was grown with the Take-all virus-attracting gene.'

'Jesus Christ,' Jak hissed like a balloon deflating. 'I don't believe it. He can't.'

She didn't know how Fear had got this evidence, and had been too scared to ask. She simply accepted its integrity, just as she accepted on faith that the Russians pulling out of any grain purchase would badly damage Hirshorn. She still had faith. That was all she had.

Sanson's original research data was the prize Jak started to reach for.

'What if Hirshorn find out about this and pull my programme funding?' he said.

'Would it matter? Next week, or the week after, you

could go on to rediscover how those genes express themselves in yeast. You wouldn't be shackled to Hirshorn. It really could go into public ownership then. Then the whole world would benefit.'

This was what would finally persuade him if anything would, she decided. Here was a scientist with a strong public duty ethic. She watched him anxiously as he stopped pacing.

'You think this will truly block Hirshorn?' he said.

'I don't know, Jak. I hope and I pray it will. That's all I can do.'

'They'd still get the wheat that fixes its own nitrogen if this development holds the key like I figure.'

'There's nothing I can do about that, Jak. It's your decision what you do with the discovery.'

He nodded ponderously.

'You better let me get a look at Sanson's original papers.'

A surge of affection rushed through her at that point. She put her arms around him and kissed him on the mouth. There was a lot of feeling in that kiss. He responded too.

A sleepless night followed for Jak. He thought about that kiss Grace had given him. He thought about her in the tiny bedroom right alongside his. Her imminent plan to move out into her own apartment. He wondered what he could do to make her change her mind. Nothing as a man, as a lover. She wasn't lying awake next door thinking about him as a man, as a lover, he was sure of that.

The following day was as stressful for him and as restless. His dilemma remained as irresolvable. What he had discovered would project him into the forefront of international plant genetics. That was something he wanted so much. But he couldn't deny the possibility that it would ultimately benefit no one but Hirshorn, which would, he slowly realized, cost everyone more than they would ever be able to afford.

Reluctantly he concluded what he had to do. Reaching for the phone in his office he punched out Herman Solkoff's number. Solkoff answered right away.

'Herman, it's Jak Redford.'

'Well, aren't you the lucky one,' Solkoff said. 'I hear you have all the funding you need and no interference from your paymaster.'

'You are exactly right, Herman. But it's not without its problems.'

'Share them with me.'

'That's what I'm calling about. Can we meet? The sooner the better. I've got something I'd like to show you.'

He knew Solkoff would be able to apply his discovery to the process of fixing nitrogen in rice. Equally other plant geneticists would find it helpful for the cereals they might be working on. That way the advance might eventually benefit the whole of mankind. It wouldn't be his exclusive discovery, for which he would get world acclaim. But that no longer mattered.

26

SELLING TWENTY PLUS MILLION TONS of wheat was no minor item. In some ways Caddy Hirshorn had been getting ready for this for three years. Possibly he had been preparing for such a deal ever since going to work for his Daddy. He checked in at the Waldorf Tower. Not a hotel he normally stayed at. On the occasions he stopped over in New York he preferred the more exclusive Mayfair Regent but hadn't the energy to waste shuttling the fifteen blocks between them. He took a one-bedroom suite. Shapiro got a room in the main hotel.

Negotiations proved long and arduous, and it felt like he needed to keep his foot in the door the whole while. He knew it was the Russian style of negotiation, but at times he was tempted to ask if they truly wanted to buy wheat, because if they didn't he was missing his family. But the moment he took such a line, he knew they would get a better deal than he was prepared to give.

As he freshened his face in one of the three bathrooms in the Russians' suite, he had no doubt why Krevenko had insisted that they dispensed with preliminary discussions conducted by their aides and made them part of the main negotiation between themselves. The head of Exportkhleb had clearly heard rumours about his health and was seeking to tire him. They had been negotiating for two days, and he was getting very tired. Only the objective kept him going. Occasionally he was pushed on by his Daddy, who sometimes seemed to be looking over his shoulder, waiting to shake his head if he wasn't getting the absolute best deal. They had agreed a sale of twenty and a half million tons, and were getting close to a price. He was holding out for the world market price of $210 a ton discounted by 10 per cent. The Russians were looking for $209.725 less ten at the port elevator. The comparatively small difference amounted to over five and a half million dollars.

The water felt good on his face. He made a point of breaking frequently during negotiations. This long established tactic that often unnerved the opposition was today essential to his staying the course. He reached for the rose he had standing in water. It had taken on a fresher appearance, though quite how it did so in New York water! He thought about Armand Bequai who had bought wheat so skilfully during the past year. Would he prove as skilful now? He thought about Gordon Dulles waiting with Hartmine at the Carlyle. Would his nerve hold out? Then about Wilf Fear – still regretting the need to rely on the CIA. What would result if he wasn't to be trusted after all?

There was not a thing he could do about it right then. He prayed it would be okay as he stepped out into the hall. He was relying on prayer more and more. A waiter came in pushing a trolley with fresh coffee and pastries. He followed him through to the negotiating table in the dining-room.

There Shapiro was receiving information over the phone and nodding solemnly. When the call was done he hesitated. Caddy met his eyes and saw the news wasn't good. His mind went at once to what the problem could be. He didn't want this here. It would be a distraction. Maybe whatever it was had a direct bearing.

Krevenko came in accompanied by his aides, with whom he had whispered discussions following any change in the world price. These often meant calls to Moscow and each call seemed to bring worsening news of their grain harvest and increased confusion in their economy. Caddy wondered if anyone could come up with the money for all this wheat. During their negotiations the price of wheat on the markets had twice opened at its up limit of twenty-five cents; physical wheat changed hands for more than the market price as traders panicked. The word was that world shortages would follow this sale.

'That was Carl Flint,' Shapiro said, sidling up to him. The lawyer had been in the District Court for the judgment in the USDA's case against Hirshorn Chicken. Shapiro shook his head. 'Our chickens were declared a hazard to health.'

He nodded and drank some coffee. 'Only our chickens?'

'Jesus Christ, Caddy, that judge was a real surprise. He was going along with our people all the way. Making all kinds of promises.'

With a glance at his aide, he said, 'I guess they misread his signals. He doesn't want to be a Supreme Court judge badly enough.'

'The dishonest bastard. We should find a way to stop him being any kind of judge at all.'

'That is foolish,' he said. 'The real fight will be before the appellate bench. We have some business here to conclude.' He glanced round at Krevenko.

'You have bad news, my friend?' Krevenko said.

'None that makes any difference here.'

'We have more bad news also. The Republics now permit me to buy twenty-two million tons in total only. This is bad. There is no more money to borrow.'

'Maybe we can steer you to a banker who might be able to help you.' He smiled. He didn't trust this Russian candour.

Krevenko smiled too. 'First we take the twenty and a half million tons of wheat, no? Then we find out how much we will borrow for this.'

'If you're coming back with $210 a ton less ten, I'm ready to make that deal.' He glanced at the monitor with the KCBT prices. Because of the deals he could make on insurance, freight and shipping, he could still discount that price for such volume.

'This is a small difference.'

'We live on tight margins, Aleksei.'

Krevenko pulled at his ears like they didn't already stick out enough from his round face and glanced at his principal aide. He whispered to him in Russian. Then they both glanced at the monitor. The price hadn't moved all day.

'In London we paid less.'

390

'I hear tell you did. Can London deliver a single bushel?' He smiled at Shapiro, enjoying the threat to his position that statement implied.

'Every day the price gets higher, Aleksei.'

'One day it bursts and comes running down. No?'

'No doubt about that. You could do worse than simply waiting for it to happen.'

With a huge intake of breath, Krevenko said, '$209.85. We save the difference with Russian shipping.'

'I could live with $209.85. The shipping arrangement wouldn't be acceptable to our longshore unions. A lot of people will be pretty steamed about you walking off with so much wheat without us getting the longshoremen mad.'

'Ah,' the Russian sighed, 'if only we dealt in a truly free market, we would not sit here for days to make many small points. First they try to take your wheat, then not let you sell to us,' ticking the points off his fingers. 'Then they say the ships you must use.'

Krevenko stood up and got himself a fresh cup and poured some coffee, then bit into a Danish pastry and came back to the table.

Each time he did that there followed another protracted element in the negotiations. Caddy glanced at his wrist-watch. It was a little after 11:00. He was seriously concerned about his level of energy, fearing it might suddenly vanish.

Negotiations continued through lunch, and following many side discussions, the Russians finally got to splitting the freight, using eighty per cent of their own ships.

'Aleksei, eighty per cent wouldn't get that grain moved from the dock.'

'But the KGB tell me this labour union is weak.'

'Corrupt is what they mean,' he said.

After lunch he went to lie down in his own suite for half an hour. It was all he'd allow himself. He took a shower, and changed into fresh clothes. Those he discarded smelt of cigarette smoke. He returned looking refreshed and impeccably tailored, but feeling more tired.

'We both have a figure in mind,' he opened with.

'Tell me your figure,' Krevenko said.

'Seventy per cent.'

'In my favour of course.'

'If our seamen allow Russian ships to carry that much wheat, you've got a deal. I'll drop to fifty per cent. But the unions will want so much compensation to give up that amount of freight, I'd need to move our price back to $210 a ton.' He checked the time. 'The markets close soon. Tomorrow the price could open up limit. That'll cost you another twenty-two million dollars, Aleksei.'

The Russians went into whispered negotiations. No one else could sell them wheat cheaper and guarantee delivery.

He waited, knowing they were close.

'$209.90 and fifty per cent of grain on Russian ships. Fifty per cent on American ships. But your government makes us the differences on American freight charges, no?'

Promising that on behalf of the US government couldn't have been easier. He smiled. 'I guess I can sneak that past, Aleksei.'

Krevenko rose and stepped round the table, extending his arms. Right then as the Russian embraced him, it occurred to him that he could never once remember his Daddy embracing or kissing him. He decided he should hug his kids more.

Everyone clapped. They had a deal.

'Tonight we celebrate,' Krevenko announced. 'Tomorrow the lawyers have the contracts ready to sign.' He gave his gap-toothed grin.

Sitting in his hotel room waiting to make his move stretched Gordon Dulles' nerves. He snapped at everybody from OH to room service. The coded call he received from his brother-in-law's private secretary telling him about the deal with the Russians made him more tense. Dulles first leaked the news to the commodity markets before calling Wilf Fear.

'Did he get a good price?' Fear asked.

'Who gives a shit,' Dulles yelled.

'Take it easy, Gordon. Everything is set.'

Dulles snorted at that.

'Make good and sure you get Dr Redford to New York to talk with the Russians. You got all the evidence?'

'Sitting right here on my desk. Redford didn't question the validity of the copies I showed him. By the time either he or the Russians figure out that every piece of it's a forgery, it'll be too late.'

'Is he all set?'

'If he hasn't changed his mind. I'm kind of running out of levers. The last thing I want to have to do is tell him what's really going down here.'

'Get him there, Wilf,' Dulles said. 'There is one hell of a lot of money at stake.'

'There's more at stake than money, Gordon,' the CIA man said. 'But then I guess money is all that ever drives those crazy bastards at the Pentagon. Those guys are between a rock and a hard place these days.'

'The commodity markets were in uproar again today,' the *Eyewitness* newsreader said, 'with news that Hirshorn, the giant grain trading company, had closed a deal with the Russians for twenty-five million tons of wheat . . .'

A smile crept through Caddy's tiredness as he watched the newscast, wondering why it was reporters never got anything exactly right. Because they were never around when it happened, he guessed.

'Very little wheat was traded on the floor. Brokers are saying the price could go higher than the quoted price of $210 a ton. There are reports of it changing hands for as high as $225 a ton as processors try to fill orders. There have been persistent complaints that the Commodities Futures Trading Commission has failed to regulate the market. Also that Hirshorn Grain broke the rules. Earlier *Eyewitness News* talked with Commissioner Margaret Meredith to ask her why the Board of Trade backed off its fight with Hirshorn.'

'Clearly they weren't in breach of the three million bushel speculative limit,' the beautiful and immaculately attired Margaret Meredith said with a tight smile.

What that smile didn't give any hint of to him, or anyone else watching, was how pissed off she was. But he

393

knew she was after the call he'd taken from Deke Turetsky at the White House, telling him the Chairman of the CFTC was lending a hand. Her anger had sprung from the fact that finally there was no true separation of powers, that all regulatory oversight was politically interdependent. What this reaction told him was that she didn't understand the fundamental nature of the free market where everything, but everything was subordinate to profit. It could work no other way. He would teach her that when he hired her. Someone as smart as she was would be quick to learn.

'Can the government block this sale to stop inflation in food prices?' the *Eyewitness* reporter asked.

'You'd need to ask the Secretary for Agriculture,' Margaret Meredith responded. Her smile remained unblemished. 'But either we have a free, if regulated market, or we don't.'

Her body language, as she stepped into a waiting auto, confirmed everything he needed to know about this woman. He had learned how to read the unconscious gestures people made. She was in control, despite losing. Anger made people useless. Shutting off the TV, he went through the hotel suite to get the door as the buzzer sounded a second time.

Gordon Dulles stepped inside.

'There's a posse of reporters in the lobby. You won't get out of here,' Dulles said.

He nodded. Going out to celebrate with the head of the Exportkhleb wasn't his idea of fun. He would have preferred dinner in the comfortable upstairs dining-room at Lutece, which served the finest French cuisine in New York. The Russians wanted something more flamboyantly American.

'We'll find a way past them.'

'Jesus, Caddy, I'm almost too scared to breathe in case this comes loose.'

'Relax.' He laid his hand on his brother-in-law's shoulder. 'What's the bottom line, Gordon? We pick up the pieces and start over. Tomorrow you'll wonder what all the fuss was about. Come on, you got work to do.'

He steered Dulles through into the sitting-room to go

over the final details of the deal. On the outside he was cool, even relaxed; on the inside a growing anxiety was eating away at him like a rat in his stomach gnawing its way out. He knew he was in for a restless night.

The number of lawyers in suite 29K for the signing almost made it crowded. Carl Flint arrived with most of those who had assisted Bill Moncton in the District Court throughout the case against Hirshorn Chicken. The Russians brought in as many legal minds, checking and rechecking every detail, wanting nothing to go wrong. The wheat price was up limit again this morning. The papers were set out in two neat piles on the table. Across the room Caddy picked at the remains of the buffet lunch. He wasn't hungry, especially after dining with the Russians at Peter Luger's steak house, which lurked in the shadows of the Williamsburgh Bridge out in Brooklyn. Not the most fashionable neighbourhood, but the Russians enjoyed seeing the sleazy side of New York life. They practically had to slaughter their T-bones right at the table. And for the first time he had been revolted by the idea of eating such food. It was the closest he had come to recognizing a dead animal on the plate. He tried telling himself the notion was ridiculous, as a whole raft of both the nation's wealth and his company's earnings were based on killing and eating like this. But last night he had only been able to manage the onions and home-fries.

He pushed celery into a dip and chewed it as Aleksei Krevenko joined him.

'You are sad to sell us so much wheat?'

'Not as long as you don't turn right the way round and sell it to my customers here at a profit, Aleksei. How bad are things for you?'

'Bad. But spring wheat down forty-seven million tons is a small problem. I think free enterprise is not so good for Russia. Out of all this confusion perhaps a fascist coup.'

'That would be a real shame.'

'You still have wheat to sell. No?'

'Some,' he said, thinking about their only buying twenty-two million tons total. The cost was all the

Russians could borrow at this stage from the World Bank. But if less than half of what they needed would keep them from starving, it wouldn't keep them from going hungry. That had been the basis for the whole revolution: not enough to eat. There had been no place for them to turn but to the capitalist system. But he feared they had left it too late. Now they were starting with a real hard lesson. He was sorry about that. Some in Russia would get mad.

'What did you pick up in London?' he said.

Across the room he noticed Shapiro immediately lose the thread of his conversation with a Russian lawyer about Porsches. He almost smiled. The time was getting close.

'We got a little over a quarter million tons.'

'Good price?'

Krevenko inclined his head non-committally.

With another oblique glance at Shapiro, seeing him totally ignoring the Russian lawyer now, he said, 'I'll discount their price by fifteen per cent if you take my wheat instead. I'll even beat Russian freight charges if you give me cargo back from Odessa.'

His offer was a serious mistake, he realized at once. His desire to get even with Shapiro had robbed him of his judgement. The Russian would have seen the whole scam in that offer – the market price was far higher than the discounted price, so why make such an offer? He saw Krevenko's eyes narrow in suspicion and he tensed, waiting for the blow. It didn't come. Instead Krevenko started to grab, seeing only a better deal than that he had made in London. A whine of surprise emerged from Shapiro. He silenced him with an impatient gesture.

'I want an answer now, Aleksei.'

The Exportkhleb boss quickly conferred in Russian with his principal aide, who produced a calculator. They then consulted with one of their lawyers.

Shapiro's anguish became naked; Caddy's gestures more impatient.

'Caddy! That deal's crazy. Wheat's making $227 on the Spot.'

'I'll make enough profit on this, Pat,' he said and glanced

at his watch. 'It's a gesture of goodwill.'

Krevenko came back, his toothy grin almost a mile wide. 'We would not lose seven million dollars on a principle. Instead we take your wheat. No?'

'Of course, you rogue.' He gripped Shapiro's arm hard, holding him fast as he tried to leave. 'Stay with me, Pat.'

The pain in his arm from his boss's vice-like grip was excruciating. Where did he find the strength? A nerve must have been pinched. It was all he could do not to cry out. Panic swelled through him and he fought the inclination to vomit. Sweat broke out on his forehead, and ran between his shoulder-blades. He couldn't breathe. He clamped his teeth together and tried to suck air in slowly and evenly as if past a matchstick as he had done in front of that window in his father's house in Philadelphia. If he didn't get out of here soon he'd fall over. It was only his boss's grip that was keeping him upright. Jesus Christ, what had happened? What had he done? How had he tipped his moves to Caddy? They wouldn't make a cent on their wheat deal. The Russians pulling out would strand them. The markets would soon close and so his partners could take no action today to salvage the situation. His boss was a devil, no doubt about it.

The clock on the bureau across the room came into focus. The time was approaching when the commodity exchanges stopped trading. Shapiro almost imagined hearing the minute-to-close warning bell. Perhaps Caddy did too for at last he released him. Then he saw his smile. It was chilling, deathlike.

Choking back his vomit he ran to the nearest bathroom. His plan to call Walter Shearing in England was delayed as he threw up into the lavatory bowl. Pain and disappointment fountained out of him, along with regret that he had ever broken the solemn trust that Caddy Hirshorn demanded of all employees. It was too late to go back, to try and salvage something. There was nothing to salvage. Caddy gave no one a second chance. Getting up off the floor, he made the call to England.

'Sell, sell. Sell our wheat, for Christsake. Sell it,' he said the moment Shearing picked up the phone.

'Slow down. What are you saying?' Shearing caught the panic from his voice like it was highly contagious. 'We've sold it to the Russians.'

'Hirshorn undercut us – they're reneging on our deal.'

'We'll be wiped out – ! They can't, we'll sue them – oh shit, shit. Tell me they didn't. They can't. The bank's got notes against the whole of my property. When the fraud's discovered we could go to prison. The banks will take my farm. They'll take it. I'll lose everything. Damn you, damn you.'

'Start selling, Walter,' he said, trying to get back in control. 'We can make more money this way with the market so bullish. They're paying $227 a ton for hard red wheat here. We sell now we'll do just great.'

'Who do I sell to? The brokers are closed. I can't do a damn thing. Are you stupid? The wheat's already been sold. Pierre d'Estaing holds all the contracts. Look, you'd better reach him and get him working pretty damn quick or I'll be completely ruined. Jesus Christ, do something, fast. Get hold of d'Estaing.'

'I can't do a thing, Walter. Not a thing,' he said in a hoarse whisper. All he could do right then was nod, confirming their hapless position. He saw Caddy's hand in everything. Certainly he wouldn't be dumb enough to leave them in a position to make more money. D'Estaing had to have been in on this with Caddy from the start. That made most sense. He wouldn't be available to resell their wheat until after the price had collapsed. Meanwhile the Board of Trade would look for payment in full to release the wheat from the certified warehouse. It wouldn't be forthcoming, and in these circumstances they would fore-close and sell them out. They were dead in the water. Shapiro dropped the phone back onto the rest.

The excitement he heard beyond the bathroom door said the contracts were ready to sign. He had no interest in seeing this.

The run for the Washington–New York shuttle was clearly

a gruesome experience for the CIA man, and several times Grace had to stop herself assisting him. Both Rory and Jak had offered to help him and had been snarled at. The poor man looked in agony and he sweated profusely. If Jak hadn't disappeared at the last moment they wouldn't have had to run. She thought about what he was playing at, if he was truly going through with this. She still wasn't sure. But from the state Wilf Fear was in she believed he might shoot Jak if he changed his mind again.

Jumping the queue for a cab at La Guardia almost got them into a fight. She suspected Wilf Fear wouldn't have been any use to anyone in a fight right then, even though he was the principal cause. His pain was compounded by the stop-go ride in from Queen's. The cab felt like it had no kind of suspension. Then the driver dropped them at the Park Avenue entrance to the main hotel, rather than the E50th Street entrance to the Tower. That meant hauling up a dozen stairs in the lobby and across to the Tower elevators. His movements were getting more laboured, she noticed. He looked at his watch a half-dozen times in the space of five minutes. She suddenly worried in case he had a time bomb set to explode in the suite if all else failed. None of them spoke as they rode to the twenty-ninth floor. There were serious and anxious looks on each of their faces.

'Jesus Christ,' Fear said, 'I don't know what you folks have to worry about.' He looked at Jak but didn't explain himself.

'We have a meeting with Gregor Zlotnikov,' Fear told the security man who opened the door.

The two-hundred-pound Russian blinked a couple of times like a message was coming out of his brain, then he slowly shook his head.

'No Gregor Zlotnikov.' He closed the door. No one rushed to put a foot in the jamb.

'Hey, what is this shit?' Fear said. 'I don't believe this.' He rang the bell again and hammered at the door.

This time it was opened on the security chain by a woman. She was smaller than her colleague.

'Now don't give us an argument, lady,' Fear said. 'We have a meeting set with Zlotnikov. It's pretty damn important. If you don't get him out here you'll go where all the bad girls go in Russia.'

'The head of Exportkhleb is signing an important contract. You must wait.'

'No, get him out here now! Before anything gets signed. Tell him Wilf Fear is here. Tell him. Now, for Christsake!'

No one could have misunderstood the urgency in his manner. Grace felt breathless just watching him.

The woman security officer said, 'Wait,' and hurried away.

Despite the obvious pain he was in, the CIA man paced. Jak paced too, hands folded over his head. Grace looked at Rory who shook his head. She had a sinking feeling. Perhaps they were too late.

With his lawyers lined up on the left-hand side of the table and Russian lawyers on the right, Caddy came to the table with Krevenko for the signing. The expectation in the air was broken by the Russians clapping. Krevenko clapped also. That was something he found moving, but it didn't reduce his feeling of impatience to get this done.

'First to show our friendship, we swap presents. Yes?'

It was like these guys didn't want to sign. Maybe they were hoping the price of wheat would collapse before they did. Maybe it would! They made a great ritual of bringing the present in. He had come suitably prepared. That wasn't his problem, rather the rat that was gnawing away inside his stomach getting nearer to the surface.

They gave him a golden ear of wheat exquisitely crafted. He examined it appreciatively, fighting his increasing impatience. His present to the head of Exportkhleb lacked imagination, even though it contained more gold – a fountain pen.

'I am deeply touched, Arkadi,' Krevenko said as he examined his present. 'We sign with this. Yes.'

There was no ink in the pen. Ink had to be sent for. The delay brought the rat inside him closer to busting out. It was then that trouble reared its head in the shape of the woman security officer entering and speaking urgently with the security boss. He hurriedly exited the room.

The hands on the quartz clock moved silently on while the rat continued to gnaw through his stomach. Every eye in the room went to the door as ink arrived and the pen was filled. With a slight tremor of the hand, Caddy signed the contracts first as the double doors to the dining-room opened and Gregor Zlotnikov rushed in.

'Aleksei Michailovich,' he said, 'an urgent matter. You must delay the signing.'

Krevenko dismissed him with a flick of his hand and took up the gold pen. Zlotnikov became more insistent, using his formal title.

'Tovarich Krevenko!' The head of security turned white in the face as his hand went out to prevent the signing.

Anger flared in Krevenko. 'Boris Ivanovich, this is not the way to conduct yourself before a business associate.' He rose sending his chair crashing over. 'What is this urgent matter?'

Zlotnikov spoke in Russian, his words galvanizing the other Russians who were present.

'Aleksei?' Caddy said, 'what's happening? Sign the contract.'

'Yes. Please, my friend. Please. We delay one moment. No? I come back and sign directly to make the deal.'

He went out with Zlotnikov.

Carl Flint looked totally bemused. 'Are they pulling some kind of stunt?'

Caddy said nothing, but had a strange, unpleasant cramping in his stomach and found himself a little breathless. He got hot and started to sweat. He closed his eyes and drew in some deep breaths, trying to ease his pain.

'Caddy?' he heard Flint say like he was a thousand miles away. 'Are you okay? Can I get you anything?'

'Some water,' he whispered.

The cramping passed.

*

Tears came into Grace's eyes as she sat on the gold and green sofa in the hallway and watched the round, boyish-looking Russian turn into an old man before her eyes as Jak outlined what had happened to the Russian wheat. She wanted to put her arms around him and comfort him. Rarely had she seen anyone so distressed without expressing it. Not even a little cry of anguish escaped him. At first there was disbelief that this had happened. 'Certainly my good friend Arkadi Hirshorn could not be held responsible for this thing. Where is the proof that this thing happened? Where?' he demanded.

Like in some well-rehearsed play, Wilf Fear produced all the evidence right on cue. Krevenko became greyer and older-looking as he examined it, while Jak explained what it all meant.

It was then that an awful thought occurred to Grace: something wasn't right here in what they were doing.

'How did the CIA get all that evidence so conveniently in place?' she whispered to Rory, who was next to her on the sofa.

'A good point, Grace.'

'My God,' she said, 'they're working for Hirshorn too – the CIA are.'

Only when Aleksei Krevenko turned and looked at her did she realize what she had said out loud.

'I agree, madam. Something is not right with this,' Krevenko said. 'We have many problems in Russia. But our people will still need wheat.'

'With their own wheat rank and dying in the fields of the Ukraine and Georgia,' Jak replied, 'won't Hirshorn wheat stick in their craw?'

Fear became more anxious, like his plan had suddenly stopped working. Grace thought he might do something desperate.

'You'd better talk with the foreign ministers of the twelve Republics before you go any further on this, sir,' he advised.

'Why I talk with them?' Krevenko said, raging now. 'I make the decisions to buy wheat, not the Republics. Only maybe this thing was done. I talk to no one. Our people still need this wheat.'

This Russian being so pragmatic, despite what may have happened to their grain, visibly disturbed Fear. 'You can't be serious about going ahead with this deal. You can't.'

More than anything now, Grace was convinced the CIA man was working for Hirshorn, but couldn't understand why they'd not want to sell the wheat. She rose and instinctively reached out to Krevenko and touched his hand.

'I'm sorry. I'm so sorry,' she said.

He smiled, and with his soft fleshy fingers he brushed her tears off her cheeks.

'This is a very brave thing you do. But we must be practical. Until this is proven why our spring wheat has failed, and perhaps even afterwards, we buy this wheat at best price. Put bread in the bakeries. That will ease one problem, I do this.' He went out.

'Jesus Christ,' Fear said. 'Jesus H Christ!'

Caddy felt sick as he waited for the Russians to return. That feeling only deepened with the belief that they wouldn't come back with the right decision. He knew that he had to take some urgent action, that if he didn't he'd be finished. The stress of all this made his physical condition worse, which was affecting his mental process, and for the first time in his life he felt powerless to act. Taking a deep breath to try and push back the sick-feeling he had, he reached across the table for the contract he had signed. The effort brought him pain and made him giddy. At first he couldn't focus his eyes on the signature pages, then when he did he tore them to shreds, startling those in the room.

'The deal is off,' he announced in a hoarse whisper.

All eyes were on him when he rose and started across the room. He didn't realize immediately that it was because he was lurching like a drunk.

'Are you okay?' Fear said, meeting him in the hallway.

For someone whose failings had potentially just cost him four billion dollars, he was thinking, this man was showing remarkable equilibrium. But then those working

403

with the government bureaucracy were rarely touched by the real world.

He paused and tried the bathroom door and found it was locked. It was then he noticed the three people who were with the CIA man. He wondered which of the two men was Dr Redford. He smiled wanly at Mrs Chance and said, 'I think you are going to succeed very well against American Chemicals. I'm going to sell my stock.'

'Excuse me?' she said.

He shook his head and went out.

The weariness he felt going along the corridor to the elevators wasn't a problem, but his giddiness was. He staggered like a drunk and needed the wall to support himself. The old guy operating the elevator looked at him as he fell inside and pressed himself against the wall. He told him which floor. He guessed the operator was close to retirement. He remembered how his Daddy had so often threatened him with the prospect of being an elevator operator if he allowed himself to fail. What do you say now, Daddy?

'Excuse me, sir?' the old guy in the maroon coat said.

He felt embarrassed, realizing he had spoken his thought.

'Thanks,' he said as he stepped out on the nineteenth floor.

There was a faintly acrid human smell inside his suite, the sweat of anxiety from Gordon Dulles. He stared at his brother-in-law for a long moment.

'Jesus Christ, Caddy.' The words burst out. 'You look like shit.'

With a nod, he sat heavily in the deep sofa.

'The Russians. The Russians,' Dulles said. 'What did they do?'

'The poor bastards didn't know what the hell to do. Still don't, I guess. They'll wake up to it pretty soon. I tore up the contract. The deal is off.'

The holler of delight that exploded from Dulles could have been heard on the twenty-ninth floor. He stomped around the room more like an Indian on the warpath than the old pirate he was.

'You mean I can start breathing again?' He laughed and drummed the table. 'Shit, Caddy. Jesus! That is magic. Pure magic. Armand Bequai has sold twenty-four million tons of our wheat like you ordered. I mean it is *sold*. Telexes exchanged on every deal.' He laughed and drummed on the table again. 'We'd have been finished if the Russians had gotten hold of that wheat. We'd've needed the President to declare war on them. He may yet have to.'

'Like my Daddy always said, Gordon, there's no profit worth having without risk.' He wondered why he was still quoting his Daddy. With this deal he had put all the humiliation he had ever suffered way behind him. 'I guess we showed a little profit?'

'We sold for better than $226.6 a ton. That is four hundred million dollars over the deal you made with the Russians.'

Caddy got up and staggered to the icebox for a Coke.

'What's wrong with you, Caddy?' Dulles asked, his tone suddenly sober.

'The hell do I know!' he responded in alarm to his brother-in-law's naked fear. He tried recovering himself as he thought about the money they had made. Fleetingly he considered whether his problem was like that crazy Chinese homoeopath suggested, that subconsciously he feared poverty. No, he decided. That was pure garbage. This was simply business, the way his Daddy had shown him.

'I'm tired, Gordon. I need to get home to my family.'

But he felt more tired than ever before in his life, and he was in pain too. He knew what the combined pain and sick feeling were that had been creeping up on him. Throughout the excitement of these negotiations he'd been able to ignore them. Now he was frightened. He suspected no amount of money or power would send his fear away.

Epilogue

THE PACE GRACE SET AS they ran through Rock Creek Park was tough, and at times Rory seemed to have a problem keeping up, but she didn't know if he was faking. Jak never ran with her lately. She had found real staying power for serious running from a diet she had developed of potatoes, raw oats and soya milk. On that she was planning to run the New York marathon, if she was still around. Taking a tiny apartment up near the Kalorama Cafe suggested she intended to be around, but keeping those closest to her guessing increased her independence. That was something she enjoyed. She had ignored advice about the district she had moved to not being safe for a single woman. It was great, she found. An interesting mix of people and cultures. It was the first time in her life that she had been truly independent. It would be a long while before she gave it up.

Running meant freedom, self-assertion, independence. She stopped at the gate on Kalorama Circle where she got off the park.

'I love watching you run, Grace,' he said when he joined her. 'You have a flowing gait like your feet don't touch the ground. Some runners hit the pavement like they were breaking concrete, burning energy without transmitting power. There's real economy to your running. Will you marry me, Grace?'

'There's no one I'd sooner marry,' she said, and smiled and took his arm. 'But you know the price. Will you come to Mexico with me to help those people?'

'Sure, I told you I would, just as soon as I get through

doing all I'm involved with here.'

'That's the problem, Rory. Your problem. You're always going to be fighting someone's battle here.'

'What would you have me do? People need help.'

'People are always going to need help. Nothing ever changes until you help people to change the way they think. The only real and worthwhile change comes from within the individual. Then the whole world changes. Do you know who taught me that?'

'It sounds familiar,' Rory said.

'It should, Rory.' She held his look. 'Why are the financial pages, along with most of the country, treating Hirshorn like some saviour? It makes no sense.'

'Sure. If the only information you get is from the media. The guy stopped a Russian cabal getting all that wheat which they were going to use to blackmail the Republics.'

'But that's according to the CIA.'

'That's how things tend to work in the freest country in the world. Grace.'

'Hirshorn and his pals should be in jail for what they did. Instead people are cheering for something they believe they can aspire to – wealth like his, beyond imagination. In fact most of their thoughts shackle them to the earth and stop their imaginations making them fabulously wealthy.'

'The problem is, and always has been, Grace, getting to all those people with the right message.'

'No. You only need to get to one person – yourself – and change his heart. He gets to another, and pretty soon we're all free.'

He wasn't listening. 'I still don't know if the Russians truly believe what happened to that wheat. I guess they have so many other problems.'

'Meanwhile the West reduces them to third world status with all their food aid.'

'Maybe,' Rory said.

They exited the park in silence. On the street, Rory said, 'Is Jak going to Mexico with you?'

'Who knows. He came by yesterday,' she said. 'We had

407

a really long talk. He's changing, Rory. Some big shifts. He's decided to go after American Chemicals over the death of his wife and child.'

'He wants Christic to help him. No problem. He's got all the help he needs.'

She stopped and looked at him. She knew he would respond like that, but paradoxically was disappointed. 'Just another fight for you, Rory. It won't really change the way American Chemicals operate.'

'It'll get a lot of folk aware of the problem.'

'A lot of people are aware of the problem now. No matter how hard Jak hits American Chemicals, no matter what I do to them, even if we put them out of business, there's always going to be another company like them. That's what people here want. That's not the way to help those field-workers in Mexico, or stop other tragedies like Rose's death.'

'I have to do what I'm best at doing.'

'What you're doing is just one more bad habit you can't break. Your rationale is sounder than most, that's all.'

'Did Jak tell you what he did with his breakthrough in his wheat project? He shared the information with every other scientist working in the same field.'

'He did? Why didn't he say? That means he won't have control of his findings.' She was surprised.

'I don't think he cares any more. At least Hirshorn won't control it.'

She thought about that, puzzled at why Jak hadn't told her. Then she thought she knew.

'I love you, Grace,' Rory said. 'Just give me some time, I'll get to Mexico with you.'

She knew that he loved her, his every gesture and look said he did, but somehow not quite enough.

'There isn't that much time left. You'll come by one morning to go running and I'll be gone.'

With that she took off along the sidewalk and didn't look back. She knew she need never look back from now on. One of these mornings she'd be gone, and sooner than she had imagined, for now she had a strong feeling which it would be out of Rory and Jak who would come on down to Mexico after her. Right then she was absolutely clear in her mind about what she was doing and why.